A MURDEROUS OPIATE FOR THE MASSES

To Katina, of the bright
smile and funny anecdotes,

May your life have as much
joy and insight as you brought
to our classes. Live long
and prosper.

Peace

J. F. Huy

A
MURDEROUS
OPIATE FOR
THE MASSES

J.F. Huey

To order additional copies of this book, contact:
Xlibris Corporation
1-888-7-XLIBRIS
www.Xlibris.com
Orders@Xlibris.com

CONTENTS

To my mother and ALL her babies.
To all women seeking justice and the truths
that have been denied.
May your goddess (or god)
treat you kindly.

/-HUEI

CHAPTER 1

Since crack hit the streets in the 1980s, peculiar murders have at some point or another been labeled "drug-related," whether they were or not. The drug-related label became an excuse for poor investigation or as an explanation for heinous acts of violence that no sane, unaltered individual would commit. Politicians, news media, social scientists, and social organizations pointed fingers at violent music and television for the glamorization of violence, corruption of the youth, the endangered black male and blatant images of sex for sale. So you can imagine the subsequent public reaction when police arrived early Sunday morning at the opulent New Faith Cathedral (aka NFC) on Church Avenue in response to a hysterical 911 call and found the charismatic minister G.P. Hearst hanging by the feet from a rafter over the baptismal, his throat sliced, most of his blood drained into the water below.

That was all the information transmitted to Ki Dicer before arriving at the scene. Cars filled the parking lot and people, probably worshippers, wept openly in the ninety degree morning heat; the weatherman had predicted that today would be the hottest day of the summer with temperatures expected to reach 105. The vulturous news media had staked out the cavernous front court of the extravagant cathedral. Building material alone must have cost a fortune, as another was spent on the stone masons who laid the intricate patterns and crafted the vortex arches and spires. For some reason, Dicer was more interested in the craftsmanship this morning than the dead preacher. She told herself it was not due to her aversion to religion, especially those that spend millions on the building and not the souls of their parishioners; but that was a personal problem. Slipping into her professional mode, Dicer tucked that idiosyncracy away and stepped into the cool marble and stainglass foyer. The Vatican would be jealous. Her thoughts wandered not only to the craftsmanship, but where they found the artists to do such work.

"Lieutenant!" a gruff male voice called from the carved mahogany door to her right.

"Johnson, why am I here?" Dicer asked the big man, a poster boy for the donut-eating-cop cliche. He frowned for that was not usually a point of discussion.

"Ayers told me to call you." He jerked his almost bald fat head inside. Johnson, at thirty-five, had spent the last two years losing nearly a hundred pounds; but his head hadn't lost anything but hair.

"Well, I told you about doing what Ayers told you." Dicer walked into the hall. Red-cushioned, highbacked pews lined each side of the blood-red carpeted aisle. Shakers they were not. Near the stage, pulpit rather, a crime scene team worked methodically as a photographer and videographer captured the process for perpetuity.

The pudgy coroner, Dr. Malcolm Roanan, knelt over the body which had been cut down from the rafters. The dangling cut rope swayed from air silently emitted from the cooling system. No sweating allowed in this place of worship.

"Murder or suicide?" Dicer asked the coroner.

He rubbed the back of his arm against his chin. "I thought you were on vacation, Dicer."

"Someone lied to both of us." Dicer squatted to take in the late preacher's final countenance. "Run a toxicology."

Roanan snorted. "They drained him like a hog, Dicer. Homicide. As a boy I remember the headless chickens running around, but I don't think this fellow did much running after they cut and hung him, especially not to his crack pipe."

"He had a crack pipe?" Dicer asked hopefully.

He sighed, shaking his head. "You're always looking for crack pipes."

"That's what they hired me for."

"And I thought it was your fancy footwork on the dance floor," a deep voice crooned behind her.

Her guts did a bellyflop, for the speaker was Aaron Norris, her arch persecutor from the state bureau. "Mr. Norris, what brings you here so quickly?" Dicer asked sweetly.

"In the area, Dicer. This isn't drug-related, I can assure you." Norris spoke in that authoritative voice that made Dicer's lips curl in a sneer.

"And what makes you think it's not?" she asked. As far as debunking drug-related myths, that task belonged to her; although why she was called was still a mystery to her. Perhaps Ayers would enlightened her when he appeared.

"You're head-line grabbing, Dicer. There's no evidence of drug activity at this scene," Norris told her in a too loud voice, as he looked over her shoulder.

Turning around, she spotted Captain Norman Buchova in full regalia speaking with a white-haired man who looked as old as the apostles. He met Dicer's eye and angrily waved her over. What the fuck was going on?

Brushing past the slender tailor-suited Norris, Dicer sauntered over as nonchalant as possible. "Morning, Captain."

His beady red eyes bored into her as his mouth opened, displacing his hog jowls. Instead of speaking, he pulled her into a corner. "What the fuck are you doing here, Dicer?"

"I—" Dicer swallowed the truth and borrowed Norris's explanation which she doubted was the truth. What's good for the state boys is good for us, she thought. "I was in the neighborhood."

"You're on vacation. Leave the scene," he commanded.

"Captain, I'm here now; you're short-handed."

He stepped closer. "Father Thomas knows who and what you are and was unhappy to see you here. This is bad enough without a drug scandal."

"With all due respect, captain, this is a murder investigation and I'm a homicide detective period."

"And you're on vacation. Now get out," he seethed.

Setting her jaw, Dicer prepared for battle until she saw detective Ayers pull his big left ear. "Fine. I'll see you in ten days, captain sir." She saluted. "Happy hunting." Turning on her heels, she strode out the side door and stopped, waiting for Ayers to join her in the side hall. Two minutes passed before he entered the hallway. "Sorry, Dicer."

"What the hell is this about?" she asked the stocky bronzed fellow.

"I don't know." He leaned against the wall, feeling in his shirt pocket for his smokes. "I told Johnson to give you a call because something, and I don't know what, is not right. The big boys responded too quickly. You saw Norris; he was here before you and made a point of noting you were on vacation." He looked both ways down the hall, then tucked a small baggie into her palm. "And you tell me what this is."

Dicer glanced down at a green crystalline substance. "Where'd you get this?" The college students' latest craze was the GreenTart, a morphed opiate encased in candy, usually apple sour.

"On the scene somewhere," he said vaguely, looking around. "The captain showed up; I went out to check—"

Someone had come into the hallway behind her, but she didn't know who. "Sure Lou, come on over, the pool is all yours. Your girls should have a good time." She glanced up as Norris drew abreast. "Guess you were right, Aaron, not drug-related. I should have kept on going."

"I've been telling you that for years, Dicer." He smiled coldly.

"Everyone doesn't use Preparation H for lipstick, comrade." Dicer slapped him on his thin shoulder. "See you this evening, Louis." She sauntered off; her mind way ahead with the sample Lou had gotten somewhere in this place and the source had disappeared when he wasn't looking. She was sure that's what he was going to tell her. And that meant coverup. Her skin prickled. Outside, the crowd had gotten larger and the temperature higher.

Taking in several tear-stained faces, Dicer wondered if she had missed anything about the Cathedral.

"Dicer!" a voice called. The lieutenant kept walking. "Be that way," the voice said closer.

At her car, Dicer opened the door before turning to the reporter, Lin Gao. "Ms. Gao."

"Was this done by a crazed addict?" she asked, again reminding Dicer of Connie Chung for her directness, though there was no resemblance.

"I don't know who did it. I was just passing through and saw the commotion. I have no evidence of drugs."

"If you did, would you tell me?" she asked, eyes sparkling.

Dicer shrugged. "I'm on vacation, Lin."

"Oh, it's Lin now." She pursed her peach lips. "I'll give you a call later. What do you know about the New Faith Cathedral?"

"They had some wonderful craftsmen; it's majestic." Dicer looked back at the building. "Beautiful."

"Yes. But I meant the people, the faith?"

"Nothing. You?" Dicer eyed her closely. Having known Gao forever, she knew her tones.

She pursed her lips. "I'll give you that call." She abruptly turned and walked away.

Resisting the urge to call her back, Dicer got in and drove away. Ayers and Gao were suspicious. About what? Fuck, she was on vacation and she still hadn't left the metro area for more than three days last weekend. Vacationing alone was not fun, especially when you had tons of work to do around your new old-house. The only problem was that it had been too hot after ten in the morning to work outside, so most of the attention had been given to the inside. The first renovation had been the small swimming pool, thankfully covered by a bamboo canopy.

Turning into her lane in a hidden southern nook of the city, Dicer saw a familiar blue Pathfinder parked in the cobblestone courtyard. As the door opened under her hand, a streak of yellow rushed towards her. "How's my girl?" Dicer asked swooping the child up into her arms. "Miss me?"

She nodded. "Mommie's here too."

"She is?" she asked walking around the corner into the room she was using as a family room until the other was finished.

"Daddy too," she added.

Dicer stopped in her tracks, scanning the empty room. "He is?"

"In the swimming pool," the child said pointing outside.

"Kerry!" Dicer called going into the kitchen where her sister busied herself making hamburger patties.

She turned reminding Dicer of their mother more than ever. "No need to yell," Kerry admonished, much as their mother had done.

"Did you bring Bart here?"

"Yes." She returned to her task.

"Kerry . . . " Dicer began, but remembered the child in her arms. "Down we go, Katie."

"Okay." She scampered down and away.

Leaning on the granite counter next to her sister, she tried to still her temper. "Kerry, what are you doing bringing him here? I asked you nicely not to. I thought we had an agreement. I won't say jackshit about the worthless sonofabitch, if you don't bring him around me."

Kerry purposely wiped her hands and turned to her, her eyes set and lips pressed together. "How can you be so heartless, Ki? He's trying very hard."

"Very hard?" Dicer jerked her head towards the window overlooking the pool. "Trying hard to get the breaststroke down."

"He came to apologize, so please behave."

"Behave? I should behave? Kerry, you may be able to forgive him for being a lying, thieving bastard; but I'm not going to forgive him for stealing my shit."

"He had a problem."

"No shit!" Dicer hissed. "I don't want his problem to be my problem. It's bad enough I have to pick up the problems he makes with you and Katie."

Her head snapped around. "What problems? You mean the money? I'll give you your fucking money back, Ki. We don't need it."

"You know damn well that's not what I mean." Dicer sighed shaking her head. How the hell did smart, beautiful women fall for worthless, unemployed men? Was the dick that good?

"You want us to leave? You think he's going to steal some of your precious stones?"

"If he could get a dollar for them, yes." Ki stared her down.

Kerry's face was purple with anger, but Ki could see in her eyes that she knew she was right. Why the hell didn't that knowledge sink lower into her heart and close it off to the bastard? "Can I use your stove at least? We'll leave after lunch." She brushed past Ki.

"My house is Katie's house." Ki walked out going upstairs to change. Love, especially that blind kind Kerry had, remained a mystery to Ki. Seeing her obsession and her continuous hurt over Bart had not been easy on their mother. Every time he pulled a stunt that cost her heartache and money, she would swear off of him; but a few months later he would weasel his way into her good graces. Like now. Crazy fucker.

GreenTarts had been on the scene about a year and a half now as party favorites for students. Rumor has it developing as a local product in the home economics department. The biggest fear of local law enforcement and drug counselors is its attractiveness to youngsters in its candy forms. There's even a lollipop form designed to help you nurse your habit, one lick at a time. However the usual form was the small hard green candy in the tiny baggies. Users would put it in their hand, or on a platter if at a party, and simply dart out their tongue to the crystals. It would dissolve slowly, reportedly causing a feeling of well-being and contentment, a euphoric effect that keeps them coming back. In the samples the police lab had examined, the purity of the opiates was incredible and dangerously high, which led to a rash of overdoses, but surprisingly no deaths. At least no deaths were reported. However, that may change for the bag Ayers recovered from the cathedral contained heroin, not the comparatively mild alkaloids of the previous batches.

"Thanks, Roger," Ki said to the chemist.

He turned to her. "Don't you want to know what was on the package?"

"What?"

He gave her a feral grin. "Baker's delight."

"And what is that?" Over the years Ki had gotten him not to give her the technical chemical jargon, but now he gave her the ingredients as though he were a chef.

"No, I literally mean Baker's delight." He held up a slide. "Cake batter. They must have made and bagged the Tarts in a kitchen. It'd be hell if they accidently sprinkled this in the icing."

Her blood ran cold as the icy hand of death gripped her arm. "Roger. . . ." She shook her head. "Thanks, I owe you one."

"Honey, it's more like one one one." He rose from his chair. "Where you want the report sent?"

"Louis Ayers, and keep a copy in the safe for me. I'm on vacation."

He gave her the evil eye. "Hate you."

"How's Mark?" she asked of his significant other.

"Busy as ever. Tis the season of love, happiness, foolish affairs and weddings. So business is booming." He removed a stuffed brown envelope. "Would you do a brother a favor, Dice, since you're on vacation and all?"

"Sure. Where you want it delivered?" She took the package from him.

"The Yemen, to Yvette Yemen herself."

"Big timing are you now?" She asked the gifted chemist who contracted with the police department.

"Gotta pay the rent. Thanks."

"No sweat." Ki tucked the package under her arm and left the building into the glaring sunlight. No wonder siestas were declared from two to four; it was practical to avoid sunstrokes. Foolishly, Ki thought, she was here doing a job that was officially not hers to do.

CHAPTER 2

The Yemen was a renovated palace, that's the best description one can give of the series of Spanish style villas formed around a courtyard of gardens and pools. A guard came out of the booth to greet her at the twelve foot gate.

"Lieutenant Ki Dicer, Metrox police." Ki held up my shield. "I'm here to see Yvette Yemen."

He gave her a cold look. "Is she expecting you?" he asked haughtily.

"Does she expect night to follow day?" Ki asked mildly. For some reason, Ki didn't think anyone like her ever expected darkness to follow their days as they pushed on.

He went back to the booth and called up, then opened the gate for her. Asshole. The only disappointing feature of the place was the rather mundane and colorless drive.

Parking next to a silver Jaguar, Ki got out and looked around the premises until another guard came out.

"Lieutenant Dicer, this way please." They walked not to the front villa but along a garden path to a smaller unit to the right and entered a side door into a simple hallway with blue oriental wallpaper. They came out in a room that resembled a den, albeit more expensively decorated, but not ostentatious. Yvette Yemen, draped in white silk, relaxed on a sofa as two conservatively dressed men took copious notes on her seemingly rambling comments. Then they abruptly stood and walked out.

"Lieutenant Dicer, please have a seat," she said without turning.

"I'm not on official business," Ki told her skirting the sofa.

"Then why did you use your credentials to get in?" she asked.

"Habit." Ki sat on the edge of the sofa facing her with the package on her lap. Yemen was approaching sixty, but good genes and probably a good physical regime had her looking an elegant forty. "What can I do for you, Dicer? No one in my household uses drugs." She called her entire business empire her household. "Not that you know of. And Roger Patak asked me to deliver this to you." Ki held up the package, and the guard who stood over her took it from her.

"Unofficially of course."

"As a favor to a friend."

She nodded and removed samples and one of Roger's patent blue covered reports from the package. Her lips twisted in displeasure as she read the first few pages. "Dom, get Pearsall on the line, tell him to proceed with the suit against Revline. This is our formula down to the drop of peyote."

"Yes, ma'am." He hurried out.

"Bad news?" Ki asked.

"For Revline." Her eyes studied Ki as if looking for the horns, the elites in this town swore she had as she chased their drugged out children as diligently as the Fifth precinct chased the black and hispanic teenagers on the eastside.

"Corporate espionage. Interesting."

"Can you imagine the proceeds if the illegal drug manufacturers patented their formulas?" she asked, a wry grin playing at her lips.

"I guess that would be a bonanza, perhaps even fueling a manufacturers' war, which would see an increase of designer products on the market, pushing down prices, pushing up use and not to mention the advertising gimmicks."

She chuckled. "You are as anal about this as reported, aren't you? The metro's own drug czar. Many people have speculated on your ardor as well as the chief permitting you to roam, nearly unchecked. Care to enlightened me?"

"Simple, I'm the most enlightened person on the force and clearly drugs are bad for individuals, community and country."

"A naive arrogance." She glanced at a woman approaching with a tray. "Or is that part of your persona? No one lasts as long as you have bucking the system, Dicer. You must remember all of those adages about nonconformists and crusaders."

"Are you warning me, Ms. Yemen?"

"Glad we understand each other. Would you like a glass of iced tea?" Yemen asked as the young woman filled two glasses.

"Yes, thank you."

"Have you had lunch?" she asked.

But before Dicer could answer a voluptuous raven haired woman entered from the patio wearing only a sheer shift over a gold bikini.

"Mother, is that a swimming pool or a sauna out there?" she asked in a slightly accented voice.

"Sauna," Yemen said dryly, watching Dicer watch her drily daughter. "Jaio, join us for tea and say hello to the good lieutenant, Ki Dicer, our city's very own super cop."

She turned and extended a hand. "Pleasure to meet you, lieutenant."

"Pleasure is all mine," Ki told her, looking into pools of onyx Jaio had for eyes. Damn. Damn. Double Damn! Talking about lust at first sight.

"Dicer, Jaio against my wishes has moved back to the city and insists on living among the people. Perhaps you have some advice as to a safe and ethnically representative neighborhoods."

"She means an integrated suburb," Jaio responded sitting next to her. "I would prefer something less bland, like Carrollton."

Dicer frowned. "I don't think you do. Carrollton is nice to visit when the police makes a sweep to clear the streets for you tourists, not to live."

"Then where would you suggest?" She crossed her legs and Ki swallowed.

"A number of places. Azure for one. Bombay Missions. Hmm, Boxtown is full of color and flavor. A couple of others too." Again Dicer's eyes fell to her long caramel legs. Again, she felt Yemen's eyes on her.

"I'll check those out." She sipped her tea. "Do you have a card? I'd like to consult you again if you don't mind."

"No, I don't mind." She felt her body for a card. "Sorry, I don't have a card; I'm on vacation and not carrying any."

Jaio reached onto the table and pulled a pad and pen to her. "Here. Just write it."

"Think I can manage that." Dicer scribbled her numbers on the pad.

"Dicer, what do you think of the death at the New Faith Cathedral?"

"I'm trying not to. It was a gruesome and unsettling death. I'm sure my colleagues are working diligently on the case. Unfortunately I'm on vacation."

"And you didn't leave town?" Jaio asked.

"A weekend. I'm working on my house; that's a sufficient respite from the department."

"Yourself?" Jaio asked, a smile teetering at her lips.

"Yes. I'm pretty good with my hands."

Her smile blossomed, showing the deep dimples that her relaxed countenance had only hinted at. "I'll have to inspect your handiwork one of these days."

"I'd be honored to give you a demonstration."

Mother Yemen cleared her throat. "It was nice of you to drop that package by, Dicer. Good to see you as well."

Ki could take an unveiled hint any day. "Nice to see you again, Ms. Yemen." Dicer rose. "Nice to meet you, Jaio."

"Same here, lieutenant." She stood as well. "I will ring you."

"I look forward to you—it." Dicer smiled, avoiding Yemen's eyes. "Good afternoon."

Driving southward to home, Dicer kept thinking of Jaio Yemen. If only she had not smiled like that. That was Yvette Yemen's daughter for crying out loud, which meant she was most likely selfish, demanding and controlling. Yet she didn't seem that way at all. Obviously her mother had not liked the idea of her moving back to town. Why?

The phone continued to ring as her key tried to stick in the lock. Shit. Finally she opened the door and answered the phone. "Hello?"

"Was that a legitimate pool invitation for my girls yesterday?" Ayers asked.

"Of course. What time are you coming? I'll start the grill if it's near dinnertime."

"How about six?"

"That's fine. How's the investigation going?"

"I wouldn't know. Captain Buchova reassigned me this morning after I questioned him about Norris claiming jurisdiction over the case. Good riddance, I didn't want to interview another NFC member only to hear what an outstanding friend, leader, and mentor Hearst was. Let them tell it, he was on the verge of eclipsing Jesus H. Christ himself. Some are even referring to his death as the crucifixion. I can't wait for these last two hours of my work week. One more week and I'm on vacation. Look the captain just came in, I'll see you at six."

"Look forward to it." Dicer hung up and looked around. The early morning had been pretty productive for her, so she could spend the evening relaxing. When the sun went down she would finish that floor in the family room, completing her interior flooring. A labor of love in which she laid every tile.

Ki Dicer checked her messages, Gao had phoned three times, her excitement or agitation increasing with each call. Calling her number at the Globe, she answered on the second ring.

"Ms. Gao, Dicer here."

"Dicer, why did they remove Ayers from the Cathedral case?" Gao asked promptly.

"I don't know."

"You and I should talk, Dicer. How about dinner?"

"I'm cooking out for my guests. You're welcome to join us."

"Maybe afterwards," Gao hedged.

"Aw come on, Gao, don't be such a fuddy duddy. I'll even throw a couple of steaks on in addition to the hotdogs."

"I'll see how my deadline is looking. But we really need to talk, Dicer."

"Then come on over; you'll be among friend."

"Uh huh. Bye." She hung up.

Again she left the impression that there was something going on and that Dicer needed to know. Over the years they had developed an effective symbiotic relationship; Gao got her stories and Dicer got her exploits covered more than any officer in the department. Additionally, the chief got a reputation for being tough on crime and his officers, for even Dicer's reprimands would be made public. And depending on the public's or the chief's mood, she was paraded out for the success or the many failings of the Metrox PD. Dicer kept two separate albums simply labeled, "Good Dicer" and "Bad Dicer." Lucky for her, there were few Bad Dicer stories written by Gao or she wouldn't have had a job.

Like Yemen, many had wondered why the chief let her "run wild," but the truth was much simpler than anyone knew or cared to know: Ki wasn't that good or that bad; she fit the politically correct bill for an officer of the 21st century. Metrox like other police departments grappled constantly with image problems on all fronts and by having the "right look" and demographic variables, Dicer was tossed to the media. In turn she pitched her ideas about crime and policing, which didn't always align with those of the police department. Yet the chief would publicly reprimand her on one hand, and privately pat her on the back. It was not uncommon for him to send her public with an idea to check the pulse of the city before implementing it.

In short Dicer was the chief's guinea pig with a lightening rod up the ass. Many colleagues didn't know whether her shooting up the ranks fairly quickly to become one of the youngest lieutenants in modern Metrox history was due to her competence or was compensation. Careful examination of her jacket would illustrate the complexities of modern policing; Ki Dicer was the epitome of what they "said" they wanted, she did the tough assignments they said would get her promoted and was under constant scrutiny. How could they deny her promotions without doing more harm to themselves? It was a political game and there were no bones about it; she was groomed for it. Or was she? Perhaps it was the simple result of time and space intersecting at this moment placing her here with all of the correct characteristics and the fortitude to withstand the onslaught. Or in the words of her good buddy Ayers, she just didn't give a shit.

At six thirty, Ayers arrived with his little entourage, his two daughters, Lisa and Lily, and the little fellow who lived with his mother in their garage apartment.

"Hello, Ryan," Dicer greeted the toddler.

"Hey." He ran across the room to Lisa who was developing so rapidly, the rambunctious youngster had become shy almost overnight.

"The pool is waiting for you," Dicer encouraged them as they stood too quietly looking around the room.

"Anyone else here?" Lisa asked.

"No, you'll have it all to yourselves. You can change in Katie's room." They trailed off and Ki turned to Lou who didn't seem in a happy mood. "What happened?"

"Don't ask. When I arrived Diane was in a state, Lily was on punishment; Lisa was teary-eyed; and Ryan had been there since nine this morning. No one knew where his mother had gone or when she was coming back." He smiled wanly. "You have a cold beer? This has not been my day."

"In the fridge."

He held up the bags in his hands. "I brought barbecue sauce and buns; you never have any."

"I knew it was something. Besides being in a state, how is the lovely Diane?" she asked as they went into the kitchen.

"Don't start, Dicer." Lou Ayers and Ki were best buddies, even after she outranked him and became his supervisor; nevertheless he didn't appreciate her flirting with his wife. He opened the fridge. "Your refrigerator's full; Kerry's been over?"

"The weekend; but I filled the fridge myself."

Taking out a beer, he closed the fridge door. "I see you've had those rocks delivered. When are we going to build that retaining wall?"

"When we get a cool spell or this weekend whichever comes first. You're volunteering to help?"

He sighed. "Diane was talking with someone who was talking with someone who saw Deana's wall you did."

"Uh oh." Ki laughed.

"Uh oh is right. I didn't tell her you were sleeping with Deana at the time."

"I was not!"

He laughed. "But that would have gotten me off the hook. So you think I could watch you when you do yours? Just to brush up on the techniques."

"Brush up, my ass; you forget you told me you never even built a birdhouse. And how many times have I offered to rebuild that wall?"

"Hey, I just don't want you showing me up in front of my girls."

"Too late," she told him with a wink. "They idolize me."

"You wish." He pulled the foil back on the top of the pan of meat. "Steaks? Who else is coming? A new girlfriend you haven't told me about?"

"Hell no, but Lin Gao said she might come over. It seems she has something to discuss about the NFC. No hint to what it is, except she keeps telling me that we need to talk. Any ideas? She knew you had been booted too." Ki glanced at him.

He washed his hands as he thought of the proper response. "Dicer. . . ." He turned to look at her. "Something is not right here and it has to do with that church."

"I know. That baggie of GreenTart's main ingredient was heroin, and pure as hell. You should let Ramonas know where you got it, so he can keep an eye out." Ki watched his reaction. Cool. She thought Ayers was the coolest man she knew and not just the bullshit way black men tended to be.

"You know where I got that shit, Dicer; and it wasn't on the street. It was in—"

As lively as Dicer was used to seeing them, the girls rushed in with Ryan in tow; he carried a limp duck floater raised to his lips. Seeing Ayers, he took it to him to blow up.

"You have an air pump?" Ayers asked as the girls held out their own ball and floats.

"Yes, it's in the corner. It's a high powered blower so be careful." Dicer checked on the chicken and links on the grill, deemed them ready and promptly removed them.

Ayers saw them safely in the pool with all of their accoutrements and came over to the grill. "When did you do that back fence?"

"Last week. Kenny lent a hand."

"In exchange for what?" Ayers asked knowing Ki's n'er-do-well cousin.

"Settling an old score." Kenny was always hitting someone up for money. Everyone else had the good sense not to lend him more than a ten spot.

"He'll be back asking for something."

"Yeah, that's what I thought too, but it's been a week and he hasn't been back."

"When is he going to marry that girl?"

"Not. She got smart and walked."

"When?" he asked surprised.

"About two weeks ago."

"That explains Kenny's urge to work. If I were him, I'd have put a ring on that girl's finger even if I had to steal the sonofabitch or get it out of a gum machine. Ask Diane."

"Don't have to ask, Lou. She has it mounted remember. Nice neon plastic."

"Yeah . . . Is that your doorbell?"

Dicer listened a second. "Yeah." She trotted to the front door.

Gao in shorts and a sleeveless yellow polo stood with a sixpack. "I filed my article fifteen minutes ago. Unless something breaks I'm here for awhile."

"Now where have I heard that before?" Dicer asked with a soft chuckle.

"Don't start, Dicer."

"Why is everyone saying that?" She closed the door behind her friend.

"Because you're at home and you get self-righteous with everyone's lovelife in here." She slowed to take in the renovations. "You have been busy."

"Told you. Want to see what I've done to the bedroom?"

"No." She walked on into the kitchen where Lou was placing the grilled meat in the oven. "Hello, Ayers."

"Gao. You're just in time."

"For what?" she asked, putting the beer in the freezer.

"Want to make a salad? Dicer can't remember the veggies."

"I resent that, Lou. I have a beautiful salad chilling in the basement fridge."

Gao glanced at Ayers suppressing a grin. "Why is the salad in the basement, Dicer?" she asked.

"There was no room in the fridge up here."

"As I recall, there's never anything but room in your fridge."

"There was always whipped cream if you bothered to look," Dicer teased.

"I don't want to hear about this," Ayers said taking the pan of steaks out to the grill.

Gao chuckled. "He's a good guy."

"Yeah."

"That's why he was taken off the case. What's going on, Dice?"

"I don't know, Lin. You saw me leave yesterday, at the captain's request."

"You could have told me that then."

"Why?" I glanced at her.

"I've been trying to get an interview with any and all of the leaders at NFC for months, but I couldn't get past their PR people. They're insulated and tight-lipped. No reporter who would dare ask a tough question is allowed an interview."

"Since when has religion been your beef, Lin?"

"Religion or a sophisticated cult?"

"No difference."

"That's where my thoughts are running on this one. Dice, there's something going on with that church and I believe that murder was related." She opened the fridge and took out a long-neck. "Did you get a good look at those grieving members outside?"

"Seemed quite devastated."

"Devastated? You left a bit too early. Devastated went to hysterical about noon."

"How so?"

"Crying, agitation, chanting. Didn't you see it on the news?"

"No, I worked on the floors last night."

"They had to open up the other assembly hall to have service in order to calm them down." Gao shook her head in disbelief. "Have you ever seen a depiction of the savior laying on hands where the sufferer is delirious from fever, the savior lays on hands and they suddenly subside into a euphoric stupor, just staring their appreciation and love?"

"I think I know what you mean. Why?"

"That's how they were acting; then after communion they suddenly became as docile as sheep. I've never seen anything like it; but it fits the reports of their midnight masses."

"Midnight masses? And what reports?"

"That's what I've been wanting to talk to you about. I've been getting these e-mail messages about the strange practices at the Cathedral."

"Like what? Virgin sacrifices?" Dicer quipped then saw her face. "You're kidding?"

"Sexual sacrifices rather of eleven and twelve year-old girls. Their translation of a tithe is half and the trinity is the three member board of governors; that's where the true power rests and to which umbrage is paid. The ministers are messengers of god alright, for the triumvirate gods. The e-mail messages hint at mind control techniques. And seeing their reaction, I don't doubt it." She paced the kitchen. "But how can this happen during these times?"

"People are always searching for meaning, Lin. Technological advances do not supplant the basic human spiritual need. If anything, it fuels it. There are answers that science just can't solve and the more we learn how things work; the more frustrated we become when we can't explain something. Take for example those highly intelligent people who thought the ship was coming with the comet. What was it called?"

"Heaven's Gate or something."

"Right. And people have all this disposable income and once they have all the new gadgets, what then? They're not happy, their souls are empty; they don't know whether they are loved for their money or not; they've been riding high for so long, there's no where else to go. Everything on the outside is done and it doesn't make them happy, so it must be on the inside. Their old church didn't provide what they believed to be the proper direction or they wouldn't have been in this spiritual turmoil, so it follows that their gods are no longer adequate; so they search for new gods, man-made or not for the bottom line is that they want to feel good. And according to your own eyewitness testimony, felt good they did."

Gao stared at her. "What the fuck are you on?"

"You asked why at the dawn of the new millennium people are buying into cults. Isn't that what all of the millennium experts said was going to happened? Apocalyptic predictions and all. Nothing surprising there."

"Dicer, I'm telling you what I saw wasn't natural. It's as if they were programmed to the communion. They actually believed in that flesh of flesh and blood of blood mantra. They were enraptured."

"Who?" Ayers asked coming in.

"The New Faith Cathedral," Dicer told him. "Gao was just telling me about their religious experience yesterday."

He shook his head. "You should have seen it, Dicer. I've never seen anything like it. If Buchova had not given them the okay to use the adjacent hall, we would have had a riot." He turned to Gao. "What was your impression?"

"Something's not right there, Lou. It was too damn weird."

"To me too. They looked high to tell you the truth. Did you notice their eyes?"

"Not really, I was paying more attention to their body language as a whole. Swaying like weeds in a gentle breeze. I swore I heard humming."

"I thought it was moaning," Ayers said.

Dicer looked from one to the other as they compared notes on the New Faith Cathedral. True, these two were trained observers, but what they were describing could not be missed easily by any outside observer. "I want to ask you both something."

"What?" they asked simultaneously.

"Do you think this was related to the minister's death?"

"Yes."

Dicer looked at Gao, but asked Ayers, "Do you think you were removed from the case to cover up something?"

He hesitated, then glanced at Gao. "You working or is this an old friends' visit?"

"You're off the case so you have nothing of relevance to add."

"Don't blow me, Gao. You in or out?"

"Fuck, I'm here; I'm in." She glared at Dicer. "What's going on?"

"This may sound far fetched, but somehow drugs may be involved." Neither offered a disgusted or surprised protest, so she continued. "I don't know how, but some high-grade heroin is involved. Now this is stranger. Cake batter residue was found on the baggie. I'm assuming the person who gave it to me had not baked a cake that morning and stuck his hands in his pocket."

"No," Ayers said.

"The NFC bakes their own breads, in fact they own several bakeries," Gao added. "In fact members have turned over sixteen plus small businesses to them, mostly service and delivery, including a pizza joint."

Both detectives stared at her. "What?"

"This is what I've been trying to tell you. They are not what they seem. The sex, the business scams, why not drugs? What better way to get your drugs than have them delivered with your favorite topping?"

A chill shot through Dicer, for that was her fear. "How are we going to go about this?" she asked absently.

"Carefully," Ayers said. "These aren't ordinary people. Just look at the brass yesterday. It reminds me of those religious fanatics in the middle east where everything is molded together with the government, trying to establish a great religious state."

Gao looked from one to the other. "Since when have you two become religious experts?"

"My concern is that I was ordered from the scene and Lou was taken off the case. My question remains, is someone in the department covering something up? If so who and why?"

"Buchova would be the obvious choice," Ayers said.

"Too obvious," Gao commented.

"Or that would be the obvious rationalization."

"How can we decide on a strategy when we can't decide on who or what we're going after?"

"That's why we're here." Dicer turned to Gao. "You have any background on the NFC you can share with us?"

"In my trunk. You have a copier?" She slipped from her stool.

"Yes." Dicer turned to Ayers. "You get that report from Roger?"

"What report?"

Dicer pursed her lips. "Roger did the lab work for me; I told him to send the report to you."

"I didn't leave until five-thirty and there was no blue folder in my box or on my desk. Yours either."

"Perhaps he was backed up."

"Perhaps it was intercepted." He glanced out to make sure the children were okay.

"Perhaps we're jumping ahead of ourselves here. There could be a logical explanation for all of this," Dicer mused.

"You're the one talking about a drug conspiracy."

"Not a drug conspiracy, but a conspiracy that may have drugs involved."

"What's the difference?"

"Motivation."

"What are you talking about now?" he asked shaking his empty bottle. "Is that lemonade cold?"

"Shit!" Dicer slipped from her stool. "There's two gallon jugs downstairs. They're probably frozen."

"Why is everything downstairs?" Ayers asked.

"I need to buy a bigger refrigerator. There's no room." Dicer went downstairs to retrieve the two gallons of lemonade from the freezer; they were icy just like the kids liked it.

The children spent the evening in the pool getting out only to eat their dinner by the poolside. Meanwhile the adults tried to come up with a plan of investigation that would side-step their supervisors and not alert the NFC to the fact that they were in their cross-hairs.

The phone rang. "I'll get it," Gao said standing next to it. "Hello?" She listened and held her hand over the mouthpiece. "Lieutenant Dicer," she said in a seductive voice.

"Thank you, darling." Dicer took the phone from her. "Hello?"

"Aw lieutenant I was under the impression you were unat-tached."

"I am, but my colleagues don't let me wallow in my own piti-ful loneliness. They even bring their adorable children to cheer me up. How are you this evening?"

"Quite well, thank you. Are you by chance available for lunch and a tour of those neighborhoods you mentioned earlier?"

"I do believe so. Where and what time?"

"I thought we'd find a place in the 'hood."

"The hood? Okay, what time and where should we meet?"

"I can pick you up. What's your address?"

"I live at the far southern tip of the city. Perhaps we should meet somewhere in between."

"A long trip doesn't bother me. Or don't you want me to know where you live?"

Dicer chuckled. "No, I don't mind. Have a pen handy?" She gave her the directions, then hung up to find both Gao and Ayers staring at her with whimsical smirks. "What?"

"What are you meeting Honey-voice for?" Gao asked.

"Mind your own business."

"Don't get distracted," Ayers warned, checking his watch. "Let me get them out of the pool."

"You have a key, Lou; the pool is theirs for the summer."

"Thanks, but we'll try not to wear out our welcome."

"No problem of that. And don't forget to tell Diane, I'll be over to assess that wall. Again. We'll do it with or without your help."

He chuckled and walked out to gather the children.

"What was that all about?" Gao asked.

"She wants that wall around her garden repaired."

"After all of these years? Why?"

"It seems I have a career after I'm fired from the department."

"Which may be soon if this blows up in your face," Gao warned.

"Now, it's my face? What happened to us? You, me and Lou?"

"But who always takes the flak? You. You've already been thrown off once. This time you're deliberately disobeying orders."

Dicer frowned at her. "Twenty minutes ago, you were all in favor of this. What's changed?"

"Nothing. I just want you to see the possible consequences of this for you and for Lou. I have a bad feeling about these people. Don't underestimate them."

"I won't. Plus, I'm not investigating the murder, but a possible drug trafficking organization based on a reliable source. Just as you're trying to get interviews with the triumvirate for an ongoing series on local religious leaders."

"If my editor buys it."

"As long as the NFC buys it."

"Yeah." Gao glanced slyly at her. "Who was she?"

"Who?"

"Miss Breathless on the phone?"

Dicer chuckled. "Jaio Yemen."

Gao choked on her lemonade. "Do you know who she is?"

"Yvette Yemen's daughter."

"Not just her daughter, her very capable successor. Don't let that beautiful smile fool you, Dicer; she's no dilettante. You be careful."

"Jealous?" Dicer asked winking.

"Shit no. I don't want you crying on my shoulder when she breaks that limestone heart of yours."

"You're cold, Gao." They looked up as the kids trailed in draped in their towels. "Enjoy yourselves?" Dicer asked.

"Yeah."

"When can we come back?" Lily asked.

"When your mom or dad has time to bring you."

"You could come get us," Lily said with those wide brown eyes that had her father wrapped around her finger.

"I guess I could when I'm not working." Dicer glanced up at Lou. "You know someone needs to watch you in the pool and I can't do that while working."

"When are you not working?" she asked.

"Good question. I'll let you know. Okay?"

"Okay."

"What do you say?" Ayers asked them as they headed out of the kitchen.

"Thank you, Dicer," they intoned.

"You're welcome." They left with Gao leaving not long afterwards.

Since a small child, Ki Dicer has always dreamed so vividly that she wakes up looking for the result of what has transpired during the dream. To her relatives this has always lent credence to their belief that she has a tenuous grip on reality; however, she prefers to think of it as a manifestation of her creative soul, if not talent. The closest she came to true artistic expression is the stonemasonry. Of course they made some inane remarks about stones, bricks and rocks. Family. You can't live with them and they won't let you live without them. She was in a creative zone of zen-stone when the bell buzzed and buzzed as she cleaned her hands and tried not to track mortar through the house to the front door at two o'clock in the morning.

Her cousin Kenny stood nervously in the shadows, looking over his shoulder. He nearly knocked her down when she unlocked the door.

"What the hell are you doing here this time of night?" Dicer growled at him.

"I owe a guy two hundred dollars. Can you help me out?"

So here it was. "No."

"Come on, Dicer. I helped you with that fence in this hot ass weather and didn't ask for a dime."

"First of all, you took breaks every fifteen minutes. I had to reset several bars and you messed up a whole batch of concrete. Not to mention—"

"Alright. Alright." He held up his hands. "Lend me two hundred dollars and I'll help with that wall and any other project. Please, I need the money." He clasped his mocha hands in a prayer.

"Who do you owe two hundred to?"

"A guy on the strip." He glanced nervously about. His otherwise handsome face was covered in a scraggly beard as if he hadn't shaved in a week.

"What guy?"

"Stop interrogating me, Dice. You gonna lend me the money or not?"

"You better not be on no shit, Kenny. I'll kick your ass and then lock you up," she threatened. And she would do it too, for his own good.

"I'm not stupid." He followed her into her study.

"But you keep gambling anyway."

"Guilty." He watched as she counted out the twenties from her stash in the money box. "Why do keep so much money here?"

She looked up at him. "Don't even think about it."

"What?" he asked innocently. "I just asked a simple question. You should know better. How much you got in there? Five thousand right."

She dropped her hand to the modified Tek-9 in the box and brought it up swiftly. "Hands up, Kenny."

"What the fuck you doing, Dice?" Beads of sweat popped up on his forehead.

"Get your fucking hands up." She closed the box with one hand and stepped from around the desk. "How many are with you?"

"How many what?"

"You're trying to set me up." She motioned him backwards. "How you planned on doing it? You left the front door open and he came in? Was he going to wait until I went to sleep or were you both going to jump me?"

"You're crazy. I wouldn't do anything like that."

"Most times I'd agree with you. Now call your friend or I'll shoot you and say I thought you were a burglar."

"No one would believe that with those locks you have on the door." He saw her realize his mistake.

"You tried my top lock and nearly tore up the spring. My key got hung today. You inept sonofabitch." She slipped off the safety for single fire. "Call him now."

He wiped his brow and licked his lips. His eyelids fluttered. "Dicer, you don't understand."

"You tried to rob me. What don't I understand about that? You think because I didn't press charges against Barry, you could fuck me too, brotherman? After all—"

"You've done for me? Is that what you were going to say, Dicer? You haven't done one fucking thing for me besides rub your self-righteous badge in my face."

"You're right I should have been rubbing shit in your face, you stupid, gambling, player wannabe. Call your fucking partner in crime." She raised the ugly ass gun.

"How do you think the rest of us feel while you're prancing

your dyke ass in the news? Who the fuck you think got the back-lash from that? Me. Me. Me. Not your man-crazy sister, not your mama. Me. Dicer. Who do you think caused my failure? You."

"Don't you blame your lazy ass on me, boy." Ki walked closer, knowing the lily-livered bastard would overplay his hand. "Lazy? Lazy!" He lunged for the gun, betting she wouldn't pull the trigger. He was right; she jerked it back, swung around and clubbed him at the base of the skull. He dropped like a sack of coal.

Stepping over him, she cautiously exited the study, gun in front. "Alright, come on out. Kenny's down, you're next." As she approached the vestibule she heard a car door. By the time she got outside, a car was spinning off down the lane. "Sonofabitch!"

Checking to make sure Kenny was still out, she picked up the phone and started to dial it in, but sat the phone back in its cradle. Knowing she would regret it, she called his mother.

"Hello?" her aunt Mae answered drowsily on the sixth ring.

"Mae, it's Ki. I just knocked the shit out of your son."

"What the hell for?" she asked now wide awake, her dislike for her niece not veiled.

"He and a friend tried to rob me."

"You're mistaken."

Ki rolled her eyes. "No, I'm not. Come get him or I'm calling it in, as I should have done in the first place."

"You wouldn't."

"Wouldn't I? Make your decision?"

"I'm on my way." She hung up.

When Kenny came to, his hands were handcuffed between his legs on the front veranda with its cool red-orange granite tile, the night light brought the colors to life. Lying face down, Kenny got an upclose view of them. At that particular moment Dicer would have given more for the tile than her ne'er do well cousin.

"Like the tile?" she asked hunkering down next to him as he rolled over. "You know how hard I had to look to find that tile?

And the time it took to put it down in this pattern? You know, I would work ten hours then come home and work five on this house. My house. My blood, sweat, and tears. Every step taken is on my floor. Every inch of flooring was laid with these two hands. Over six thousand square feet, inside and out. That's not including the courtyard. Have you any idea how much money I saved doing this myself and begging for discounts? Of course you do, you just tried to steal it. You wanted to know why I had that money right? That's why. Every dollar I save, I put it in the box to be used on renovations that I can't do myself. Now do you want to tell me why you felt entitled to that money?"

"Fuck you, Dicer."

"You tried that but you couldn't get it up. Why Kenny? What do they have over you?"

"You should be worried about yourself, Dice. You're not so hot you can't be touched. One of these days, someone is going to put your ass in place."

"I'm in my place now. But you invaded it. Why Kenny? What did I do to you?"

"Just shut the fuck up, Dicer!"

"Will do. From now on, I'm not going to say one goddamn thing to you. Forget we're family. Forget we're in the same town, in the same country, in the same universe. From now on you don't exist for me. Next time I see you, I'll shoot first and fuck the questions."

"Yeah, I'm scared." He was sitting up as best he could.

"Don't be. Just stay away." She settled back as a car came up the lane. Mae's white Roadmaster pulled into the courtyard. Both front doors opened, Ki's mother getting out of the passenger side.

"Help me! She's gone fucking crazy!" Kenny yelled to them.

"Uncuff him, Ki," her mother said softly.

"Gladly." Ki released him, dropping the cuffs into her pocket.

"What happened?" she asked checking his wrists.

"I came to borrow a few dollars from her and then she stuck a gun in my face, hit me over the head, and cuffed me out here. She's fucking certifiable, auntie."

Ki rolled her eyes. "Auntie, please. Would you explain what happened to your ride?"

"He probably left when you came out waving that big ass gun." His balls were back.

"Kenny, just get the fuck away from here and remember what I told you." Ki turned back to her front door. "Nice seeing you, mother."

"Aren't you going to invite me in?" she asked.

"It's three o'clock in the morning, mother; but if you insist, come in." Ki held the heavy Scottish door for her. She entered looking around. Ki knew what she was doing: giving Mae time to get Kenny's version. And of course, they would concoct some excuse for his criminal behavior, as they would for any man in their family. Wait until Lou heard about this one.

"You've done a lot of work since the last time I was here," her mother finally said.

"Yes, I've enjoyed every minute of it."

"Your father said he offered to come down and help you, but you refused his help."

Ki didn't feel like justifying this project to her again. "I really wanted to do this myself, mother. He understood that."

"There's no shame in asking for help when you need it, Ki."

Ki ran her fingers through her hair. "Mom, I didn't need help to lay flooring. I've done that since I was ten." Why was she arguing with her?

"Perhaps he wanted to spend a little time with you. You ever think about that?"

"To be honest, I didn't. Satisfied?"

"Your grandfather would have been proud of what you've done to this place."

"Well I've done my best to remain true to the natural material."

"Best dollar you ever spent?" she asked.

"Yeah." A car horn blew. "Your chariot awaits."

She nodded. "Don't be such a hardass, Ki. Call me sometimes."

"I will," Ki promised, then walked her out.

Her family. What could be said about them that was not jaded by her many years of semi-estrangement? When she came out, they went in. When she joined the police department, five of her male relatives were in jail or prison. When trouble befell her, they cheered. When the old man sold her the house for a dollar, they grumbled. When he died and left what little he had to her, they openly assaulted her good name and her taste in lovers. Yet when they had problems, they came to her which made them resent her more which she didn't understand.

There were a lot of things about her family she didn't understand and she usually had to get Lou to explain them to her. One case in point is her father, Kirk, who runs a construction company. She worked there all through high school and college, not in the office like Kerry, but doing flooring and painting. Every unemployed relative on her mother's side of the family has worked there at one time or another. They know the man; he was part of their family once and still gives them a fat check for their annual picnic. Yet when someone wants a summer job, they call her to ask for them. They like him more than they like her. Why go through her anyway?

When Ki awoke the following morning, late of course, her father was on her mind. Why? She didn't know. So she phoned him when she came out of the shower, putting him on speaker phone. She loved those things.

"How's business, Slicer?" she asked when he answered.

"Booming. You ready to quit chasing the bad guys and do something constructive?"

"Ha. Ha. No. What have you been doing?"

"I bought a boat. When you come up this weekend, we'll take her out."

"Is Father's Day this weekend?"

"Sure is. You aren't changing your mind are you?"

"No. I've been so busy, I haven't kept track of the time."

"I hope you're getting needed rest. They should have forced you to take six weeks off long ago. Whoever heard of a cop not getting sick from eating donuts or taking a day off to go to a donut convention. Shame on you."

"What can I say, I like my work."

"And that's what's important. Your mother called me Friday. You should call her."

"I saw her last night."

"Good for you. Was there anything you needed? David is pointing at his watch like he's mute. Say hey to Ki, David." A gruff greeting came over the line.

"Tell him, howdy. And no I didn't want anything."

"Did that load suit your needs, honey?"

"Yes, they did. But it's been too hot to get to it. But I'm going to start next week. I may need another load."

"I got a load of rubble to dispose of. Do you want it?"

"Sure; you know me. I can find something to use it on."

"That's my girl. Gotta go honey. See you Friday."

"Saturday morning."

He chuckled. "Thought I'd steal an evening with my favorite ladies. Ta.Ta."

"Ta.Ta." She hung up wondering what ladies he meant. Kerry wasn't going; she worked Saturdays.

A wimpy car horn blew below. Glancing in the mirror, she trotted downstairs as the doorbell buzzed away. When she opened the door, Jaio Yemen stood in a short white skirt and backless blouse looking out into the courtyard.

"Have trouble finding the place?" Ki asked, eyes admiring the view.

"No trouble, you give excellent directions." She then turned, half-smiling. "I must admit I did not expect to find a Mediterranean villa tucked in the canyon."

"Or me living in it?"

Her smile blossomed. "Touche. You did come across as a split-level Jim Walter type."

Ki laughed. "Just a step above the double-wide trailer. Come in, I need a few more minutes to find my shoes."

"Late night?"

"It shows?"

"A little. Mind if I give myself a tour?"

"Help yourself, I'll be right down."

"No hurry."

They toured several neighborhoods close to what was still called downtown although most of the original business operations were long gone to the suburbs and beyond. Many of the city departments remained along with utility companies' main offices. Yet major investments over the last two years had done much to attract several businesses back, including a home improvement center which coincided with the home repair business, a major chain and a strip of specialty stores in the fashionable Boxtown district. Of all the neighborhoods, Jaio found Boxtown the most interesting with its boxcar accents and criss-crossing train tracks along the sidewalks. Boxtown, originally a shanty town dating back to the 19th century, had a number of houses built around actual boxcars, a few remarkably preserved.

Ki directed her to a bright red caboose attached to a low building. "I'm starving and you promised me lunch."

"As you wish." She negotiated her little Austin Healy into the nearly empty parking lot. "Not much of a lunch crowd."

"Jaio, it's nearly three."

"So it is. And not one complaint about my company."

"No reason to." Ki got out and stretched.

"Do you know a real estate agent who handles the Boxtown area?" They walked up the crosstie ramp to the bistro.

"I know an agent in Oldtown, where we're going next; she should know what's available or about to become available if you're in no hurry." Ki opened the door. "Are you?"

"No. Before the fall though."

"Are you staying with your mother?" They took a seat in one of the red velvet booths as a porter dressed waiter appeared. Ordering drinks they perused the menu.

"I'm staying in an apartment at the Globe building. As you may know, my mother's personality takes up an entire city block." She chuckled.

"I've heard that."

"So how do you know my mother?" she asked abruptly, eyes piercing.

"A friend of mine works at the Globe."

"Aw, the razor penned Lin Gao."

Ki raised an eyebrow. "How did you make that connection?"

"I spent last evening reading up on you from the Globe's archives."

"Oh. Wish I had the opportunity to return the favor." Ki managed a smile. "Don't believe everything you read."

"Even from your personal publicist? My mother likes one of you to have allowed that to continue for ten years."

"And you would not?"

"No, I would not."

"And what would you have done differently?"

"What I'm going to do now, remove her from the crime beat."

Ki blinked rapidly trying to process the information just given me. One, Jaio was taking over the Globe; two, she was gunning for Gao.

"You can't remove Gao from the crime beat, she's the best crime reporter in the city."

"You are in error, Dicer."

"Bullshit, Gao can write circles around any reporter you have on staff or at any newspaper in the state."

"If that's so, why is she writing articles like this morning's?" She cleared her throat. "The crimes of illusion: Broken dreams and family violence."

"That was an insightful cultural piece on the country's bankrupt value system and how it contributes to frustration and violence. It was the non-linear process she was getting at."

Jaio sipped her water. "Now how many people got it?"

"More than you think."

"How do you know what I think?"

"Then why are you moving Gao? She loves the crime beat."

"Or do you love having your own mouthpiece in the media? Are you afraid if she were moved, you'd actually have to work?"

Ki glared at her. "What the fuck are doing? I work my ass off. Gao knows it, the chief knows it and the public knows it. I don't give a fuck what you think."

She smiled. She actually smiled. "Didn't mean to touch a nerve there."

The waiter reappeared and they ordered lunch, Ki's appetite nearly gone now.

"One question?" she said, suddenly looking serious.

"What?" Ki snapped, harsher than she meant to. Perhaps lack of sleep, that Kenny thing, and now Gao's transfer had suddenly gotten to her.

"Have you slept with her?"

Ki blinked rapidly. "None of your fucking business if I have or not." Ki raised the glass to her lips to get the sour taste out of her mouth.

She chuckled. "I can see by the disgust in your face that you have not. So I won't feel bad by asking you into my bed."

Yes, the liquid spewed from her mouth. "What?!"

Jaio wiped the 7-Up from the table. "Don't deny you haven't thought of us between the sheets. There's something cosmic between us; even my mother saw it. She cautioned me to leave you alone, by the way. Why would she do that?"

"Perhaps you're a vindictive bitch."

"Now you're angry at me." She reached for Ki's hand and she snatched it back. "Dicer . . . Can I call you Ki?"

"No." Only her mother calls her that.

"Dicer, I'm not going after Gao; I'm going to offer her a promotion, well an expanded area. And you are right, she's insightful and full of ideas. I want to turn her loose on editorials, allow her to focus that sharp wit on everybody, not just the lowly criminals."

"Why are you telling me this?" And she knew Gao and Dicer were friends before Dicer told her.

"I felt as though I owed you an explanation for my earlier comments." The stick then the honey. Real smooth, Ms. Yemen.

"Is that an apology?" Dicer asked.

"If you need one, yes. I didn't mean to upset you."

"Oh so you're just rude and enjoy pricking people to see if they bleed?"

She raised her hands in surrender. "I'm guilty. The more people bleed, the more the shark comes out in them. I like to know whether I'm dealing with a hammerhead or a bottle-nosed dolphin. I prefer not to have sharks in my bed. You can understand the necessity of that."

"You think I'm safe?" This was sounding like a very bad late movie; but Gao had already warned Dicer about her. Still she wasn't prepared for her blatant invitation to sleep with her after knowing her only 24 hours, regardless on whether she was right or not about her wanting to sleep with her.

"I would hope so, for my sake." This time Dicer didn't jerk her hand back when she reached for it.

"What's that supposed to mean?" Then she smiled, dimples in full bloom. And Dicer knew she was about to make a fool out of herself if she didn't watch it.

One thing about her family that always puzzled Dicer was their ability to get into bad, unproductive, sick, even violent relationships. One uncle left a hardworking state employee for a woman with four kids and a minimum wage job. Another one preferred crackheads over the mother of his children. One aunt was married to a man who rumors had it had another whole family in Shortsville. One cousin was known throughout the city for giving fantastic blowjobs; another had no qualms about asking strangers for money and a little more. One had reported eight children by eight different women and those were the ones known. Even her sister Kerry was in love with a habitual thief. Their family history was replete with such bad choices and infidelities, and so few examples of normal, healthy, long-term relationships. It's easy to understand why her relationships were kept to a minimum. Fear of stupidity is a strong motivator; but lust can be even stronger.

It was nearly six when Jaio drove into her courtyard and cut the engine. "Are you going to invite me in for a swim?"

"I'm sure your mother's pool is larger."

"But not as inviting." She ran a nail along her arm.

"Don't you have a company or something to run?" Ki asked in a squeaky voice.

"Like you, I'm on vacation. My sole intention for the week was to survey the city to see what it has to offer." She took Dicer's hand in hers. "And what I have to offer it."

"So which neighborhood you liked the best?" Dicer asked extracting her hand from hers and reaching for the door handle.

"Boxtown and Oldtown." Yemen got out as well. "How much acreage you have with this, Dicer?"

"Seven and a half."

"Not bad. That little cottage over there yours?" She pointed to a small log and stone cabin sitting in a hollow of trees.

"Yes. I rent it to a college student. Half the time I forget she's there." Half the time Dicer forgets to collect the rent. In the summer she doesn't bother at all, for the tenant keeps the grass down to a manageable height. When she does it, Dicer didn't know; daybreak most likely when she was dead to the world.

"A landlord, I'm impressed," Jaio teased.

"Hardly. It's two rooms with a half-bath and a two-foot square shower where a closet used to be."

"But it's snug and dry."

"That it is." Ki unlocked the door.

"What are you going to do with that pile of rocks and blocks?" she asked following Dicer into the cool foyer.

"Build a retaining wall around the courtyard."

"You have your work cut out for you."

"Not work, art." Dicer walked back to the kitchen for drinks.

"Yes, I believe you." She stood at the patio doors looking out. "Yes, your pool is quite inviting. May I?"

"Of course, I'll look for you a suit."

"Don't bother." Yemen turned to Dicer with an inviting smile. "Or are you expecting company?" Her skirt came off with one tug.

"No," Ki croaked. She wore only a slither of a black bikini, leaving little to the imagination of the secrets held between those long caramel thighs. The backless blouse came off just as easily. Her nipples jutted out from the open-cup bra. No secrets there either as Dicer's mouth watered and pulse quickened.

"You like?" she asked and turned slowly.

Dicer reminded herself that this was a very dangerous woman for her. "What would you like to drink?" she asked when her voice returned.

Her smile lit up the room. "Water will do," she said chuckling. "And you don't think you're safe?"

"Not from you. Do you always come on so brazenly?"

"Yes and no."

"Which translates into sometimes?" Dicer filled glasses with ice.

"When necessary." She looped her arms around Dicer.

Dicer turned in her grasp and realized that she was as tall as she was and there was strength in her arms as she tightened them around her. "Jaio, I'm not going to be your toy."

"You're only a toy if you want to be. You're a healthy adult exploring sexual pleasures with a similarly endowed person, playing together." Then she kissed her, literally taking her breath away as she held her in a lip-lock. Frantically Dicer pushed the glasses on the counter before dropping them. Jaio shivered involuntarily as Dicer wrapped her cold hands around her exploring her exposed back and buttocks.

In the distance Dicer heard the phone rang and the answering machine pick up. She had not switched over from working late. Gao's voice drifted through the kitchen.

"Dicer, pick up the phone. There's been another one and Lou took the kids to SeaTown. Buchova and Norris got into a shouting match that could be heard outside; then Buchova stormed off. Will you wipe your hands and pick up the damn phone. I hate these things."

Heart-throbbing Dicer broke the kiss and reached for the phone. "Lin?"

"You sound funny. What part did you hear?"

"Buchova and Norris. There's been another what?" Jaio slowly unbuttoned her blouse.

"Hanging at NFC. The second minister Warren Gomez. They are down to one now. How do you think he feels about now?"

"I. Don't. Know," Dicer said through gritted teeth as Jaio suckled her nipple.

"I'd be scared shitless. And your brothers in blue aren't saying a damn thing to the press."

"What do you want. Me to do? I'm out. Of the loop." Jaio pushed her shorts down.

"Try to get something, like why Buchova stormed off from the crime scene. I'll call about nine. You think you'll have something?"

"I hope so."

"Bye," she said, the frown in her voice.

"Bye." It took Dicer several tries to put the phone back on the hook. "Upstairs," she breathed, paying for the suggestion as Jaio bit down, stopping short of pure pain.

When Jaio drifted off to sleep, Dicer made several phone calls trying to see what was going on with the New Faith Cathedral murders. All they knew was that Warren Gomez had been found naked in his chambers tied spreadeagle to his desk. His body had been mutilated but they didn't know how. No one knew what Buchova and Norris were shouting over, except Buchova kept saying, "No more." No more what? Dicer closed her eyes, trying to get into Buchova's head. What would inspire him to lose his temper and shout, "no more" in front of bystanders?

"No more what?" Jaio asked drowsily pulling Dicer back down.

"Just talking to myself."

"Should I be worried about that?" she asked, then kissed her.

"About what?"

"You talking to yourself and/or regretting sleeping with me?"

"Neither." Dicer rolled her onto her back and lowered her head to her nipples.

Night had fallen completely when the phone rang in the darkness. "Hello?"

"You sound as though you were asleep," Ayers said.

"I was. What's up?"

"Norris nabbed Gao trying to sneak into Gomez's chamber. Buchova is nowhere to be found, Dicer. Aviles has put a soft warrant out for him."

"Where are you?"

"Downtown, she called me in wanting to know why I was taken off the case and you pitched from the scene Sunday."

"What did you tell her?"

"What do you think I told her? She had Roger's report, the one you told him to send to me."

"How the hell did she get that?"

"How the hell should I know? She wants us in her office at seven-thirty in the morning. Now, I'll have to find a babysitter." He sighed. "Ryan is still here. I got a feeling she's flown the coop. Diane wants to call social services."

"Can you blame her?"

"No. But he's almost family."

"I know. You won't believe what Kenny did last night."

"Yes, I would. Mae called me this morning accusing you of trying to destroy her son and that I should do something about you."

"Geez!"

He chuckled. "Looks like we both have family trouble."

"At least Ryan didn't try to rob you."

"Not of money. You think Diane would agree to being a foster parent?"

"You won't know until you ask her."

"A lot of help you are, Dicer. Look, I'm heading home. See you at seven-thirty."

"Hey, what about Gao?"

He chuckled. "She went to the Globe to write an angry article on the public's right to know and the state's Draconian assholes, or something to that effect. Night."

Dicer hung up and rose to go to the bathroom.

"What about Gao?" Jaio asked in the darkness, scaring her shitless for a split second.

"She tried to cross police tape and a state boy nailed her. She went to the Globe to write up her experience."

"Good for her."

Dicer went on into the bathroom. When she turned on the shower, the door opened and Jaio entered. She stood looking at herself through the mirror.

"Looking to see if the spell has worn off and returned your body to its original dumpy frog form?" Dicer asked stepping into the shower.

She gave a belly laugh Dicer didn't think she was capable of. Perhaps she had underestimated her depth. "Now who's a vindictive bitch?"

"Not I, said the frog." Dicer melted under the pulsing fingers of the shower. After hearing the toilet flush and the door close, Dicer thought she was alone until a soapy hand trailed down her back.

"What do you have to eat in the kitchen?" she asked, moving Dicer aside to get under the shower.

"I'm sure we can find something to suit your refined tastes."

"I'm not as refined as you think; my mother worked hard for everything she has and expected me to do the same."

"Is that a fact?"

"Fact. That line about my returning here against her will was full of crap. What she was against was my opting for normalcy, for choosing not to take over the reigns of the Globe two years ago." She chuckled.

"What?" Dicer asked lathering her back.

"I saw you then."

"When?"

"Two years ago. Let's see, you had on these tight baseball shorts, a white tank over a purple sports bra and your hair had been freshly cut just off your shoulder." She laughed. "And you broke your finger."

"At the kiddie carnival! That was the worst day of my life. Actually that started the worst week of my life." Dicer stared at her smiling. "You saw that?"

"Every embarrassing moment that you played off so well. For the life of me I couldn't think of why you didn't quit when your finger snapped."

"All I could think about was finishing. It was for the kids right."

"What I remember most, was how you bit your lip to keep from crying out when the paramedic snapped it back under the tent." She tugged at Ki's lip with her teeth. "I thought those were the most kissable lips I had ever seen on the craziest woman I had ever seen."

"You didn't dig that bit of info from your archives did you?"

She chuckled. "I have made a bad impression on you. Let me remedy that." She gently pushed Dicer against the shower wall and tried to dry her with her tongue.

CHAPTER 3

The big blue clock flashed 7:27 as Dicer ran up the steps to the third floor. A frown etched on his forehead, Ayers stopped in his tracks. He opened his mouth then turned around and walked towards the end of the hall. Dicer followed him as he entered the glass door and walked to the counter where a young man in shirt sleeves and blue tie waited patiently.

"Tell the deputy chief, Ayers and Dicer are here."

"She'll be with you in a second, please have a seat." He pointed to the hard benches.

Ayers sat cutting his eyes at Dicer. "You could have worn a blouse with a collar to cover up that hickey; it's bad enough you're dressed like you're on the road with the circus," he hissed under his breath.

"I don't have a hickey. Do I?" Dicer felt her neck.

"No, but that goofy smile is enough evidence. Was that the person you had lunch with yesterday?"

"Mind your own business."

"Was that why you were in bed at 9:30 and were heavy breathing when Gao called?" He glanced at Dicer. "Yeah, she noticed."

"No, I had run to the phone."

"Liar."

Aviles' door opened and she stepped out in a white pinstripe pantsuit with her gold badge worn more as a piece of jewelry. "Let's go," she said, not bothering to greet them.

Everyone in the department knew that it wasn't the chief you had to fear, but Aviles. The chief would hand feed you and occasionally whack you with a stick; Aviles fed no one and she carried a big ass stick. Downstairs in the garage the department's reigning sharp shooter, Alexis Guzman waited next to Aviles' Crown Vic.

She flashed them a quick 'don't know either' smile, when Aviles wasn't looking. Ayers and Dicer debated seating arrangements.

"Just get in," Aviles snapped.

Somehow Dicer ended up in the back seat with her. "Hot enough for you, deputy chief?" she asked.

"Shut the fuck up, Dicer. You can't stay out of trouble on vacation." She tapped on the back of the driver's seat. "14555 Hampton Road."

Ayers met Guzman's eyes in the rearview mirror. "That's the Beaver Lodge."

"I'm impressed. Now why are we going there?"

"Hell if I know. I'm on vacation." Dicer reached for her sleeve. "May I?" She felt the material between her fingers. "Very nice. 85 percent silk."

"Ninety," she corrected.

"My apologies, I've been handling marble and slate too long." Dicer ignored Ayers' snort. "You want my assessment of the situation?"

"Do you ever just shut up?" Aviles asked.

"No," Ayers said a warning for her in his voice.

"Hey, I had plans for this morning. I have tons of rock in my yard." Dicer turned to Aviles. "Have you thought of a natural rock wall for your home? I'm looking for someone willing to let me experiment on a high wall."

Aviles tapped on the headrest in front of her. "Pullover, Guzman." The car pulled into a parking lot. "Get out," she told Dicer.

Dicer got out of the car and waited on her to join her at the rear. "What's up?"

"If it were up to me, you would be walking a beat at a nursery school since you're such a damn clown." She was in her face.

"You want to kiss me, don't you?" Dicer asked with a straight face.

She laughed. "You've been around that shit too much. The next time your jacket comes across my desk, you're going out to Siberia."

Siberia was the stretch of warehouses and wasteland between the sixth
and seventh precincts.

"Why not now?" Dicer asked. "I could use the regular hours."

Aviles walked away from the car, shaking her head, throwing
her hands in the air. And Dicer knew she was in trouble. She
started towards the deputy chief when she spotted a van slowing
down and the door sliding open.

"Get down, Cat!" Dicer yelled reaching for her weapon. The
Crown Vic was thrown into reverse as Dicer raced for the deputy
chief. Knowing Ayers and Guzman, they had let the window down
to hear Dicer fuck up.

A bullet slammed into Dicer's shoulder spinning her around.

"It's you. It's you!" Dicer heard before darkness fell around her.

Dicer sat up and pain shot through her. A hand gently pushed her
backwards into softness.

"You're at County General."

"I can't see," Dicer complained.

"Open your eyes," the voice instructed as something was pulled
from her face.

"What happened?" The room was a typical ugly white box.

"I'll get your partner." The woman checked her eyes before
walking out.

Ayers walked in, his face drawn and blue shirt rumpled. "How
you feel?"

"Like I've been kicked by Aviles."

"She saved your ass, took the shooter out from the ground. He
only managed to get two bullets in you."

"I warned her."

"They weren't after her, Dice. They were gunning for you."

"Me? I'm on vacation."

He rolled his eyes much like his daughters. "That's not the
issue. What is is how they knew you were with Aviles. We left from
the garage remember."

"Meaning?"

"How many people we passed going down?"

"I don't know. Give me some water will you?"

He poured the water and carefully let up the bed. "I want to talk to Kenny; this may be related."

"What do you mean? Rob, yes. Shoot me, no."

"Kenny no. His new friends may not be so discriminating."

"What do you mean his new friends?"

"Darren Wallace is out with a bigger purse and nastier friends. One of whom is now lying on a morgue slab."

Ki's insides turned over. "She stopped the car and walked off, leaving a free shot at me."

"She took out the shooter."

"Get rid of a witness."

"Dicer, you can't possibly think Aviles of all people set you up."

"Why not, I'd think the same thing in her place," Aviles said from the doorway. "How are you, Dicer?"

"Better if I knew whose side you were on?"

She nodded. "Yours. Buchova was at the lodge. We have him in protective custody."

Ayers and Dicer locked eyes. "NCF?"

"Yes. Norris disappeared from his suite last night."

"And Buchova? What is his role?"

"He's claiming professional courtesy to the state boys. I wanted him to tell that to you two." She looked from one to the other. "Let's compare notes, shall we?"

The short of it was Aviles was investigating Buchova for his questionable relationship to Norris who was under investigation by his bureau's internal affairs unit for his association with organizations like NFC that paid him substantial consulting fees. Those consultations were believed to consist of how to avoid detection in their illegal practices. At the same time, the sex crimes unit was receiving tips of strange sexual practices at NFC, apparently the same tips Gao had been receiving. Drugs did not enter the picture until an intern misinterpreted Roger's hand scripted Ayers as Aviles on the confidential report. She noted the sample had originated with a vacationing Dicer. It didn't take her long to associate Dicer with Ayers, who had been abruptly tossed from the NFC investigation. Then Buchova went missing for four hours after a shouting match. If nothing else he was guilty of dereliction of duty and she wanted him in hand. When he reappeared they moved him to the Beaver Lodge, a favorite spot for caching material witnesses and questioning officers under investigation in lieu of taking them downtown prior to formal charges.

Then the doctor chased them out of Dicer's rooms and explained the extent of her wounds. She had been hit twice, a flesh wound in her upper arm and again in the shoulder. He had repaired most of the damage, but he predicted an extended recovery period because the bullet sliced through muscle and tendon before bouncing of the upper scapula. After a shot from a big ass needle, Dicer drifted off, thinking grass would claim her stones before she could get to them.

Her eyes slowly came open, focusing on the trim male figure at the window, looking out at the waning day. Shit two days had passed without productivity. "Dad?"

"No." He turned.

"Kip?"

"Yeah. One for two." He sat on the bed.

"You look like dad from behind."

"Don't insult me." He reached for a cup of ice. "Want me to feed you?"

"Your hands clean?"

"Are they ever?" He picked up a spoon. "You got yourself shot, kiddo. As I recall, you told me you would quit if you ever got shot."

"In the line of duty. This may not have been."

"Ayers told me about Kenny. I know they're your relatives, Ki; but those people are going to be the death of you."

"Those people? Your racism is pushing through Uncle Kip."

"You know that's not what I mean."

"Wasn't it?"

"I didn't come here to argue race with you, Ki. I told your father I would check on you to see if he needed to come down. What do you think?"

"No. I'm going up there Friday. If I can find a driver. Or I can borrow your new 6359 many lettered Mercedes that practically drives itself."

"You can ride with me or Kerry."

"What are you going up there for?"

"He wanted to talk to me about something."

"What?"

"He didn't say. All he said was he bought a boat."

"Yeah. You think he's getting married?"

"Noo." He sighed. "I hope not."

"Why not? Everyone needs a chance at happiness."

"Your father's chances costs us money. You money."

There was a soft knock on the door and Jaio stuck her head in. "Are you awake?"

"Yes, come in," Kip said rising from the bed.

Jaio came in with a small blue teddy bear. "I told them I was your sister."

"You could be. You are as beautiful as they are," Kip said extending his hand. "I'm Kip Dicer, Ki's very young uncle."

"Jaio Yemen, Ki's very new friend." She extracted his hand.

"Any relation to Yvette?" he asked.

"Daughter." She sat on the bed next to Dicer "You gave me such a fright."

"Scared me too. Sorry I missed lunch." Ki chuckled. "Can I have a raincheck?"

"Anyday."

Kip cleared his throat. "I'll leave you two alone. I'll inform your father that you are in good hands. Ms. Yemen, it was a plea-

sure to meet you and hopefully we'll have occasion to dine together." He bent and kissed Ki's forehead. "Hang tough, Kiki."

"Thanks for stopping by, Kipper."

"Bye." He slipped from the room.

"Kiki?" Jaio asked.

"Don't go there, Jaio."

She traced Dicer's lips with her finger. "You're not so tough
lying on your back." She kissed her softly. "I was so looking forward to a repeat of last night, if only the cuddling."

"We'll have plenty of time. At least until your significant other
arrives in town."

"But why should we let that ruin our fun?" She chuckled and
kissed her again. "Your uncle is quite a charmer, handsome too."

"He's full of shit and himself; but he can lay a foundation with
the best of them."

"He's in construction too?"

"No, he's in real estate and development."

"And you didn't recommend him to me?"

"I recommended you to his daughter. Did you call her?"

"I talked to her on the phone this morning; I have an appointment with her tomorrow morning. I thought you would come
with me, but that was before you were shot." She rubbed Ki's
good arm. "Are you sure you're okay?"

"Yeah. I'll never pitch left-handed for the Colorado Rockies."

"You can pitch to me any time." Jaio stroked her cheek. "Ki, I
really do want to get to know you better. All jokes and innuendo
aside. This incident underscores how tenuous life can be. And I
don't want to lose the opportunity to get to know you because of
some obscure adherence to propriety and time."

"Last night didn't count for anything?"

"For more than you know." She suddenly smiled. "Whew! Now
you know. You want to rush into a whirlwind affair?"

"Whirlwind may be a bit fast for me at the moment. How
about a breezy one? We can build up to whirlwind."

"Good enough."

When she left, Dicer's mother arrived shortly afterwards and she was not in a good mood. Her hair was disheveled and she still wore her work clothes. Worst she paced the room like an addict waiting for his fix.

"Mother, you're making me dizzy, sit down."

"For once, don't call me, mother. Mom, mommie, or mama would do just fine."

"Sorry, moms, didn't mean to offend. Rough day at work, mom?"

"No, the rough day occurred when I returned home from a trip to Canton to find out you had been shot. Then Mae calls blessing me out saying you had Kenny picked up, blaming him for your shooting."

"Mo-mom, I had nothing to do with that. I've been out of it most of the day and know nothing of anyone picking up Kenny. All I know is the shooter is dead and no one has a clue why I was shot. I told no one about Kenny, because Mae beat me to it, calling Lou Ayers complaining about me harassing her son."

"She didn't?"

"Oh yes, she did. Anything comes of that, it's her own fault."

"See this is the petty shit that burns by drawers." She sighed loudly. "You talk to your father?"

"No, he sent Kip."

"Typical Kirk."

"Mom, I told him I was fine and would go up there Friday for Father's Day."

"You can't be driving with a broken clavicle."

"It's not broken."

"May as well be. You're not going anywhere and I'm staying with you until you recover." Now those are the words she had feared since moving down the canyon.

"That's not necessary, mother."

"Of course it is. You're barely functional with two good hands."

"Gee, thanks for the putdown."

She chuckled. "I didn't mean it like that, Ki."

"You never do, mom." Ki tried to get comfortable, but her shoulder throbbed. A big needle would have done her just fine about now.

Kris Marlowe is the quintessential perky white girl, always putting the happy face on the issue, one who always wonders what the race and gender problem is all about, because in her world everyone is equal, unless of course they are not in her world. In earlier times she would have been one of those christian missionaries sent out to save the savages from their uncivilized ways. She meant no harm, but her wake could be costly. She had only had her real estate license about two years, but was doing okay with that bubbly optimism that drove her more cynical cousin mad.

And she was up and running when she appeared in the doorway of the hospital room before lunch. "How's my favorite cousin?" she crooned.

"I don't know, I haven't seen Kerry."

"You know I meant you." It was the voice one would use just before pinching a baby's cheeks.

"How's business, Kris?"

"Slow this week, but last month was overflowing. I tell you, Ki, I never thought I'd get tired of seeing a house. But that place on Landau is driving me bonkers. No one can close on it." True to form, Kris inspected Dicer's bandaging and declared it suitable.

"So what else is going on in Oldtown?"

"A few community events. The pool has reopened in the nick of time." She sat on the edge of the chair. "I met with a new client this morning."

"Really?"

"Really. She said you referred her. Jaio Yemen. Do you know her?"

"Yes."

"Perhaps I should ask how well you know her?" she asked her eyes twinkling.

"Why?"

"Nothing, just thinking if you didn't know her so well, perhaps you ought to get to know her better."

Ki laughed. "That makes two of you. You have anything she might like?"

She nodded emphatically, head bobbing like a puppy. "Two or three properties in Boxtown, but there are several estates that would suit her needs just south of there in what they are calling Park Manors now, the old Midtown area. You know where they closed off that stretch of 85 after they widened Mercury Drive? They've put up a wall and converting the section to a park vista."

"Protected from the little people by a wall of course."

She frowned. "You make it sound bad."

"No, I'm just commenting on how that wall just happens to fall between low-income neighborhoods and those big houses, that's all."

She gave Dicer a speculative glance. "Why did you get shot?"

"I don't know."

"Dad said Kenny had something to do with it. I don't believe that." She glanced down then back up at Dicer. "Do you?"

"I don't know anything about that, Kris. I'm in the dark here."

"But do you believe he's capable?" she asked.

Ki shifted uncomfortably. "Kris, people are capable of a lot of things, Kenny included. On a good day, I'd say no, Kenny would not be involved with shooting someone, not even me." She watched her curiously relax. "Kris, what's going on?"

"Nothing."

"You can't lie, Kris. What is it?"

She expelled a long breath and rose. "He came by the house early Tuesday morning. Mom gave him two hundred dollars, just to get rid of him. He was ranting about you pulling a gun on him and letting his friend take care of you."

Her blood ran cold. "You sure that's what he said?"

"No. I wasn't paying attention to what he was saying. He was high." Her nose wrinkled. "And he smelled."

"Why'd your mother give him money?"

She stared at me with those green eyes. "To get rid of him."

"Why did he come there to begin with?"

Kris shrugged. "She loans him a few dollars here and there." She pushed a stray lock behind her ear. "Family responsibility."

"He's not her family."

"He was once; and for her that's good enough." Her beeper went off. "I have a lunch appointment. When are you getting out?"

"Either this evening or early tomorrow. He wants to take a few x-rays and such for some reason. Insurance money probably."

"For once I agree with you, but better safe than sorry." She jumped back into her perky mode. "Toodeeloo."

"Toodeeloo to you too." Dicer watched her flounce out, again wondering how they were in the same family.

Ki's family? One branch white and the other black. The racial differences in economic and socio-cultural outlooks were so sharp and classical that they could be subjects in a study on the psychological effects of race and racial identification. The attitudes toward certain issues were also sharply divided along racial and often economic lines. They would look at the same situation, or their own interactions, and would attach totally different meanings. For instance family jobs would be a case in point. Kerry, David, Malik, DeShawna, Lavell and Ki worked their way through college off and on at the construction company. David and DeShawna are still there, one white and one black, no problem. Malik and Lavell, both black, worked until their graduation and they found better jobs, no problem. However in the last few years there have been problems with the jobs given the black side of the family, or so reported to Ki's mother. Their complaints have centered on the job assignments at work sites resulting in their walking off. Somewhere along the way, they got the impression that they should receive skilled positions or indoor jobs like David and DeShawna who have worked there since they were teenagers and developed skills and knowledge of the industry. In that the black side sees racism in putting them in the lowest skilled positions and the white side sees laziness in not wanting to put in hard labor to learn the business. Yet neither side bothers to tell the other what they expected and where their difference were. This misperception has gone so deep that no black family member is currently working his or her way through college there and no one else works there unless they have to and then never for more than a couple of paychecks.

To her father this is puzzling since his side of the family is small and few are coming through the pipeline and those consider construction beneath them; yet her mom's side is larger, with able-bodied men and women in need of work but on the surface refuse to work. No one listens to Ki and when DeShawna who handles the accounts and spends her days in a plush office tries to explain why they're outside spreading cement, she gets the "oreo" response. She's even been accused of sleeping with Ki's father to keep her plush office, which Ki must admit is the most extravagant in the company; but then DeShawna does hold the purse strings and it doesn't take much to be more extravagant than Kirk Dicer. Kerry should know that; she was the only person in the family to start off inside, working from a card table and folding chair.

Perhaps Ki, like Kris, was blind to certain racial undertones; but it seemed like history and the culture of racism were extraneous factors that somehow insinuated themselves in all relationships between blacks and whites even when race played no role; however the perceptions of a racial motive—

"Are you in pain, Kiwi?"

Ki's eyes flew open for the shocker of the week, of the year, making her forget the pain. "I must be delirious." She tried to sit up to get a better look at him and a pain shot through her.

"Whoa, easy." He pushed her back down and adjusted the bed.

"Kylar?"

He chuckled. "Yeah, it's me."

"What are you doing here?"

"Hoping to find a place to crash. When I got there I found the place tight as a drum. Your boarder said you were in the hospital with a gunshot. Was it self-inflicted?"

"You think I'd miss so badly?" She couldn't believe her eyes. "What are you doing here really?"

"Dad asked me to come. I thought I'd crash a couple of days at your place before having to see him. What's going on with him? He even sent me a credit card, my name and everything." Her brother Kylar, almost exactly a year younger was different and had always been so. He had a mystical thing going and swore he was Chinese and lived in Chinatown in San Francisco where he studied Daoism and other isms of the Far East. He had not been home in over a decade and Kerry or Ki usually visited him over the holidays. Kerry had begged out the last time and Ki was working. He had refused her invitation to come here.

"You look good." His hair was combed back in a high ponytail and he had that thin long Manchu moustache thing going.

"Despite your blood loss, so do you." He looked around. "When are they letting you out of this sick place?"

"This evening or tomorrow morning. I just came back from lab."

"How about we spring you ASAP?"

He didn't sound like a mystic. "Spring me?"

"Yeah, I'll get the doctor to release you. What's his or her name?"

"Him and it's Banaradi."

"Back soon." He slipped from the room.

Has your life ever been going so smoothly then all of a sudden the world turns upside down and you're walking on what was once the ceiling? Adding two and two gets you six and everyone around you is speaking in code while mere strangers become your best friends and old friends become even stranger. That's how Ki saw things when Kylar sprung her from the hospital and drove home. Everything was happening all at once; even the drive home seemed different from the thousand times she'd done it before. What was her dad up to? Why had her mom gone to Canton? Why was she shot? Was Kenny involved? If not, what was he involved in? Was Buchova dirty? Norris? What was the deal on NFC? Were they trafficking drugs? Were they involved in some bizarre sexual rituals? And who was killing their preachers? All these questions were swirling around in Ki's head as she entered her house.

"You should learn to shut off your mind," Kylar said as he helped her up the stairs.

"What are you talking about?"

"You're a worrier, Kiwi. When you get your teeth into something you don't want to let go. Usually you focus on that and you're off. Now, there are several things vying for your attention and you can't grasp either one. Am I right?"

"I guess. Why?"

"We'll work on it after your nap."

"I'm not sleepy."

"You will be."

And he was right, but that didn't shut off her mind as he put it. Something was going on around her and she wanted to know what it was. First, however, she needed a nap.

CHAPTER 4

Growing up, she remembered her female relatives' discussions on love, sex, and man-hunting, which dominated much of their interaction. To her young ears they sounded as if their entire lives revolved around finding a man to reinforce their womanhood. It's interesting to think where they would be if they spent less time thinking and talking about men and focused more on themselves. Some have spent years and thousands of dollars on worthless men no one else would want. Let's rephrase that, men no one with good sense should want. Due to the lack or perceived lack of men, too many women are willing to put up with all kinds of shit from their men, young and old; and her family was no exception. Over the years, they have given her such a hard time over her sexuality (and other things) that whenever one of them had "mantrouble," Ki conveniently dropped them a sympathy card that reminded them that they wouldn't have this problem if they were a lesbian. So when her favorite teenage cousin came over with a multiple signed get well card, someone had thoughtfully reminded her in green ink that she would not have this problem if she were heterosexual.

"I didn't write it," Nikki said sitting on the edge of the bed.

"Of course you didn't; you wouldn't have misspelled heterosexual."

She laughed. "You're right."

"So your mom let you have the car?"

Her sensuous lips pursed. "No. I borrowed Uncle Kip's Pathfinder. I have it most of the time anyway."

"You like working for him?"

She rolled those big brown eyes. "He's a trip; he has me getting women's telephone numbers and sending them lingerie."

"Nuh uh."

"Yes, he does." She drew her feet up on the bed. "This one woman came to the office, I swear she didn't have on underwear when she left. And you should see the condoms he has."

Dicer frowned. "Where?" He had better not be showing her sex items.

"In a locked cabinet in his office. I found it one day he was out of town and needed a file out the cabinet. I opened the wrong one." She shook her head. "Man. I hope he looks at the expiration date, 'cause there ain't no way he could use all those unless he's on triple doses of Viagra."

"Maybe he collects them."

"Maybe, but he's using his share too." The teenager gave her a knowing nod.

"So besides the lessons in Kip's sex life, how is the rest of it?"

"Not too boring. I spend most of my time looking through architectural magazines and on the internet looking at houses. He tells me I should think of architecture as a career since I like his CAD programs so much. By the end of summer, I'll be an expert anyway." She giggled.

"So you're having a good time there?"

"Yes, except he calls me you at least twice a day." She giggled again.

"And you're insulted?" Ki teased.

"Noooo. It's just he looks so funny when he apologizes. He really is a nice man," she said as if she had doubts before.

"Yeah, he can be."

"He asks a lot of questions though."

"Yes, he is inquisitive. Does that upsets you?" Ki was getting the distinct impression she was wanting to ask her something.

"No, but it makes you think."

"About what?"

She wrapped her arms around her long legs. "Lots of things. About race, class, the future, the things you're always mumbling about. I guess that's where you got it from."

"Maybe."

"Did you know he had offered Uncle Joe a job and Joe punched him for it?"

Ki nodded. "I heard the story." The incident had happened a few years ago at a family picnic. Joe had gotten laid off at the plant after a strike. Kip, the insensitive lout, offered Joe a minimum wage job in front of the entire brood. His manhood offended, Joe punched him, knocking him across the table. Until Nikki, Kip never offered another person on her mother's side a job, not even for the summer, which furthered his reputation as a racist among the black part of the family, which was what Nikki probably expected. "I don't get it; mom says it's because I hung around you too much and forgot I was black. She tells me I shouldn't let Kip swell my head up with ideas and that if he keeps letting me use his truck he's going to want something in return."

"Whooaa!" There it was. "Kip made a pass at you?"

Nikki shook her head vigorously. "Nooo, but I can't convince mom of that."

"Why would she think that?"

"She's crazy. She thinks I'm her. She's the one who threw herself at him." She fell back on the bed.

"Is that why you called me last weekend?" Ki had never caught up with her.

"Some of it."

"What's the other?"

"Nothing major. I was thinking of moving out; I could barely study last year with all those kids running through the house. How am I suppose to do college level work this fall?"

She had a point. "Have you thought about how you're going to finance living on your own? Rent is not cheap."

"Uncle Kip said if I want I can work part-time, though mostly on the weekends when school starts. And I was thinking. . . ."

"What?"

"Connie said she was graduating in the fall. She'll probably get a job and move away. You'll need a new tenant." She glanced at Dicer. "I can mow your yard and trim the hedges."

"And what do you plan to do in the fall?"

"I'll stay on campus; it'll be a good experience for me. What do you think?"

"Sounds like a plan. Think about it when you're not mad at your mother."

"I don't know when that will be. You know she asks me for money when I get paid, says living ain't free and she's done her part. I don't do nothing and she starts yelling at me as soon as I walk through the door. And those lazy ass niggers are sitting around in the air-conditioning watching cable all day." She wiped her eyes. "It ain't my fault I don't want to be like her. I can't stand going home anymore, Dice." She buried her face in the pillow, her body racked with sobs.

"Nikki." Ki soothed her as best as she could. When Kylar came up to tell her dinner was ready, she waved him away. Apparently everything was not going as well for Nikki as Ki had assumed. "Nikki, why didn't you tell me things were going bad for you?"

"You were so proud of me, I didn't want you to know I wasn't strong; I couldn't handle my own problems."

"Sometimes talking about your problems helps to solve them. And you know you can come to me about anything."

"Mom says I'm always running to you; you probably get tired of me complaining, but won't say nothing."

Now Ki was angry. "Nikki! Sit up. One arm or not, if I ever hear such drivel again, I'm going to kick your ass. Don't ever let someone else's stupid ass notions keep you from doing what you know is good for you. Mother or no. And when have you known me to hold my tongue? Go wash your face. It's time for dinner."

See that's the type of negativity that gets on her last nerve, black, white, red or yellow. Parents undermining their children's self-esteem, placing barriers before them because of their own in-

powerlessness. And not just in their family either.
everywhere these days; parents exploiting, abusing
˻ ˼ˬ their children in some form or another. Often it's
for reasons as simple and stupid as jealousy; that's Betty's problem. She sees in Nikki what she could have been, should have been
if she had not made wrong choices at a time when she shouldn't
have been making those choices anyway, including bad choices in
men. And here she was playing psych games with her smartest
daughter, the only one of four to make it out of high school without a baby. A hardworking, solid B student with a fabulous future
ahead of her, being sabotaged by her own mother, after years of
being used as a free babysitter while her sisters went about their
merry lives. This shit got on Ki's last nerves.

She was still steaming when she made it into the kitchen,
discovering Kylar was not alone; her mother and Lin Gao sat at the
table, both giving her a disapproving look.

"That arm rots off, don't expect me to wipe your ass," her
mother told her.

"I'm right handed, mother."

"Don't get flip with me, young lady."

"Oooh, shivery me timbers, mother's getting, motherly." Ki
kicked out a chair and sat down. "Ms. Gao, you want to say something?"

"You're full of it."

"Thank you, thank you very much," she did her best Elvis,
then looked down at the plate Kylar placed before her. "What the
hell is this?"

"Onions, garlic, bean sprouts over diced beef, seasoned for
your rapid recovery," Kylar informed her.

"It stinks. Why can't I have what they have?"

"Because you're injured." He dashed pepper on the plate of
gruel. "Bon appetit."

"You're heartless." Ki saw Nikki ease into the doorway.
"Come on over Nikki and watch my total humiliation by my
family and my ex-friend."

"I should be getting back."

"Nonsense, your plate is on the table," Kylar told her, taking her by the hand. "And we haven't had a chance to talk. I haven't seen you since you came out with Kiwi what three-four years ago. You must tell me your plans to take NSU by storm. And go through my bags to find your graduation present. Will you stay?"

"Sure." Nikki sat down between Dicer and Gao.

"Hold your chin up," Gao told her. "What's a pretty and smart girl like you doing with teary eyes?"

"Just worried about Dice."

"Honey, Dicer is the last person you should shed a tear over. She can take care of herself." Gao winked at her. "On the other hand, Dicer should worry about what she's putting the rest of us through."

"What am I putting you through, Ms. Gao?" Ki asked trying to delay eating her gruel.

"Heartaches and tribulations," her mother said, nodding her head slowly.

"See Nikki, you would think I could get a moment of sympathy from my mother, but nooo. You just have to bear it and keep going. Parents are a child's ball and chain, always there tugging at you, trying to hold you back."

Her mother eyed her coldly as if knowing specifically what she was referring to. "Baby, don't let Ki's queer philosophy get your behind in a jam with your mother; when she's off getting shot at, you'll need your mother. And Betty will always be your mother."

So the family grapevine had reached out and touched her mother again. "My queer philosophy, as you call it, does not advocate allowing another, mother or not, to undermine a person's self-development."

"Does your philosophy say anything about disobedient and impudent children not living out their days?"

"I don't believe it does. Are you hoping for my speedy demise?" Ki asked close to laughter.

"One of these days, Ki," her mother warned waving her fork.

"I'm at a pretty good disadvantage now, mother." Ki laughed.

And her mother threw a roll at her, hitting her square on the nose. "Mother!"

"You asked for it," Kylar said raising his beer to his lips as Gao and Nikki tried unsuccessfully not to laugh.

"Whose side you on?" Ki asked him.

"No one." He quietly returned to his meal as they settled into companionable banter. Her mother filled them in on the latest gossip.

After dinner Gao and Ki went out on the veranda. Outside she relaxed, but only to notice Lin Gao looked pale and tired. "You've getting enough sleep, Lin?"

"No. I'm trying to work on NFC and a new project that was tossed into my lap. All my editor says is it came from above."

"What's the subject?"

"It's internal; somebody wants to try out ideas because it's summer. At least I got an intern out of it."

"Oh. So how's the NFC coming? Ayers dropped by for five minutes and said nothing about the case, that one or mine."

"The police has the third minister in a safe house while they investigate. There is no physical evidence linking anyone to the murders. Hundreds of interviews have turned up no suspects."

"So they have nothing?"

"That's about it."

"And the drugs?"

"Not a trace. With the disappearance of Norris the case went dead in the water, which he most likely killed."

"Yeah. Any more e-mail on them?"

"Not a word, a curtain of silence has fallen over this case."

"Maybe everyone is going about it all wrong."

"Yeah, I'm sure they are; you can't force people to talk."

"No, but you can create an opportunity for them."

"What do you have in mind?"

"I don't know, let me sleep on it. What do they know?"

"Both preachers were from Miami and their throats were cut with a thin blade."

"And what does the toxicology report say?"

"I haven't seen one."

"Call Roanan to see when the results will be back." Ki drummed her fingers on the arm of the chair. "And you may want to talk to Aviles."

"She hasn't returned my calls." She smacked her lips. "I sure could use a smoke."

"No, you can't."

"You want to comment, on the record, about your shooting?" She waved her trusty tape recorder at Ki.

"Okay, although I have nothing much to say. I regret that the shooter lost his life, but not that he was stopped before he found his range or I'd be on that slab. I don't know why I was targeted and the police will investigate the shooting as diligently as possible given our limited staff. The police have long been targets of young assholes looking to make their paper; however shooting for cover is a cowardly act. As demonstrated by Aviles actions we are—" She clicked off her recorder. "What you do that for?"

"I'm not going to listen to you issue a public challenge. I have enough."

"But it'll be out of context. What happened to your journalistic integrity? I want my side presented."

"Very well. Did you sleep with Jaio Yemen and why is she fucking with me?"

"None of your business and I don't know."

"You are and you're lying."

Ki sighed. "Okay, one night, all night, and she did mention a promotion for you when she takes over the Globe. She's afraid you won't take it."

"So she's making my life miserable now." Gao laid back her head. "But I can handle Jaio; you be careful."

"Why, does she have a history of seducing shallow officers and leaving them satiated, but heart broken?"

"No, she has a reputation for getting what she wants." She shook her head. "And I can't for the life of me understand why she wants you."

"That hurts, Gao."

"I didn't mean that like it sounded. Minus the bandages you're attractive enough; however with Jaio there's always some intangible that you don't see until it's too late. Besides the obvious, what does she want from you?"

"Isn't that enough?"

"I don't know, Dice. I'll ask some of your old flames who obviously didn't think so."

"Oh, it's beat up on Dicer night. Maybe I should sell tickets tomorrow; at least it's Friday."

Nikki came to the door. "Dice, you have company. Want me to send them out here or are you coming in?"

"I'll come in; it's getting a little sticky for me." Ki took her time getting up and going in.

Jaio waited on the sofa in the front room flipping through a magazine. Her eyes shifted from Ki to Gao. "Good evening Ki, Ms. Gao."

"Ms. Yemen." Gao chucked Ki on her good arm. "Later, Dice."

"Get some sleep, Gao."

"Not with three jobs to keep me busy." She winked and let herself out.

"Do you think you should be up?" Jaio asked.

"No." Ki sat down. "Why are you jerking Gao around?"

"I'm doing no such thing."

"Why don't I believe you?"

"She came running to you didn't she?"

"No. I'm psychic. Are you fucking with her because of me or are you just a nasty bitch?"

She chuckled. "A nasty bitch. And what goes on at the Globe is independent of our relationship. I hope you remember that in the future."

"Oooh, everyone is putting me in my place tonight. My mother, brother, Gao, and now you. Perhaps I should have stayed in the hospital, being out is detrimental to my mental health."

"Honestly, Ki. I'm not fucking with her as you say, just scouting out my talent. I need to know how flexible my staff is. Your friend is a professional and doesn't need you to fight her battles even as you seduce her employer."

"Oh, I'm seducing you? You virtually attacked me in my kitchen."

Despite her bravado the day before, when Ki awoke Friday morning she knew that she would not be making the three hour trip to Canton or anywhere else for that matter. Her entire body felt drained and made of lead, the lethargy the doc was talking about. Frankly it may have been withdrawal from those big ass shots he had given her. No telling what was in that shit. Now paranoia? Yep, drugs alright. They were trying to make her a drug addict. Now how would she look an addict? Not that an officer working the drug scene becoming an addict was uncommon; but she didn't even have a bottle of aspirin in the house and rarely suffered the modern maladies of headaches, stress, backaches and fatigue. Until that asshole decided to put two bullets in her arm and shoulder, she was in perfect health, her body toned and agile with low body fat, with enough muscle to do what she wanted, but not enough to ruin the symmetry of her clothing.

Pulling herself to the bathroom, she looked into the mirror, nearly scaring herself at the sight of her pasty complexion, the unruly mane of dark brown hair, eyes sunk into the sockets making her cheekbones more prominent. The only thing that remained hers was the lips, no collagen there as she blew herself a kiss. "You look like shit!"

"Yes, you do."

Letting out a yelp, Ki spun around hurting her shoulder. "Don't you know how to knock?"

"I did," her mom said. "Your talking to yourself obviously drowned it out."

"You and Kylar finally went to bed?" Even with Kylar here, she had insisted on staying, catching up on her eldest son. Her youngest was the complete opposite of the gentle Kylar; Keven with a Rambo mentality had joined the military and was somewhere in Europe on exercises.

"Yes. Now, let's get you cleaned up." She reached for her arm. Ki stepped back. "I can do it."

She laughed. "Those are your famous words. Now shut up and let me help you for once. I don't have all day; I have to go to work sometime this morning."

Sighing she gave in, too exhausted to put up much of a fight; her mom was as tall and thirty pounds heavier and didn't mind throwing it around.

After a day of Kylar's administering of various potions and techniques, Ki felt pretty good by early evening and was looking forward to someone's, anyone's visit. Kylar enticed Connie from her cottage to join him in the pool. Taking his cue, Ki dialed Ayers.

"Hello?" his wife Diane answered.

"Hi, Diane, it's Dicer."

"Lou's not home yet. How are you doing?"

"Tired."

"You lost a lot of blood and had surgery; you shouldn't have left the hospital."

Ki raised her eyes to the ceiling. "So everyone keeps telling me. Where are the girls?"

"Upstairs cleaning up. Why?"

"Kylar's here and the pool is free. If you wanted to drop them off to run a few errands or spend the evening with your hubby, feel free."

"Did you get hit in the head too?" She chuckled.

"In some ways yeah. Do you still have Ryan?"

Ki could hear her whole demeanor change in the silence. "Yes."

"Then I know you need a couple of hours to yourself. Drop them off; they're no trouble."

"I do need to run a few errands for two hours," she hedged.

"Great. I'll be expecting you soon."

"Alrighty then. Bye."

"Bye."

Okay, so maybe Ki was a little crazed inviting three children over. However, they were indeed no trouble once in the pool.

Half an hour later Diane arrived with the children who rushed right on past Ki with the merest of greetings. Diane shook her close cropped head at her normally well-behaved children.

"It's the weather," Ki offered with a half-smile.

"No excuse." Her eyes took in Ki blue tank top over her heavily bandaged arm. "How does it feel?"

Ki wriggled the fingers of her left hand. "Good, but don't ask me to play volleyball."

"Wouldn't dream of it." She handed over Ryan's bag. "I should be back in two hours; but I left a note for Lou telling him where they are, so he may pick them up if he comes home on time. But I doubt it."

"No problem, take your time. We have plenty of snacks to keep them four or five hours."

"Then you would never let them back in." She glanced up at me. "Thanks, Dicer."

"Don't mentioned it. I was kind of selfish wanting a little fun and mayhem around."

"Mayhem maybe." She checked her watch. "Gotta go. Two hours."

"Three hours, and stop worrying. This isn't the first time you've left them with me."

"No, but then you had two good arms."

Ki chuckled. "Go'on."

She walked out into the courtyard and turned around. "Okay. If you have any trouble, beep me."

Ki rolled my eyes. "I know." Ki watched her leave, thinking about all she and Lou had been through over the years; Lou's ill advised affair, the loss of a child, the long illness of parents, the violent death of a brother. This last year had been the first time since Ki had known her that she had been free of some other obligation or grief and the change was noticeable in manner as well as appearance. She was toning up, dressing sharper and sported the very short afro instead of the ponytail. Diane always had a beautiful though shy smile, but now there was a light in her eyes to match it.

Ki caught sunlight on a car window down the lane; then Kip's new Mercedes came into view. For a moment she thought he wasn't going to stop as he came to an abrupt halt, inches from Kylar's rental Ford. His face was as red as the stain on his undershirt as he got out of the car slamming the door.

"What happened to you?" Ki asked, squinting against the sunlight.

"That crazy bitch took a bottle of ketchup to me!" He stamped his feet.

"Who?"

"Betty!" He pranced like he was going somewhere then stopped in front of her. "You tell her if she does that again, woman or not, I'm decking her black ass."

Ki raised an eyebrow. "I'm not telling her black ass nothing. What happened?"

"Nikki left early, something she ate. Knowing I had to pass their neighborhood to get here, I decided to drop off her check. What did I get for my trouble?" He tugged at his shirt. "Fucking ketchup! That woman's crazy; your whole fucking family's crazy."

"Yes, both sides. Why did she squirt ketchup on you?"

He looked at Ki as if she had asked if the sun was in the sky. "I don't know."

Ki kicked a loose pebble. "Let me ask you this, Kip. Have you done anything to make her think you were trying to seduce Nikki?"

"What?" he hissed at her. "You can't be serious, Kiki. I treat that girl like my own, like I would you. She's had my Pathfinder since I got the Benz. I give her career and financial advice as I did you and Kris. The girl's too smart to be at the mercy of that wench. I regret the day I ever . . . " His voice faded and his glance slid away.

"What?" She asked, sensing something important there.

"Nothing. I need a drink. Can I borrow a tee-shirt?" He headed for the house.

Glancing at the car, Ki followed him into the kitchen. "Kylar did tell you I wasn't going up with you?"

"Yeah. Yeah." He opened a bottle of Brazilian brandy. "Why don't you have on the air conditioner?"

"Because it's only eight-two degrees and the ceiling fans work just fine. You on the other hand are still steaming from your encounter with Betty. What is it with you two anyway?"

"She's a crazy bitch."

They both jumped as the front door slammed. Neither had heard anyone drive up. Ki was trying to think where she had moved the kitchen gun to with all the children in the house, when Nikki called Kip's name. When she entered the kitchen, her eyes were red and hair full of white sticky clumps. She glanced from Ki to Kip, then back to Ki.

"Did you know?" she asked Ki in a hurt voice.

"Know what?" Ki asked more alarmed at the sound of her voice than her sudden appearance.

She motioned to Kip. "Betty says he's my father," she said in a strangled voice.

Stepping back as if from a blow, Ki stared at Kip. "No, can't be, Nikki. Tell her Kip." He didn't move. "Kip?"

He sighed, slumping against the counter. "I'm willing to take a blood test to see."

"What the fuck do you mean!" Somehow, Ki had acquired a paring knife when crossing the room.

"Christ, Kiki, put that down." He took the small knife from her. "Look, both of you sit down."

"No," Nikki shook her head.

"Sit down please. Let me explain my position here." He reached for her; she slapped his hand away. "Nikki. Kiki?" He looked from one to the other.

"You better explain fast, Kip," Ki told him. "And none of your bullshit!"

He filled his brandy glass and glanced at Ki. "I didn't know she was mine. I suspected, even asked, but Betty denied it. Afterall she was married to that trailer park white trash at the time." He glanced at Nikki. "No offense, sweetie."

"That it?" Ki asked frowning, for this was far too flimsy to accept.

"She would never agree to paternity tests and I didn't pursue it because . . . " He hunched his shoulders. "I thought if Nikki were mine, she'd waste no time trying to get something out of me. So . . . " He shrugged.

Nikki glanced at Ki and her iron heart broke. "Nikki, are you okay?"

She wiped her face. "But my mom hates you. How did this happen?"

He shook his head. "I can't."

"You owe me that much."

He glanced at Ki again. "After a New Year's Eve party, she became a little tipsy, your mother asked me to drive her home. I did. However, before we arrived we were intimate."

"In the back seat?" Nikki sneered.

Kip shrugged. "Front or back. I don't remember. I'm willing to take a paternity test, one way or the other."

"I can't fucking believe this," Ki groaned, looking from one to the other. Her favorite cousin and favorite uncle on different sides of the family may be father and daughter. That could explain alot, one being their uncanny resemblance, although she believed Nikki was much prettier. Ki couldn't ever remember seeing Nikki and Kris together enough to notice a resemblance. Geez, what would this do to Kris? What if they were father and daughter?

As they stood staring from one to the other, Ki's mother walked in carrying three pizza boxes. "I didn't know we were having a party," she said, spotting the children in the pool with Kylar and Connie as she put the boxes on the counter. Dropping her purse, she turned to them. "What's wrong?"

Nikki only pointed at Kip and burst into tears which was enough to get her flying towards him. He moved to put the table between them. "Carolyn!" he cried.

"Mom!" Ki restrained her with her one good arm. "It's not what you think. Betty told Nikki that Kip was her father."

"What?!" Now she rubbernecked from one to the other.

"Betty never allowed a paternity test," Ki went on glancing at Kip. "He's willing to take one if Nikki wants."

Carolyn turned on Kip. "How the hell you let this happen?"

"Me, ask your crazy ass sister. She told me Nikki wasn't mine. What was I suppose to do?"

"Make her." Ki swore smoke came out of her ears. "You are both damn idiots. How the hell did this happen?"

"That New Year's party when I drove her home."

Carolyn paused for a good minute before exploding, "She was drunk for Christ's sake!"

"Not that drunk," he murmured.

Then Carolyn leveled her steely gaze at her daughter. "You know about this?"

"Nothing." Ki glanced at Nikki. "Are you okay?"

She nodded. "Yes."

"Would you help me upstairs?" Ki asked her.

"Sure." Nikki grabbed her arm and nearly dragged her upstairs.

What the hell was going on with her family? And why were they all bringing their troubles to her doorstep? When Ki came out of the bathroom, Nikki lay curled up in her bed. "Nikki, honey."

"Huh?" She didn't move.

"I don't know what to say." What could you say to a seven-teen-year-old who was just told that her employer may or may not be her father, that she may have been the product of not even a one night stand, but a drunken coupling after a party?

"Why would she do that to me, Dice? All these years. Why tell me now?"

"Because she thought he would seduce you or vice versa." Now what did that say about Kip and Betty and her thoughts of him? Not much.

"I don't know why she'd think that when she was . . . " Nikki sighed and sat up. "Dicer, can i spend the night here? I don't think I can face her after what she said to me."

"You want to talk about it?"

"No." She raised teary eyes to Dicer. "I just need time to myself."

"Okay. Stay as long as you want." Flipping the switch for the ceiling fan, Dicer walked out and back down to the kitchen.

The two girls with their hair glistening in small braids and towels around their waists sat at the granite counter where Carolyn had just placed slices of pizza in front of them. Ryan sat in Connie's lap as she wiped his face. For a second everything appeared calm and normal as Kip filled glasses with ice and soft drink. Kylar removed a steaming bowl from the microwave, then glanced at his sister questioningly.

"Do you have any chips?" Lily asked.

"I think so. Kylar, try that cabinet over you." Dicer swiped one of Kip's glasses and hitched herself on the remaining stool. "Having fun?"

"Kylar lives on the ocean," Lily said reasonably impressed. "He said we could stay at his house if we ever come that way. You think dad will take us?"

Kip chuckled as he placed their drinks in front of them. "I don't think your father would appreciate your wanting to go across country to see a man at your tender age." He made a face at them. "And why don't you ever visit me? My pool is not as large as an ocean, but it's bigger than Kiki's."

"Oh now we're playing 'mine is bigger than yours' here. If that's the case, Lou is bigger than you. So be careful." Dicer sipped her soda. "What brought you over here anyway? I told you I wasn't riding to Canton with you this evening."

He glanced at her mother. "I was just coming by to check on you. You didn't sound yourself this morning on the phone. Until I saw you I had every intent of taking you back to the hospital."

Ki winked at him. "Not as bad as you thought."

Nearly four hours after Diane dropped the children off, she returned apologizing profusely that she had lost track of time. Her hair was freshly trimmed, her makeup and nails done. She looked too good to waste the night in front of the television where her children already were.

"Diane, leave them here. They're already in big t-shirts and in the midst of a sci-fi marathon. Drag Ayers from whatever he's doing and make a night of it. Nikki's here and so is my mother; they won't be any trouble."

She was torn. "But Ryan?"

"Best buddies with Kylar."

"You have three houseguests, there's no room."

"I have an air mattress and plenty of pillows." Dicer watched her come to a reluctant decision to leave them with her, which was always the case. Normally Ki was the safest person she would consider leaving them for any length of time or at all. Diane's distrust wasn't Ki per se, but her overall distrust of people in general and her tendency to do everything herself, including keeping her two daughters from an accidental death while in the custody of someone else. She didn't want to lose another child to that fate.

"Okay. I'll be by first thing in the morning to get them."

"Not too early, they'll want their early morning swim." Ki gently nudged her out the door. After a few more brief instructions, she left with her mind on dancing the night away.

CHAPTER 5

The waves broke on the rocks spraying Dicer with foam. Then someone laughing grabbed her arms pushing, yet holding her tight.

"Kiwi!" Kylar's voice floated from the tide, then into her ear. Her eyes flew open to see him standing over her, his face creased in worry. "The kids?"

"No. Lou's downstairs." He held her robe out.

"Just pass me those shorts," she said shaking her head. "What's he doing here this time of night?"

"An explosion at their house," he whispered.

"What?! Where's Diane?" Ki stepped into the shorts, her nightshirt half in.

"Downstairs too." He waited for her by the door as if she had forgotten the way downstairs.

Kylar was staying in the big downstairs guest bedroom. Nikki had taken the bedroom Ki referred to as Katie's room and her mom was in the spare bed upstairs, next to hers. The children were in the parlor she had been using as a den until the completion of the large family room. Someone had closed the doubledoors leading to the front room where Diane in a short blue party dress lay curled into a corner of the sofa holding onto a pillow. Ayers in a nicely cut beige suit, now stained, paced, his heels clickety-clacking on the tile.

"What happened?" Ki asked.

"Someone blew up our fucking house!" Ayers exploded. "If we had been there. . . ." He shook his head, moving his mouth as if to speak. "My kids could have been there." Then he sank into the sofa. Carolyn came in looking at everyone as if discerning their thoughts.

"When did this happen?"

"About one-thirty. When we arrived a little after two the fire department had put out the fire, such as it was." It was nearly five now. "Then we went through everything with arson, the bombsquad, every fucking bureaucrat downtown. The fuckers wanted to know why we weren't home as if they were fucking disappointed we didn't become crispy critters!"

"Mother, would you take Diane upstairs and find something clean for her to put on?" Ki asked her mother.

Mother nodded. "I'll change the sheets while she's taking a bath, then make breakfast." She bodily pulled Diane to her feet. "A good long soak will do you good."

Ki sat down next to Ayers. "What's this about?" Ki asked slowly.

"I'm too close to something, Dicer." He shook his head. "This morning I met with the governing board of the NFC, with a list of complaints filed and those of Gao. I pushed, pushed hard. They may have just pushed back. Ughh!! You don't mess with a cop's family!"

"No, you don't. What's Aviles saying?"

"She yanked me." He glanced at his watch. "About half an hour ago, saying I was part of the case now, as you are. There's a patrol out front. All I could think about was my kids; they could have been there. I'm gonna get those sonsofbitches and make sure they fry in hell!"

Ki touched his arm to bring him back. "Lou, who's on the case if she yanked you?"

"Pearson and the new fed liason, Gravel or something." He rubbed his hands over his face. "And I'm not off the case; no one knows more about this case than I do; they're going to need my help."

"First you need sleep, man," Kylar said returning with a cup of tea for him.

"I can't sleep." Lou stood up stretching.

"Then just rest." Kylar handed him the cup.

Lou sniffed at it. "Got something to go in here?" He strode towards the kitchen.

Kylar turned to Ki. "What's going on? You, Kip and mom have been whispering around me. What am I missing?"

Ki gave him the short of it. And his advice was not profound, nor his observation keen.

In the kitchen, Lou rifled through the fridge mumbling. "What happened to the beer?"

"Downstairs. There's brandy and bourbon over the fridge." Ki slipped onto a stool, as he took down a bottle.

"Want one?"

"No." It wouldn't mix with her meds nor whatever Kylar was doctoring her with. "What are we going to do?"

Ayers downed his drink. "You aren't going to do a damn thing. I don't see why that fool doctor let you out of the hospital. You have no idea how you were tore up. Your fucking blood was everywhere." He ranted a good ten minutes about her shortcomings until her mother entered the kitchen. Now the myth about black women cooking is exaggerated; Ki's mother cannot cook anything beyond breakfast and never made any apologies for it. She never babied any of them which made her presence now all the more surreal. Growing up, Kip lived with them most of the time and played the resourceful uncle to the hilt. Of course it was a ruse in public to get the girls; nothing but a loving, sensitive man would take his nieces and nephews around and prepare their meals; as evident race was not an issue. Even businesswise it played out with his investors and clients being a significantly high percentage of women. He was everything a so-called modern independent woman would want, except monogamous.

Carolyn, on the other hand, was the so-called modern woman fighting her way through a large family, working her way through college, marrying interracially, having four children and a career, not to mention her family obligations to her siblings and their respective families. At times she would complain about how her children turned out (which she blamed on Kip); then she would make an about face to put out how her relatives children went so wrong by explaining what she did so right. As an individual Carolyn Goddard-Dicer was a stranger to Ki, and Kylar as well. When she walked in last night with the three pizza boxes, it was how Ki thought of her growing up, coming in with those three boxes of pizza.

"Ki, go to bed or snap out of it," she said pushing her aside to look through the cabinets. "Who organized this?"

"Kerry," Ki told her.

"That explains it," she said dryly.

"Can I use your shower, Dicer?" Ayers asked hanging onto the bottle.

"Yeah. Let me get you some towels."

He waved her off. "I know where they are. Or have you moved the linen closet since the other day?"

"No."

"I put Diane in the other room at the end of the hall," her mother told him as he left. Then she turned to Ki. "I put my things in your room."

"Thanks, mom." Ki watched her mother study her for a long moment. "What?"

"Nothing."

"No, what is it?" I hated when she did that.

"There's so much you could be doing besides being a cop."

"Like what?" Here we go again.

"Look at these floors. They pay top dollar for work like this. Your father has to contract people to do this sort of work. Your love for the work is evident in every tile and stone here. You have a graduate degree. Your father or Kip would love to turn over part of their business to you. And you wouldn't have lunatics shooting you or blowing up your friend's house."

Arguing with her mother would just give her a headache. "Mother, how do you know what dad is paying contractors and what he'd love for me to do? And since we're on the subject, what were you doing in Canton on the day I was shot?"

"You worry me, Ki. If I want to know something about you I have to call Kirk. You don't talk to me, your own mother."

"And that's my fault too, I imagine."

"Not solely." Now that was quite an admission for her.

"Well, I'm sorry mother, but you and I never seem able to get past certain issues. To you I will always be the impudent kid you throw rolls at."

She chuckled. "I apologize."

"You oughta. No one else gets a roll thrown at them. Why me?"

"Because no one else would appreciate it. Kylar would be offended, Kerry would be traumatized, and well that boy would be angry." She cracked open eggs. "I'm fifty-odd years old and my children are all adults with their own lives; yet I still worry as if they were the age of Lou's children. One grandchild and no promises of more. I've missed so much of their growing up."

"What are you talking about?"

She chuckled again. "An old woman's babbling."

"Old my ass." A few strings of grey, but little had changed over the years. She still stood proud and straight, her eyes alert and measuring.

"I'm going to talk to Betty this morning and clear this whole thing up with Nikki. That child deserves to know the truth one way or another."

"You've never been more right in your life."

"She's my sister true enough, but . . . " She shook her head. The burdens, disappointments, heartaches for a moment were evident on her still smooth skin; that part she guarded ever so closely was bare for the briefest of moments. "She's a lot like you; I've always said that."

"Nikki?"

"Yes." She glanced at Ki. "I guess that's why you gravitated to her when you so pointedly avoided the rest of your cousins."

"I do not avoid them. Their interests and mine are dissimilar, not to forego the fact that they hate me."

She suppressed her smile. "I love when you get haughty and drop that goddamn twang. Where did you pick it up anyway?"

Switching horses in the middle of the stream again and people wonder why Ki jumped from subject to subject. "Mom, just what are you making with a dozen eggs?"

She looked down at the mixing bowl full of eggs. "I guess omelets. Didn't I see some ham in there?"

"Yeah."

"Now here's what I want you to do for Lou."

Ki tried not to roll her eyes, but couldn't help it. "What mother?"

"He's family, so don't get that tone with me. I changed his diapers before I changed yours."

"Yes, mother. What would you like me to do?"

"Call Kris to find them a furnished house. The sooner they get some normalcy for the children, the better. Those little girls lost everything they knew. We must settle them as soon as possible." She chose a knife from the block and balanced it in her hand. "I'll take them shopping later today. They'll want their own things."

"Sure mother, whatever you say."

"Don't get flip. I mean it."

"Which part?"

"All of it. I'm sure Kip has a love nest they can borrow until their insurance settles."

"Alright. I'll find them a house."

"The least you can do," she mumbled, taking out her frustration on the ham.

The house was quiet when Ki came down later that morning. The house never seemed as lonesome than after a full house has come and gone. Carolyn left a note on the fridge telling everyone she took the children shopping, along with Connie and Nikki. Somewhere along the way Connie had been conscripted as the children's nanny. Next time she wouldn't answer the phone when Kylar calls her. Pouring a cup of juice, Ki picked it up with her left hand. Not bad, but raising it over her head would have been foolhardy, if not painful.

Now in the silence and not in a drug-induced stupor, Ki had time to think about this last week with its strange revelations and violence. Being a sitting duck was not her forte; she wanted back in. Checking the clock, she dialed the chief's private number.

"This had better be good, lieutenant," he said gruffly after thirteen rings.

"Chief, I want back on the case and my remaining vacation days extended to Thanksgiving."

"Goddammit Dicer, you've been shot and your partner's house was blown to smithereens. I've got reporters yelping at my heels and a stack of restraining orders against your outfit. Aviles wants you assigned to Siberia, the Russian one. Girl, you cause more problems on vacation than you did running around here on duty."

"With all due respect, chief, I've just been minding my own business."

"You've never just minded your own business. You're cocky, pig-headed, and insubordinate. I've never been able to stop you from doing what you wanted, even as I in no uncertain terms instructed you not to. And I'm instructing you not to interfere with this case, lieutenant. Do you understand me, you hardheaded sonofabitch?"

"Yes sir, I understand perfectly."

"Good, Gravelli is staying at the BQ. I don't want you anywhere near there." He hung up with a click.

"You didn't have to lay it on so thick, chief," Ki murmured hanging up the phone. Then she went upstairs to dress.

The BQ, only ten minutes away next to the Seventh precinct, housed all of the state and federal officials who came through the shining city. If it looked like a Travelodge, it was because that's what it was before it fell into the hands of the city. The two-story red-roofed adobe building had forty-three rooms which were more often than not three quarters full as it was efficiently operated by reform-minded offenders unable to find work elsewhere.

This morning the grounds crew was in full throttle, which was unfortunate for those wanting to sleep in. In the office, an obese young woman sat typing at a terminal with two fingers.

"How's tricks, Gloria?" Ki asked leaning her good arm on the counter.

"Dicer, honey. How ya doing?" She wobbled around the counter.

"Just winged me. How's Ginny?"

"Good. Smart as a whip. Whatcha doing up?"

"Can't keep a good woman down." Ki winked at her.

"But while she's down you might as well enjoy her." She laughed uproariously.

"The problem is finding a good woman."

This time she winked. "When you're tired of looking, I know where a bad one is." Her booming laugh filled the office.

"Too much woman for me, Gloria."

She was about to respond when the phone rang. She told them to hold on. "Who you looking for, Dice?"

"Gravelli, working with Pearson."

"Twenty-seven."

"Thanks."

She waved as she picked up a pen. Gloria was one of the success stories, infamous around the department as a "big girl" stripper prostitute and now manager of the BQ for the last five years. Twenty-seven was upstairs on the left wing behind the office, so Ki didn't move Kip's Pathfinder which she commandeered since it was an automatic. She police-knocked on the door. Someone said something which she couldn't hear over the mower that chose that moment to pass along the thin strip of grass below.

A long minute passed before the door opened on a woman with her hair in a towel and a red nose from crying or sneezing. "Yeah?"

"Gravelli?"

"Yeah."

"I'm Ki Dicer; you're on my case."

She stepped back. "Pearson said you wouldn't stay away, especially after last night."

"He was right." The oblong room lay out before her, with a work table and low sofa separated from the bedroom by a half partition hiding on the head of the first bed.

She sneezed. "Allergies and they're cutting the damn grass. What do you want?"

"Everything you have."

"That's not a helluva lot. I'm still catching up. Until Wednesday I was chasing car parts. Thursday I was on the road." She went into the bathroom.

"Who did you piss off to get that assignment?"

"The director's adjutant."

"Miss Gardner?"

She stuck her head out the door, the trestles of black hair falling free. "You know her?"

"Not in the biblical sense. She's known as Gabor around here." Dicer whistled the Green Acres theme song.

"You had breakfast?" she asked unwinding her hair dryer. "I was settled into fifteen until they decided to move me to this lovely suite."

"I ate about five-thirty."

"I didn't go to bed until six." She stopped and looked at Dicer. "You can sit down."

"If you don't mind, I'll stand for a few more minutes."

"Suit yourself." She went into the bathroom to dry her hair. Ki scanned the room for files but saw none. She had probably hid them before opening the door instead of putting on clothing as she had thought. She had packed relatively light although there were several pastel blouses hanging in the open closet. Ki's fingers were just itching to lift her wallet from her purse when the dryer stopped.

"What were your instructions on this case?"

"Instructions?"

"Regarding cooperation with the yokals? Norris' preferred not to."

"I'm not Norris and my instructions are to assist in the investigation of the NFC murders and prevent more if necessary. I don't think I can do that without cooperation from the yokals and the rest of the Metrox officers, especially your partner. Where is he by the way?"

"My house."

"You were babysitting his girls?"

"Yep." Then Dicer realized she was being interrogated. "Cute."

She didn't bother to turn away as she pulled off her t-shirt, put on her bra, then her blouse. "Why did you choose yesterday to invite them over?"

"They were over Monday and Lily, his youngest said I could always come get them if their parents were unavailable. I was moping around doing absolutely nothing and my brother was there. He's a fish and so it seemed the logical thing to do."

"You've been with Ayers a long time?"

"Ten years."

"How many people under you?"

"Five officers and two staff."

She glanced at Dicer. "You warrant two staff members?"

Dicer shrugged. "I'm very important you know. Some would say full of shit. One staff member is a drug counselor and the other is an all purpose drug researcher."

"And this is in addition to the narcotics unit?"

"Yes, but we're not totally separate, just more visible; we're the strategy arm of the department's war on drugs."

"I thought you were homicide?"

"I am, drug-related homicides, which have been declining steadily over the last five years."

"And you're responsible?" she asked eyeing Dicer closely as if their entire relationship depended on the answer.

"No, but we'll take the credit, just like we take the blame for any upward trend."

She nodded. "And a place serving breakfast at ten-thirty?"

"Just around the corner. Mind driving?"

"Not at all." They left for a cafe two blocks away.

Listening to her recounting the facts as presented to her, Dicer's apprehension increased; either she was playing extremely close to the vest as she swore she would not do or the state boys had sent her in blind, which meant her cooperation with Metrox was out of necessity. They were going over her list of contact people; with Norris on the lamb and his partner called back to the capital, there was no one to give her a proper briefing because they were a part of the case. Dicer looked up as two female officers in white-shirted summer uniform entered the cafe, scanned the crowd and headed their way.

"Yours?" Gravelli asked.

"Yep." Dicer looked up as the officers stopped at the table. "How'd you find me?"

"Deduction," the shorter one replied, pushing a tendril of red hair behind her ear.

"Uh huh. Agent Gravelli, officers Della Mumford and Sy Gomez. Truly the metro's finest. Getting them assigned to me took an act of Congress which meant it took years."

"She was my training officer and after that no one would work with me," the youthful Gomez said taking a seat.

"Not true. Now how did you find me?"

"Ayers called Johnson and dispatched us pronto." Mumford extracted a folded note from her pocket. "Desk sarge had this for you."

"Thanks. Are you coming on or going off?" Dicer unfolded the note.

"On since seven."

Gomez waved a waiter over. "This is lunch."

Memorizing the note, Dicer tore it up. "Have you seen any-thing interesting on the westside?"

"Interesting how?" They worked out of the Fourth precinct which included the larger university NSU and some of the new more fashionable family communities.

"Not sure. Anything. Mextown or Newton?"

"The usual. School is out, kids are hanging out everywhere doing stupid shit," Mumford said, opening her menu.

"What about the prevalence of GreenTarts?"

"We've noticed a few older people scoring packages in Mextown. Mickey's on that."

Dicer turned to Gravelli. "Mickey's the other member of our crackerjack team. He's young but promising and should be a big help to you in learning the city. I'll buzz him to let him know to expect your call."

Mumford glanced at Gomez. "You're back calling the shots?"

"You have a problem with that?" Dicer asked mildly.

"No, not at all."

"Gomez?"

"Nope. Where do you want us to start and can we ditch the uniforms?"

"Not yet. I want my presence felt and you're my incarnation until I'm physically able to do this." Dicer pulled out a pad. "Here's how I want you to work this, starting this afternoon. I'm sure Johnson has alerted Cafferty to take you off the rotation."

"Yes," Mumford agreed.

"Good. Do you think you can find Darren Wallace?"

Gomez shifted. "Not hard, he's set up at a storefront on Harper."

"You're kidding?" Dicer chuckled without mirth. The fella did have balls.

"No."

"Then you should have no problem finding a cool spot to watch him and let him see you taking note of visitors. You got film or have you used it up shooting softball games between the local gangs?"

"Doc Otu just received a shipment of supplies."

"She has a pair of interns, so don't throw a fit when you see two wide-eyed co-eds underfoot."

"Underfoot is right," Gomez agreed with her partner.

"You check them out before letting them in our space?"

"Yes."

A waiter came over. "There's a fight in the parking lot if you're interested."

"Shit," Gomez grumbled. "Hold my fries."

Gravelli and Dicer had long finished their meal so they packed up and followed them out into the bright sunlight. A small crowd from the carwash next door had gathered around the two women fighting. One woman's blouse had been torn off and she fought in her leopard print bra. The second woman wore a miniskirt that was hitched around her waist showing all of her half-naked ass.

"Alright, girls, break it up." Gomez tried to step in between them, then stepped back barely escaping a shoe. "Enough, dammit!" Mumford grabbed one and Gomez grabbed the other, neither bigger than a gnat.

"Let me go, I'm going to kill the bitch!" Miniskirt shouted.

"Bring it own you stanking 'ho!" Bra shouted back.

"Who a'ho, you short piece of puppy chow?!"

Bra grabbed her crouch. "Don't stop yo' man from munching all night." The small crowd snickered as Miniskirt struggled in Gomez's grasp.

Dicer stepped into the circle of bystanders. "Ladies, now no man is worth making a public spectacle of yourself. If anything you oughta be whooping his ass or going on Jerry Springer. Since you can do neither here, why don't you go home and let these officers get their daily dose of donuts. Hmmm, what do you say?"

"Who the fuck are you, you yella bitch?" Bra asked.

Dicer fished out her shield. "That's Lt. Bitch, and you should try to cover up those flea tits. Now go on before another cruiser come up and haul your nasty ass off."

"Fuck you bitch!" Bra shouted, then winced as Mumford tightened her grip. "Police brutality! Police brutality!"

Dicer laughed. "Let them go officers. Now run along."

The two women glared at each other as if calculating their chances of doing bodily harm to the other before the officers could restrain them. Then a cruiser pulled up letting out a short burst of the siren. The crowd quickly dispersed as two lumberjack officers got out. They took in the two women trying to get their clothing straightened up.

"Lt. Dicer," the sandy-haired officer greeted.

"Sean. What's the story on those two?"

"Gimp ass Gregg's mess. They've been at it for the last two weeks. Terry and I alone have broke it up four or five times, once in the liquor store down the street." He glanced around. "Sorry to hear about your shooting and Ayers' house. What are you two into?"

"Nothing, that's what's so mind-boggling. You heard anything relevant?"

"No. This is the most excitement we get around here."

Back at home only Kylar remained in the pool as usual. The Ayers had gone to pick up toiletries and Carolyn had not returned with the children. A dozen messages waited Dicer's attention including one from Kris and her father. After returning the most important ones, she took a nap and dreamed of fighting women, getting shot and exploding houses. To say the least, her nap was not refreshing at all.

Down below instead of Kris, her mother Irene sat at the breakfast nook with Diane Ayers. Kip and Irene's marriage lasted only two years, but she refused to be cut out of the family, securing her place as the mother of Kip's only child and thus guardian of his legacy, whatever that meant. In reality, she had no other family and had immediately claimed them as her own forever more, even bringing husbands two and three to Goddard family reunions and introducing Ki's mother as her sister. Although a bit dingy and gullible, Irene was always there in a family crisis; one of those people who needed to be needed.

"What's shaking, Irene?" Ki said opening the fridge.

"The open house is running late, so I came over instead with our list of available properties to suit Diane's needs. It's not very long and I apologize for that, but we don't usually handle this sort of thing."

"That's okay, Irene. I'm sure we'll do just fine." When Ki turned around Diane's eyes were riveted on her. "Don't look at me like that, Diane; if you want to blame someone for interfering, blame my mother."

Diane shook her head. "I wasn't thinking of blaming anyone, just wondering about all of this. Any other night we would have been there. What possessed you to invite the girls over, then keep them?"

Holding her bottle tightly, Dicer exhaled slowly. "Like I said, it was a whimsical idea at the time. Kylar was in the pool and would be there for awhile and they had so enjoyed it the other day and wanted to come back. What better motivation is there?"

She waved a tired arm in the air. "All of this still has not registered on me. My house is gone. Our lives ripped apart for reasons we do not know. Everything my children knew and loved is gone. And for what? Some terrorist tactics? We knew the dangers of being a police family, but not this. Definitely not this. They came after my family, Dicer. You don't do that."

Diane wasn't hysterical as she continued, but angry, fighting mad. And no one could blame her; instead of taking her children to the park or a ball game, she was looking for a place to stay after her home had been obliterated the night before.

"We'll get them, Diane," Dicer said rather weakly under her tirade.

"That won't do a damn bit of good in replacing what we lost, Dicer. Our memories, our photographs, items from our mothers."

"I guess it won't."

Irene patted her hands. "Which is why we should get you into a new home as soon as possible to start building new memories."

Diane turned to her. "Thank you, but we can't afford these houses. We'll find an apartment until the insurance pays off."

"Now you let me worry about that, Diane. There won't be any commission." She smiled reassuringly. "And at least two of these are Kip's and since you're family and all, he can float you a very low interest rate. Say one percent."

Diane frowned and looked at Ki. She only shrugged as Kylar came into the kitchen on his way back to the pool.

"I thought you were going to Canton," she said to him.

He leaned on the counter. "Didn't you get dad's message?"

"No. What did it say?"

He rifled through the blue message slips by the phone, turned over a couple and handed her one. "For you."

"Couldn't you have just told me?" Dicer wrinkled her nose at him and tried to read his scrawl. "He's driving down? When?"

"Should be on his way now."

"Why?"

"To see you obviously." He walked out to the pool.

"As if things couldn't get worst," she grumbled. Her dad was okay on his own turf, but elsewhere he was a fish out of water flapping around looking for something to do. He would probably stay with Kerry who lived in their old house, which would bring him in contact and conflict with Barry, one of the few people he did not bother hiding his dislike.

"They can always get worst. And before they do, let's find Diane's family a home." Irene flipped open a second notebook of glossy photos. "This one is near Newton an actually belongs to Kip; he must have thought it a good location for a love nest or bought it for one of his bimbos and the no-taste bitch didn't want it."

Diane and Ki looked at each other and laughed. Irene could be rather bitchy in a comical sort of way when it came to Kip's women, which of course was the reason for their breakup more than twenty years ago. Ki was wondering how she would take the news that Nikki may be Kip's when Lisa and Lily came in jabbering away. Seeing them, Diane burst into tears and pulled them close.

When Lou returned, they went to take a look at a couple of houses with Irene. Carolyn loaded her bags in the trunk of her car and returned to stand over Ki as she puzzled over pieces of this case.

"What are you up to now mom?" Ki asked.

"I'm going to see Betty about Nikki and Kip. I called her earlier but she refused to come to the telephone. Nikki doesn't want to return home. I'm not sure how much is due to Betty's nastiness with the girl or to her wanting to spread her wings. I told her this morning that she is welcome to stay with me until your house is less crowded."

"I'm sure she appreciated it." Hell, she hadn't even invited Kylar to stay. What was going on with her?

"She would appreciate it more if Betty didn't treat her like a stepchild. Sometimes I don't understand my sisters." She smiled. "And definitely not my brothers."

"Mom, sit down. I keep thinking you're going to swat me one."

"Is it time for your pills?" she asked going instead to the cabinet, taking down a pair of glasses.

"I just had them, but thanks for remembering."

"Was I really such a bad mother to you, Ki?"

Dicer shook my head. "No mother, you were not a bad mother to any of us."

"But I could have been more attentive?"

"You were attentive enough." Mother's idea of attention was corrective instructions on diction, posture, attitudes and the like. Her motto was simple: At least look and sound intelligent. That was the calm version, the other one was: Act like you got some damn sense!

"I'm afraid to probe that response, Ki." She placed a glass of lemonade before her daughter.

"Thank you."

"It's always hard being a mother; but I definitely wouldn't want to raise a teenager today. Keven is proof of that and I still worry he's going to do something stupid and get court-martialed. And Kerry. If she could just tear herself from Barry, maybe she would be alright. Maybe." She sipped her lemonade. "Looking at your family, have you ever felt guilty of your success?"

Ki carefully closed her notebook while pondering that, not so much the question, but the fact that her mother asked it. Of me or herself? "No." Ki looked at her. "Why should I? It's not like we didn't have the same opportunities; granted we had you breathing down our necks. We went to the same schools, had the same teachers, and took the same courses. I even had to take more shit, even from them. Still do. It's not that I don't feel for them, disappointment, frustration, and disgust for different ones."

"Do you wish that you could have done more for some of them?"

"Like what? No one ever listens to me when I try to give them a little friendly advice." Ki sat back. "Now why are you feeling guilty for not doing more for your siblings?"

"Family . . . " She shook her head. "It used to be so simple. You help someone, someone help you and it went around. Now. We were all so close once."

"Physically and financially if not ideologically," Ki mumbled.

"Perhaps."

"Perhaps? Hah!" Ki held her glass up to look through at my mother. "If I said anymore you would call me racial or something as damning."

"No. And you intentionally use racially antagonistic language around them."

"Like their homophobic statements aren't intentional."

"Let's not start that again."

Ki rolled my eyes. "Yes, mother. I will allow them to constantly degrade me while not saying anything about their whoremongering, chicken-eating, hogmaw slurping, chittling-licking—" Her mother burst into laughter. "And I'm just getting started. Those pig-tail munching, rib gnawing, potlicker drinking—"

She raised her hands, palms outward. "Stop, Ki."

"Stop, Ki," Ki mimicked. "It was always me."

"Yes, you thrived on a good fight, Ki."

"Thrive or take shit and I don't like the taste." And she was not about change diets now.

CHAPTER 6

Chaotic noise, scents and movement ruled the warehouse size Fifth precinct stationhouse where the only visible distinction between the police officers and criminals was the yellow ID card the officers wore, for three offenders wore grimy fake police uniforms. A many pierced and tattooed officer handcuffed a well-dressed young man to a chair. A paper airplane flew through the air as a roly-poly sergeant bellowed out names from a roster. When people spoke of the police under siege, they were referring to the Fifth, the front-line enveloped in chaos.

Captain Mitch Leiberman, impervious to the mayhem around him, sliced through the crowd to the elevator which would take him to his office. A student of department history, Leiberman knew that every captain of the Fifth became a deputy chief or was indicted, bowing to one set of crooks or the other. Entering his outer office, he hesitated at the secretary's desk and turned slowly to glance at the three people sitting along the wall, then he walked around the counter without saying a word to them.

"Hold all calls and send them in in ten minutes."

"Yes, sir," she said to his back.

Leiberman made an effort not to slam the door as he went directly for his phone, dialing the chief's private number.

"What can I do for you, Mitch?" the chief's deal-making voice asked on the thirteenth ring, always the thirteenth if at all.

"Why is Dicer in my waiting room?"

"I would hazard to guess that she was waiting for you."

"You didn't send her?"

"No."

"I'm not cooperating with whatever scheme she's cooking, chief."

My people are overworked as is in this heat; I can't have her luring them into overtime which would come out of my budget."

"Then give her somebody whose overtime won't come out your budget."

Leiberman took a deep breath at his chief's doublespeak. "So you do know why she's here?"

"You asked if I sent her. I did not. She's infirmed, be nice." The chief hung up.

Leiberman sat back. "Crazy bitch." He didn't know what she had on the chief that allowed her free movement throughout the city and their almost forced cooperation with her brainstorms. Yet he couldn't complain too much, she had an equipment budget that every captain in the city vied for a piece of. He indexed his problems to see which he could push off on her in exchange for whatever she was wanting.

Smiling triumphantly, he picked up the phone. "Penny, tell Sgt. Fenkel to send up that rookie."

"Which one?"

"The female that stutters. Let me know when she arrives and send in Dicer alone."

"Yes sir."

The officer did not normally stutter but when he brought her in to reprimand her for personal politicking, she had been so angry she stuttered her defense. There were more liberal minded precincts in the city, but he had more pressing issues than a rookie's freedom to express her sexuality.

A knock sounded and the door opened to a dapper Dicer and her cryptic smile. "Captain Leiberman."

"Lieutenant, have a seat. It's a madhouse down below. How's the shoulder healing?"

"Extremely well, thank you."

"What brings you across Broadway?"

"We're investigating the New Faith Cathedral murders."

"I hear they've hit a brick wall. You're here for my expert advice?" he asked smiling.

"As a matter of fact I am, but I also wanted you to meet the new bureau agent. She's green and on Gabor's shit list, here without a proper briefing or backup."

"Is that why you have your puppy with you?" Their eyes met. "Hound dog, I mean."

"Yes, you can say that."

"And you want me to assign her a liaison from the Fifth?"

Dicer nodded. "A contact, at least."

"And at most?" He steepled his fingers.

Dicer shifted. "Captain, let me rephrase her situation. She's flying solo without a net and the usual restrictions placed on the local agent. Before I left there was talk about allowing a permanent assignment here in metro, in the Fifth to be more precise. You're tripping over the FBI and the DEA. Do you really want another Norris underfoot?"

Leiberman sat up. "And this agent would be more amenable to our goals?" More malleable to his touch.

"From what I understand, the director is quite embarrassed about Norris and is reluctant to place a more intractable agent here. Agent Gravelli's background includes three years on the meanest streets of the state. She's one of us in a suit."

Leiberman nodded. "Which doesn't explain your presence here. What do you have in mind, Dicer?"

"Your endorsement for a metro bureau office." She extracted a sheaf of papers from a portfolio. "Not in your precinct."

Leiberman sat back studying her, not sure of where she was coming from. "Where?"

"The Gamin Station."

"You're fucking crazy." The Gamin Station was the two-story stationhouse Dicer worked out of in the Fourth, adjacent to the university. There were twenty-four or so people there and she had a third or more of them and half the space.

"That's pretty much the consensus these days, captain; nevertheless—"

"You want the state bureau in your pocket." Leiberman rose. No, he didn't see that coming. The state's fledgling bureau of investigation branched off from the state police several years ago and was still trying to establish its position in the law enforcement community. Heretofore, the bureau had been a tool of the state attorney general, investigating high profile cases and state-wide organized criminal activity. When Norris got under metro's skin, the chief had pushed Dicer in his face which resulted in several memorable and public shouting matches. He may dislike her carte blanche access, but he cheered for the home team.

"I do have the space," Dicer said as his eyes refocused. She didn't know what he had been thinking but she saw the devious light in his cold gray eyes. She knew he didn't like her but he was forthright about it and that was cool with her; they knew where they stood with each other and she came prepared to deal.

"What do I get for supporting your little coup?"

"Coup?" She chuckled. "Captain, that implies the powers that be are completely uninformed on this."

"Plausible deniability," he said dryly. He may not know what she had over the chief, but he did know the chief's standard operating procedure with her. Something blows up, it's her fault; a strategy works beautifully, the chief gets the publicity; nevertheless she was handsomely rewarded.

"Did I tell you, Colonel Bower from the armory was getting new equipment?"

"They just got new equipment with those bases closing in—" He smiled. "You have an inventory list?"

"Uh huh. I get first shot." She wriggled a green folder.

"Let's make a deal," he said as his phone buzzed. "Yes, Penny?"

"The rookie is here."

"Tell her to have a seat." Leiberman released the button. "Perhaps, I can help you out on another matter as well, Dicer." He walked around the desk and took the equipment list from her.

"What matter is that, captain?"

"I have a rookie that needs a more politically correct environment and an understanding role model."

"You have an out rookie," she said tonelessly.

"Why yes." He pulled a pen from his pocket to initial a couple of surplus items. "We have openly gay officers in the 5th but they aren't as political, that's more of the 4th's purview. And I was thinking—"

"You want me to take her off your hands and prevent a complaint against a homophobic lieutenant."

Leiberman smiled thinly. "I would not have put it that way, lieutenant," he said stressing the rank.

"No sir, you'd called it developmental management."

"Shall we meet the new agent and the rookie. I'd like to know who I'm condemning to you."

"And who I'm saving you from. Looks like you're getting the best of this deal, captain."

"I doubt that seriously, Dicer." He opened the door, then followed her out.

"Time will tell," she said softly rounding the counter.

The young officer with the crewcut jumped to her feet as they approached and saluted.

"This isn't the military, officer," Leiberman told her, lazily returning the salute. "As of this moment, you are reassigned to the Gamin House in the 4th precinct under Lt. Dicer here. She'll see to your training for the remainder of your probationary period."

Jill Merlo glanced from the captain to the lieutenant. "Sir, is this a disciplinary transfer?"

"No. Lt. Dicer has a standing request for officers with your talents and obvious potential," he told her with a smile.

"What talents may those be?" Merlo asked.

Dicer laughed. "Officer, didn't your mother tell you not to look a gift horse in the mouth. What's your name?"

"Jill Merlo, sir—ma'am."

"Dicer will do fine." She extended her hand. "Welcome to heaven. We have the latest technologies and our own researcher, website, and space."

"And we are now two-thirds female," Mickey told her extending his hand. "I'm Mickey Sharp, Jill. This is Agent Laura Gravelli." Dicer introduced Gravelli and Leiberman then quickly ushered out her team, dispatching the rookie to clean out her locker. Paperwork would catch up later.

The Gamin Station, a two-story adobe building, stood on the edge of the university across from the intramural center and art center. Behind the stationhouse sat one of the oldest housing projects in the city that for years had been a hotbed of drug activity behind the wooden graffiti-covered walls. The walls were now gone and the only space not converted to gardens was the chain-linked playground. The only parking lot ran parallel to the police lot, with only handicap parking at the front of the building. The tenants and officers tended the gardens. The courtyard where older residents now sat under a tent was laid by Dicer and a couple of officers on an off weekend. The renovation of the Gamin projects was Dicer's most rewarding achievement in her relatively short career; all of the work had been done by volunteers and tenants.

The Gamin Station officers, by some estimates, were the most idealistic and strangest officers on the force. The officers considered themselves public servants which was enforced by the station's commanding officer, Myra Cafferty, affably called Mary Poppins behind her back. Adding to the station's "softy" reputation was the amount of greenery decorating the building's common areas with its soothing pastel blue and green walls.

It was to this thankfully cool building that Dicer with Gravelli and Sharp returned for the first time after a month's vacation, although she had been shot the week before and was not scheduled to return until Wednesday instead of Monday. Despite the number of employees, the Gamin Station was actually a barebones operation with only four officers per shift on patrol. Since communications were centralized downtown, the in-house dispatcher was the communications officer in a room of computer monitors and communications equipment.

Dicer entered the glass nerve center. "Peggy."

The chubby woman looked up from her computer screen. "Lieutenant!" She pushed the headset down. "Welcome back."

"Thanks, Peggy. I want you to meet Agent Laura Gravelli; she'll be working out of 2G, so will you hook her up with a phone, number and everything."

"Anything you say, lieutenant." Peggy shook Dicer's hand then Gravelli's. "Welcome to Wonderland. You give me your other numbers and I'll tie them in anyway you want."

"Don't do that," Dicer told Gravelli. "She once tied me into a sex line."

Peggy chuckled. "I'll just hook up voicemail for you and get you a portable."

"Okay, we'll be upstairs."

"I'll send everything up by an intern," Peggy told them.

"Thank you." Dicer guided Gravelli out and introduced her to the other's on the first floor before leading her upstairs to 2G which was across the hall from her office.

Expecting a bare interrogation style room with an old metal desk and folding chair, Gravelli blinked at the polished desk, credenza and small conference table, the burgundy executive chair, the built-in bookshelves full of books and manuals, the royal blue carpet and the computer set-up. "A cop definitely didn't decorate this office."

"I take offense." Dicer moved to the computer and switched it on. "Peggy will send up the password to this which you should change immediately. If you want we can have the lock changed."

"No, that won't be necessary."

Dicer unhooked the key from her keyring. "Don't lose it."

"Try not to." Gravelli placed her bag and purse in the chair. "Now let's see yours and this lab you keep bragging about."

"This way." She waited for Gravelli to check the lock mechanisms and to finally lock the door.

"It's quite different from the 5th."

"In a lot of ways." Dicer unlocked her office and stepped inside. "This is the bridge."

Gravelli turned slowly in the large office with a desk pushed into a corner. Large monitors and maps occupied the walls with a conference table in front of a large screen television. A row of shelves held boxes of discs and tapes. "And you are what again?"

"A plain detective."

"Those books in 2G are yours, aren't they?"

"Yes."

"Asset seizures?"

Dicer laughed. "The big screen is."

"Now I'm ready for that lab."

The phone rang. "Duty." Dicer picked up the phone. "Dicer here."

"Lieutenant, that reporter lady is here to see you."

"Gao?"

"Yes, ma'am."

"Send her up, we're headed to Otu's lair."

"Yes, ma'am."

Dicer hung up, then fitted herself with a telephone headset. "Full speed ahead, agent."

Otu's office and lab at the other end occupied half of the second floor. The lab was more of a computer lab and library with bookshelves occupying a fourth of the space, with computer workstations liberally distributed around the central command center of a high tech mapping system. Four of the ten workstations were occupied and a fifth person sat at a table strewn with books.

Dicer walked up the three steps to the central unit and waved a hand in front of the diaphanous city map. "When everything is working we can see where every patrol car is and where every car has been dispatched. Every piece of information available is tracked, including type of call." She chuckled. "That is when everything is working. Now looks like we have a traffic problem downtown and half our officers are at the donut shop."

"Only a third are at the donut shop." A short woman in a white polo and baggy shorts and sandals quickstepped onto the platform. "You're not looking much worst for wear, Dicer."

"Just the thought of seeing you brought a smile to my heart and a song to my lips, my dear doc." Dicer laughed. "Gravelli, this is Dr. GT Otu, our resident professor and jack of all-trades. Anything you want to know about the history of drug use here and around the world, she knows. And what she doesn't know, she'll make up."

"She strokes my ego so that I'll keep PATSI up and running."

"PATSI?"

"Police all tracking systems integrated. Nothing too creative for this bunch. We have the dispatchers' radio, computer, and telephone traffic integrated, coded and fed into a databank here. We have a few cruisers wired for direct videofeed in addition to computer." Otu gave her a half hour tour while Dicer returned to her office with Lin Gao.

"What have you been up to, Gao?" Dicer asked her.

"Trying to stay out of your girlfriend's sight," Gao told her.

"I meant about NFC." The investigation into the cathedral murders lay dead in the water and the toll on the investigating team stood with one bureau agent on the run, a captain in protective custody, one officer shot and the house of another blown to bits. Although the two latter incidents had not proven to be directly related, the collateral damage significantly impeded the investigation. Winged or not Dicer was hellbent on solving the case, one way or another.

"My contacts are scared, Dice."

"Of what?"

"I don't know. At first I thought it was someone in the church, now it sounds more like someone on the outside."

"Did you at least get confirmation?"

"That's all. No detail. Nothing more than I already had. No names, dates, or shoe sizes. I can't even get to Brother Thomas."

"He didn't say anything when Ayers interviewed him." Which was right before someone blew his house up.

"Are you going to give him a shot?" Gao asked.

"You know it, as soon as Gravelli checks in."

"She seems more palatable than Norris."

"No comparison; it's hard to believe they come from the same agency."

"Norris was dirty," Gao reminded her.

"Right."

"What's the latest on Buchova? Is it possible for me to get an interview with him?"

"I haven't spoken to Aviles and I seriously doubt an interview is possible at this moment," Dicer told her regrettably.

"You aren't trying to forestall the public's right to know are you?"

"Of course not. Aviles is handling this and keeping a pretty tight lid on it."

"Very well, but I want first go at him."

"I'll pass that along." She too wanted another go at Buchova. His actions the first few hours after the discovery of the first body irreparably damaged the investigation.

"Where's Cafferty?" Gao asked as Dicer stared into space.

"She was bustling out when we arrived."

Watching her zone out again, Gao questioned whether Dicer should be up and going full speed ahead, which was the only speed she had.

"Are you okay, Dice?"

"Yes." Dicer rose. "Do you know if there are any non-affiliated detractors of the NFC? Like a watchdog group or anything?"

"No, I can check with the religious editor. What are you thinking?"

"Nothing concrete, just ideas floating around, trying to approach this as thoroughly and logically as possible." There was no telling how much evidence Norris destroyed or conceivably planted, although the latter seemed unlikely given that very little physical evidence was found at all.

"Toss out some ideas and—" The phone shrilled.

Still wearing the headset, Dicer flicked it on. "Dicer."

"Lieutenant, a call just came in from the New Faith Cathedral. A man just fell from the balcony during midday services," Peggy told her.

"I'm on my way, get Sharp and Ayers over there."

"I'm on it."

Dicer informed Gao as she buzzed Otu's office for Gravelli. She chastised herself as she rejoiced at the prospect of getting a fresh start on the crime scene. No stone would go unturned in her effort to prevent a fourth victim in the case which had been sabotaged from the start.

As Jill Merlo queried the desk sergeant about Dicer's location, Dicer and Gravelli hurriedly came down the stairs. Gao had left immediately while the others gathered their things.

"Lieutenant!" Merlo called as the women rounded the corner towards the back doors.

"Toss Davis your gear bag and come on; you're driving," Dicer called back.

Merlo handed her duffel bag to the squat man and trotted back through the lounge to catch up as they exited into the parking lot. "Where?"

"New Faith Cathedral," Dicer told her tossing the keys over the hood of the tiger striped Chevy Suburban.

"I'm following you out of here," Gravelli called getting into her regimental Mercury.

"In case you get lost just go straight up Sixteenth until Wyoming and go west." Dicer slipped into the passenger seat of the Catmobile, as the neighborhood children referred to the vehicle with the satellite dish on top and all the bells and whistles inside.

"What's the quickest way?" Merlo asked pulling out of the parking lot.

"Take Delaware over to eleventh, take it up to Church Avenue. That should avoid most of the midday traffic." Dicer pulled the video display terminal (VDT) to her and plugged in her headset. "Patch me through to Pearson," she instructed the dispatcher.

Heart-racing, Merlo concentrated on driving while listening to Dicer's end of the rapid discussion of the case and how to proceed. Driving over from the 5th, she had gone over her little speech to Dicer in protest of her abrupt transfer in the middle of the shift no less. For the last two months she had been alternately ignored in the most tedious of jobs and placed in the most grueling of exercises. Every complaint drew her footpatrol in Carrollton, yet not once had she complained about her duties, only the environment.

"Slow down," Dicer told her when she braked to avoid a service van slowing to turn suddenly without a signal. "He's not going anywhere."

"Sorry, sir—ma'am."

"Just relax, Merlo. This baby can get away from you if she senses you don't have the reins tight. Your turn is coming up."

"Yes, ma'am."

"And stop saying that."

"Yes, ma—" She glanced at Dicer. "Sorry."

"And that too." Dicer opened the center compartment and took out several pairs of gloves.

As they approached the cathedral, an officer waved them through as he blocked off the street. A firetruck and two ambulances were on the scene as fire licked at a stone statue on the side lawn.

"I didn't think stone burned," Merlo said slipping on her gloves as she matched step with Dicer.

"It doesn't. Someone must have poured an incendiary compound over it, probably an emollient of some sort to keep burning like that." Dicer hesitated only a second before climbing the steps.

"Maybe it's like the burning bush," Merlo said softly getting a whimsical glance from Dicer.

"Don't make me call you Mulder, officer." Dicer walked up to a thin man in plaid pants and golfing shoes, his hair slicked back. "What's with the burning virgin, Pearson?"

"Not ten minutes ago, it just went up in flames. The fire boys just rolled on down the street."

"And the ambulances?"

"Several members collapsed."

"Where is the body?" Dicer asked, detecting a faint indefinable musty odor she did not remember from the last time. "What's that smell?"

"Don't know." He led them down the hall to the left of the main assembly hall. "The body's in their little theater."

The body lay twisted over seats in the fifth row from the back next to the aisle. On its back the head and shoulders hung over the back of two seats, the fingers of the right hand brushed against the floor. Like the others, it was naked and the throat slit. Very little blood drained from the deadly wound.

"Blood upstairs?" Dicer asked.

"Yes, in one of the curtained booths."

"And who is he?"

"Antoine Soliris. According to Brother Thomas, he arrived Saturday to fill in for the two deceased men."

"Where was Brother Thomas when he came tumbling down?" Dicer asked.

Merlo standing apart noted the exchange of glances among the onlookers at Dicer's question.

"He was on stage," a plainclothes officer said stepping forward. His badge clipped to the brown leather belt in his chinos, his blue oxford shirt crisp, his loafers shiny.

"He see anything?"

"Not until he fell."

"Where was he supposed to be?"

"Who?"

"Mr. Soliris."

"Working in his chamber preparing for the evening sermon."

"How you know that?" Dicer asked standing up as the crime scene team came in.

"Thomas told me."

Dicer removed her gloves. "How many people were here for the noonday service?"

"About one hundred."

"Where are they?"

"In the assembly hall."

"Have you interviewed everyone?"

"Not everyone. Most had their backs to the balcony."

"Did you get their vitals?"

"Working on it now."

"And when that is done, you run checks on everyone that was here, looking for any history of mental illness or abnormal religiosity. I want this church closed while we do a search of the entire compound from step to steeple." Dicer looked up. "Mickey, is the perimeter secure?"

"It is."

"Where's Ayers?"

"Explaining the securing of the perimeter to the administrator," Mickey said with a half-smile.

"Good, I won't have to repeat myself. Mulder, you're with Mickey. Gleason, take your team and coordinate with Ayers. Leave no pillar of salt unturned." She walked up to Mickey. "Understand me, Mickey?"

"Gotcha, boss." He waved Merlo to him.

Gleason hesitated glancing at Pearson who was instructing the criminalists. If Pearson had no quarrel with Dicer taking the investigation from them and barking orders at his team, he would offer no objections either, for the moment.

"Where's Thomas?" Dicer asked Gleason before he could leave.

"In his chamber with one of the board members. It's in the other wing."

"Thank you," Dicer dismissed him, informed Pearson of her intentions and left the theater. Again she caught a whiff of the scent, now sickly sweet as she crossed the front hall. "What the hell is that?"

"Smells like my baby's shit, after Jr sprays air freshener in his room to kill the smell," Johnson said suddenly at her side. "But it doesn't."

Dicer's footsteps faltered as she took a deeper breath. "Naw, it can't be. Find the custodian or someone who knows how this ventilation system works." She grabbed his sleeve. "And order in a K-9 unit."

"You want to bring dogs in here?" Johnson asked, just to clarify her order.

"Yes. This smell bothers me too damn much."

Johnson, eyes wide, looked around as if to avoid falling tiles or lightening. "Okay." He walked off throwing a glance back at Dicer.

CHAPTER 7

Chief Andrew Harmon scanned the precincts' budgets with the accompanying charts and graphs illustrating distributions and changes. As usual the 5th outstripped the others by a quarter, even with the 4th's experimental programs sapping resources. Thinking of the 4th and its myriad of community-oriented programs, he thought of Ki Dicer and her tons of ideas which invariably found their way via memo to his desk, not infrequently from a detractor complaining of her disregard for protocol or more accurately the slipping of her leash. He was well aware of the widespread belief that Dicer had something on him which afforded her such latitude in her handling of cases, special projects, and her superior officers, rather officers of superior rank.

Nevertheless no one would believe his response if they ever dared to directly ask him about it as Aviles had. To him the answer was simple, he allowed Dicer free rein because he could; in other words she was no threat. Oh he wasn't underestimating her for one second. When she became a bit too creative, he allowed Aviles a swift kick; beyond that no one touched her. They understood each other on a cosmic plane almost; each allowing the other a freedom that went beyond experimental programs. To say he lived vicariously through her would not be incorrect though inadequate. And she did what she did because he would support her to no end, even as Aviles took a chunk out of her on occasion.

And what of Aviles who alternately referred to Dicer as his heir apparent and his red herring? He knew the animosity between the two women was largely a facade which both needed to effectively do their jobs. In a real sense, it was Aviles not he who was her mentor in a convoluted way. How else had Dicer so skillfully avoided the subtle political traps her detractors laid for her?

Suddenly aware his mind had drifted off, he yanked his attention back to the dull budget reports which would send him into a peaceful slumber unlike reading the newspaper which gave him nightmares. Unable to keep his mind on the report in hand, he switched off the light vowing to get up early.

After a late swim in the apartment complex's pool, Jill Merlo returned to the apartment she shared with Toni Jensen, her partner of two years. At the moment they were at odds over moving into a larger place. Jill wanted to wait to see if she survived her probationary period, while Toni brooded over her lover's lack of self-confidence in a job she obviously could and liked to do. The aroma of freshly popped popcorn and the sound of an action movie filled the tiny apartment when Jill returned.

"What are you watching?"

"Predator2," Toni told her, her eyes following Jill into the bedroom. She had arrived home late, but only a half hour after Jill; they had gotten into an argument almost immediately, picking up where they had left off at breakfast. The tiny apartment had been their home for a year and she was tired of tripping over herself and Jill's gear, although neatly stacked. But it felt like a submarine, even moreso with the shower running.

A rapid knocking on the front door startled her. She quickly closed the bedroom door before going to the door, looking out the peephole. She did not recognize the woman, so made sure the chain was on the door before opening it.

"Yes?"

"I'm looking for Jill Merlo. Does she live here?"

"Who are you?"

"Sy Gomez, metro police." Gomez held up her shield.

"Oh, come in." Toni unlocked the door and stepped back.

Gomez stepped in carrying a gear bag. "I apologize for the late hour, but our lieutenant is in battle mode and time is irrelevant."

"That's okay, have a seat. Can I get you something to drink?"
"No, thanks." Gomez sat down in the recliner, taking in the
room and the closed door that undoubtedly led to the bedroom.
"Jill is in the shower." Toni smiled shyly. "I guess you hear
that."
"I had an upstairs neighbor who showered at four o'clock ev-
ery morning. Drove me crazy."
"Tell me about it. We're looking for a larger place, but we can't
seem to agree on anything."
"What are you looking for, an apartment, house?"
"House, but Jill's still uncertain about her probationary pe-
riod."
"I guess her abrupt transfer this morning didn't help, huh?"
Jill frowned at her. "What transfer?"
Gomez looked guiltily around the room. "Oops. Guess I let
something slip."
"Well I got home late, then she went swimming." Toni won-
dered why she was talking to this officer like a friend. Yet she
seemed different from the few other officers she had met.
"How long have you two been together?" Gomez asked.
"Two years." Definitely not like the others.
"Good start. I've been with Monica for four years and she's
still adjusting to my being a police officer."
Toni smiled, sighing silently at the revelation. "Jill's had a
tough time; I'm glad she's found someone who understands."
"Actually we've never met. We kept missing each other this
evening."
"Oh." Toni raised an eyebrow. "Can I ask you something?"
"Sure."
"How has it been on you? Are you out? Does your supervisor
ignore your complaints?"
Gomez chuckled. "I've had a very good run due in large part
to the lieutenant who is herself out which is one of the reasons I
gather Merlo was transferred. However I'm not privy to the circumstances, but it makes sense."

"Which precinct do you work out of?"

"The 4th in the Gamin Station near the university."

"There should be affordable housing near there then."

"Yes, it is and you'd be closer." They both noted the shower stopped.

Toni jumped up. "I'll let her know you're here."

"Thank you." Again Gomez studied the tiny room, looking through into the dark kitchen. What was their relationship like? From what Mickey had told her about Merlo's demeanor, she would have expected her to have a more domineering partner or at least someone not as sweet-seeming as . . . her partner. She had not even gotten the woman's name, a piss poor job she had done. Dicer would have been disappointed in her technique. They were a close and handpicked lot with high expectations of themselves even as others thought they were pampered in Dicer's wake, but that wasn't the case. They worked ten hour shifts and often longer. Dicer's vacation had been a vacation for them all and now it was definitely over as her presence here indicated.

In shorts and tee, Jill Merlo came out of the bedroom with Toni on her heels. "Dicer sent you?"

Gomez rose extending her hand. "Yes. I'm Sy Gomez; nice to meet you."

"You too." Jill glanced at Toni then back at Gomez. "Is this private?"

"No. I just brought equipment Dicer wanted you to familiarize yourself with before you returned in the morning, six o'clock." Gomez watched her reaction, merely a shrug. "She doesn't believe in employee training on the clock, but this won't take long. Mind if we go to the table."

"Sure. You want something to drink?" Jill walked into the kitchen flipping on the light. The table and refrigerator dominated the small room.

"You've drawn the pleasurable duty of becoming Dicer's left arm." Gomez unpacked a computer and communication equipment, and a box containing a .38 S&W Lady Smith. "Compliments of Dicer herself. Welcome aboard."

Jill picked up the gun, inspecting in slowly. "This is a personal weapon. Why?"

"Nostalgia. She likes to have the security of a revolver. And she expects you to carry it too, in addition to your department issue." Gomez pulled out hers, identical to the one Jill had in her hands. "We all have them, even Dr. Otu. Now enough of the past, here's what you need to keep up with Dicer."

Gomez stayed for an hour explaining the codes and equipment to not only Jill but Toni who was a tad quicker than her lover and more comfortable with technology.

Dicer drove into the parking lot ten minutes before six as Mickey pulled up on his Kawasaki. They met at the back door. "Beautiful morning!" Dicer greeted him.

"If you say so, lieutenant."

"Ah Mickey, you guys got lazy while I was away. No use wasting a glorious morning in bed."

"Unless its with someone who makes it more glorious."

"Absolutely. Six-thirty for briefing," she told him as she took the stairs.

"Want me to get donuts?" he asked tongue-in-cheek.

"No, let the rookie get them."

Mickey chuckled and walked into the communication booth.

Dicer didn't arrive home until midnight after a ten o'clock meeting with Aviles, who had spent the better part of the evening keeping politicos off their back. After Dicer closed the cathedral, the church's board made several calls up the city's political ladder, resulting in a flood of calls to the chief who redirected them to Aviles who informed them if it were her decision she would have halled the church's upper echelon downtown. She had told Dicer much of the same thing if they didn't get a break in the case soon.

Dicer spotted a buff folder on her desk that had not been there the night before. Picking it up, she sat at the conference table. Five minutes later she was slipping on a kevlar vest when Jill knocked on the door.

"Come in!" Dicer called, noting that Ayers and Johnson were technically off today but they would be at NFC.

"I've checked—"

"Do you have civilian clothing?"

"Not really. I could go home—"

"No time." Dicer walked over to a closet and flung open the doors revealing three stacks of pants and polos and several blazers. "Find yourself something in there and put on a vest."

"We're expecting trouble?"

"I sure as hell hope not, because you're the only backup I'm taking with me."

Merlo found a pair of jeans and an olive polo in her size. "Where?"

"I'll tell you on the way. You can change in here; I need to talk to Otu."

Twenty minutes later Merlo negotiated the dirt switchback road up a ridge on the outskirts of town. When the terrain leveled off, a magnificent stone and half-timber house stood atop a knoll before them behind a split log fence that was more for design than protection against anything but cattle or sheep. The road switched to shell as they passed the gate. A row of sports utility vehicles stood in the courtyard. Merlo parked at the end of the row next to a custom painted jeep. The two police officers got out and looked around.

"Let's go in." Dicer walked up the steps of the wide veranda and knocked with the brass knocker. The door swung open and they entered a marble foyer.

"This way please," a woman in a maid's uniform said near the wide staircase. She led them behind the stairs to a doorway that led to descending stairs. They followed the woman down the stairs to a room decorated for comfort in strong masculine taste. "Have a seat, he'll be with you shortly."

"Thank you," Dicer said sitting on a leather sofa.

A side panel slid back and a man in his early fifties with charcoal colored hair and bushy moustache entered in blue silk pajamas. "You are the early bird, Dicer."

"I like catching worms. Are you volunteering?" she asked.

He threw back his head and laughed, then turned his attention to Merlo. "You are new. What did you do to get sentenced to Dicer's squad? Did you hit a supervisor? Shoot an unarmed suspect? Sleep with a suspect?"

"I wanted my rights," Merlo told him.

"Oh, you're a lesbian." His eyes darted back to Dicer. "You do like them fit. I always thought I'd be the one to put a bullet in you, Dicer."

"As I thought of you."

"I searched my soul on whether to send you that note. There was no way of knowing what you would think of me if I did."

"We both know you don't care what I or anyone think of you?"

"Not so. I care in a way that allows me to know how an individual will react. Take you for example. We're mirror images of each other trying to bring order into our chaotic worlds. Both considered by our contemporaries to be mavericks of the worst sort. Furthermore, we're both suspicious of wise men bearing gifts. And I know what I'd think of you if you called offering assistance to one of my cases. I'd think you had either stared death in the face and realized everything you believed in was a crock of shit or you were playing an angle that would net you substantial rewards. Seeing your bored expression, it's the latter." He chuckled. "You may or may not be right. That's irrelevant because you know what I have could be instrumental to your case."

"Yes, it could be."

"And you want to know my price."

"No. You're going to give it to me freely," Dicer told him with a half-smile.

Blue Pajamas turned to Merlo. "How long have you worked for Dicer?"

"This is my second day."

"What do you think of her?"

"She's efficient," Merlo replied.

"Efficient yes. But you have some impression of her. What is it?"

"I have not had the time to formulate an opinion."

He glanced from Merlo to Dicer. "You're losing your touch, Dice. How many guns do you have between you?"

"Four."

"And you're both wearing vests I presume?" he directed the question to Merlo.

"Yes."

He watched Dicer. "Yes, you do expect the information free."

The maid returned. "Breakfast is ready, sir."

He rose fluidly. "Ladies, please join me."

Dicer rose. "Thank you, but no. The information please."

His smile was steely. "You shouldn't insult your gracious host, young lady. You will make your officer think you are an uncouth flatfoot unable to separate your job from your life and everyday civility." The mirth came back. "Plus, I have a story to tell."

"Very well, but make it quick. None of that long-winded bullshit."

"I'll make it as short as possible."

The small dining room was surrounded by glass and mirrors with the table set for three.

Judge Victoria Seeley was not a favorite of the police officers. She frequently rebuked officers in court for sloppy procedure in a case. Yet when Dicer was told she had a choice between Seeley and rubberstamp Rosenberg, she skipped upstairs to Seeley's office. The perfectionist judge waved Dicer to a chair as she finished whatever she was typing.

"I rearranged my schedule to match Rosenberg's in order to get this done." The elderly judge, her hair in a bun, removed her horn rimmed glasses and looked squarely at Dicer. "What have you gotten yourself into, Lt. Dicer?"

Dicer gave her most reassuring smile. "I need a wiretap for Nathaniel Balsam's estate as well as Gideon Travette's."

"Is that all?" Seeley sat back.

"No. All of their communications devices, cell phones, mistresses phones and—"

"What are you looking for, Dicer?" She beckoned the officer closer.

"Their connection to the Mexican mafia." Dicer slid the chair closer.

"What's your evidence?"

"Ruben Fuentes."

Seeley stared at her. "Ruben Fuentes?"

"Yes."

"You want me to allow you unbridled wiretapping to Balsam and Travette based on Fuentes?"

"Yes?"

"As part of a deal with whom?"

"No deal. Fuentes came to me, rather I drove up to his house."

"Alone."

"I had a rookie."

"What is he getting out of this?"

"Nothing from us."

"Fuentes?" Seeley rose, walked to a file cabinet and removed a thick green folder, then returned to her desk. She thumbed through several pages before looking up. "I'll need a statement from Fuentes."

"Would a microcassette do?" Dicer pulled out a pair of cassettes. "One is Travette reportedly approaching Fuentes for a partnership. The second is Fuentes' statement to me taken this morning."

"And you don't believe that in itself is enough for an arrest warrant?"

"If I did, I'd have it. I want evidence." Dicer rose. "Judge, one of my men found a box of GreenTarts in the New Faith Cathedral.

When he returned to the room, it was gone with only law enforcement personnel and church officials onsite. The packet he did confiscate was pure heroin. If what Fuentes say is true, they are responsible for my shooting and the bombing of Ayers' house."

"Those are serious accusations, lieutenant."

"Which is why I'm here, judge, and not ripping apart the finely laid floors of the cathedral."

"Which was your first inclination." It wasn't a question.

"My people are still on-site. I don't plan on removing them anytime soon."

Seeley shook her head. "No, you remove them this afternoon. Is the cathedral named in your request for a wiretap?"

"No."

"Very well, i want specifics of what you're looking for and how many taps and for how long you want them. I want each piece of equipment you intend to use, including that directional mike. You know how this works. I'll be expecting your return."

Dicer leaped to her feet. "Yes, ma'am."

"And lieutenant?"

"Yes."

"What is Fuentes getting out of snitching?"

"The elimination of murderous competition. He's a superstitious man, your honor." She paused. "He's scared."

"If that's true, you be careful."

"No doubt." Dicer left, snagging Merlo. They had a job that Aviles would need to approve.

Jill Merlo arrived home after eight, tired but in a good mood after a fourteen hour day. Toni sat in front of the television with an array of apartment brochures spread out on the coffeetable next to a pizza box.

"How was work?" Jill asked, sitting a small box in front of Toni.

"Okay." She picked up the box. "What's this?"

"Nothing much." Jill walked into the bedroom. Over lunch

Dicer had gotten her to talk about herself which led to Toni and their problem of late. When Gomez came on duty, again the conversation got around to relationships to which everyone had opinions on how to help their significant others cope with their job. They all had trying stories, all except Dicer who swore her private life was as dull as the rubber plants in the lobby. Yet when they went downtown for the third time that day, she pestered Jill into picking up a "little something" for Toni.

She was stepping into the shower when Toni came in with a frown. "Where's your uniform? Those aren't your clothing?"

Jill winked. "My first plainclothes assignment. The lieutenant has a closet of clothing in her office. She told me to keep a set or two in my locker, as well as workout gear. We have passes to the intramural center."

Toni watched her closely. She looked tired, but not frustrated and angry as she usually was. "You like your new assignment?"

"Yes. You won't believe this place and the people. You met Gomez. You should meet the others."

"I look forward to it, now stop wetting the floor." Toni pushed her into the shower. "And thanks for the earrings."

"Welcome." Grinning Jill reached out and pulled Toni into the small shower.

"Aye!" Toni exclaimed laughingly as her t-shirt was soaked.

Toni awoke wrapped in Jill's arm. It had been two weeks since they had made love and even longer since it meant something. The alarm would go off in twelve minutes so she snuggled back into Jill wishing last night was not an anomaly. It was her day off and she was going apartment shopping near the university. With summer school in session, there should be an abundance of housing.

"What are you thinking?" Jill asked sleepily.

"Apartment shopping," Toni said softly.

"Where?"

"Near the university."

There was a lengthy silence. "What about a house?" Jill said finally.

Toni sat up, disbelieving her ears. "What?"

"I was talking with my squad. They all have houses which they got cheap and fixed up. I was thinking that maybe we could do the same, if you're willing."

"How much fix-up are we talking about?"

"We could choose." Jill sat up. "After my probation is over, I can get a low interest loan from the credit union with no hassle. I know you are in a hurry to get out of here, but if we start looking now, seriously, we could have everything ready by then."

"Your probation is over in six months?"

"Five actually."

Toni glanced at her warily. "This isn't a ploy to keep me here is it?"

"No. You think I like living in these cramped quarters? The money we spend on deposits and rent, we could use for down payment on a house. Maybe we can take some of those homebuyers seminars, see how much house we can afford."

"You're serious?"

"Yes." Jill turned to her. "I know it's what you want and so do I, but you had to see my point. Until I was transferred, I didn't think I was going to make it through in the 5th. So many times I just wanted to quit, give up."

To Toni that revelation was a shocker. Sure she was having problems, but she thrived on the fight. Didn't she? "Why didn't you tell me things were that bad?"

"I thought it was me, that I was over-reacting, that maybe I wasn't good enough and had to blame something."

Although Toni didn't like what she was hearing, she was glad to hear the old Jill sharing her ideas. Could a change of locale have had such a dramatic effect after only two days? Or was this just a passing phase? She hoped not. They had been through much together as friends before they were lovers. She had given up a job she had held for four years to follow Jill here and it had taken her three months to find a comparable though not fulfilling job here. They had moved into the apartment to save money, pure and simple.

Disentangling herself from her sheets, Dicer reached to turn off the alarm with her left hand. Realizing what she had done, she switched on the light and stared at her shoulder, then peeled off the dressing Kylar had put on the night before. The wound was healing rapidly and the soreness was gone. Slowly she rotated the shoulder, discovering she had pretty good movement.

When she returned from the shower, Nikki waited on her bed watching the early morning news. "Ready?"

"I don't think it needs anything?" Dicer said.

"Of course it does," Nikki said rising as Dicer sat in a chair. Her eyes focused on Dicer's left shoulder above the blue towel wrapped around her body. "Jesus, Dicer. What happened?"

"Kylar wrapped it with some foul smelling ointment."

"Whatever it was it worked. We need to patent that."

"I doubt he'd give you the recipe." Dicer looked down at her shoulder.

"Still you should wrap it lightly."

"Okay, go ahead." Dicer sat as the teenager bandaged her up. "Guess those summers at the Y paid off. Thank you."

"Welcome." Nikki went back down for another two hours of sleep.

As Dicer dressed, fragments of her dreams came back to her. Fuentes and Brother Thomas were prominently featured in them. What was Fuentes sending them into? Why had he made that recording in the first place? On the surface what she told Seeley was true: Fuentes would be handing over the competition if the NFC were indeed dealing in GreenTarts. Scared? Of a sorts, but not for his personal safety, but there was something, which was why he rolled over so willingly. If she brought down the NFC, it would net him something incredible that far outweighed his personal concerns with the legal system.

As she left, she passed Connie running down the lane, then she waited remembering she needed to talk to her. She stopped the vehicle waiting for her tenant.

"Morning, Dice," she said leaning on the top.

"Morning, Connie. Are you going out to Wango's today?"

"Yes. I'll be back at three. Why?"

"I need you to feel up the freezer."

"No problem. The usual?"

"Yeah and a little extra for the grill."

"Mind if I start it up this evening?"

"Help yourself, just do up a little extra. Hopefully I'll be home for dinner."

"I'll call you at six to make sure." Connie tapped the top of the vehicle and trotted back to the side of the lane.

Dicer drove on, knowing she would miss Connie when she left. She was a worry-free tenant who easily worked out her rent when she couldn't pay.

At the Gamin stationhouse, Jill Merlo was assigned a desk behind a row of file cabinets, from which she spent the entire morning calling witnesses clarifying points in their earlier statements. In her office upstairs, Dicer caught up on her paperwork leaving Merlo on her own for the first time since her transfer. In the previous four days she had worked fifty hours and nearly all of it directly with Dicer at a pace that kept her double-stepping to keep up; so a return to more mundane tasks was a welcome respite.

A shadow fell over her desk as Mickey leaned against the file cabinet. "Find anything out of the ordinary?"

"No." Merlo placed the files in an empty drawer. "They just really love their NFC," she said in a syrupy sweet falsetto.

"Yeah, it's driving Dicer bonkers." He checked his watch. "Are you eating lunch?"

Merlo checked her own watch, but the tug in her stomach told her it was way past lunch. "Let me buzz, Dicer."

"Don't bother, she's gone."

Merlo blinked. "When? Where?"

"Two minutes ago and with Lou, so you have no reason to stay." He motioned her up. "Come on, I'm starved. We need every ounce of energy we can get around here."

"How many hours a week do you average?"

"Sixty."

"That's eighty hours a month in over time. I could use that." Mickey chuckled. "Dicer doesn't authorize overtime."

"Huh?"

He slapped her on the back. "Just kidding, but only half. You can also opt for a four-day week with her, but I'd advise you not to do that just yet. She doesn't take kindly to an officer unwilling to give a wee bit extra."

"I gathered that much, but . . . " She followed him toward the front door.

"You can't work for free. Is that what you were about to say?" He gave her a boyish grin.

"I can't."

"Don't worry, she'll make sure you get what's yours."

"Y'all like her, don't you? Not just as a supervisor?" They crossed the street before he answered. "Yeah, Dicer sticks up for her people, none of that bullshit the rest of them put you through." He chuckled. "Don't get me wrong, Merlo; she will work your ass off and expect you to hold up your end of the bargain. And trust me, it is a bargain to get sent over here, though sometimes it doesn't seem like it."

"I hear she has a direct line to the chief?" Merlo ventured as they hit the path taking them around the intramural center.

"Also means the chief has a direct line to her and there are no buffers when something is screwed up which is why she busts our chops. We screw up, she's screwed. You got it?"

"Yeah. I got it." A green, red, and white sub shop loomed before them.

"I'm not trying to scare you, Merlo. Just how it is over here."

He held the door for a middle age woman laden with bags and a cup box.

"Thank you, officer," the woman said and went on.

Taking their orders to a back booth of the half full shop, they watched the summer students discuss their courses or love interests.

"Do you guys do anything off-duty together?" Merlo asked, stealing an onion ring from him.

"Socially?" He swallowed reaching for a pickle. "Yeah. Mumford and Gomez are always having something. They live on the same street by the way. Lou has a family, so does Vic, so there are family outings like a picnic or something. Dicer barbecues and just calls people up out of the blue."

"She said something this morning at roll call about Sunday."

"I was late. Her brother is still here so maybe she will, now that Lou has a house. She likes his girls."

"How old are they?"

"I don't know nine, ten, twelve, something like that. They've known each other since they were kids, same street I think. He joined the force first."

"They're the same age?"

"He's a couple of years older."

"What don't you know about your colleagues?"

"Very little." He winked at her. "They know as much but I talk the most."

Merlo opened her mouth, then closed it, looking out the window at two youngsters on rollerblades.

"What?" he prompted. "When everything is back to normal, we're going to be paired together so we may as well get on the ball now."

She chuckled. "Thatta fact?"

"Yeah, Lou and Vic, Mumford and Gomez, that leaves me and you."

"I thought we were just her assistants."

He feigned offense. "Me, an assistant? Don't think so. You maybe, miss thang."

She suppressed her laughter at his antics and her unasked questioned was answered. "You have a steady?"

"Steady job?"

She laughed. "No, steady partner?"

He sobered. "Yes. Not long-term, but I'm hoping. He works at the AIDS hospice, he's a nurse."

"How'd you meet him?"

"A friend of mine stayed there before his death."

"Recent?"

Mickey nodded. "March. We were running buddies." A chill went through him. "Some of us are damn lucky."

"Yes." They were silent awhile. "Seven of us and four are . . . "

He winked at her again. "Cool isn't it. And don't forget Otu."

"And Mumford?"

He chuckled. "She does act the part doesn't she? But she's been married six years, which doesn't stop her from advising me to settle down."

"Doesn't mean she hasn't drank from our cup of tea either." This time she winked at him.

"No, sure as hell don't." Mickey spotted a man in gingham pants and a frayed polo taking a seat two tables in front of them. "Professor Duncan!"

The middle age man looked up. "Mickey, hi."

"They have you working this summer?"

"Fool that I am." He sat his tray down and pulled over a chair. "I hear Dicer is back."

"Yes. Peter Duncan, Jill Merlo, she's our newest addition."

He wiped his hand on his shirt and extended it to Merlo. "Pleasure, young lady."

"Same here, professor."

"Duncan supplies us with interns, which means we get the smart ones."

"I wouldn't dare send Otu anyone else. How are Wanda and Karen doing? I haven't seen them in two weeks." Duncan took a big bite of his sub.

"Good, they were running around the city with Levins this week."

"What do you teach?" Merlo asked.

"Research and social policy. Have either of you been to the Sunset?"

"Yes!" Mickey exclaimed. "It is absolutely to die for. And you won't believe who is playing there."

"Yes, I would. That's why I'm asking you." He took another bite.

"Who?" Merlo asked.

"Xorron."

"Who's that?" Merlo asked.

Duncan and Mickey exchanged glances. "What are you doing at ten o'clock tonight?" Mickey asked his soon-to-be partner.

"Probably just getting off."

"Nope, you're going to the Sunset Club with me. Jon's working and I need a date," Mickey told her. "Are you going Duncan?"

"Yes. I guess I'll see you there."

"Count on it," Mickey assured him.

"Unless we have to work," Merlo hedged. She had to call Toni who would no doubt be overjoyed.

Six o'clock, Ki Dicer came down the stairs ending her first week back, not quite satisfied with the progress made, but had put several things in motion that would hopefully land them concrete evidence or at least point them towards that evidence. Merlo and Mickey were sitting at Mickey's desk in front of the computer.

"You're not paid to play computer games. Go home and do it on your own time."

The two looked up with guilty smiles. "We clocked out half an hour ago." Mickey rose. "Are we done?"

"I am, but you're welcome to remain. You two getting along?" Dicer glanced from one to the other.

"Peachy," Mickey told her, taking his helmet off the file cabinet.

"Good. Enjoy your weekend, you've earn it." Dicer started off.

"What about that barbecue, Dice?" Mickey asked.

Dicer turned around. "I'm home Sunday. You're welcome to start the grill."

"Me?"

Dicer laughed. "I'll give you a call. Night."

Merlo watched the easy exchange as she shouldered her bag. "We're picking you up right?"

"Yeah. You sure you don't mind?"

"No, like you said it's on the way."

"You think she wants to go?" Merlo motioned towards Dicer filling out a form at the front desk.

"She has a date."

"How do you know that?"

"I took the message when she went downtown."

"What kind of women does she date?"

Mickey laughed. "Hell if I know."

"I thought you trained under her."

"Yeah, but rumor has it she's celibate."

"Seriously doubt that." The two officers exited the back speculating on their lieutenant's sex life.

The southwest style Sunset Club stood on Laredo Drive with a large horse and rider mural on the side of the adobe building. Each of the lobby's interior walls contained vivid sunset murals depicting different seasons. A row of paintings attracted viewers around the ticket booth.

"Twenty-five dollars!" a woman exclaimed.

"She's donating the proceeds to the children's AIDS fund," someone told her.

"That's what they all say," someone else said.

Merlo glanced at Mickey. "You didn't tell us it costs so much."

"What else do you spend your money on, Jill?"

"We're saving for a house."

"And fifty dollars could be the difference between your ranch and villa. Yeah." He reached into his pocket. "Besides, I got connections." He held up three tickets.

"Where did you get those?" Toni asked moving closer to him to allow a wheelchair safe passage.

"I know people in low places remember." He led them to the door. "Come ladies."

Merlo shook her head at her colleague who looked quite dashing in his summerweight blue suit. More than a few heads turned as he made his way through the closely arranged tables to the front to a reserved table where a buxom blonde talked to a tuxedoed waiter.

"Lovey," Mickey said kissing at the blonde's cheek.

"Mickey, nice to see you in one piece." Her eyes roamed the two women.

"Too fine to be blown to bits. Lovey, this is my partner Jill and her mate Toni." They greeted each other and took their seats.

Ten minutes after they took their seats, the club lights dimmed and a teenage girl came on stage.

"Good evening, welcome to the Sunset Club and thank you for contributing to the Metrox Children's AIDS Fund. This is our eleventh concert in the tri-state area with all proceeds going to local children's fund. We have three acts for you tonight, so I hope you came prepared to jam until the sun comes up. Ladies and gentlemen, I am proud to introduce your first band, Vibora!"

When the stage lights came on, the audience discovered that Vibora was an all-girl band whose members were all under twenty-one years old. The six young women were simply dressed in tuxedo pants and lavender blouses. By the second acid jazz number, everyone forgot their age. After the third number while the audience applauded their performance, the pianist rose and moved to the microphone at the edge of the stage to the center.

"Good evening. More than a dozen years ago a tribute album of Cole Porter songs was made to benefit AIDS. That disc was my first exposure to Cole Porter and several songs have since become favorites of mine and we'd like to perform them for you." She chuckled. "Don't hold our ages against us."

Someone shouted, "Just play your music girl!"

In response the band began to play and the youngster began

to slowly unbutton her blouse and began a racy rendition to several catcalls. Five songs later, she returned to the piano after a standing ovation. After three bluesy numbers with the guitarist singing lead, the band unplugged their instruments and left the stage amidst thunderous applause.

The teenage MC returned to the stage. "Too darn hot for me," she said with a giggle. "Our second band tonight doesn't have a name yet so we just call them Bandies. The members come from our local schools and clubs. By some estimates they're the best we have to offer. I like them because they sound like Motowners. For instance, they do the Supremes. Baby love, ooh baby love . . . " The audience chuckled at her off-key singing. "Now you know why they have me here." She told a few jokes until the other band was plugged up and read. Obviously after ten performances they had the quick interchange down to an art.

In addition to the band, four women in sequined dresses and big hairdos came out for five numbers followed by four young men in pastel blue suits. They finished up together with a long medley that had the crowd up on their feet.

The youngster came on stage yawning. "It's past my bedtime and they're taking me to the hotel as soon as I introduce your last act. I'm supposed to tell you to go to the bathroom and fill up pitchers because they're going to play until they drop. She's in a mellow mood tonight and I have fifteen minutes to kill. Although I can't sing and Bandie won't let me play with them, I am a musician. For those of you with big bladders, I'll keep you company with my flute." The youngster pulled out a flute from the bag at her feet and began to play horribly. "Sorry, it doesn't feel too well. I'll try something else." She went through the routine several times as the audience laughed until they cried.

When a drummer let loose on a long tympani, the youngster gathered up her instruments and accompanying gags. "Ladies and gentlemen, I am proud to introduce my band and uh..what's your name?" she asked the piano player still in shadow.

"Rex, sweetie."

The youngster fanned herself, pretending to swoon. "She called me sweetie."

"She's a real ham," Toni said laughing.

"Yes, she blew us away," Lovey said.

"Graven Images featuring Rex Xorron!" the youngster shouted and ran from the stage as the lead guitarist kicked into a long soul-stirring solo and the lights slowly came up to reveal another six woman band, full-grown women, all except the pianist scantily dressed.

"*When my baby leaves me alone. . . . and my heart loses its song, that's when I need to return where my soul can be free. . . .*" sang the gritty-honey laced piano player. The long two-hour session interspersed bluesy favorites and their own recordings.

"Thank you. Thank you for coming out tonight," Rex Xorron said to the thunderous, standing crowd. "Many years ago when I was young, single and carefree, I always closed with a particular number. For the last couple of years, my daughter has virtually stolen my audience and because of her diversity has gained one of her own. I have been given credit for this little tour, but I must give credit where credit is due. The tour was Dorie's brainchild and she organized the Bandies and talked everyone else into donating their weekends for the tour. So if it pleases you, I'd like Dorie to finish out tonight's show for me. Dorie, are you awake?"

The teenager trotted out to the audience's standing ovation. "Thanks, mom." She picked up a mike. "Here's for to everyone who wants a friend as well as a lover, woman or not." The youngster sung two songs before leaving the stage.

"Damn!" Jill Merlo exclaimed, exhausted from the emotional rollercoaster.

"That about sums it up," Mickey said remaining seated.

"Do you have any of their albums?" Toni asked Mickey.

"They have a live version taped two weeks ago out front for free and at the Triple X music store," Lovey told them. "I believe your city has one located in Boxtown."

"For free?" Toni asked.

"Tonight they're free. He'll give you one when you exit, if you want it that is. Twenty-five dollars was quite a steep price for Xorron who still plays for free or for causes such as this."

"How can she afford it?" Toni asked, looking around at the dispersing crowd. Afterall it was getting close to three in the morning.

"She likes to sing without all the bullshit of the music industry; she has other interests."

"What about Dorie? Is she going professional?"

"She can make her own decision at twenty-one."

"Helluva lot better than a lot of the people making millions."

"Her day will come. For them, it's not about the money." Lovey rose. "It was nice meeting you both." She made her goodbyes and left through the side entrance.

"Say thank you, Mickey," Mickey told them grinning.

"Thank you, Mickey," Toni said with a smile.

"You're welcome. Now take my ass home." He yawned and stretched.

They chatted about the show all the way across town. "How do you know Lovey?" Toni asked him.

"Lovey's my brother," he said offhandedly.

"Your brother?!" Jill exclaimed. "That was not a man."

"Yes, it was. And you should have seen him when he was younger. Man, he was drop dead gorgeous."

"He's staying in town?"

"Yes, then he'll fly back with them Sunday."

"Maybe you can talk him into coming to Dicer's with you?" Jill suggested.

"I'll ask, but they're on their own plane."

"A charter or their own plane?"

"Xorron's plane." He looked at them as Jill pulled into his yard. "You really haven't heard of Xorron. Where are you from again?"

"Texas."

"That explains it." He chuckled. "Thanks for the ride. Good night."

"Night." The two women drove home discussing their evening and how neither had to get up the next morning.

CHAPTER 8

Dicer feeling good when she awoke Saturday morning decided to finish the floor in the family room which would complete the flooring in the entire house. Four hours of intense work was all she was needing to complete the project which would have been finished over her vacation if she had not been shot. In a way the failure to finish the floor had been the worst result of the shooting. When Kylar offered to assist she shooed him away. Nikki didn't bother to offer as she went about her Saturday routine: sleep late, errands, and softball.

"Tomorrow, we celebrate!" Dicer shouted when the last tile had been laid.

"Whoopie," Kylar said chuckling. "And now you feel like a natural woman."

"Damn straight, I do." Dicer laughed. "You have any idea how long this took?"

"Yes. I do." He nodded emphatically. "I hate to bring you from the clouds, but I think I should tell you before he walks in."

"Who?" Dicer asked, bending over her tools.

"Dad."

Dicer straightened up. "Maybe he got distracted like he did last week and changed his mind." Her father was scheduled to come last weekend, but he was called back to the office before he made it out of town good.

"No, he's at Kip's already."

"Well, we'll make every effort to be nice to him, won't we." Dicer dropped tools in a bucket to clean them.

"It's not you he's always harassing." Kylar leaned against the wall. "You two have a perfect relationship."

Dicer guffawed for that had always been his perception of their relationship. "Not even close." True she was closer to her father than the other three.

"Speaking of close." He reached down to fold the small drop cloth. "I didn't expect you home last night."

"Why wouldn't you?" she asked, glancing up at him.

"Didn't think you were the love'em and leave'em type. Do the do and go about business."

Dicer chuckled. "To settle your curiosity, we had a pleasant dinner, stimulating conversation, and a relaxing nightcap. We parted in the parking lot."

"Bet she was disappointed."

Dicer laughed. "You may be right."

"She seemed nice enough. What fault do you find with her that you just can't live with?"

"I know what you're thinking, Kylar, and I'm not looking for the perfect woman, just a perfect match."

"Same difference, Kiwi. Plus you're looking for an impossible combination."

"Am I?" she asked.

"Yes. A strong, assertive woman who bends to your will. Impossible. Once she bends, she loses respect in your eyes."

"Well thank you, Dr. Ruth. Why don't you finish the statement and tell me that I'm doomed to wander this big house alone for the rest of my life."

"I wouldn't go that far, just right now." He picked up the two buckets. "I'll take this out to the shed."

"Thanks. And what do you mean not just right now?"

"If you keep adding to the criteria for your perfect lady, you'll need six different women to meet them all."

She followed him out. "What does that suppose to mean?"

"You go daffy all of a sudden? No woman can possibly meet your standards."

"Why not? I do."

Kylar guffawed, much like his sister earlier. "I pity the fool who falls in love with you."

"You should lay off the music, Kylar."

"Don't change the subject."

"I didn't start this."

"Yes, you're the one who left Miss Jaio all hot and bothered last night."

"Oh alright then. Tell me why you're single if you have all the relationship answers."

"Simple. Having you as a sister raised my expectations of women too high. Every woman I meet I end up comparing to you."

Dicer laughed. "That's sick, Kylar. Don't tell no one else that."

"Perfection, you can't find it, even if you look in the mirror."

"When did you say you were leaving?"

"Tuesday, but that's not going to change the fact that you're too damn choosy for your own good." Kylar looked around the neatly arranged workshop. His sister was not as unyielding as he was accusing her of being; furthermore he understood her point of view in setting certain criteria for friendship.

Kirk Dicer in his fifties stood lean and fit, burnished a deep tan from years of working outside alongside his employees. His four children all had abandoned the business he loved, but he did not hold it against them nor had he given up hope on Ki and Keven returning. Kylar? He did not understand his eldest son who had grown up in Ki's shadow; but there was more to it than he could not understand. He had been a sickly baby and small child who Ki felt compelled to protect. Ki. So much like her mother neither could stand the other, although things were better between them. Both strong, demanding women who insisted the world operated a certain way and made a concerted effort to make it so.

Kirk took in the villa and the improvements made since his last visit. The lawn was impeccable as usual and the hedges shooting up like sentries would soon obscure the view down the lane.

He knelt to examine the fittings of a low stone wall around a flower bed of Japanese iris and lilies.

"Can't you ever not work?" Kylar asked.

"No." Kirk rose to scrutinize his son, a small delicate man with that damn moustache and ponytail in the top of his head. "You're looking healthy, son."

"I am healthy. How are you?"

"Can't complain. Have you enjoyed your stay with Ki?"

"It's been peaceful."

"Until now you mean?" Kirk asked raising an eyebrow.

"We shall see won't we."

Kirk looked back at the piles of rocks waiting to be transformed into a retaining wall. "Why hadn't you started on that wall?"

Kylar gave him a mocking look. "That's Ki's wall."

Kirk nodded, understanding his meaning. "Have you seen, Kerry?"

"Thursday." They moved towards the front door.

"If your mother and Ki can call a truce, why can't we?"

"Because they are alike, we are not," Kylar told him.

"Yes, they are, but I'm sure we share commonalities." Kirk stopped in the doorway to study the flooring laid out before him in the foyer and front room. "Gorgeous."

"The whole house is like this," Kylar told him. "You should see the room she finished not too long ago. All she allowed me to do was clean up after her."

"You poor boy," Kirk said, laying a hand on his son's shoulder. "One day, I'd like to see what you did with that little place in San Francisco."

"I'm leaving Tuesday, you're welcome to join me."

"Make it Friday and you have a deal," Kirk said and walked off.

Kylar stood looking at him; the man had never been past the Rockies and never expressed a wish to do so. "What?"

"I'm taking a vacation; I need to go somewhere. I've never been to San Francisco. We could get a convertible and ride the coast. What you say?"

Kylar didn't know what to say. "Why?"

"I want to go to the Napa Valley too."

"Are you dying?"

Kirk laughed. "No, but I am more aware of death lately. Do you have a beer or something?"

"In the kitchen." Kylar headed that way, glancing back at his father as he followed taking in the flooring.

"Where is Ki?"

"Someone called and she left an hour ago, said she'd be back in an hour."

"The shooting didn't slow her down did it?"

"Only for a couple of days. You know how she is? Like you." Kylar pulled out one of the local brews.

"Yes. You don't approve."

"Your lives."

"Your mother said you once considered moving back."

Kylar frowned. "Once or twice. I've also considered China."

"You ever been?"

"No."

"Want to go? We could go together. Don't you speak Chinese or something?"

"Some." This conversation was getting stranger and stranger. Perhaps when Ki arrived, things would return to normal.

Kirk shook his head. "Maybe I'm stretching it for me. Why haven't you gone, son?"

"I'm a poor man, dad."

"Hell, it can't be that expensive. Make out an itinerary and cost of the trip and fax it to me. No, we'll do it when we go to San Francisco. I'll foot the bill if you'll bring back videotapes for me and yourself of course. Do you have a companion to take with you? I'm sure it's more exciting with two people and safer."

Kylar watched him warily. "What's all of this about, dad? You want to come to the bay area and now you want to pay my way to China. I haven't worked for it as you say."

Kirk opened the fridge and snagged a second beer then went towards the patio door. "But you have, son. You have." He walked out, skirting the pool and directly to the wrought iron back fence where he stood looking down the sloping hill of wildflowers and clumps of blue rug juniper. He lost track of time until he sensed the change in the air and turned to see Ki sitting on a stone bench watching him.

"Kylar said you were acting strangely," she said rising.

"Just reflective." He pulled her into a long hug. "How's my girl?"

"Don't know, I'll ask Katie."

He chuckled. "You look good. Kip said you did, but I had to see for myself."

"What are you reflecting so much on, dear old dad?"

"Just life." He sighed.

"What's going on dad?" She didn't expect him to say much more than he already had.

Toni Jensen checked her watch, then made a right turn at the light taking her into Boxtown proper and down to the strip that housed Triple X music store. Inside the colorful store, soft jazz played over the large store that featured a clothing line upstairs. A soda fountain counter stretched across the back wall. And someone was holding court in an adjacent corner, signing autographs. Curious Toni sliced through the small crowd; Rex Xorron sitting at a card table chatted with a pair of HSU students about Brazil.

"If you're interested, by all means go," she told them as she pulled a flyer to her. "Call this lady, and tell her what your ideas are. Sometimes there are vacant seats on their plane and you can hop a ride if you're going for academic purposes. But make sure your passports and visas are in order; they do go through customs and all that."

"Thank you," they said rising.

Xorron looked up at the small crowd. "And you guys just stand here listening to whatever I say." She counted them. "Seventeen. I think I can afford seventeen coke floats for your being such an adoring audience." She handed out coupons. "Thank you, enjoy."

"No, thank you," Toni said stepping aside for two identically dressed teenagers.

After giving away everything else on the table, Xorron looked up to see Toni still lingering. "There's a pizza parlor two doors down. Would you join me for dinner?"

"Sorry, I'm meeting someone for dinner."

"Call her up and invite her over." Xorron handed her a phone.

"How do you know it's a her?"

"Short buzzcut, military bearing, nice eyes?" Xorron chuckled.

"Yes." Toni studied her.

"Front table last night or were we so bad you totally dismissed us as a nightmare?" Xorron asked with a lopsided grin.

"No, no. You were great. It's just I didn't think you would notice anyone in the audience."

"Oh, I noticed. Make the call, I'll be right back." She walked through a pair of swing doors.

Toni excitedly dialed home. No one answered, so she checked her messages, finding one from Jill telling her to have dinner without her. Leaving a hurried message of her own, Toni scanned the nearby stacks of music. Wow! Who would believe this?

Xorron came out with a fresh shirt. "Ready?"

"Yes. She wasn't home yet."

"Well, looks like it's just you and me."

Toni followed her out. "Don't you have an entourage or something?"

"Something, but I'm just a normal person. If you hadn't seen me last night, you wouldn't notice me at all."

Toni took in the long legs, the caramel skin and the dancing eyes and sensuous lips. Oh yes, she would have noticed alright. Definitely noticed.

They entered the dim pizza parlor and took a seat in the back corner. "I'm Rex," Xorron extended her hand across the table. "What's your name?"

"Oh. Toni, Toni Jensen." Toni shook her hand, and swore she felt an electric current in the woman's hand.

"I'm pleased to make your acquaintance, Toni."

"Yours as well." Toni tried to take her eyes off the woman but couldn't. There was something about her.

A waiter came over, did a double take at Xorron, and immediately apologized for the slow service. Their drinks arrived in a short minute as well as light salads they hadn't ordered.

"Does this happen alot?" Toni asked.

"Only when they realize they've been screwing up." Xorron raised the cranberry juice to her lips. "We're in the restaurant business and our success has always rested on the quality of service."

"Some places do not know what quality service is." She was remembering a rude waiter from last week at an Italian restaurant of all places.

"True. What business are you in, Toni?"

Toni sighed. "Healthcare claims processor."

"You don't sound enthused about it."

"Four days a week, the hours are great but the pay isn't."

"How long have you done that?"

"Almost five years now. Four back home."

"What brings you to middle America?"

"Jill, that's my girlfriend, was hired by Metrox PD and I decided I'd take a chance on her here rather than Texas without her."

"You love her?"

"Yes, more than she knows."

"Then it wasn't a chance then was it?"

"No."

"But?"

"But it's been rough the last few months." Toni wondered why she was revealing herself to this woman she didn't know; yet it felt so right, so easy to do so. She hadn't made many friends since she'd been here and definitely no one she could trust her inner thoughts to.

"Why?"

"We live in this cramped apartment because I wasn't too sure how soon I could find a job here. The economy wasn't so great last year. Then Jill was having problems at her precinct." Toni smiled suddenly. "Then she was transferred and it's made all of the difference in the world. You wouldn't think changing locale and supervisors could affect an individual so much."

"But it does, especially if the person is a sensitive individual. Is she?"

"Yes, though she tries to act tough. She's a real sweetheart and I love her to death." Toni smiled fondly, her eyes slightly out of focus. "She feels like she's found her niche."

"And you, Toni, what is it that you need to feel like you've found your niche?"

"I don't know. We're thinking about buying a house when she's off her probationary period."

"Will a house be enough to fill that void you've been feeling? You can't blame Jill's problems for all of your discomfiture." Xorron lifted her glass to her lips.

Toni stared at her. "No, I can't."

Their pizza arrived and they dug in.

"What do you want?" Xorron asked after a lengthy silence.

Toni shrugged. "I don't know."

"Consider me your fairy godmother. If you could have anything what would it be? Anything at all?"

Toni chuckled. "When you grow up like I did, you learn not to want, that unmet desires lead to frustration and subsequent abuses of alcohol, drugs or your family. If you don't want anything, you can't be disappointed. As you learn to expect very little from your fellow humans, you fixate on those who are decent and treat you well for they are truly unique in your world."

"Sounds like you're pretty good at dissecting situations. Ever thought about becoming a counselor or psychologist?" Xorron's success was based on her ability to quickly assess her personnel and their abilities then utilize it in the most productive manner possible.

"Yes, I have, but. . . ." No dream, no disappointment.

"But what?" Her stock in trade was making dreams come true for young women who had seen the rough side of life and were willing to work. Her companies were full of such women; furthermore they were drawn to her, as this one was.

"I . . . I don't know. Sometimes I just can't think straight. It's like I see what I want but not the road to get there. Like the obstacles are so profound that I can't even conceive of them. It's so much easier growing up knowing you want to be a botanist, architect, police officer or something you can shoot for. Me, I don't know. Sometimes I feel so inadequate, so alone."

"You talk to Jill about this?"

"No, I try, but . . . it's like she knows but doesn't understand either. I need stimulation, but I just can't seem to get it from the world, thus I find myself reading incessantly or watching movies to keep from facing my own frustration." She chuckled bitterly. "Wallowing in my own pity, not very flattering is it?"

"Not pity, insight. Sometimes talking to someone who has no emotional ties helps clarify things in your own mind. Now let me see if I can sum up what I'm hearing." Xorron took a long sip of her juice and lightly drummed her fingers on the glass. "You're frustrated because you're underutilizing your potential and intellect. You don't feel challenged and the big kicker is, you refuse to acknowledge your desires. Now let's discuss this wanting to be something with the big BUT on the end. First let's get back to my original question. What do you want?"

Toni wiped her hands. "I want to feel like I'm growing, like I'm doing something worthwhile. Processing forms all day is not creative and takes almost no brain power."

"If you want to grow, go to grad school."

"Hah! Have you seen the tuition at NSU? You'd think it was an Ivy League school or something."

Xorron grinned. "So you have checked it out?"

Toni shrugged, despite herself she continued to dream that she could continue her education. "On one of my days off."

"Then the deadline for fall should be rapidly approaching. You should get your admissions material in."

"I'll last right until tuition is due."

"Where there's a will there's a way."

"Tuition costs more than half of what I make a year." Why was she even having this conversation? The let down will be even greater when she returns to the reality of her life.

"You believe in Fate, luck or whatever?"

Toni nodded. "Guess I do, in some form or another."

"You have a pen and paper?" Xorron asked pushing her plate aside after only two slices of the large pizza.

"I should." Toni dug into her purse, the one that Jill said contained a voodoo doll. She placed the pen and small notebook on the table.

"You get yourself admitted to the program of your choice at NSU, these people will find every tuition, fee and book cent you need. If you need anything else, the woman to talk to is Ms. Parker. I'll email her so she'll be expecting your call. Don't procrastinate, call her Tuesday. She'll want to get things started on your end. She'll want a personal statement from you, so you might as well start working on it."

Toni looked at her incredulous. "You're kidding?"

"No. The bottom number is my personal assistant's office number. If you have any problems whatsoever, she's the one who can fix them. When I check Friday, I expect to see your name on that list, Ms. Jensen."

Toni tried hard to look past the celestial smile to see the guile inherent in such an offer. "What's the catch?"

Xorron nodded. "You gotta volunteer a few hours each week somewhere and make satisfactory progress."

"Why me?"

"Why not you? Good guys do win on occasion."

The waiter approached. "Can I get you anything else?" he asked.

"A box for the pizza and bring a salad to go," Xorron told him.

"Right away." He scampered off.

"I'm sorry to cut dinner shorter than usual, but the kids are playing at Azure high school. How that came about, I don't know."

"Dorie is very talented," Toni said still in a daze.

Rex laughed. "Yes, Dorie is many things, not the least a pain in the butt."

"Is she your only daughter?"

Xorron shook her head. "No, I have them ranging from three to thirty. And a grandbaby.""

"Three to thirty?" Toni blinked. This woman before her was no one's grandmother.

"And there are others who consider me their mother of a fashion, but everyone agrees that Dorie is definitely mine."

Toni agreed. "And she seemed to have a good time on stage."

"She does."

The waiter returned, quickly slipping the pizza into the box. Then held out the ticket for Xorron to sign. "Would you like to see the manager?" he finally asked.

"No, I've seen all I need to see," Xorron told him rising. "The pizza was good, thank you."

The two women strolled out into the early summer evening. "Thank you for everything," Toni said, taking the boxed salad and pizza.

"You're welcome, Toni. Don't have me calling you; you call Parker."

"I will." Toni got into her car and watched as a young man fell into step next to Xorron.

Dicer hung up the phone after sending Mickey and Merlo back home after their contact failed to show. She should have known that was too good to be true, but she was going to nail Darren Wallace to the wall. Back downstairs she could hear little Katie's peals of laughter above the din of voices in the front room where their impromptu family reunion was taking place. Her father had not let Katie out of sight since they had arrived. He had brought her a giant block building set and had commandeered a corner of the room to play. She took the most pleasure in destroying his creations. Kip had a blonde on his arm who drank every word he said. Kerry and Kris were recounting some office hijinks from the week. Kylar listened as his mother's youngest brother, Frank Goddard, entreated him to come back the following month for the real family reunion which was sure to be the best ever because he was in charge. Her mother, Carolyn, was deep in conversation with Nikki.

Ki circumnavigated to the corner with her father and niece. "Can I play?"

"Okay!" Katie exclaimed pushing several blocks to her.

"Thank you, sweetie." Ki pulled the child's ponytail.

The doorbell cut through the house.

"I'll get it," Kylar said rising quickly.

Alexis Guzman, deputy chief Aviles' adjutant, stood in the doorway. "Hi, is Lieutenant Dicer here?"

"Yes, come in."

"No, you have company. Would you ask her out? Guzman."

"Sure." Kylar crossed to his sister. "Guzman wants to see you outside."

"Give me a hand." Ki extended a hand for him to pull her to her feet. She walked out into the courtyard to the pile of rocks where Guzman and Aviles stood in the shadows. "Evening, ladies."

"Dicer," Aviles greeted her. "They found Norris, a bullet at the base of the skull in Memphis."

"What was he doing in Memphis?"

"Whatever, the fact is their reach extends outside of the city limits."

"Anything on those phone taps?"

"Two hours ago, they started using a descrambler after a lengthy conversation of how the devil was eavesdropping."

Dicer pursed her lips. "Mickey was meeting an informant in Siberia, he never showed."

"Shit, this all may be related." Aviles paced. "I hope his informant was just lost, because the way things are going, we'll find him floating in the reservoir."

"You talked to Gravelli?"

"We were having dinner when she got the call. She's on her way to Memphis."

Dicer wasn't going to ask why she was having dinner with Gravelli. "He wasn't hung up or tied down or anything? Throat cut?"

"No. Nice and clean as you please, that was the word."

Dicer raised her hands above her head. "This is going from bad to worst."

"Technically Norris is not our problem."

"Like hell he isn't." Ki paced, reaching down to pick up a smooth round rock. "I need more people, Aviles."

"Can't do, Dicer"

"Shit! You want this case closed or not?"

"There have been other murders in the city and frankly I . . . " Aviles trailed off.

"Yeah. What am I supposed to do with my hands tied?"

"Use your feet," she said softly. "I'll see if I can get Leiberman to spare a man or two. And they will be men, Dicer."

"I have no problem with men; men have problems with me."

"I need more ideas, evidence or something to keep this up."

"Doesn't the scramblers tell you something is not right here?" Dicer asked.

"Maybe if you pull that car off of Wallace, you can tell me more."

"Cannot do. He's in this."

Aviles stared through the dark. "Come again."

"The snitch Mickey was going to meet was going to verify that Wallace was either supplying the raw material for the GreenTarts to the NFC or was distributing for them."

"Or both," Guzman said thoughtfully.

Both turned to look at the sharpshooter. "What do you mean?"

"Your people reports that Wallace has new friends with deep pockets. No one knows who those friends are, no one sees him interact with anyone beyond the usual. Maybe his connection to NFC is more than skin deep if he's working both ends with them." Dicer mulled that over. "That would explain how he ended up on Harper. The church is nothing more than a front for drugs."

"Much more remember. Your friend Gao has a nasty piece coming out in tomorrow's Globe."

"And how would you know that?" Dicer asked suspiciously.

"I too have my contacts and I will undoubtedly have to defend the department in the fallout. You may be setting things in motion that you can't control. But the death of Norris has brought that to the forefront." She exhaled. "Let's go, Guzman."

"Is that all?" Dicer asked.

"Isn't that enough?" Aviles said softly. "Your team will have much to discuss over barbecue tomorrow."

Dicer chuckled. "I don't want to know how you know that. You're welcome to come, both of you."

"Can't fraternize with you." Aviles opened the car door. "Sorry to take you away from your family."

"No problem." Dicer walked back inside and into the kitchen just in time to catch her parents in a furtive embrace and kiss.

Toni sat in bed going through the NSU catalog as Jill came out of the shower. "What do you think about astronomy?"

"Yes, that's you. And where did you get the catalog?"

"Carlton upstairs. He borrowed some sugar."

"Does he buy sugar?"

"No, he fills up his pockets at restaurants." She giggled, getting a wry look from Jill.

"Want something to drink?"

"Whatever you have." Toni flipped through the descriptions, returning to one program in particular where three professors ran a communications center that used some of the equipment Jill had been given.

"Wine cooler okay?" Jill asked sitting on the edge of the bed.
"Yes."

"Now tell me again what's going on?" Jill had been besides herself with excitement when she arrived, telling her about having pizza with Xorron and going back to school. Then her aunt had called and Jill had gone into the shower.

"She'll pay for graduate school if I get accepted." Toni turned up the bottle.

"Why?"

"Why not me? I'm smart and creative. It's time I used that."

"Yeah, but I meant why is she willing to pay for it?"

"That was her answer."

"That's no answer, Toni."

"It made sense at the time."

Jill sat behind her on the bed, looping an arm around her waist. "Maybe it did, but think about it. No one gives something for nothing."

"Your new lieutenant gave you a gun."

"Yeah, but that was part of an identity ritual or something. We're talking about thousands of dollars here."

"I'll check out this foundation first to see if they've done this before. What if it's legit?"

"What if it's not?"

"Why would she lead me on?"

"Power trip maybe. She mesmerized the audience last night, why not you one on one over pizza?"

"Yeah, but to what end."

"To exploit your insecurities. People get a kick out of everything these days, not the least being mindfucking. Mickey knows this professor, maybe he knows about this foundation or maybe Otu. Yeah, Otu can find out."

"She wants me to call these people Tuesday."

"Why Tuesday? Why not Monday?"

"Isn't it the Fourth?"

"No, that's next week."

"Oh." Toni leaned back against her, enjoying the meandering caresses.

"Are you still going out to Dicer's with me?"

"Yes." Toni closed the catalog and notebook, placing them on the nightstand. "What should we take?"

"A side dish is what Mickey said. Everyone usually brings the same thing, but we're new." She watched Toni rise from the bed. "Where are you going?"

"Bathroom, is that okay?"

"Well . . . " Jill turned back the covers on the bed and removed her robe.

Dicer awoke after a fitful night of exhaustive vivid dreams. She had gone to bed leaving Kylar and their father up, so she hadn't discussed the intimacy of their parents with Kylar. Nikki was reading the paper at the kitchen table when she entered.

"Sleep well, Nik?" Dicer asked.

"Yeah." Nikki looked at her. "You didn't."

"I know. I'm going to eat and try to get two hours of dreamless sleep." Dicer opened the fridge. "Where's Kylar?"

"He went for a walk."

"What time did dad leave?"

"I don't know; I went to bed not long after you."

"Want an omelette?"

"I had cereal."

"My omelette's are very good."

"Oh, okay." Nikki laughed.

"What's funny?" Dicer glanced back at her.

Still laughing, Nikki snapped the section of the paper she was reading. "Listen to this, 'In a Miami cafe, a would-be robber reached for the revolver stuck in the front of his pants. When the gun snagged, the robber tugged, accidently pulling the trigger and shooting his penis.'" The teenager wiped her eyes.

"Crime hurts," Dicer said dryly. "What were you and Kip talking about so intensely before he left?"

"School and stuff."

"Talked to your mother?"

"No."

"Your sisters?"

"Some."

"Want me to mind my own business?" Dicer asked.

"No," Nikki said at length. "Just the same old same old over there, people coming in and out and children running everywhere."

"Not much difference from over here lately."

"Oh yes, it is. Your family doesn't yell and curse at each other nonstop. Janky ass men don't show up looking for your sisters."

"Naw, she keeps him close."

"Can I tell you something?"

"Of course, you can tell me anything."

"Famous last words."

"Nooo, think of me as a priest." The words sparked another fit of laughter from Nikki. "What was in that cereal?"

"My life is so fucked up that I have to laugh to keep from crying," the teenager said, folding the paper.

Dicer turned from the omelettes to look at her. "I know it's rough, but your life is definitely not fucked up."

"I don't even know who I am," Nikki moaned, wrapping her arms around herself.

"How would you be different if the tests came back that Kip is your father? Would you be smarter, taller, less compassionate, a better ball player, less beautiful, more silly, bolder, weaker or what?"

"You don't get it because you had a real family."

"What's a real family? Blood or people who love each other?"

"Like I said I didn't have a real family. I was the babysitter, the maid, the whipping post for their nasty tongues."

"Haven't we had this conversation before? Look, you're out. You never ever have to go back there."

"What if Kip is not my father? Then I'll only have my mama."

"What do you mean you'll only have your mama? You have your sisters, your cousins, aunts and uncles."

"Nobody!"

"I'm nobody? Kylar is nobody?"

"Noo, you're missing the point, Kiwi."

"What is your point then, Nikki because I am missing it this morning?"

"I feel so alone. No one understands. I have no home; I can't go home. You're only letting me stay here because you're feeling sorry for me."

Dicer waved a spatula at her. "Bullshit, Nikki. Just put that delusion out of your head right now. I sympathize with you, but I don't feel sorry for you. If I didn't want you here, you'd be staying with my mother and that's something I would feel sorry for you about." Dicer looked at her younger cousin, so much like her. "Nikki, we're as close as sisters, at the moment you're closer than Kerry. My door is always open to you."

"Then how come you didn't offer to let me stay here this fall when I told you I wanted to leave home?"

Dicer's jaw dropped. "What? Is this what all this is about? Nikki, you told me what your plans were. How did I know that you wanted to move in? I'm not a mindreader you know. Do you want to stay here this fall instead of the dorm?"

"I don't know." She sat with her head in her hands. "Kip said regardless of the results of the test, I could stay at his house in Orleans because it's closer than yours."

Dicer nodded, understanding dawning on her. Kip was making grandiose promises which had her thinking how her life could have been knowing he was her father. "Nikki, do you like who you are?"

The teenager looked up. "Yeah."

"You wouldn't be who you are if things had been different growing up."

"I may have been even more of me."

"A richer you, you mean?"

Nikki shrugged averting her eyes. "Maybe."

"Maybe not."

"I'll never know will I?"

"No, and no use dwelling on it either."

"Your skillet's smoking," Nikki told her.

"Shit!" Dicer turned around to remove the skillet from the tap.

"Just like my life."

"Will you stop it, Nikki. No one's life is perfect. You may as well understand that now. Everyone has problems, obstacles, regrets. What matters is how you deal with it and at the moment you are not dealing with it at all. No, I take that back, you're sounding like a sniveling spoiled brat."

"And what are you sounding like, giving all that accept and be happy bullshit. I know life is hard, you're the one who doesn't know. Everything comes easy to you."

"Hah! A lot you know, kiddo. You think it's easy being me? I've scrapped and scraped for everything I have. You think it was easy living with my mom too? With dad? When I was your age, I was a skilled laborer, with emphasis on labor. I didn't go to play on Kip's computers and sit in air conditioning offices; I was outside pouring concrete or building walls."

"At least you had a dad to teach you something. I had nothing."

"Okay, Nikki, if it helps I'll concede that you had absolutely nothing growing up. Now the question is: What do you have now? What does the future hold for you? Stop looking back and see your future with or without Kip. This is your life and you just can't depend on others to make you happy, not your mother, not Kip, not your sisters, not me. You are responsible for your happiness, no one else. Don't ever think someone else can make you happy and that you should sacrifice yourself for them, like so many of your relatives are doing. You're a wonderful, smart, beautiful girl, don't go settling for some deadbeat motherfucker with kids strewn across the midwest."

"Talking about Tisha?" Nikki asked, breaking Dicer's diatribe.

"Not particular, but that a good example. There are all these together women settling for these dead beat guys. I don't get it."

"What don't you get?" Kylar asked closing the patio screendoor behind him.

"Why good women fall for no good motherfuckers," Nikki informed him with a laugh.

"Good man shortage," Kylar said going to the sink to wash his hands.

"If that's so, why are you single?" Nikki asked.

"Good woman shortage."

"Now that I must agree with," Dicer said turning back to her breakfast making. "Kylar, you want an omelette?"

"She's been cooking them for thirty minutes," Nikki said.

"She's slow sometimes. So you and Kip are going car shopping today?"

"What?" Dicer turned around again to look at them.

Nikki rolled her eyes at Kylar. "He asked if I wanted another car or just keep his Pathfinder."

"What did you say?"

"What do you think I would say if someone offered me a new car?"

"I hope you'd say that you could find better use for the money, like your college education."

"I'm not stupid, Kiwi."

"So what did you tell him?"

"Kiwi, leave the girl alone," Kylar said softly.

"Stay out of this," she snapped at her brother, then immediately felt contrite. "This is an ongoing dialogue."

"Yeah, she wants me to be responsible for my own happiness and not depend on anyone," Nikki said dryly.

"She's right about that."

The doorbell sounded and they all looked at each other, for it was not eight yet. "I'll get it," Nikki said rising, thankful for the respite. She was not ready to have both of them on her case.

Jill and Toni trailed Mickey south to Dicer's house where they parked behind a large blue fourdoor pickup with a toolbox. The aroma of charred hickory filled the overcast day. Taking a deep breath, Toni took in her surroundings, noting they were above the city after a slow incline.

"Seems so peaceful here."

"It can be." Mickey walked over to the rocks. "Remind me to get some of these rocks for my flower bed. You don't mind carrying them do you?"

Jill chuckled. "Only if you don't steal them."

"She won't miss a dozen or so." He turned back toward the veranda where Nikki had greeted Toni and Jill.

"Mr. Mickey!" Nikki saluted him.

"Miss Nikita, how many hearts have you broken this week?" Mickey gave her a courtly bow.

"None."

"That you know of, my lady." He slinked an arm around her waist. "Every man and half the women who have laid eyes on you now have broken hearts. Even I out of respect for Dicer carry my broken heart like a man."

"And that has nothing to do with Jon?"

"Who?" He danced her around.

Kirk Dicer walked into the room seeing Mickey holding Nikki close. "Who the hell are you?" he demanded.

Nikki giggled. "Uncle Kirk, this is Mickey, one of Ki's officers. He taught me how to samba and rumba."

Kirk smiled suddenly and extended a hand. "Right kind of you, son; however you're not teaching right now so unhand her."

Mickey stepped back and bowed. "As you wish sir. May I add that you have the most beautiful eyes."

"Shit, you're a gay-boy. Just remember that when you're groping my niece."

"Yes, sir, but it is definitely hard." Michey chuckled and stuck out his hand. "Now you, makes me glad that I'm a man. May I have this dance?"

"Hell no," Kirk told him and walked out.

Mickey turned to Nikki. "That is one fine man."

"And Ki's dad."

"Where is our fearless leader?" Mickey asked.

"On the terrace."

"Oh it's a terrace now?" He followed her out to the terrace. Ayers' children and Johnson's oldest frolicked in the water as everyone else socialized around the pool strung out from the bench by the door to the fence.

Ki Dicer guided Toni around introducing her to each and every one of her guests, including the children in the pool. "You have a lovely home," Toni said standing near the fence looking back at the house.

"Thank you. Merlo says you're looking for one. Any ideas?"

"Maybe on the west side, but coming here we passed a few lovely neighborhoods, so we may consider the south. I just want a little space to call my own. We both have stuff, you know."

"There's nothing like having your own to do with as you please."

"How often do you have these get-togethers?"

"Ever so often, we're not on any schedule, someone just decides we should barbecue."

"Kiwi!" Kylar called waving a phone.

"Excuse me. Help yourself to the drinks in the big box in the corner." Ki snagged the phone from her brother and entered the house.

Toni helped herself to a coke and joined Jill and Gomez who had just arrived. As the afternoon wore on, Toni relaxed and enjoyed the outing, coming to understand why Jill spoke so highly of her new squad.

As the party drew to a close, only Louis Ayers' family remained along with Jill and Toni. Toni found herself in the kitchen with Kirk Dicer who was tanking up on caffeine before his long drive back home.

"You're not a cop, right?" Kirk said leaning on the counter.

"No."

"What do you do?"

"Healthcare processor."

"Sounds unproductive."

"For me, yes; but not for the people needing their claims processed in a timely manner."

"Guess you're right. Does your parents know you're gay?" he asked out of the blue.

"Yes," Toni said raising her glass to her lips, wondering why she hadn't gone outside.

"Do they approve?"

"No." Toni met his eyes. "No, they don't. Do you approve of your daughter?"

He laughed, shaking his head. "The issue never came up."

"Never?" Toni asked.

"Not to me."

"That's rare. My parents are not so open-minded."

"Give them a chance, they'll come around eventually." He opened a cabinet taking out plastic wrap and foil. "You take some of this food. And give your parents a call, if just to see how they're doing."

"You see where Kiwi gets her habit of giving unsolicited advice," Kylar said walking into the kitchen. "Toni, nice to meet you. I hope you will enjoy the city more in the coming year."

"I'll try. You stay out of beehives."

Kylar chuckled and winked. "Can't, that's where the honey is."

Ki entered the kitchen from the terrace, looked from her brother to her father and back. "I can't believe you're going with him."

"Jealous?" Kirk Dicer asked of his daughter.

"Yes, very." She hugged her brother. "Don't let him get to you, Ky; he's a mutant clone."

"I've always known that." Kylar touched her on the nose. "Hang tough, big sis."

"Hang loose, little bro."

"Let's go before you make me cry," Kirk told his children, then pulled his daughter into his arms. "You stay out of trouble."

"Can't do that; trouble is my life." Ki walked them out.

Toni had watched the entire exchange between the family members with a strange sense of longing.

CHAPTER 9

When Ki Dicer left for work Monday morning, she found it wet and threatening more rain. Gamin Station stood quietly waiting as the day shift arrived making a lazy rush for the back door before the rain returned. Mickey trotted in just ahead of a downpour and into a tempest as two half-dressed uniform officers fought in the open lounge knocking over the chairs. A third officer snatched a fresh box of donuts from the side counter a split second before the smaller officer was tossed against it. Two officers rushed in from the adjacent lockerroom.

Jill Merlo came in from the squadroom. Her eyes met Mickey's across the disheveled room.

"Break them up," Dicer said over her shoulder.

As Merlo stepped towards them so did the others as if waiting for a signal.

"Stay away from my wife!" the smaller one yelled trying to break away from the restraining hands.

"Carson, in my office in five minutes," Dicer told him. "Grant, what are you doing here?" she asked the larger man, who was bleeding from scratches on his cheek.

"Deputy Chief Aviles." Phil Grant tucked his undershirt in his pants.

Dicer inwardly groaned, remembering Aviles' words about sending her men, and knew she was being warned. Grant was a notorious womanizer and troublemaker. "Put something on those scratches. The rest of you put this room back together." There was a moan from the four officers. "You should not have waited for me to tell you to separate them."

"Yeah," said the officer eating donuts from the box.

"Who the hell are you?" Dicer asked.

"Martin Geddes, Lt. Dicer. I've been trying to get assigned to you for months." He extended a white powdered hand to her.

"Put those down and help Grant out." Dicer spun on her booted heels. "Fifteen minutes people. Merlo in my office."

Jill followed her out and up the stairs to her office where a pudgy man with earphones sat at a table untangling a tape.

"What was that all about?" Dicer asked, rifling through her desk.

"I don't know."

"So you were just going to let them knock each other out?"

Jill shrugged. "No. I . . . "

"Did nothing." Dicer looked up. "Afterall there were others there, right."

"I suppose."

"And you were all waiting until the others acted."

"Looked that way."

"And a damn shame it was too. Don't let it happen again." Dicer handed her a folder. "Your paperwork came over. I've placed stickers where corrections are necessary."

"Yes." Taking the folder, Jill cleared her throat. "What time did you get here?"

"About five. I have a lot to do today. It'll only take a couple of minutes, just sit over there with Sam." Dicer picked up her phone and pressed two buttons. "Put me through to Hernandez."

Jill tried not to listen as Dicer spoke rapid idiomatic Spanish; but when her voice increased then fell into a string of curses, she gave up all pretense of filling out the forms to listen. As Dicer turned around, her eyes fell back to the forms.

"Are you finished?" Dicer asked Jill after hanging up.

"Almost."

"You would have been if you had not been eavesdropping."

Sam laughed. "It was hard not to."

"You get that address?" Dicer asked him.

"Yep. 4633 Coronado."

Dicer moved to her computer and typed in the address, then waited a few seconds. "I'll be damn. Finally a break. Sam, you're genius!"

"Yes. Can I go home now?"

"Yes. Yes. Have a dream on me." Dicer reached for the phone. "Tell the squad, we're going on a little exercise; I'll be down in ten." She hung up and turned to her computer, typing rapidly. Sam slipped out without disturbing her.

Jill finished her paperwork, noting she was waiving her rights to a probationary appeal in exchange for confidential access to the Gamin's secrets. "Lieutenant?"

Dicer looked up, took a second to focus. "Yes?"

"What do you want me to do now?"

"Oh, go down stairs, Mickey will outfit you with riot gear."

"Riot gear?"

"Yes. Yes. We're conducting a raid. I'll give everyone the details below."

"Okay." Jill left feeling the first stingers of excitement.

Ten minutes later Dicer came down into the briefing room with her raincoat over her arm. "Do I need to dress you two down or can we get on with the business at hand?" she asked Grant and Carson.

"Business," Carson said looking at Grant.

"Very well. Grant, you are on notice. We run a tight ship here."

"In other words, don't rock the boat?" he asked settling down.

Dicer glared at him, then counted her team. Six as Gomez and Mumford entered dressed in black, helmets under their arm. "We are going to visit a residence at 4633 Coronado." She flipped on the screen showing the schematics of the residence. "Mickey and I are going to knock on the front door. Mumford, I want you and Merlo stationed in the back. Gomez, you and Geddes position yourselves to watch the side entrance by the garage. Grant, you are covering our approach. I expect no trouble, but we are dealing with an unknown here, so be careful. Do not. Do not rush the house."

"Shouldn't we surveille first?" Grant said slapping the clip into his weapon.

"This is surveillance with an attitude."

"Do you have a warrant?" he countered.

"Shut the fuck up!" Mickey snapped.

"This is an exercise in precaution," Dicer told him. "Set your headsets to channel 9. It is cleared exclusively for our use. Check your weapons now. Any questions so far?"

"What are we looking for?" Mumford asked.

"Mickey's lost snitch. We have reason to believe he is in the residence or someone there knows where he is." She glanced at her watch. "It's getting late."

"The use of force?" Gomez asked.

"None unless the danger is imminent and I do mean imminent. Do not fire first, not even a warning shot."

"Then why are we in riot gear?" Grant asked.

"Because it's rainproof," Dicer told him.

"What about backup?" Gomez asked.

"There are seven of us. If we encounter something we can't handle, we'll fall back here." She pointed to a spot on the map.

"I don't like this," Grant said.

"Neither do I, but we have only one chance at this and due to the nature of this investigation we must do this ourselves."

"Sure wish Lou was here," Gomez said.

"So do I, but he's not. Gomez, Merlo, Mumford, Geddes take the CatMobile; we're taking the van. This is a routine exercise, do not lose your judgment." Her words conveyed the opposite to her team. "Let's go."

"I can't believe we're doing this without a warrant," Grant said falling back with Merlo. "We'll be all up shitcreek if this blows up, because we all know this is illegal."

"We're just backup to a routine questioning," Merlo told him.

"Since when has a routine questioning used riot gear?"

"Merlo!" Mumford called.

The Coronado address was a Tudor-style on a corner lot

approximately two miles north of the Gamin Station in the affluent Astair community. The rain had slacked to a drizzle as Dicer positioned her vehicles blocking both entrances to the property.

"Hold your position," Dicer told them from the back of the van as she checked the paper in the fax, then pressed a series of buttons. "Come on," she muttered.

"What was that?" Mumford said in her ear.

"Hang on, I'm waiting on a fax."

"Understood."

"Uh, Dicer, we have company. The chopper's approaching," Mickey told her.

Dicer switched channels. "Hernandez, that you?"

"Yes, ma'am. Let's get this show on the road."

"We're on 9 and thanks for the support."

"Air out."

Dicer turned her attention to the fax and removed the first sheet and handed it to Mickey. "Is this your snitch?"

Mickey studied the dead man with a thin trail of blood on his neck. "Yes. When?"

"Early this morning." Dicer checked the gun in her shoulder holster. "Mumford and Merlo, move into position. You got us on screen, Hernandez?"

"That's affirmative."

"Let's go people." Snagging the fax in one hand and opening the side door with the other, Dicer got out, her black trench coat flapping behind as was Mickey's who was outpacing her to the door. "Be cool, Mickey," she said softly.

"I am." He walked up the steps and knocked heavily on the door and rang the doorbell. A half minute later, he repeated the process.

The door, with the chain on, opened slowly. "Yes?" a middle-age woman asked.

"Police, would you open the door, ma'am?" Mickey asked holding up his shield.

She looked past him at Dicer, then the police van. "What are your names?"

"Ki Dicer," Dicer said holding up her identification, then the fax. "We have a search warrant, Mrs. Aberdeen. No need to call downtown." There were several murmurs in her ear as the name registered on her team.

"May I see it?" she asked, extending a hand through the crack in the door.

"Of course." Dicer handed her the warrant. "Open the door."

The door closed then opened wider. A shot rang out and the woman flinched started to turn towards the interior just as an explosion rocked the house knocking the two officers back down the stoop.

"Clear out!" Grant shouted running up the walkway towards the down officers.

"We have a runner on the westside," Hernandez called as the chopper veered away.

"Get the fucker!" Dicer called sitting up. "Merlo, you there?"

"On it!"

"Go, Grant! Gomez maintain position."

"Within reason," Hernandez countered. "I've alerted HQ and the fire department," he said calmly.

Dicer stood up checking her body. "How's she doing?" she asked Mickey.

"Took some debris in the back and hit her head." They both knew her body had shielded them from the explosion. "She'll make it if nothing went in too deep." Together they gingerly moved her down the walk as people cautiously came outside.

Meanwhile, Mumford and Merlo were losing ground on the suspect as he cut then jumped a fence that took them two tries to clear in their excess gear. They cleared the fence in time to see him head into a wooded area. "He's in the park," Mumford said huffing.

"On my way," Grant nearly shouted as he raced through the quiet streets in the van.

Merlo saw a figure in green converge on the spot the suspect had entered a good fifty yards ahead of them. "Who is that?"

"Hell if I know," Mumford shouted and redoubled her efforts as they entered the trees.

"We've lost them," Merlo said coming to a stop to listen, but the ground was wet and a drizzle had started up. No sounds were detected.

Both officers heard the low whistle, drew their weapons and proceeded with caution.

"Talk to me, Mumford," Dicer said in their ear.

"Suspect in the trees, but so is someone in green."

"Go carefully. Grant?"

"I'm on the opposite side, getting out now."

The three officers could hear the sirens filling the early morning calm as they stalked their prey through the dripping trees. Merlo said a silent prayer for the high boots she wore as her foot sunk four inches in an unseen hole. "There's the other one!" she hissed and started toward the streaking figure to the right.

"No!" Mumford called. "Look!" She pointed where their suspect, unconscious or dead, hung over a small tree, doubling it over. Blood dripped onto the ground.

"We need an ambulance out here!" Merlo called.

"Where?" Dicer asked.

"About a hundred, a hundred fifty yards inside from the— which way did we come in?"

"From the eastside," Mumford said.

"Say something," Grant said.

Merlo shouted. "Over here!"

"Damn!" Several murmurs came back.

"Sorry," she said. "You hear me, Grant?"

"Yes. Again, and put your hand over the mike."

Merlo shouted again. A half minute later Grant arrived and took a look at the perp. "I'll be damn."

"Who is it?" Merlo asked, as he had said the same thing Dicer had said when she pulled up the address on the computer.

"Darren Wallace."

"Who?"

"The biggest wannabe gangster in the city. He just came back into town a few weeks ago. Dicer had us bulldogging his Harper street storefront."

"And the woman was the deputy mayor," Grant told her. Shit, Aviles had put him in it this time. "This is trouble."

"Sure is. Mumford, an EMT team is on the way, switch your comm to 15, ignore the beep in your ear; they'll hone in on your signal.

"Ten-four, Dicer." Mumford switched her comm link.

At eleven o'clock Dicer and Aviles entered the chief's panelled office with its view of city hall. The two women took seats in the matching straightback chairs across from the chief who eyed them crossly as he answered negatively to the caller's questions.

"Yes, sir. I'll do that." He hung up. "What the hell were you thinking, Dicer? You got a warrant for the deputy mayor's house and were prepared to raid it with that goddamn gestapo goon squad. I oughta dissemble it right now and send you over to Leiberman. But no, I know you had help. Am I right, Catherine?"

"Yes, sir."

"You could have warned me?"

"I did, sir."

"You could have been more specific." He rubbed a hand over his face. "Mr. Mayor is calling for an inquiry into your actions. He is blaming you and/or Hernandez for the explosion, with the possibility of a conspiracy to implicate Aberdeen."

"That's ludicrous!" Dicer exploded. "She had a fucking convicted drug dealer fucking her brains out."

"Not one of your people saw him exit the house."

"Hernandez—"

"Only saw him on the grounds, not the house itself."

"And what is Aberdeen saying?" Aviles asked.

Chief Harmon rose from his desk. "Two people demanded she

open the door and shove a paper in her face that may or may not
have been a warrant for she didn't have time to read it before someone hit her upside the head."

"What? The lying bitch!" Aviles exploded this time, getting a
surprised look from Dicer and the chief.

The chief came to a decision on how to handle this but turned
to Dicer. "I take it you have everything on tape?"

"And video from the van."

"Leak the video." He nailed her with his eyes. "I trust you can
do that without fucking up."

"Yes sir."

"Go execute the remainder of your search warrants." They rose.
"Not you, Catherine. You got us in this fine political mess; now
you'll have to carry it to the outhouse."

Dicer quickly left headquarters and returned to the Gamin
house in the pouring rain. What was up with Aviles? The chief was
clearly upset with her over something. She had directed this investigation since Norris went missing, every step. She had Buchova in
her sights before that. No doubt Aviles was pulling her strings.
Had her shooter mistook her for Aviles after all? And who was the
person who took out Wallace?

She entered Gamin station and noted the quietness and lack
of personnel. Perhaps her team had gone to lunch. She headed for
the desk sergeant. "Pete, where's everyone?"

"Gravelli and Pearson conscripted them for a raid on Brigham
Fortier's estate." He handed her a folder. "Aviles authorized it."

Dicer stared. "I'll be fucked."

"That would sum it up." He reached for a drink can. "Told
them you'd be pissed."

"When Gao gets here send her up."

"Will do."

Dicer went upstairs to her office to splice the tape for her
"leak." Aviles? On a impulse Dicer dialed Guzman.

"Aviles' office," she answered.

"Your boss back?"

"No, she's still upstairs. Where are you?"

"At the Gamin. Alex, you keep a vigilant eye on your boss. I get the impression she's treading in dangerous waters."

"I'll take that under advisement. Follow your own advice. Thanks for calling." She hung up.

So someone had come in. Was it Aviles? No, she would have let her know. Who then?

Toni worked only five minutes from their apartment and often went home on her lunch break where she nuked a lunch prepared the night before. With the leftovers from their outing yesterday, she could eat most of the week. Seeing her notebook on the counter, she took it to the table, opening to the numbers Xorron had given her and decided to call the bottom number.

The phone rang three times before it was picked up to a hurried, "Hold on," and soft jazz oozed in her ear. Thirty seconds later, the phone clicked. "Sorry about that. What do you need?" she asked.

"Uhh, I'm Toni Jensen from Metrox. I met Rex Xorron the other day."

"Toni Jensen, let me see here. . . . Okay, Ms. Jensen, I have you right here. Let me decipher these notes . . . tuition, books, computer, low-interest loan. Loan? Hold on." She was put on hold again.

A few seconds later, a male spoke, "Ms. Jensen, Artis here. I need a fax number and your address. Then I'll give you a pair of local numbers you'll need. Now that fax number."

"Okay, but can I get more information on your program?"

"Of course, I'll enclose a packet about the company and the foundation." They exchanged information and Toni returned to her lunch.

By four o'clock Toni had a stack of faxes half an inch thick; most were forms but several were information sheets about seemingly innocuous subjects like Brazil, a women's studies program and mythology. She had put them aside to finish her work. The phone in her cubicle rang.

"Jensen here," she answered expecting her supervisor who made it a point to call them to ensure they were at their desks working.

"Ms. Jensen, this is Brenda Falvo with Eagle Realty. Do you have time later this evening?"

Toni blinked. "Excuse me?"

"Eagle Realty is a subsidiary of Vengar International, we're just moving into the Metrox area but have acquired choice pieces of property, most for our employees. Artis e-mailed me to expect your call, but I had a few minutes and thought I'd give you a call instead."

"Oh."

"Are you free this evening?"

"I can be."

"Very good. I'm working out of the Vengar office at 7999 East Laredo. What time can I expect you?"

"Is six too late?"

"No, I'm on the first floor to your left. You'll see the flag above my door."

"Then six it is."

"Look forward to meeting you, Ms. Jensen."

"You too, Ms. Falvo." Toni hung up wondering what the hell she had gotten herself into. Jill would not be happy, having warned her about these people.

Five-fifteen Toni called home and surprisingly Jill answered on the first ring. "You're home."

"Not for long, we've been out all day and I came home to change into something drier."

"I thought you had clothing in your locker."

"It's wet. I'll be back around seven. Are you working over?"

"I have a meeting at six."

"Then I'll see you at home."

"Yes. Want me to pick up something?"

"No, leftovers are fine. Gotta go."

"Me too. Love you."

"Love you too."

Toni checked her watch and scanned several of the faxes to kill time before her appointment which was surprisingly close to them.

Vengar-Metrox housed a four story rose brick building surrounded by a lush garden. The parking lot was full for close to six in the evening. Toni parked and hurried into the building through the rain.

"Looks like it's going to rain all night," the young man at the counter said as she wiped her feet thoroughly on the rug before stepping onto the slick looking marble.

"It does. The realtor is left?"

"Yes, ma'am."

* * *

At eight, Dicer sent her weary team home, telling them to arrive no later than seven instead of six. She could not work them this brutally without some flexibility on her part. They couldn't serve two masters when one was operating in the shadow.

"Lieutenant?"

Dicer turned around to see Grant standing in her open doorway. "Yes?"

"About this morning with Carson." He stepped into the office, eyes taking in the setup.

"Yes, please enlighten me." She waved him to a seat. He was a large man, looking larger in civvies.

"He's married to my ex-wife. We were once partners."

"Ouch. And what triggered this morning?"

"I helped her out the other day when he was off fishing or whatever." He smiled.

Dicer rolled her eyes. "You didn't."

"I did and the magic was still there."

Dicer exhaled. "Is Aviles aware of your former relation with Carson's wife?"

Grant tugged at his watch. "Yes, she is."

"And what was your assignment before this?"

"The deputy chief's adjutant since your shooting."

"And you were sent to spy on me?"

"No."

Dicer pursed her lips. "Simply cause chaos with Carson in the lunchroom."

Grant shrugged. "You requested personnel; I was available."

"And loyal to Aviles. How many times has she saved your ass from those stunts you pull?"

"Not as often as you may think."

"But when it counted." She watched him closely. "Thanks for being straight with me."

His lips twitched. "Yes, lieutenant."

"Stay away from Carson's wife during your stay with us."

"No promises." He grinned lecherously.

"No promises that Aviles can save you from me. Now go home and get some rest."

"And you, lieutenant? You should leave as well." He knew her reputation and today had done nothing to detract from it.

"I'll go when I'm done." She dismissed him with a slight shoo of her right hand.

Jill unlocked the door, expecting to hear the television or the stereo as she entered, but the apartment was quiet and empty. There was no message so she pulled out the peach pie for dessert and hunkered down on the sofa to watch one of Toni's tearjerker movies. She had dozed when the door opened and Toni came in with an armload.

"It's raining cats and dogs."

Jill sat up. "Where have you been?"

"Vengar-Metrox to Eagle Realty." Toni placed the packages on the table.

"What's all that?"

"Pictures, a couple of videos and brochures."

Jill yawned. "For what?"

Toni went into the kitchen. "Want something to drink?"

"Whatever you're having." Curious Jill pulled an envelope from the shopping bag. An address was printed on the flap. She counted seven of them and opened the first one to reveal photos, plans, and information on the property. "Where'd you get these?"

"Eagle Realty."

"Where'd you find them?"

"Artis."

"Who?"

"He works for Rex Xorron. They have an office on East Laredo." Toni sat down next to her on the sofa.

"I thought we agreed to check this out."

"That's why I called them today and they already had me in their system and on a list for housing and other stuff."

"Why?"

"Jill . . . " Toni couldn't explain it beyond what she had already.

Jill took a deep breath. "Toni, I'm not trying to burst your bubble, but stop and think about this. You had one pizza with this woman and now she wants to give you the world. Why?"

"I don't know. You'll have to ask her."

"I will. Where's her number?"

"I don't have her number per se."

"Then what do you have?" Toni took the info and went to the phone. When there was no answer, she called information and got Rex Xorron's home number.

"Don't do this," Toni entreated putting her hand over the phone.

"If someone is doing all of this for you; surely they can take a call at home." Jill shook her off and dialed.

A youngster answered then yelled that she had it when a second person picked up. Toni listened as the two bickered and the younger sounding one hung up.

"Sorry about that. Who are you calling for?" the person inquired.

"Rex Xorron."

"Mom? I don't know if she's here. What's your name?"

"Toni Jensen," Jill told her.

"Okay, I'll zap her. Hold on."

Twenty seconds later, the phone clicked. "Ms. Jensen, I hope you're finding everyone helpful."

"Too helpful. Could you inform me of your intentions, please."

"Ms. Merlo, how are you this evening?"

"Better if you tell me what the hell's going on?"

Xorron's sigh spoke volumes. "I'm just trying to help a sister pursue her goals. No strings attached, only that she helps another along the way. We make money, we spend money where it does women good. There's nothing untoward, although our efficiency is sometimes overwhelming, but it is our stock in trade. We are relatively new to the Metrox area and are trying to build a base there. Ms. Jensen has all the qualities that we look for in people. She wants a future that we can provide."

"At what price though?"

"Hard work and a commitment to humanity."

"You're a philanthropist?"

"If you insist on identifying with a label, that one is doable."

There was a commotion in the background. "I'm on the phone, sweetie."

"Read!" a small voice piped up.

"Okay, five minutes."

"Five minutes," the child said.

Jill smiled despite herself.

"I apologize," Xorron said into the phone. "The long days keep them up past their bedtime."

"How old are they?"

"Three and four. Ms. Merlo, you're only four or five hours away. If you want to reassure yourself that we are not trying to buy your partner and are legitimate, drive over one day and check us out. Ask around in the community, well certain communities." She chuckled softly.

"I can do that from here."

"Yes, you can. Now if you'll excuse me, I have a story or two to read to my girls."

"Thanks for taking my call."

"Sure, I hope I have allayed your most pressing fears."

"Yes. Goodnight."

"Goodnight."

Jill hung up and turned to Toni. "She's smooth alright. I'll check her out tomorrow." If she had time.

"I'm taking a shower." Toni headed for the bedroom.

Jill followed her. "Toni. Toni. I'm just trying to protect you."

Toni turned on her. "No, what you're saying is that you don't trust my judgment."

"No. no." Jill shook her head. "You do the same for me, always, keeping me from acting without thinking. We only have each other. We have to take care of us, together, individually. Women, these powerful women don't care about us. They just don't care and when they do it's for their own reason or image. Charity is more for their benefit and standing than for helping people."

"That's so damn cynical, Jill."

"I'm a cop, I'm s'pose to be cynical."

"No, circumspect, Jill." Toni poked her in the chest.

"That's what I was doing, not trying to undermine you or anything." Toni raised and dropped her arms. "You know what they say, if it seems too good to be true then it usually is."

"Usually, not always."

"What if I came home tomorrow and told you I was chief? Would you believe me?"

"Probably."

Jill rolled her eyes. "Not hardly. And that's how I feel with this deal. Just go slow." She took Toni's hands. "Please. Like it took you two years to give me the time of day. Take it slow, please?"

Toni extracted her hands. "Stop begging."

Jill kissed her quickly. "Take your shower."

"Thank you, your majesty." Toni entered for a long shower, thinking about the possibilities. Life had not been easy on either of them.

Dicer sat up in bed, then realized the phone was ringing. "Hello?"

"Am I calling too late?" Jaio Yemen asked.

The clock showed 12;02. "It was a long day." She had arrived home about 10:30, showered and climbed into bed.

"Yes. A few nasty barbs were hurled your way."

"I hadn't noticed; I have a case to solve."

"You mean it's not?"

"I can't discuss an ongoing investigation with you."

"I was calling to see how you were holding up."

"At midnight?"

"I'm concerned around the clock."

"Nice to hear. Why did you really call?"

Jaio chuckled. "Are you suspicious of everyone?"

"Yes."

"When are you free for dinner?"

"I don't know."

"Are you brushing me off, lieutenant?"

"No, I'm in the middle of a . . . dicey investigation. I don't need distractions."

"Is that what I am?" Jaio teased.

Dicer rolled over. "Not all that you are, but yes definitely distracting."

"And what else am I?"

"Not getting into this."

"Into what?"

"Good night, Jaio."

"You do need to eat, Ki. Lunch tomorrow?"

"I can't promise that."

"A late dinner then. Around six-thirty?"

"I can't.."

"Seven then."

Dicer chuckled. "Okay, but I'm warning you up front that I may have to cancel."

"Understood. Is the Trudotte okay?"

"Yes, sure."

"Now that wasn't a vote of confidence. Would the Whattaburger be more to your liking?"

Dicer laughed. "Too much grease. Boleros?"

Jaio laughed with her. "Yes. Should we consider that our bistro from now on?"

"Now on? Dinner only."

"And I thought you were recuperating quite well."

"Night, Jaio."

"Night, Ki."

Dicer hung up the phone and tried to get comfortable but Jaio's image would not disappear easily, nor the memory of her touch.

CHAPTER 10

Conflicting stories on the front page of the morning paper landed Dicer in the chief's office. Chief Harmon studied her as she read the scathing private memo from the mayor's office. Not a muscle twitched, not an eye blinked.

"Well?" he asked when she looked up.

"He needs to proofread." She placed the two sheets neatly on the edge of the desk.

He nodded once. "No one truly understands the political nature of my position, that I must compromise, and make sacrifices for the greater good. There are budget and personnel decisions that guide my actions. I like any leader must choose my battles wisely. One hates to lose good soldiers but at times it is necessary. These decisions are not made lightly or selfishly, but strategically. When you enter a battle and find your enemy greatly outnumbers you, you must decide whether to fight or flee. There is no shame in retreating; none at all. I've done it and will likely do it in the future." He rose and walked around to the front of the desk.

Dicer waited patiently for him to continue.

Harmon tapped the memo with his knuckled. "When I received this, I relayed a copy of your proofread report. Combined with your statements and the comments of several reliable sources in the upper echelon of the mayor's office, I have no choice in what I'm about to do." He held her eyes. "You fail on this, Dicer, you hit the ground; there's no safety net. I don't want to see you in here until this is over. Do we understand each other?"

"Perfectly sir." Dicer rose fluidly.

"Get out so I can tell the mayor of your reprimand, to which you reacted badly."

"Yes, sir."

"And Dicer?"

"Yes?"

"Don't sacrifice your soldiers."

"No sir, I won't."

Indeed her team thought they had been sacrificed as two officers from IAD hovered over them as they typed up individual reports of the previous day's events. Dicer came in, took in the scene and blew her stack.

"What the hell are you people doing in here? Everyone upstairs in my office now." She clapped her hands together. "Don't look at them. It's my wrath you have to worry about. Go. Go. Go." They scrambled to save, delete or print their reports.

One of the suits turned to her. "That wasn't very cooperative, lieutenant."

"No one asked for my cooperation. In fact you are impeding my investigation. Those officers submitted their reports last night; they are free to supplement at any time, except on mine. If you boys had bothered to adhere to procedure, you wouldn't be here."

"You're a fine one to talk about procedure, Dicer." Ben Mallory told her. "You subvert it at every turn."

"Subvert? Oh we all know who you're taking your orders from, which makes your presence here even more confounding." Dicer clucked her tongue. "This is like a counterattack huh? Well, I can't fight city hall can I? Bullshit. You take your muck-raking asses back across town and tell your honor's whipping boy to either shit or get off the pot. I'm going to do my job until I no longer have one."

Mallory walked up on her, but every word was clear to the bystanders. "I always said your fucking mouth would hand your ass to me. The chief is cutting his losses and will not save you this time. You're as good as gone, Dicer. Maybe you should have your team pack your office while they're up there."

"I may be gone, but I'm taking your friend with me. Now get the fuck out so we can do real investigating, not witch- hunting."

Everyone heard the tape recorder click off. The young man slouched in a chair stood up as all eyes turned towards him. "Lieutenant Dicer, I'm Eduardo Trujillo, investigative reporter for the Virada. Can I ask you a few questions about the charges levied against you?"

"No, she can't. This is an internal matter," Mallory told him. The Virada was a growing midtown newspaper with an acute bias for the fringe and the underdog. They would paint Dicer as the lone ranger fighting against the blue curtain of silence and corruption. They had done it before, during their inaugural year.

"That is obviously interfering with her investigation. Is it true the only reason Lt. Dicer is underfire is because a drug investigation led her to the door of the deputy mayor? Is it true that forces have worked to keep Dicer's team off the case from the beginning? Was that because someone knew where the trail would lead? Moreover the public wants to know whether it stops at Aberdeen or not. If not, then Dicer's removal is tantamount to accessory after the fact isn't it?" Trujillo held the silver recorder out to him. "Care to comment, sir?"

"Let's go, Feinstein." Mallory turned on his heels, retrieved his briefcase and walked out.

Trujillo turned back to Dicer. "About those charges?"

"I'm not aware of any formal charges."

"I mean in the Globe this morning."

"Pure fantasy. If you'll excuse me."

"About an interview?"

"Later." After setting a time for the interview, Dicer went upstairs as her team assembled.

Toni debated whether to call the Parker woman or not. What if Jill was right and this was some scam? But why? How? But how would she know? Taking out her calling card, she dialed.

"Futures, how can I help you?"

"I'm looking for Ms. Parker."

"She's in with students. Leave your name and number, she'll return your call ASAP." Toni gave her the information. "Are you a student?" the receptionist asked.

"I'm trying to get in at NSU."

"NSU?"

"Nuvalle State In Metrox."

"Yes, I didn't associate. I don't think we have many students in Metrox or applications for that matter. Is that what you need or do you just need to talk to Parker?"

"Well, yes and yes. Xorron told me to call her today."

"Rex Xorron said call?" the receptionist said dropping her air of southern charm.

"Yes."

"Hold on, I'll see if you're in the system."

Toni listened to the clicking of a keyboard, then the phone clicked.

"Ms. Jensen?" a second voice came on the line.

"Yes?"

"Parker here. Everything is set up on this end, we're just waiting for your admissions letter from NSU. However, I don't believe that will be much of a problem since our liaison there is the associate dean of graduate studies, Elizabeth Arana. Her number's 555-8347. You should contact her as soon as possible. August will be here before we know it."

"Yes, tomorrow is my day off. Is there anything else I should do?"

"I'll fax you an info sheet that you should fill out for our records. I'll send you a larger information packet by mail. Why don't you call Arana for an early morning appointment. She'll be ecstatic to hear from you since we're just getting started at NSU." Parker laughed softly. "As a mature student, you may find yourself conscripted into her service. You'll find Arana to be quite a dynamo." The phone buzzed. "My time's up, Ms. Jensen. I'll give you a call later in the week to see how things are going. If you have any questions, just email or call us."

"I will thank you."

"That's why I'm here. Good luck and I look forward to seeing you during our orientation next month."

"What orientation?"

"It's in your packet. We try to have a small retreat for our new participants to orient them to their new roles and responsibilities. Take care. Goodbye."

"Goodbye." Toni hung up and immediately dialed Arana. Getting her assistant she made an appointment for the following morning.

When Toni arrived home at a quarter after six she found Jill there with a pair of unopened boxes. "You're home early."

"No authorized overtime for us. Dicer is staggering us again." Jill shook her head. "She's working sixteen hour days while they're trying to fuck her. They would get eight hours out of me and not one second more. All she's trying to do is her job and they're trying to stop her because of who the criminal is, rich and powerful. Rich people think they're above the law. And the way they try to flaunt it, that's what gets me. The sheer boldness of it. 'Oh sure, I had the drugs but you don't understand, I have privileges because I'm rich.' It makes me sick."

Toni stared at her. "What happened?"

"IAD nosing around harassing Dicer because of the investigation and yesterday's explosion at the deputy mayor's house."

"Oh boy."

"Oh boy is right." Jill went into the kitchen. "What do you want for dinner?"

"Pasta and fish." Toni raised the bag from the fish market in her hand.

"Fried or baked?"

"I was going to bake it; but if you're going to fry, I'd prefer that."

"I'd prefer that," Jill mimicked taking the bag from her.

"What's in the boxes?" Toni asked leaning on the counter.

"Don't know, they're yours. Kinda heavy too, I had to drive around to get them from the office." Jill began her dinner preparations.

"Let's see then." She was expecting an info package from Artis, but nothing this size nor in two boxes. The first box did contain information packets along with how-to-succeed books, CDs, an array of polo shirts and caps with the VENX designer label and/or Triple X Music logo. She unfolded a handwritten note. "Courtesy of your sponsors. Yes, it's flagrant advertising, but they are footing the bill.—Artis T," she read aloud.

"How many shirts?"

"Nine." Toni held up one to her, then another. Three were larger than the others. "I guess the large is yours."

"I won't be a billboard for those people."

"Oh, but you're one for Nike, Adidas and Levi's?"

"Not the same thing."

"No? They could keep the labels on the inside. No one cares."

"Where's the garlic salt?"

"In the refrigerator."

"I'm not going to ask." Jill removed the garlic salt and pepper from the refrigerator door. "What's in the second box, pants?"

"Funny." Toni slit the other box containing green foam pellets. Reaching in she extracted a notebook computer case which judging its heft contained a computer. Accessories were wrapped in a heavy green plastic bag.

After Toni had said nothing for ten minutes, Jill walked over to see what had her so enraptured. "Send it back."

"It's not new and it's wired for their network." Toni was reading the instructions. "It's loaded to the teeth. Let's see if we can get online with them."

"Don't get too attached." Jill returned to the kitchen not seeing the look Toni gave her.

Early Wednesday morning, Toni drove across town to the NSU campus and the central Tremont Hall which housed graduate studies on the sixth floor. After getting lost twice in the oddly numbered floor, she was directed to a suite at the end of the building. No one was at the reception desk, but a young black woman with a stylishly cut silk suit was watering plants when she entered.

"Good morning," Toni said.

"Good morning," she replied in a slight accent. "Every time I leave this chore to someone else, the plants suffer. They require more moisture than most and the ventilation system keeps the air too dry, which is good for the paperwork, but not the plants."

"They are beautiful," Toni conceded.

"Thank you." She sat the watering can behind a cabinet. "What can I do for you?"

"I have an appointment at eight with the associate dean, Elizabeth Arana. I'm a bit early, but I wanted to leave in plenty of time not knowing what the traffic was like. I work five minutes from my apartment." Toni didn't know why she was so nervous, babbling on.

"Only by ten minutes. Who made the appointment?"

"She didn't say."

"Nevermind. What was the appointment for Ms . . . ?"

"Oh, Toni Jensen. I'm applying to graduate school and Ms. Parker at Futures says Elizabeth Arana is their liaison and would help with the admissions process as well as . . . " She trailed off at the woman's raised eyebrow.

The woman extended a hand. "Ms. Jensen, I'm Elizabeth Arana."

"Oh." Toni shook her hand.

"You're cutting it pretty close, but it's doable. Since Parker sent you, you will not need financial aid which makes it easier." She began to gather forms from a stand. "Have you taken the GRE in the last three years?"

"No."

"That in a way makes it easier to admit you as a conditional student, but you should take it ASAP for the spring semester. Which program are you applying for?"

"I'm undecided however, the Interdisciplinary communications program held my interest with the institute and all."

"This is sounding better and better."

"How so?"

"No need to get a particular programs approval. I handle those

myself which means I most likely will double as your advisor unless you have others in mind?"

"No. This has all been a little fast for me. Last week this time,
I had no idea I would be trying to get in."

"What changed?"

"I had dinner with Rex Xorron."

Arana nodded understandably. "Yes, that would account for
your being undecided but interested in the Institute. She has a
particular knack for getting her people in her programs."

"Excuse me? Her program?"

Arana smiled. "Not technically. Last year she made a sizeable
contribution to the Institute for Brazilian topics in communication. Preferably women. What interests you?"

"The equipment. We see all of these images and words every
day, every hour, every minute; yet we never think about how it is
produced, how it is made. What goes into it from the idea stage to
the end product."

"So in other words you're interested in production?"

Toni shrugged. "I suppose I am."

"You watch a lot of movies?"

"I'm ashamed to admit that I do." Toni chuckled.

"Nothing to be ashamed of. Now the reason you watch may
be though." They looked up as an older woman entered the office.
"Morning Ms. Rossi."

"Morning Dr. Arana. You have an early appointment."

"She's here." Arana waved a hand at Toni. "Ms. Jensen will
need her application expedited. Better still, she's interested in our
IC program and infatuated with our equipment."

Ms. Rossi nodded. "Welcome aboard. You bring those back at
one-thirty and I'll walk them through. Do you have official transcripts?"

"No."

"Unofficial?"

"Yes."

"You call them this afternoon; they should arrive well before the deadline. Is there something I should know about that would disqualify you from the university?"

"No."

"One-thirty." The woman entered a side door.

Toni raised an eyebrow at Arana.

"The projected enrollment for the graduate programs is less than ideal. Some are literally recruiting off the streets. No offense."

"None taken."

"I have brochures and plans of study for the IC in my office." Arana showed her into her office.

Toni felt more reassured about the rapid changes in her life as Arana essentially validated Rex Xorron. Yet she didn't think that would be enough for Jill. "What can you tell me about Rex Xorron?"

Arana gathered brochures and more information sheets before settling in a chair at the side of her desk. "I'll admit to being biased; nevertheless Rex Xorron is an extraordinary woman of deep passions and commitment. She has enormous power, but even that is surpassed by her compassion and unassuming manner. One wonders what iron discipline it takes to keep her ego in check, especially with that fan club she has all but praising her." Arana chuckled. "You could realistically believe that she is the most adored woman in that town while at the same time being the most dis-liked. Like I said, I'm biased."

"But I'm glad to have an independent perception. My partner is suspicious of her motive and the speed at which this is going; however she's a police officer."

Arana nodded. "Understandable. She has this uncanny ability to identify an individual who will make the most of an opportu-nity, even after knowing them for only a short time. I believe she throws the opportunity at you at such a rapid speed to see whether that individual is serious or just blowing smoke. You would be amazed at how many people say they want to go to Paris, but if you offer them the opportunity to leave tomorrow morning, most will not go."

"Do you think?"

Arana nodded. "Want to go Paris tomorrow?"

"I have to work."

Arana chuckled. "Don't we all. Are you going to Ydyllic for the orientation?"

"It's on the weekend and I will try."

"If you want to ride with me, you're welcome."

"Do you know how many there are?"

"Between four and six usually, plus those in the other programs who will have a picnic that same weekend." The phone rang. "Excuse me."

Toni flipped through the brochures and more lengthy descriptions of the graduate programs. She felt more comfortable with every passing minute and she admitted that Arana's age had a lot to do with it.

Dicer slammed down the phone. "Fucking pencil pushers." She stood up abruptly. "I'm hungry, let's go eat something unhealthy."

"Blue Fry?" Mickey asked rising.

"Why the hell not. Merlo, up for an injection of cholesterol?"

"Show me the fries." Merlo exited her program.

"Is whatever camp they had going on over?" Dicer asked Mickey.

"Probably, but another has surely taken its place." Mickey groaned as his beeper went off. Recognizing the number, he trotted back to the phone. "I need to get this, I'll meet you downstairs."

"We'll see if Otu wants to clog her arteries too," Dicer told him.

Walking excitedly up to Dicer and Merlo, Mickey danced in place. "Let's go out."

Dicer cut her eyes at Merlo and followed him out the front door. "What is it?"

"Fuentes is getting ready to book," he told them.

"Come again," Dicer said grabbing his sleeve.

"You heard me. Fire sale. He's selling off his real estate, paying off his soldiers and calling in favors before heading south. Exactly where is not known."

"How reliable is your source?"

"First tip from Records and Deeds that someone was verifying the titles and dimensions of the properties. I got the rest from someone else."

"Why?"

"That's the billion dollar question. No one knows, but isn't it grand!" Mickey danced across the street, drawing the attention of passersby.

Dicer wanted more information before beginning her own celebration, for Fuentes was a devil they knew and on some ways more humane than most. True the majority of his business was legitimate now, but he built his small empire on illegal gains. Abandoning it now made no sense. Perhaps he wanted a clean legitimate start elsewhere, to put his illicit past behind him. Yet people like Fuentes thrived on their infamy allowing their illegal reputation to affect their legitimate business interaction, often for the better.

CHAPTER 11

Arriving home more exhausted than at the end of a work day, Toni plucked the yellow note off the door. Dumping her bags, she walked around to the front office to pick up her package. Back in the apartment she spread all the information she had received on the kitchen table and contemplated the enormity of the decision to return to school. They liked to play it safe, but at the moment they, no, she was gambling on their security with an unknown. Had she been bedazzled and charmed by Xorron's promises and smile? Had Jill been right that this was too good to be true? And what of the two people she had met, Falvo and Arana? There was something about them that she couldn't quite put her finger on. She had seen them both interact with others and their manners were civil and efficient, but not as forthcoming and chatty as they were with her. Why? Was that Xorron's influence? Both had called her sister and given her a friendly one-arm half-hug when she left them.

And the houses Falvo had shown her! Her favorite was the one near Mextown, which they could possibly afford if they ate beans and rice. Toni pushed that out of her mind as she heard the key in the door, locking then unlocking the deadbolt. Growing up in Houston, they had a habit of keeping the door locked at all times.

Jill came in carrying grocery bags. "There's more," she said setting them on the counter.

"Were you hungry when you went in?" Toni teased.

"Only a little," Jill conceded. "But I thought, what the hell I might as well get this over with. Must have been everyone else's idea too. Did you know the Fourth was Saturday?"

"Yeah." Toni removed bags from the car. "What do you want to do?"

"I don't know. Gomez invited us over to their house. We could go to the park if you're tired of being around cops?"

"No, that's fine."

Jill looked at her. "What's the matter?"

"Coming down from all the excitement, I guess." Toni waved a hand at the table of booklets, brochures, packets and forms. "Life is nothing but a series of forms. I must have filled out ten thousand forms today. It's amazing how on paper your life can be reduced to nothing but a list and numbers. Sorry, your life score is only 42, you ain't living, you're existing."

"I take it you filled out a lot of forms today," Jill said suppressing a grin.

Toni rolled her eyes and took out a package of Oreos. "Bless your soul."

"You eat too many and break out, don't blame me."

"Would I do that?"

"Yes, you would." Jill nodded to the table. "What's all the forms for?"

"Those are mostly mortgage applications and school-related forms."

"You went on campus?"

"Yes, I told you that this morning?"

"So?"

"So what? I filled out two hundred forms, to get transcripts, to take the GRE, fifty different forms just to get in, one for the university, one for the graduate school, one for the program, one because I'm female, one because I'm ethnic, one because I'm out-of-state, one because I'm undecided about which program, one because I'm leaning towards IC, one because I won't need financial aid, one because I just might, one because I'm late applying, one because I'm early registering, and one because of all of the above and many, many more."

"Okay I can understand your repulsion to forms. Now what is this about mortgage forms?"

"After I finally left campus about three, I—"

"You should have come by for a tour," Jill interrupted. "Now you offer," Toni said dryly. "Anyway, I went by Eagle Realty to pick up a video. She was on her way out to show this couple a house in Newton and dragged me along to tell me about a new house that would be perfect for us. Well it wasn't. Neither was the house for the couple, so we all took a whirlwind tour of several houses in the area; they insist on living in Newton. I don't know why; it's so suburbia, so new, no character. When they decided enough was enough for the day, they left; but instead of going back to the office, we went by three houses she had just gotten today."

Jill took the six-pack from her hands. "No need to help."

"Sorry." Toni reached for a bag. "Anyway one house, goodness, Jill, it was perfect for us. I mean I could see us in that house. You know the color Dicer had in her bedroom, the pearly blue? That's the color of the house. Almost, maybe darker."

"Inside or out?"

"Out."

Jill groaned. "I was afraid you'd say that. What else?" When Toni got to talking, she had learned to keep her comments to a minimum.

"Oh, it's south of Mextown in an old neighborhood where the people had the most beautiful yards, full of flowers and sculpted bushes. Our house has four bedrooms, a study, a rec room and a sunroom."

"How many bathrooms?"

"Three. And the master bedroom . . . Why tell you about it when you can see for yourself?" Toni fished a key out of her pocket. "Ta da."

"Oh, you bought it already, how nice."

"If I could have, I would have." Toni giggled, the fatigue fading fast. "Come on, I'll even buy dinner."

"What? You're buying. Where's my calendar? I need to write this down."

"You're so damn funny." Toni lightly punched her on the shoulder.

"Hey, up until this last month, you were as tight with a dollar as a virgin with her pussy."

"Ugh!" Toni rolled her eyes at Jill's analogy.

"Oh don't get all prudish on me now, Ms. Thang."

Toni shook her head. "I take it your day went pretty well."

"It did actually. We were stuck indoors most of the day doing of all things inventory."

"What about the case on Aberdeen and Wallace?"

"Oh, Wallace made bail and upstairs again did a bellyflop and pulled us off Aberdeen, then declared that somehow all of the files on the second floor inventory had been lost and had to be redone; that included Dicer's office and Otu's lab. Shit, Otu probably has a million things in there. If Dicer wasn't such a nitpicker we would have been up shit creek. Obviously they had done a similar thing before."

"Really?"

"Yeah. A lot of Otu's equipment does not belong to the department per se." The phone rang. "I'll get it," Jill said moving towards the phone. "Hello."

"Good evening, Ms. Merlo. Is Ms. Jensen there?" Rex Xorron asked.

"One second." Jill held out the phone. "Your fairy godmother."

Slipping past, Toni pinched her buttocks before taking the phone. "Hello."

"Good evening, Ms. Jensen. You have been a busy woman today. A minimum of six memos with your name on them came across my desk today. What are you doing over there? Testing my people and their resources?"

Toni chuckled. "No, they keep giving me forms to fill out."

"I apologize for that, but the people around me insist on accountability which unfortunately means paperwork."

"Lots of it."

"I know you've had a long day, so I'll get to the point. We've just acquired a number of properties in Metrox, which normally wouldn't be a problem. The whys of the problem does not concern

you, however what we're doing about them may very well be your
bargain of the century. We have six houses that we're dumping at
cost—" There was an outburst in her office, to which she responded
in a rapid dialect Toni didn't quite catch. "Now where were we?"

"Six houses at cost." Toni motioned for Jill to pick up the
extension.

"Right, Carla Eagle got carried away with her charge and I
have six houses that I need to unload immediately. I have two
families that are moving there next week, but that's all of my people
we've found housing for which leaves four. Three if you and Ms.
Merlo can allow Brenda Falvo to sell you on one, I can get you a
low-interest loan with MissTennArk Bank which handles most of
our employee's mortgages there for us."

"How low?"

Xorron chuckled. "That depends on the house. I spoke with
Carla earlier today and houses ranged from an appraised $80,000
to $2.3 million. What she was thinking on the $2.3 million I have
no idea. But that one has to hit the market to recoup our invest-
ment; we can't let that go for half-price."

"Half-price?"

"We buy cheap, usually half price. Now here is where you
come in. If you have time to tomorrow, let Falvo show you those
six, well five of those houses to see if you like any of them. Whatever the appraised price is, think half. I—"

"What if I've seen one that's not of those six?"

There was a pause. "Hmm. I'm sure we can switch out some
kind of way, though the discount may not be so large. These six
were in a special account that I'm trying to free up. Don't worry
about that, we'll handle that. Just find what you like. As you see,
I have a tendency to offer unsolicited advice and offer my people
first choice at the spoils." There was another outburst of angry
voices. "You would think that at this time of the evening, people
would behave in a more civil manner. Give Falvo a call to view
those houses, then give me a ring. Take care."

"You too, and thanks for thinking of me."

"How can I not, you've been showing up on my desk all day. Good night."

"Good night."

Jill stared at her. "And what the hell was that about showing up on her desk?"

"Memos, Jill. She said earlier memos concerning me were crossing her desk, that's what she was referring to all day." Toni walked to the counter. "Geez. You can be so paranoid. And for what?"

"For what? Now she's offering you a house at half-price. How deep must she sink her claws in your neck before she wants to sink her fingers in other places."

"Jill."

"Can't you see she's buying you."

"You think I'm that cheap?" Toni asked angrily. "Not once has she asked for anything."

"Not yet. Women like that—"

"You don't know her."

"And you do? For chrissakes Toni, open your eyes. The majority of people who works for her are women. She likes women. You're a woman. Duh!"

"Oh yeah, she want's an educated harem."

"Then what does she want?"

"I don't know!"

"Exactly! She puts you in a house and she thinks you will be eternally grateful and willing to show it." Jill made a lewd gesture, snapping her hips at Toni.

"Fuck you!" Toni stormed into the bedroom and slammed the door.

"Guess she won't buy dinner," Jill murmured.

Dicer entered the side door of the furniture warehouse and waited for her eyes to adjust to the dark. Seconds later she walked down the hallway to a door with a sliver of light shining under the door. She knocked softly scanning the length of the hallway; no one was in sight which unnerved her more than anything. The door opened and she entered.

"Lt. Dicer, welcome," a voice greeted her from behind the door.

"Fuentes," Dicer said turning as he closed the door. She had not expected him, but then she should have, given the confounding news of his imminent departure.

"Have a seat please." He waved her to a leather sofa.

"Thanks. Are you going to tell me what's going on?" Dicer sat making sure her gun was easily accessible.

"As much as I can, but you know most of it."

Dicer nodded. "You're liquidating and jumping ship. But why? Not that I'm not happy to see you leave."

He gave her his infamous smile. "I'll miss pitting wits against you as well. Aviles, however, I will not miss. I made her career you know." He took a deep breath and sat in the secretarial chair in front of the desk.

"So you've said. Why now? Why not last year?" Sitting across from her in his wrinkled Dickies and workshirt with a baseball cap pulled low, he seemed less malevolent than she had ever seen him, looking like a simple middle-age worker with two days growth of beard.

"Someone made me an offer I couldn't refuse."

"Leave town or else what?"

"Leave town or never leave town."

"Meaning?"

"Meaning I had no option to leaving town."

"Someone scared you that much?"

Fuentes studied her. "Scared is not operable here. Let us say explained in no uncertain terms where the continuation of my enterprises would lead. I did not care for the images conjured. And I do mean conjured."

"Conjured as in spells?" Had he gotten ahold of his own bad shit?

"After a fashion." He rose, removed an amulet from his neck

and held it out to her. "Take it. At this point in your life, you need it more than I do. Evil is real señorita; we all need protection." He grabbed her hand as she reached for it. "You have always had mine, even as you sought to destroy me, my niece."

Dicer yanked her hands back. "You're crazy."

He shook his head. "No. You're living in my father's house. Kip and Kirk are my brothers. My mother was the old man Dicer's housekeeper. Nothing original there." He smiled. "Kip has made a fortune selling me overpriced properties."

"Kip wouldn't launder your money!" Dicer stood up abruptly.

"No, but he would take advantage of an unsuspecting client, which many of my buyers posed to be."

She stared at him as he had always stared at her and the realization shocked her. Had he always arranged their encounters just to see her? No, that would have been suicidal. "Do they know?"

He shook his head. "No. Then again they may."

"Why tell me now?" Dicer sat down.

"I have a daughter." He laughed, a new sight for her. "She's coming to NSU in the fall. Perhaps she and Nikki can be friends."

"What do you know about Nikki?" The hackles rose on her back.

"She and Katie are the most important people in your life." He winked at her. "Although Jaio Yemen is making an effort to win you over. Isn't she?"

Dicer only stared. "If something happens to them—"

He waved a dismissing hand. "You're forgetting, they are my nieces as well. And Jaio can take care of herself."

"What do you want?"

"I want you to look out for Demetria. She's not so tough that hearing her old man trashed won't hurt her." He raised an eyebrow. "Plus she thinks I'm a simple entrepreneur."

"You have a daughter, why would you peddle shit to kids?"

"I can say I never peddled to kids, but that won't satisfy you. I could also say it was simple business, though not my only or most lucrative. That still would not get me off the hook. Now as we sit here and my plane awaits me, I can't tell you why; all I can say is that Evil exists, and it had me in its grip." He moved closer. "I offer no excuses for anything I did. I did what I felt necessary to make a living. But the purpose for calling you here wasn't to make apologies for my behavior but to warn you. I want you to be careful, Dice. The NFC is Evil."

"And you're not?"

Fuentes shook his head. "They're feeding their congregation opiates in their communion." He nodded as if she had disagreed with him. "Flesh of my flesh and blood of my blood indeed contains opiates for the masses. That's what Wallace, not I was willing to do, to slowly addict the congregation."

"That's barbaric."

"I can see in your eyes, that you know I speak the truth."

"Then who is killing their preachers?"

"Perhaps they expressed their disapproval too vociferously."

"I need proof."

"I have none to offer." He splayed his arms. "That's all I have."

A double knock sounded on the side door. Fuentes rose, reaching for a briefcase. Quickly he removed an envelope from the inside. "They're waiting for me. Here's information on Demetria." He held it out to her, then pulled her in a quick hug, kissing both cheeks. "This place is going to blow in three minutes. I suggest you get the hell out."

"Where are you going?"

He hesitated. "South America. I can't tell you which country." He flashed her one last smile. "I'll send you a postcard. Go!" He slipped out of the door.

Dicer headed for the door, but heard a burst of gunfire. "Fuentes!" She turned to the side door as it crashed open. Fuentes, carrying a lanky man badly bleeding, stumbled back in.

"Ambush!"

Dicer, gun in hand, pushed open the other door and checked the halls. Still clear. "Let's go." She waved them out.

"Take the case." Fuentes shoved the case at her. "For Demetria.

If I make it, I'll send for it. If I don't, you got to take care of her for me. Promise me." He searched her eyes. "Promise!"

"Promise." Dicer hooked the case under her arm and stepped out. A bullet clipped the door frame and she returned fire to the left. Shots came from the right. "We're fucked."

"Where's the amulet?" Fuentes asked.

"In my pocket." Dicer withdrew it and held it out.

"No, put it on and hold it, make sure your thumb is on the groove in the back."

She did as she was told. Five seconds later explosions rocked the warehouse.

"Our three minutes aren't up!" Dicer yelled, fearing being crushed to death.

Gunfire erupted from the side door and they turned towards the door as it burst inward. An auburn haired woman stood there with a submachine gun. Dicer had her finger on the trigger when Fuentes knocked down her hand.

"Our side."

"Come on," the woman said, not taking her eyes off of Dicer. Dicer hesitated only a split second and followed Fuentes out. A large hole had been torn from the exterior wall and a thick sediment haze filled the air. Five bodies lay under and over the debris. The woman led them to the loading dock where a van was backed up with its doors open. Fuentes with his comrade tumbled in. When Dicer hesitated, the woman shoved her from behind, sending her tumbling into the van and onto the floor. The door slammed shut before she could regain her balance and by then the van was spinning off. The van rocked as it made a sharp turn around the corner, just as a tremendous concussion sounded.

"I hope you had insurance on that car," the auburn haired woman said holding on to a strap at the back of the van.

"Who are you?" Dicer asked.

"Sparrow." She tugged at a filament running along the ceiling. "Let her off here."

The van stopped and Sparrow flung open the door.

"Thank you," Fuentes said taking the briefcase.

"Don't make me regret this." Dicer stepped out of the van, then realized she was still wearing the amulet. Had she set off the explosions or was it a signal to the woman that they were in deep shit? As she headed back towards the warehouse, sirens sounded in the distance. How would she explain this? The truth? As much as she could.

Toni came out of the bedroom after a long nap and a news show that was interrupted by a report on the explosion. Jill looked up from her own notebook computer.

"I made hamburgers but you were asleep."

"Okay, turn on the TV; Dicer was at the scene of the explosion."

Jill stood up. "Where?"

"I don't know. Somewhere in Siberia."

"What channel?"

"Three." Hunger pangs led Toni to the kitchen as Jill found the station.

"I wonder why she didn't call us."

"Perhaps because you're off."

Jill shot her a long look and reached for the phone, dialing Mickey. He answered on the sixth ring and had not heard of the explosion or from Dicer since they had left her a couple of hours earlier in her office. She was going to eat dinner at her desk and work until. Mickey told her he was on his way to pick her up and they would head to the site.

Dicer sat in a patrol car, drinking water when Aviles arrived. Someone hurriedly pointed Aviles in her direction.

Dicer spotting the deputy chief, got out of the car and met her in a cleared area. No one said anything for a long moment.

"Why were you out here?" Aviles asked.

"To meet someone."

"Who?"

"I didn't know who until I arrived. It was Rubin Fuentes who was in there."

"What did he want?"

Dicer massaged her neck. "To tell me he was leaving the city."

"But before he wanted to blow up a building?"

Dicer counted to ten. "No. One last bit of info. He alleges that the NFC is feeding opiates to its members through communion and the deaths of its preachers may have been internal controls."

Aviles stuck her hand in Dicer's face. "Don't repeat that to anyone."

"Which part?"

"None of it."

"Come on, you know I've had suspicions along that line, all he did was confirm it."

"He didn't confirm a damn thing. Where's the evidence? All he's doing is fanning your obsession."

"My obsession? Every time I get close, someone upstairs yanks my chain. I get the greenlight from you and some asshole cuts me off. I'm not obsessed, I'm pissed that the most cooperation I can get is from a goddamn gangster! On top of that Stein has me doing inventory. Don't tell me that's not a calculated roadblock to upset us. Perhaps you should start investigating upstairs or has Aberdeen used up all of her free passes? Shit, you people can't even do a cover-up right."

"You're bordering on insubordination, Dicer," Aviles hissed.

"Fuck it. I'm going to do my job despite the yahoos trying to pull my strings. You suspend me right now, or get the fuck out of my way."

"Don't fuck up, Dicer. I'm the only friend you got upstairs at the moment if you hadn't noticed. You force me to put you on suspension, they've beat you. Now shut the fuck up and tell me what happened or you'll have plenty of time to play with your blocks."

To reign in her anger, Dicer took a long drink from the water bottle. "Can we go somewhere? There are ears everywhere out here."

"Yeah. There's a diner down the street." Aviles pulled at her sleeve.

In the diner, Dicer recounted the discovery of the identity of her mystery contact, the edited conversation, and the two aborted departures before the auburn haired rescuer appeared leading them out. Aviles took notes even as her tape recorder rolled.

"Kidnapping," she interjected as Dicer told of the shove into the van.

Dicer reached across the table and took the pen. "It was necessary to avoid getting blown to bits."

"It's kidnapping to avoid an aiding and abetting the escape of a felon."

"Of course he's a felon, but he wasn't wanted."

"Didn't he tell you the building was about to blow? Arson at least, destruction of property. Not to mention we have six dead. No telling how many of those kills were his. You should have tried to bring him in."

"Of course you're right. No matter that a third party was trying to kill us both." Dicer raised a hand to the bandaid the medic had put on her forehead where a splinter had caught her.

"Did you at least get out of him where he was going?"

"South America was all he said."

"No other clues?"

"No." She looked up as Mickey and Merlo entered the diner, scanned the few patrons and headed their way. "I guess my team watches the news."

Aviles glanced back at them. "I want a full report on my desk at 10 o'clock. Don't make another foolish raid without consulting me."

"Sure."

Aviles nailed her with her eyes. "Don't get your ass in something that flippant mouth can't get you out of. I'm not wasting another marker on you." She rose, nodded to the officers and left the diner.

Mickey and Merlo sat down across from Dicer. "Hey."

Dicer sighed. "What are you doing here?"

"We come to help," Mickey told her glancing at Merlo for agreement.

"Then take me home."

"And you can tell us all about it."

Dicer groaned as she picked up the ticket. "Let's go."

When they reached Dicer's, she got out and leaned in and told them, "If I don't show up tomorrow, take the Cat-mobile and camp out across from the NFC."

"Where are you going?"

"Get my ass in a crack."

"Sure you don't need us?"

"No, I need you on the NFC."

"Anyone particular?"

"The bigwigs. One down, two to go." Dicer went into the house without looking back.

Nikki met her at the door, a gun in her hand.

"What the hell are you doing?" Dicer took the gun from her.

"You had a message; the man said they followed you and to watch your ass." Nikki visibly relaxed.

"Okay, but I'm worried about my chest and your gun." Dicer went through the house checking the windows and doors, then turned on the security system, fully.

"I'm going to bed now," Nikki said. "Will you be okay?"

"Yeah. What you want for breakfast?"

"Pancakes," Nikki said chuckling. "Night."

"Night, sweetie." Dicer went upstairs, removed Fuentes' letter from the small of her back, and tossed it on her bed before going into the bathroom for a long shower where she finally allowed her mind to consider what Fuentes had told her. The fact that he could be her grandfather's son was not the issue; but whether the issue was their relationship to each other over the last ten years. The game of cat and mouse, the deadly encounters. Had he been involved in her success on the streets as he had implied? And what of young Demetria?

CHAPTER 12

By seven o'clock the following morning Dicer had not arrived, so Mickey and Merlo took the Cat-mobile and parked right across from the main entrance to the New Faith Cathedral. They had only been there an hour when two young men rolled up in a gold Mercedes and went in.

"I'll be goddamn." Mickey sat up.

"Who are they?"

"Dicer's cousin Kenny and Wallace's brother Damon." Mickey reached for the phone, then paused as a van slowed down to a near stop. The auburn haired driver turned and looked directly at them then drove on down the street. "You see that? She had auburn hair like Dicer described."

"Coincidence?"

"See if you can get a hardcopy of her from the tape."

"You get the license plates?" Merlo asked.

"Yes." He was pulling the console to him to run the plates.

Toni Jensen ensconced in her cubbyhole reached for the phone. "Jensen."

"Brenda Falvo here, Toni. My supervisor just sent me a memo about those last houses we seen yesterday."

"Really?" Excitement crept up her spine.

"Yes. Between you and me, I think you can get a damn good deal on SunRay." She took a deep breath. "I don't mean to pressure you, but we have to unload them and if you want to get an appraiser over there you can. But I can start the paperwork now and give Xorron a call to inform her of your interest."

Toni drummed her fingers thinking. "Okay. But I need to talk to Jill and get her to go over there."

"Okay. I'll call you later this afternoon."

Toni hung up from Falvo and dialed Jill. When the dispatcher informed her Jill was out in the field, she paged her, then waited anxiously for her call which came five minutes later.

"I need you to meet me for lunch."

"I can't. I'm on a stakeout."

"But I need to show you something."

"What?"

"That house on SunRay. Apparently Falvo jumped the gun in showing me those houses. The one I liked is on Xorron's list."

"Oh what a coincidence." Jill rolled her eyes at the phone. "We're talking about the deal of the century here. Half price and—"

"Give me the address; I'll drive by when we get time."

"Just call me, I'll take off then; it's slow here."

"Okay. What's the address?" Jill pulled out her pen.

"4655 SunRay. It's south of Mextown."

Jill thought that sounded familiar. "I can find it. But I can't promise you what time. It maybe after three." Gomez and Mumford was relieving them at two.

"Okay." Toni paused. "Thanks."

"Don't thank me yet. I may hate it." She was definitely beginning to hate this situation and that damn Xorron woman. Who the fuck did she think she was interfering with their lives?

"You won't."

"I'll try. Bye."

"Bye."

Jill hung up and stared at Mickey. "All of this is your fault."

"What?"

"Xorron and this house thing." She hadn't spoken with him about it although she had been meaning to. "Man, Toni's head is so full of sugarplums, my head is spinning. Xorron is offering to foot the bill for graduate school. When she found out we were considering looking for a house, she set Toni up with a real estate agent who now has these houses they bought up and now have to unload at a deep discount. I never heard of anything like that."

"It happens, especially in an area like this where there are more houses with all the new construction."

"Well Xorron even offered to get her a low interest loan with MissTennArk Bank."

"At least you know their reputation."

"I know, but the whole thing just gives me the creeps. She spent all of yesterday planning her future with people she just met. Now she wants me to look at a house she wants to buy."

"You're feeling left out?" Mickey asked.

"Don't even try it. It's like she's checked her brain at the door with these people." Jill sighed. "What time are we taking a break? The biggest purchase of our lives and she's. . . ."

"She's what?"

Jill lifted the pad she had written the address on. "Run 4655 SunRay for me for you. That sounds so familiar."

Mickey stared hard at her. "It should, that's one of the houses Fuentes unloaded." He turned to the terminal.

"Are you sure?"

"Yes. What was the name of that realtor?"

"Eagle Realty."

"Eagle? I've never heard of them." His hands flew over the keyboard. "This is too fucking unbelievable."

"What?" Jill moved to where she could look over his shoulder.

"Xorron owns Vengar and Vengar owns part of Eagle. Get this . . . No, guess who owns the Virada?"

"Vengar?"

"Vengar-Metrox to be exact." He scrolled through the list. "Lookit. They virtually own south Boxtown."

"Toni said they have a building on East Laredo."

"Yep. Two of them." He looked back at Jill. "It could be a coincidence."

"I thought you didn't believe in coincidences."

"That's Dicer."

"I think we should tell her."

"You're right, if for no other reason than to cover your ass." He reached for the phone. Dicer didn't answer any of her numbers. "She must be in with Aviles now."

Indeed Dicer was in with Aviles and the sparks were flying as they fought over the proper course of action.

When Dicer left Aviles she drove to Kip's agency where she enticed Nikki and Kerry to lunch. Kris had an appointment but promised to meet them afterwards. Kip only raised an eyebrow when he passed all four in a group in the hallway, for that could be a wicked combination under certain circumstances.

"Nice car," Kerry said getting into the passenger seat of the Chrysler.

"Rental."

"You should get one of these," Kerry told her.

"Can't afford it. I'm on a tight budget."

"Right. You're walking on your money."

"Let's not start, Kerry."

"You ever thought of hitting mom up for money?" Kerry asked her sister.

"No."

"Me neither. I'm afraid she'd say no and I don't think I could handle that rejection."

"You can't handle any rejection. That's why . . . " Ki trailed off. "I didn't invite you out to fight."

"We never intend to fight; it just happens." Kerry sat back. "So what's so important that drags you away from your precious work to save the universe?"

"Demetria Hawkins." Ki pulled the small graduation photo from her shirt pocket. "Here."

"Oh my god, she looks like me," Kerry said holding the photo to Nikki. "Don't she?"

"Yes," Nikki concurred.

"Does mom know that dad had another daughter?" Kerry asked.

"She's not dad's."

"How many children have Kip fathered?" Nikki asked.

"She's not Kip's either."

"She's our aunt?" Kerry asked.

"No, but close." Ki pulled into their restaurant. "It appears grandfather had a son who had a daughter, Demetria, who is coming to NSU in the fall. Her father asked me to keep an eye out for her after telling me who he was. I didn't believe him until I saw the photo and the family resemblance. He somehow knew that Nikki was going to NSU this fall and thought it a swell idea if they could be friends."

"It's bad enough finding out Kris may be my sister and now this? Didn't anyone in your family keep their pants up?" Nikki asked.

"Apparently not." Ki got out, the others following.

"So what is it you want us to do about this girl?" Kerry asked.

"That's what I'm asking you. It's more complicated."

"How?" Nikki asked as they entered the bustling restaurant of suits.

"I'll explain." Ki turned to the hostess. "Is the back table available?"

She glanced down at a screen. "Yes." The three followed her back through the tables of young executives who didn't fail to notice the three tall attractive women. Neither did Ki Dicer fail to register a number of familiar faces.

When they were alone again, Ki glanced from one to the other. "How's it going?"

"We're both okay. Now explain," Kerry said impatiently.

"You too?" Ki asked Nikki. The teenager nodded. "I'm not asking you to take an oath of secrecy; however I am asking you to be discreet and sensitive to the situation."

Kerry waved a lazy hand at her. "Fine. Now tell us. You're so damn strange."

"According to the information I have, her mother is dead and she grew up in New Mexico. Her father well . . . her father is a sort of persona non grata, which she may not know of his illegal activities."

"All my friends have jailbird daddies or uncles or mamas for that matter," Nikki said reaching for a roll. "Big deal."

"Maybe not, but it could be dangerous for her which is why I'd like you not to mention her father to her."

"Then why did you tell us?" Kerry asked.

"Because you would have complained if I had not. Look, I just found out and I thought you'd want to know. I shouldn't have told you, but the resemblance is so striking what kind of explanation could I have come up with?"

"How do we know this is the truth? You could be covering for dad," Kerry accused.

"Why would I do that?"

"Who is this fella? Let's go see him."

"That's the complicated part; he's gone and she doesn't know yet." Ki expelled a long breath. "She's expecting him to meet her at the airport at seven-fifteen."

"What a heel, he's part of the family alright," Kerry sneered.

Ki frowning stared at her. "What's wrong with you?"

"Nothing, the men in this family gets on my fucking nerves."

Ki looked at Nikki who stared into her glass of tea. "Okay, don't tell me. But does either of you want to go to the airport with me?"

"Why should you go at all?" Kerry asked.

"Family?" Ki said.

"Fine fucking family we have. If you're so concerned about family then . . . " Kerry waved the waiter over and ordered a martini.

Against her better judgment Ki pulled out her checkbook. "How much do you need?"

Kerry shot her a withering glance. "I don't need your money, Ki. You've made it perfectly clear you don't want me to have it."

"Fine, don't tell mother I didn't offer." Ki replaced her check-book.

"Don't tell mother," Kerry mimicked.

"Why don't you grow up, Kerry. What kind of example are you setting for Katie?"

"You're saying I'm an unfit mother?" Kerry hissed.

Nikki put a hand on her arm. "No, she didn't say that. Can we order now?"

"Yes, please." Ki waved the waiter over. When he was gone, she turned back to Kerry. "What happened? And don't say nothing."

Kerry rose. "Which way is the ladies room?"

"Through there." Ki pointed the way, then watched her sashay off. "You tell me," she said softly to Nikki.

"She just found out Kylar is still in Canton and your father is going back with him tomorrow. And she asked Kip for a raise, he said no because she just received one in March."

"That it?" For Kerry that was enough.

Nikki shrugged. "Something with Barry."

Ki groaned. "That's it then. She gets mad at the world when he screws over her. Well, I'm tired of talking to her about it." What more could she do? Kerry didn't pay rent, student loans or a car note because she drove a company Pathfinder and their mother paid Katie's daycare. Everyone was taking care of Kerry, but Kerry.

"I'll go with you," Nikki said suddenly.

"What?" Ki asked.

"I'll go with you to the airport to pickup Demetria. It's not so great to think you're all alone, even if you aren't."

"No, it's not." Ki was grateful neither had yet asked for Fuentes' name. "So what do you think it is between Kerry and Barry this time?"

Nikki smiled. "I thought you were tired of talking about it?"

"With her."

"Well, from what I gathered out of the raised voices he split with her bill money with another woman."

"What?"

Nikki nodded. "Your father called Kip, I was in the office. He was asking him about Kerry because someone was trying to buy Kerry's house."

"What?!"

Nikki nodded gravely. "Barry. That's when she found he was gone."

"I bet dad was pissed."

"Yep, especially when Kerry tried to cover for him. I don't think she dissuaded him from pressing charges."

"No, she wouldn't, not dad, not this time." What was surprising was the relatively calm manner in which Kerry was taking it. Ki watched her stop at a table and flirt with two men. Unlike her, Kerry was good with men in the flirtatious way which made her even more upset of why she would put up with Barry's shit. If their dad had anything to do with it, she wouldn't be putting up with him anymore.

"There's your mother," Nikki said pointing.

Ki turned to see her mother approaching with clear intent. "Uh oh, one of us is in deep doodoo."

Nikki giggled.

"Hello mother," Ki said as her mother took the vacant seat.

"Hello Ki, Nikki."

"How'd you find us?"

"Kip. He saw you and made a guess."

"I left him a note," Nikki said.

Carolyn flashed her a smile. "I thought as much." Her eyes roamed the dining room spotting Kerry, giving the two men her card. "Your father called me about Barry. What has she said?"

"Nothing. Nikki was filling me in."

"I don't know what's wrong with that girl."

"The Goddard genes," Nikki said seriously.

"Don't you start about those genes too, young lady. You have been with Ki too long," Carolyn admonished.

"As good a reason as any," Ki said. "So what brings you by?"

"Katie. I'm off tomorrow and thought a stay with me would do her some good. I was going to pick her up at daycare today."

"Before or after this drama unfolded?" Ki asked as Kerry headed their way.

"Before. You have a problem with it?" Carolyn asked her oldest daughter.

"No, mother. Although you do have a tendency to distort temporal order."

"Yes, my second daughter." Carolyn watched her real second daughter warily take her seat. "Hello, Kerry."

"Hello, mom. Is that a new ring?"

Carolyn Goddard-Dicer held out her left hand. "Yes. You like it?"

"It looks like an engagement ring." Nikki took her hand. "You're not getting married are you, aunt Carolyn?"

"Maybe, maybe not."

"Make sure he knows you have four children and a grandchild and that they come first," Kerry told her.

"He knows all about my four wonderful, petulant children and little Katie. Speaking of Katie, Kerry. Would you be terribly upset if I took her for the holiday weekend?"

"We were going to spend the weekend with Ki, but if it's okay with her, then it's okay with me," Kerry said smoothly.

Carolyn glanced at Ki. "I didn't know it was your weekend with her. Do you mind?"

"No, mother. I don't mind; I can drown my disappointment in mortar." Again Ki acted as the intermediary between them. It was not her weekend with Katie, but Kerry didn't want to seem too eager for her mother to take her daughter.

Toni worked right through lunch with the intention of leaving at three to meet Brenda Falvo and hopefully Jill at the SunRay house. She was packing her things for the week when her supervisor, Milt Coombs knocked and entered.

"Do you have a few minutes, Toni?" he asked taking the other seat in the cramped quarters.

"Yes." Toni settled into her seat wondering what this was all about. Like any supervisor he had his favorites and his doormats; he had pretty much left her alone.

"I understand you're not happy with us."

Toni looked him in the eye. "I haven't expressed any unhappiness with the company."

"You aren't looking for new employment?"

"No." The job was so routine and the hours flexible that she believed she could do it and go to school full-time. She would have to if they bought a house.

"There's been a few inquiries today about you. Care to inform me?"

"I'm applying to graduate school and trying to get financial support."

"Oh, I see. Are you planning to go full time?"

"I'm going to try."

"And work here?"

"Yes."

"Hmmm." He crossed his legs.

"Is that a problem?"

"Past experience has proved that the quality of work has suffered when the employee has returned to school."

"I assure you, my work will not suffer."

"Yes. Yes. Easier said than done." He rose. "We'll see. We'll see. Enjoy the Fourth." He left.

Toni shook her head, made sure her computer was off, and left, ignoring several sly glances.

Mickey and Jill, in separate vehicles, arrived at the SunRay house, parking behind Toni's car in the circular drive. Getting off his bike, Mickey let out a low whistle at the immaculate pearly blue exterior with the white trim and railing.

"How much you say this is?" he asked Jill.

"I don't know. Half of whatever the list price is, according to Toni." Jill walked up the two steps to the door.

Toni opened it before she could knock. "You came!" she exclaimed pulling her in.

"You left me no choice," Toni said, but immediately regretted her words. "In time."

Mickey followed her in. "Which one of you has the green thumb? That yard will be a bitch to maintain."

The three toured the four bedroom/three bathroom partially furnished house. Jill grudgingly conceding that Toni had made an astute choice that would meet their needs; yet she doubted that they could afford it, even if she worked double shifts for the next ten years.

Dicer picked up Nikki and headed for the airport, her apprehension growing with each mile. Parking in a short-term lot they crossed to the terminal taking in the travelers.

"Isn't that Rebecca?" Nikki asked pointing down to an athletic woman with a backpack and a baseball cap as they went up the escalator.

Dicer looked down and muttered a curse. "Yeah."

"Want me to go catch her?" Nikki asked but was already running up the last steps to take the stairs back down.

"Shit!" Dicer checked her watch, seeing she had plenty of time, took the escalator back down. Nikki had caught the woman and was pointing back toward Dicer. Some days you should not get out of bed.

"Must be fate," Rebecca said, then gave Dicer a quick, chaste hug.

"Twisted," Dicer said. "What brings you back to Metrox?"

"Obviously a misguided sense of hope we could be civil to each other."

"At least let us take you to your hotel," Dicer said.

"Don't bother."

"Fine." Dicer turned away.

Nikki caught her arm. "Come on, Dice. She came all this way."
Nikki darted to Rebecca. "She's under a lot of pressure and she's
still recovering from the shooting."

Rebecca's expressive eyes widen. "Shooting? What shooting?
No one told me about a shooting?"

"In the shoulder and arm," Nikki told her pointing.

"Are you okay?" Rebecca asked.

"Of course."

"Always the toughie."

"She's finished the floors in the house," Nikki said. "You should
see them. Tonight."

"Nikki, she obviously does not want me there."

"Yes, she does." Nikki turned to Dicer. "Don't you, Ki?"

"No."

Nikki stared at her. "How can you be so cold?"

Dicer threw up her hands. "Fine. Rebecca would you like to
stay in the guest room? Perhaps we can discuss this rationally like
adults over tea."

"Not much of an invitation."

"Please?" Nikki entreated. "I'm staying with her. You don't
have to be alone with her."

Dicer took a deep breath. "Yes, you're welcome to stay there.
I'd feel better knowing you were there and not at some fleabag
motel."

"I'm flattered with that one. But why would I expect more
from you."

"Great!" Nikki exclaimed. "Do you have anymore bags?"

"No. I travel light remember."

Nikki hooked an arm through Rebecca's. "Come on, we have
to meet Demetria's plane."

"Who's Demetria? Dicer's new love?"

"No. You'll see." They followed Dicer back up, Nikki filling
Rebecca in on the events since she had been gone.

The plane arrived half an hour late which for most travelers
during the holiday rush was right on schedule. Nikki and Dicer

positioned themselves directly in front of the gate, studying each female face. As the stream of passengers slowed, they were giving up hope and afraid they had missed her.

"Maybe she changed her mind or he told her he was gone," Nikki said as two young males deplaned.

"Maybe." Dicer felt a stab of disappointment.

"Maybe she took a later flight," Nikki consoled.

"Maybe, but I am—" Dicer stopped midsentence as a young woman in shorts and sleeveless blouse ambled out. She swept the area with a keen eye; the second sweep she keyed in on Dicer and Nikki and headed directly for them.

"I'm Demetria Hawkins. I believe you're expecting me."

Dicer forced her jaw not to drop open. "I'm Ki Dicer, Demetria and this is Nikki and Rebecca. How may I ask did you know we were waiting on you?"

"Little things, not the least that I have your face burned into my memory. My father sent me newspaper clippings and other photos of you. Since you're here, I take it his deeds finally caught up with him."

"You know?" Dicer asked.

Demetria shrugged. "Information age. I read the Globe daily."

"Well shame on him for underestimating you. You have other baggage?" Dicer asked.

"Yes."

"Then to the baggage claim we ago." Dicer led her small group out.

Going over a report in bed, Dicer responded to a light tap at her door, "It's open."

Rebecca, in short pajamas, entered quietly and sat cross-legged at the foot of the big bed. "Would you really have let me stayed at a hotel?"

Dicer placed the report on the nightstand. "Yes, I would have. You walked out on me remember."

"That's not entirely true."

"No? What part of that is false?"

"Okay, I left but I thought you understood that it had nothing to do with us, that this was a journey I had to take alone. It would have been unfair to ask you to wait, not knowing how long it would take me to complete it. As it was it took seven months."

"Seemed like seven days," Dicer sneered; but in all honesty the months rolled back as soon as Rebecca sat on the bed.

"Then I shouldn't be out of your system." Rebecca straddled her legs. "The fit is the same."

"What are you doing?" Dicer asked disinterestedly, but reached for the light all the same.

Dressed for work Jill Merlo stood in the doorway to the bathroom as Toni wiped her mouth and flushed the toilet. "You sure you aren't pregnant?"

Toni shot her a withering glance as she reached for her toothbrush. "Aren't you late for work?"

"No. You need anything?"

"For you to stop pestering me. Go. I'm fine."

"It gets worst, you go to the doctor."

"Yes, mother," Toni intoned.

"I put the gatorade in the freezer."

"Thank you. Go."

"I'll come by at lunch."

"That's okay, Jill."

"I'll call you then." Jill reluctantly pushed away from the doorway. As she walked towards the door the phone rang. She headed for the phone in the living room but saw the line still connected to Toni's computer. She reached the one in the kitchen on the third ring. "Hello?" she answered.

"Good, I caught you," Mickey said.

"What's up?"

"Holiday deployment. You and I are reassigned to the 7th. Hope you are in uniform."

"I am."

"Then I'll pick you up in the Catmobile in fifteen."

"Is this okay with Dicer?"

"Yeah. She'll be out there too."

"And they couldn't tell us that yesterday?"

"You know we're in Stein's doghouse."

"Right. See you." Jill hung up and returned to the bathroom. "We're on patrol in the 7th, so we won't be at the station. Just beep me if you need me. Mickey's coming by to pick me up."

"Okay." Toni leaned against the counter. "I think it's nerves about everything that's changing so quickly."

"Could be."

"I hope you understand, Jill."

"I'm trying, Toni. I just wish you could see this from my point of view."

"I'm trying too. What I'm trying to do is beneficial to both of us, but you make it sound as though I'm acting selfishly."

Jill took a deep breath and exhaled slowly. "I know that; I just don't want to get caught up in something without knowing the score."

"Next weekend you can go to Ydyllic with us. Spouses are welcome; we'll have our own room. There you can drill Xorron or anyone all you want."

Jill saw the light in her eyes. She hadn't asked before. "I'll see what my schedule looks like. Maybe if I volunteer to work a shift tomorrow, Dicer will let me off early Saturday. How are you going to swing it at work?"

"Working Wednesday." Toni stared ahead for a long moment. "What should I tell Brenda Falvo about the house?"

"See how long she can hold it. I just want to check and make sure everything is clear and legal. Okay?"

Toni refused to smile. "Okay. I'm sure that's understandable." She let out a mental sigh. "Did you get in the papers?"

"No." Jill headed for the door. With Toni puking over everything, she hadn't had time to do much of anything except get dressed.

"I'm tired; I'm going back to bed." Toni veered towards the kitchen.

"You should, but drink the Gatorade first and don't eat."

"No need to tell me not to eat." Toni took the chilled bottle of Gatorade out of the freezer. Toni swore by the stuff.

"Lookee. Lookee. Speak of the devil." Jill held up the smaller Virada paper whose headlines declared, "Xorron Benefactor of Children's AIDS Fund."

"Kind of late isn't it." Toni took the paper scanning the story of the proceeds from last week's concert as well as the donation of a renovated building for a hospice and a team of nurses to staff the hospice.

"How do you donate people?" Jill asked after Toni read the passage aloud.

"Maybe it's part of their program. Pay for their training and send them where you want them to go." She had read that somewhere in all of the information she had been flooded with, at her request of course.

"Like you?"

"If someone guaranteed me a job, I wouldn't mind."

"But to tell you where and when to go."

"We all have to pay a price to get what we want, Jill. You do it."

"Knowingly and voluntarily."

"Same here."

"But to what extent do they allow you to know."

"I know enough." A horn blew. "Is that Mickey?"

"Must me." Jill rose, hesitated and gave her a quick peck on the cheek. "Love you."

"Love you, despite you," Toni told her with a wink. "Be careful out there."

"I will. Take care of yourself." Jill hurried out the door to the striped suburban.

Dicer met one team then the other at an East LaFitte diner for an update on their other case. Grant and Geddes were sent back to the Sixth Precinct to oversee a waterpark of kids. Mickey and Merlo ordered lunch as Dicer sipped tea and briefed them in succinct statements, easy for them to digest. Nothing had changed much, however they were going to church Sunday with evidence bags. Nevertheless Dicer speculated that the communion would not be adulterated. After Pearson and Gravelli raided Brigham Fortier's estate, the NFC had gone into defense mode, protecting themselves against any detection which made the meeting with young Damon Wallace more significant. She just didn't know how or why.

Mickey watched Dicer closely when she completed their briefings. "Not sleeping again?"

Dicer smiled slyly. "No." With Rebecca back, she had a slight problem: Jaio Yemen. What would she do about her? It had never crossed her mind to give up Rebecca for Jaio. Keeping them both was not an option given the personalities of the women involved. Neither did she have the time and energy to do it.

"Well obviously, you don't want to tell us," Mickey said.

"No, strange night is all."

After a long pause, each in their individual thoughts, Merlo put down her fork. "Next weekend Toni has that orientation in Ydyllic. I want to go and check all of this out. Is it possible to get Friday evening off? I can work tomorrow if necessary or Sunday."

"No need, take the whole day off. We'll just keep you a couple of extra hours the rest of the days. With our present load, that makes more sense. Unless you want the overtime."

Jill paused. "You think I could get the morning shift? That way I'm home at three."

Dicer nodded. "I'll sign you up then. If there are no more questions or requests, I'm going downtown to complain to deaf ears."

"Wait, about the house on SunRay?" Mickey asked. "You hear anything? My guy said everything was done proper, the realtor bought it outright."

Dicer shook her head. "No problems except appearances. They are in the real estate business. You just happen to pick the right one."

"That will make Toni's day," Merlo said.

"So you're going ahead?" Mickey asked.

"Yes, I suppose I am. We're not real estate geniuses, but the deal is unbelievable. We couldn't possibly afford that much house otherwise."

"You're okay for closing costs and everything?" Dicer asked.

Jill nodded. "Toni's a miser usually, which is why we're living in that box. We're tripping over each other now and it's time to get a bigger place."

"Is she older than you are?" Dicer asked.

"Yes. She's had a rough go of it growing up."

"Then it's time she enjoys a little of the good life."

Jill shook her head. "Going to grad school and working full time. I don't know how good it will be. But if anyone can handle it, she can."

"Funny, she said the same thing about you," Mickey told her with a companionable squeeze of the arms. "Leiberman doesn't know what a favor he did you."

Dicer nodded her head in agreement. She had read the notes in Merlo's file. None of the behavior the complaints pointed out had arisen during her short stay there. Mickey, who preferred to work alone or with her, had asked to be partnered with her after the first day. Perhaps he had found a kindred spirit; he too had been labeled a trouble-maker and dumped on her after a serious row in the 5th too. A team of misfits was what they were and she had no complaints as long as they did their work, which they did and then some. What had Cafferty called her team? Left shoes for left feet.

Brenda Falvo walked towards Toni in the lobby with her hands extended. "I can tell by the look on your face, that you have good news for me."

Toni chuckled. "Yes."

"Great, then I don't feel so bad about being late. Carla is over at MissTennArk with a client, two actually. We're on a roll this week. You don't have a friend needing a house do you?"

"No, they all have houses."

"I have no problem selling to your enemies either." Falvo laughed. "Come on, I have something that's going to make you very happy. I asked about that extension and no problem, take all the time you need. While you're deciding you can rent it for the amount of your mortgage payment and it'll go into a special ac-count—" Falvo caught herself. "But you've decided right?"

"Right."

"Then my harassing has not been in vain. I got your rate and your payments all spelled out for you. All we need is your signa-tures. The loan is going through the Vengar accounts which mean if you find a lower interest rate in the state, it's illegal." Falvo nearly dragged her into the office. "And it's ready to move in. With Xorron backing you, I see no reason you can't move in as soon as next week."

"That's quick," Toni admitted.

"Right. Since this is almost an in-house deal, we could skip a number of the procedures."

"What do you mean by an in-house deal?"

"Just a deal handled within the company, which is one of the advantages of being an affiliate of Vengar. A lot of the things a small company would go to an outsider for, they can get from another Vengar affiliate at an extremely low cost-high quality rate. Guaranteed. As they say, 'Membership has it's privileges.' Definitely."

"Yeah."

"And there's a few things we need to go over and we can get you copies. Get your lawyer to review it and just give me a holler when you're ready to deal. We can go over to MissTennArk and that's that. We can handle everything from there. How does that sound?"

"Too easy?"

Falvo laughed. "We try to make it as painless as possible. When you get ready for that mansion, come to us and let us get a real commission off of you." Falvo winked and pulled out a folder with Toni's name on it.

Dicer returned to the Gamin Station to begin what was essentially her second shift. The highlight of the day was writing an indecent exposure ticket to a topless buxom blond. There she found several messages from a petty downtown bureaucrat. Three hours of incessant paperwork, she broke for dinner.

Preferring to wear her uniform when patrolling, she received several wry though appraising looks when she entered the Mextown bistro. She had barely taken her seat when Eduardo Trujillo sat down across from her.

"Busted you back to patrol?"

Dicer shook her head and studied the young man. "How long have you been with the Virada?"

"Two years learning operations. I've written a few commentaries, but the police beat is my first assignment as a reporter. It's more political than I imagined it to be and I don't mean police versus citizens. The internal politics, especially downtown and in the 2nd and 3rd. Power plays galore and it's so obvious; it's almost laughable."

Dicer nodded. "You've been busy."

He returned her nod. "I try to do my homework. For instance, your relationship with Ruben Fuentes. It makes me wonder what was said in that meeting before it was interrupted. Want to enlighten me?"

"No."

"Did it have anything to do with NFC?"

"Mr. Trujillo, may I order?" she asked as the waiter approached.

"By all means."

"Thank you." Dicer ordered.

"Ever heard of Pablo Menendez?"

"Didn't he kill his parents?" Dicer quipped.

"He is capable of that, but I don't think he did."

"Nice man?"

"Makes Fuentes look like a saint. You sure you never heard of him?"

"No, I never heard of him."

"So you wouldn't know he was head of a Mexican mafia and he has a church in San Diego that bears a striking resemblance to New Faith's Cathedral?" He watched her closely. "In fact, they are identical."

That peaked her interest. "How did you find that out?"

"Not the usual channels; I consulted a psychic." He winked at her.

"Maybe I should get the name of this psychic."

"You're welcome to use me as an intermediary."

"How generous." Dicer studied him, thinking the most remarkable thing about him was the light behind his eyes giving him a rather ethereal appeal, making his story about the psychic almost believable.

"Yes, it was."

Jill Merlo stretched out in bed as Toni chattered on about the next few weeks, making a to-do list that was already three pages long. Jill yawned.

"Am I boring you?" Toni asked closing her tablet.

"No, you kept me up all last night and I need to go to sleep so I can work an extra shift so we can afford that mansion." She turned over on her side. "I hope you aren't hoping for furniture in the next few years. Nor butter to go with that bread. Shit we'll need to shop the week-old bread bin."

CHAPTER 13

Toni awoke nervous about their four hour trip to Ydyllic with Jill and Elizabeth Arana who had never met. Given Jill's enmity towards everything having to do with Xorron, Toni feared a trip laden with barbs and innuendos. She had gone to bed complaining about riding with Arana and being stuck in a cheesy hotel room all weekend. All week, they had done little beyond argue, about any and everything. "I know you're awake, so get up," Jill said from the doorway. Accustomed to getting up at four-thirty, she had been up for two hours reading through Toni's information packets on Vengar and the foundation.

"I'm still sleepy," Toni groaned and rolled over.

"Tough titty. You wanted to go, so get a move on it. Up. Up." Jill clapped her hands sharply.

Toni sat up looking across at her. "What you on?"

"Just want to get this over with. And breakfast is on the table."

"How kind." Toni rolled out of bed.

Jill loaded her bag into the trunk of Arana's black Chrysler. Strangely she felt deflated that the car was not one of the foreign luxury models that symbolized success. Arana gained another point in her book with the offer to drive the first two hours and she would take the last two into Ydyllic which she knew. Jill gladly took the wheel as Arana and Toni kept up a string of conversation on their trek towards Ydyllic.

Nearly five hours later, after sitting for half an hour on I55, Arana rounded a sharp bend in the road. The colorful vine encircled sign welcomed them to Ydyllic.

"Beautiful city," Jill quipped, seeing nothing but the forest they had seen for the last ten miles.

Arana glanced at her through the mirror. "It really is, we have less than a mile to go before it's evident."

"What is there to do in this town on a Friday night?" Jill asked.

"About anything you want. There should be an event calendar in the rooms."

"Look a gas station!" Jill quipped pointing at the X-Mart.

"Quit, please," Toni murmured.

Arana glanced back at Jill. "I'm taking it as a personal challenge to ensure that this town wins you over before we head back Sunday."

"Oh, I'm overjoyed now," Jill told her.

Toni shot her a withering glance. "I'm sure the bus comes through here."

"Just kidding." Jill reached across and touched her shoulder.

Arana didn't miss the gesture or the tone of voice. They would have to be treated as a pair, not just a student with a spouse. She drove across town through the tree-lined streets to the Ydyllic Inn with its blue banners blowing in the hot wind. A yellow shirted valet and bellhop came out and unloaded their bags.

Jill noted Arana's familiar exchange with the bellhop. The lobby, thankfully cool, was all marble and exposed beams with live green plants. The young blonde woman at the front desk waited with a patient smile for them to cross the lobby, as they side-stepped a group of Chinese women.

"May your goddess treat you kindly," Arana greeted the clerk.

"May your goddess be just," came her response. The clerk slid a small folder and signature card to Arana. "1428."

"Thank you." Arana stepped aside.

"Toni Jensen."

The clerk extracted two folders from a file box. "1416. Please check the info, correct if necessary, and sign the cards. Registration is in 1400. Everything is taken care of except long distance phone calls. Would you like to leave your credit card imprint or shall we bill you?"

"We have phone cards," Jill told her, sliding the card back.

"Very well. Enjoy your stay, Ms. Merlo."

"I'll be sure to try. Do you have a swimming pool?"

"Yes. There is a full gym as well."

"Thank you," Toni said pushing her card across the counter.

"Enjoy your stay, Ms. Jensen."

The three women went up to the fourteenth floor where the bellhop waited on the elevator. "If you need anything, my name is Juan," he said, nodded slightly and stepped onto the elevator.

"Right nice of you, Juan," Jill told him.

"You want to meet in half an hour at registration? It'll give us time to freshen up and we can decide on where to go for lunch," Arana said.

"Yes. I'll see you then." Toni followed Jill around the corner to their room.

Jill unlocked the door and stepped into the airy suite. "Damn," she said. "It's bigger than our apartment."

"And better furnished." Toni sat down on the sofa as Jill checked out the kitchenette, opening cabinets and the refrigerator.

"Want something to drink? Looks like the beverage of choice is something called Brezzo and we have a shitload of it. Peach, cranberry, strawberry, pineapple-orange and something I never heard of. Ba-cu-ri and Mu-ru-ci or some shit."

"Probably four bucks a bottle."

"No, it's complimentary, says so right here on the tray. Here, you try the Bacuri and I'll try the muruci." Jill took the pint-size bottles to the sofa, glancing at the fruit basket on the table. "Fruit too."

"Yep." She took the bottle from Jill and stood up. "I'm going to the bathroom."

"I'll just sit here, turn on the tube, and see what this Ydyllic place have to offer big city girls like us." Jill pulled the stack of brochures and circulars on the coffee table to her. It didn't take her long to realize the city was not only women-friendly, but the mayor, chief of police and most of the leading businessowners were women. Holding up the flyer for the Mexicali festival starting today, not far from them, Jill walked to the bedroom. "Toni, is your thing all day tomorrow because I . . . " she trailed to a stop, appreciating Toni's body as she changed her blouse.

"You what?"

"Huh?"

"You want to do what tomorrow?" Toni slipped on her blouse.

"Oh, go to this Mexicali festival tomorrow."

"I don't know, that's why we're going to registration." Toni checked her watch.

"What were you doing in here so long anyway?" Jill asked.

"Upset stomach."

"Again?"

"You know how I am."

Jill nodded. "You take something?"

"Yeah. That Brezzo thing and Tums."

"Oh, mine was good. Yours?"

"Yeah. Let's go."

"Wait, I need to go." Jill went into the bathroom, immediately comparing it to the Sunray house and not their apartment. They had moved most of their unessential things and would move the rest during the week. Of course, Toni was more excited than she was, although she wouldn't admit to any excitement at all.

The registration room, 1400, was a meeting room where half a dozen young people were seated filling out forms and/or talking to a purple shirted individual. Arana detached herself from a purple-shirt when she saw them.

"There you are. There are a couple of people I want to introduce you to." She led them across the room to two woman at a computer terminal, processing a young man's forms. "Got a second, Parker?" Arana asked.

The gray-haired woman looked up. "Of course." She turned to the young man. "You're all taken care of, just wait for your printout." She walked around the table, a half-smile on her lips, as if she was born with it and would die with it there.

"This is Toni Jensen and her partner Jill Merlo. Ladies, the venerable Ms. Parker. She's taken care of everyone for twenty years, making life so much easier for us, always finding that little extra to tide us over."

Parker took Toni's hand. "Welcome aboard, Toni. Glad you could make it." She glanced at Jill. "You as well, Ms. Merlo. Perhaps we can find a program for you as well."

"No thanks, one recipient of your largesse is enough in the family," Jill said in a tone just short of a sneer.

Parker appraised her with a lazy eye. "I hope it is us and not Toni you resent; it will be quite difficult for her to battle you and adapt to her new environment. Either you allow us to alleviate your fears or you adopt a new attitude, young lady."

Jill glanced at Toni who suppressed her grin and Arana who turned away. "Then you can start with this hotel. How much money are you blowing by having your meeting here as opposed to the Motel 7?"

"It's not costing us anything and Motel 7 wouldn't give us a break. Our normal meeting hall is closed for renovations and the manager was kind enough to lend us the 14th floor."

"Isn't the hotel losing money by letting you use an entire floor?" Jill asked.

"No, it's a special floor and would be empty otherwise."

"Why?"

Annoyed Toni touched Jill's arm. "She's a police officer," she said as a manner of explanation.

Parker shook her head. "No need to apologize, her points are valid." She waved a woman with braids and wire-rimmed glasses over. "Ladies this is the new director of the DIC Foundation, just appointed July first, Randi Woodson. Randi this is Toni and Jill;

Jill is a police officer and worried about our intentions towards Toni."

Randi shook their hands warmly. "I can understand your concern. Not too long ago I had them as well, but Ms. Parker walked me through the process, holding my hand with each step."

"Now she holds my hand, making sure Futures has a future."

"It will as long as the foundation exists for Futures is the epitome of our existence."

"Am I understanding that you were a recipient of one of these scholarships?" Toni asked.

"Yes. Undergraduate. I was twenty-five and giving up the roaming life. I ended up here with an aunt who knew of this program. I applied and here I am."

Parker nodded. "Don't let her nonchalance fool you. There was a lot of hard work in between applying and becoming director of the foundation."

"A labor of love," Randi assured them. "Parker would say the same."

"Definitely," Parker agreed.

"Well rehearsed," Jill said.

Parker laughed. "You're a tough cookie, Ms. Merlo."

Randi glanced from Parker to Jill. "Have I missed something?"

"Toni is on a Rex special and Jill is a bit leery of us," Parker explained.

Randi nodded. "Ah, the Rex-treatment. She can be like a steamroller at times. Trust me, I know; but when it comes to the participants in the programs, you are safer than you can imagine."

"Spoken like a true apostle," Jill said. "You've come up through the system and you're now head huncho, what else can you say but good things about the program."

Randi chuckled. "You're right and I can say those things because I did come up through it and I am now director which means I'm going to insure that students with special needs and talents get what they need to succeed. It took me a long time to understand that my goals in life were not contradictory to the foundation which is fundamentally the ideals of Rex Xorron. Ten years ago, I had no idea that I'd be running a multimillion dollar international foundation. And whatever Rex is up to with you, don't let it interfere with the simple fact that, improbable as it seems, she does care about you and your education; and your responsibility is to your studies, not Rex. She may think of you as her children, but you're not required to act like a petulant child."

"Was I just reprimanded?" Jill asked lightly.

"Yes, so chill," Toni told her. "You promised."

"Must be my empty stomach complaining. Don't you feed your children?"

Randi suppressed a grin. "Tonight, but for now the restaurant downstairs will gladly fill your empty stomach. Now if you'll go over to that table in the corner with that bored young man, you can get your packets, which will tell you all about the weekend's events. Now if you'll excuse me, I have a meeting. Nice meeting you and I'll see you back here tonight." Randi slipped away before Jill could go on the offensive again. Parker had been gently pulled away and Arana was at a table with a middle-age woman.

"I can't believe you're acting like this," Toni hissed under her breath. "These people have been nothing but kind to us and you're cutting up like this. You have any idea how that makes me look?"

"Like I won't give you up without a fight."

Toni turned to her. "You're not giving me up, Jill. This isn't a contest of loyalty either." Shaking her head she walked over to the freckled young man with the sandy hair. "Good afternoon, I'm Toni Jensen." She realized he was just a teenager.

"Hi, I'm Geoff." He reached for a leather planner with her name emblazoned on it. "Inside is everything you need including your Foundation card which will get you into several places listed on the back and even some that aren't. You are in Group G which has nine members which are listed here along with the other groups members." He slid her a sheet of names.

A woman in her forties with short hair walked over, placed a hand on the young man's shoulder. "How is it going, sweetie?"

"Just fine, mom. I was just telling Ms. Toni how it all worked." He glanced down at a list, then reached for another planner. "Where's your partner, this is hers."

Toni turned to see where Jill had escaped to and saw that she had been cornered by a small child about six or seven. "With that little girl."

"Freda!" the young man called. "Leave her alone, she needs to come over here."

"Don't yell at me, boy," the child called back.

"Don't make me send you both home," the woman told them quietly without ire.

"What are these other groups?" Toni asked, noting five groups.

"One is our new undergraduate students, one is our gender studies students from three campuses, one is our exchange students from two campuses, one is our graduate student group and the fifth group is a mixed group of former and current participants. The latter two are staying here."

"And the others?"

"They're staying at home or at a boarding house-style dorm near campus. They've been here all week and are about tired of our friendly advice and forced comraderie."

"I didn't get your name," Toni said.

"Opal West, program coordinator."

"Which means what?" Jill asked.

"Which means I make sure we have programs to fit the needs of targeted groups."

"Say again."

"I find the money and reason for Ms. Parker to give it away. I also review the programs use of funds and whether or not they should receive less or more."

"Then what does Ms. Woodson do?" Jill asked.

"The Foundation has obligations other than our academic programs and she is responsible for those as well."

"Here," Toni handed Jill her dayplanner.

"And you are?" West asked Jill.

"Jill Merlo, Toni's partner."

"Welcome to Ydyllic." West shook her hand. "There are t-shirts over here. Why don't you select your favorite size and color to wear to the picnic tomorrow. Your nametags are in the back of the planner."

Geoff came over. "Can I go to the festival now?"

"Yes, thanks for subbing for me."

"No problem, mamacita." He handed her a key from around his neck. "Later."

Fifteen minutes later, Jill, Toni and Arana left the hotel and drove down to a Thai restaurant next to the university, then a quick car tour of the campus.

"Where would you like to go now?" Arana asked.

"Where does Xorron live and work?" Jill asked.

"Please don't start, Jill," Toni said. Jill had been relatively civil since leaving the hotel.

"I'm just asking."

"She lives to the south, near where the picnic is tomorrow; but Vengar is just northwest of the Inn on the lake. I'm sure we could finagle a tour." Arana headed the car northward.

Xorron was in a long meeting when they arrived, but a young purple-clad pager gave them the five-dollar tour of the three-story villa with the enclosed courtyard, the daycare, and spectacular view of the lake. They were leaving the media center when an auburn haired woman passed them on the hall. Jill stopped in her tracks, frowned then headed for the woman.

"Excuse me!" she called as the woman placed a hand on a door at the end of the hall.

The woman turned. "Yes?"

"Have you ever been to Metrox?"

"Metrox? Not that I recall. Why?"

"I could have sworn I saw you outside of a church."

She laughed. "Then that definitely was not me."

"Then you have a twin out there."

"So I've been told." Her wristwatch beeped. "If you'll excuse me, I'm wanted inside."

"My apologies." Jill stepped back as the woman entered the door, noting the small plaque on the wall simply said, "security." Deep in thought she returned to Toni and Arana who were back in the lobby.

"Where did you run off to?" Toni asked.

"I thought I saw someone I knew."

"Was it them?"

"No, but it could have been her sister." Or she was lying. She indeed matched the description of Fuentes' rescuer and looked like the woman they got on film in front of the NFC. Was there a way to get a photograph of the woman as she left the building? She had to let Dicer know about this. "Are we headed back to the hotel?"

"Yes. Dinner's at seven." Arana led them out into the heat which felt hotter than when they entered the building.

"At least they had the good sense to have the picnic early tomorrow," Jill mused.

"Yes. It gives the students time to make the festival in the evening before they head out Sunday."

"Where can I rent a car?" Jill said suddenly.

"At the Inn. Since you're making such an impression on the foundation people, I'm sure they'll lend you one."

"Funny," Jill said.

Arana glanced back at her. "I'm serious, especially tomorrow."

"No thanks, I don't want them doing me any favors."

"Suit yourself." Arana drove them back to the hotel.

Jill called Dicer to fill her in on the auburn-haired woman and to get an update on what she had missed in the last twenty-four hours. As expected very little had changed.

When Toni emerged from the shower, Jill lay in bed reading with her feet up. "All yours."

"I'm not going," Jill said without looking up.

"Let's not start this again."

"I'm damned if I do and damned if I don't. All your smarty friends talking to me like I'm an idiot."

"Who? And if you think that, it's because you've been acting like one. What's wrong with you anyway? You said you would come to check them out, not harass them."

"I'm sick of all of this syrupy sweet shit. 'Believe it or not Xorron really cares.' Yeah right. I'd prefer to see a foreign film without subtitles rather than spend two more hours hearing how great everything is."

"I don't think they're going to do that. Come one, get up."

Jill stared at her then sat up. "I hope you realize how much I love you to put up with these people."

Toni embraced her. "I do baby. I do."

Dinner was buffet-style with three tables laden with food. Another section of 1400 was open and the guests mingled freely exchanging numbers with each other. Jill and Toni joined Parker and two students near the nonalcoholic bar. As the guests settled down Opal West moved to the podium.

"Good evening, I just want to welcome you this evening. I know how much you love speeches so I've asked a few long-winded friends—" Several groans went up from the younger students. "Okay, some of you have had a week of long-winded speeches. And we've appreciated your bearing with us, so I won't subject you to anymore. So without further ado, I present to you the woman who made this whole week bearable for you, vice-president of Vengar, Dizzy Dean."

"Here we go again," Jill whispered. "My teeth are already aching.

Dizzy Dean was a cafe au lait woman in casual attire with her hair pulled loosely back. "I want to talk to you this evening about the devil and Elvis Presley. Once upon a town not too too far away, a white boy thought he could rock, but the only roll he had was on his mother's dimestore table. . . ."

Jill found herself laughing hysterically with the others as the VP continued her little story, making frequent rambling asides that somehow tied into the story making it even more hilarious.

" . . . and the devil responded, a hunk-a-hunk of burning love," Dean finished and took her seat to wild applause and catcalls.

Wiping her eyes West took the podium. "What can I say but enjoy your dinner, mingle, and I'll see you in the morning."

Toni leaned into Jill. "Enough of a nasty edge for you?"

"Yes." Jill rose. "Can I bring you anything?"

"No, I'm stuffed."

At the bar Jill ordered their drinks and turned. Her eyes fell on a long-legged woman slicing between the tables. Rex Xorron stopped at the table with West and several students.

"Here you are," the bartender said behind her.

"Thanks." Jill took the glasses back to her table where another woman had replaced Parker. She would make it her business to speak with Xorron before the trip was over.

CHAPTER 14

Sunday morning Dicer stared at the white board with her colored scribbles. Everything she knew about the case was on that board, the case literally laid out for her. She knew who, what, where but not when and how. The NFC had eluded their traps and wiretaps. Now it was a war of stamina. Could the NFC curtail their activities long enough to outlast police surveillance? Hopefully the pressure would get to them forcing them to make a mistake; if not she would have to force their hand somehow.

As she stared at the board, a pattern began to form but there was a random element that didn't quite fit. Who had caught and downed Wallace? Who was the auburn-haired woman with Fuentes? And why was Trujillo camping out downstairs? What if Merlo was right and the auburn-haired woman worked for Xorron? Trujillo worked for Xorron. Xorron bought much of the Fuentes real estate. According to Mickey she had bought up much of Boxtown. Why?

Rising, she pulled down a map of the 5th precinct which incorporated Boxtown. Getting the colored pins and Mickey's list, she plotted Xorron's incursion into the area against the NFC and its leaders' holdings. Nothing, Xorron was concentrating in the older neighborhoods like Boxtown, Oldtown, and Mextown, but the NFC people were in the newer, more expensive areas of the city.

"Ugh! I need a fucking clue!" Dicer slapped her chest, feeling the amulet Fuentes had given her beneath her shirt. Inexplicably she had put it on after Demetria arrived. Demetria, sweet and too wise. Fuentes had been both right and wrong about her. No, she wasn't hardened, but she wasn't innocent either. She freely condemned her father's illegal activities, but she did not for a minute consider giving up the condo he had left for her. Lately Demetria and Nikki had come up with the idea of their sharing the condo. Dicer had remained silent on the subject of her favorite cousin moving into a dwelling most likely purchased with illegal earnings from a notorious crime figure, relative or not.

A knock sounded on her door which she had locked. Dicer unlocked the door to admit Mickey. "What are you doing here?" she asked him.

"Knew I'd find you here." He closed the door behind him. "Lab results are negative on the bread and juice. Sorry."

"I didn't expect anything else." But she had hoped.

"We said someone is either getting hurt by our vigilance or they're dumping it somewhere else. Where do you suppose that would be?" He rocked back on his heels. "That was our problem. Yesterday."

Dicer slowly raised her eyes to meet his. "What you know?"

He glanced at her board and the map. "I did what you said about putting out the word that some adulterated shit had hit the streets."

"Where?"

"Carrollton." Carrollton contained the ghetto of the city.

"And?" she said tempering her excitement.

"Word came out of Mextown that GreenTarts were dirt cheap."

"Who?"

"Scott Thorn's people. Only . . . " He frowned.

"Only what?"

"Only Thorn's people have a new ally, some serious latino muscle."

"Pablo Menendez!" Dicer blurted out.

"You've been holding out on me!" he accused.

"No. No. A little birdie told me that." Trujillo. Why hadn't she thought he'd move east. "Look, I haven't run across any vice reports on Pablo Menendez in this town. I need you to find out everything you can on his time here. I'll give you the report from San Diego on him."

"You have a jacket on him?"

"Mexican mafia." Dicer dug the file out of her locked desk drawer. "He's a nasty s.o.b. and we should alert Shuler and Leiberman to the likelihood of increased violence in Mextown, OldTown and perhaps Boxtown." Dicer spun towards the map. "Shit!"

"What?"

"Those were the places Xorron was buying up. Was that a defensive move?" Dicer tripped over a chair getting to the table and Mickey's Xorron files. "Didn't you have a security firm listed somewhere?"

Mickey followed her to the table, fishing through the file. "V-Sec was bonded here last year, but not listed as a Vengar company, but it is headquartered in Ydyllic. I thought that wasn't a coincidence."

"Fuck! Why hadn't no one seen this pattern?"

"It's a large city and a lot of business is going down. Companies coming and going." He picked up a report he had gotten from the YPD. "They usually keep a somewhat mellow profile when it comes to their business dealings."

"But with a security firm, they can legally arm a small army," Dicer mused.

"And have all kinds of clients," Mickey finished her thought.

Dicer's hand reflexively went to the amulet under her shirt. On closer examination of the amulet, she had discovered it was a tiny beacon-style transmitter that would activate if pressed in a certain manner. Otu had checked to see whether it was a standard bug as well. More and more she wondered who would respond if she activated it. First she would try the direct approach. "Mickey get me the number and address for this security firm. It's time we became familiar."

Toni, Jill, and Arana had a significantly larger load than when they arrived after visiting the World Bazaar in St. Maria's Li'l Rio.

"Admit you had a good time," Toni teased Jill after a round of goodbyes in the lobby. They had had a three hour working lunch before checking out. By then everyone was quite familiar, thus comfortable with each other after a day of frolicking, shopping, and carousing together.

"I'll admit to nothing," Jill said with her wry smile.

"You don't need to; it's written all over your face." Toni hooked her arm through hers. Whatever Opal West said to her at the picnic when she had taken her aside had worked a miracle on Jill's attitude.

"Okay, so I enjoyed the picnic games and the club last night." They had borrowed a hotel minibus and gone to St. Maria's to a blues club.

"Good, you should be much better company the next few days."

"Which means I had been bad company?" Jill asked sardonically.

"I wouldn't say that."

"You don't have to."

Elizabeth Arana separated from a small group and joined them. "Ready, ladies?"

"As ready as ever," Jill retorted.

"Let's hit it then."

"Is there a place in Metrox where we can get that Brezzo?" Jill asked Arana.

"Boxtown, at the market off of Topaz at Pacific."

"Near the music store?" Toni asked.

"Yes."

"What are they going to put in that gray building on the corner?" Toni asked when they were seated in the car.

"A restaurant and office space, I believe. A gallery had been proposed at one point." Arana eased out of the tight parking slot the valet had squeezed the car into. "I don't know what happened to that idea," she said when the car was clear.

Jill leaned on the front seat. "Dr. Arana, what is your relationship to that gorgeous young man you had breakfast with this morning?"

Arana laughed. "One of my many cousins."

"Most of whom migrated to St. Maria's," Jill said. They had met a half dozen Aranas while in Li'l Rio the day before; one woman worked in the World Bazaar and gave them employee discounts; another managed the restaurant where they had dinner; and still another managed a lakeshore hotel that overlooked the human-enhanced beach.

"Many, yes."

"And why aren't you running a store or restaurant or something?" Jill asked.

"What makes you think I'm not?" Arana asked with a glint in her eye. Jill had asked little if anything about her the entire weekend.

"Well nothing. Being a dean must be time consuming?"

"Associate dean and it does keep me busy with the IC center."

"What kind of business do you have?" Jill asked.

"I don't. Education is my business."

"You're awfully young to be a dean of any kind aren't you?"

Arana chuckled.

"Get that a lot do you?" Toni asked.

"Yes. I'm not as young as I look and not easily impressed or intimidated, which comes in handy in Metrox."

"Anywhere these days."

"Got that right." They settled into easy banter as they headed back to Metrox.

All afternoon Dicer called the V-Sec number and got only a recording, finally giving up and going home to get a little rest before beginning the week.

In the early morning darkness, Dicer reached for the ringing phone. "Dicer," she said sleepily.

"Lieutenant, Sgt. Abrams from the Fifth, we've got a situation at Commerce and Wyoming. Your presence is deemed necessary."

"What kind of situation?" Dicer asked, switching hands as she turned on the light to look for her clothing.

"Your GreenTarts."

"On my way, Wyoming and Commerce?"

"That's it."

Dicer hurriedly dressed and drove to the downtown intersection which was unusually lit by police strobes. A yellow van had collided with a steel light pole and its rear doors stood open. Two men shouted at the officers from inside of the van.

"What are they saying?" Dicer asked the officer with the microphone.

Exasperated, he glanced at her. "About the aliens or about their cargo which is strewn for fifty yards?"

"The cargo?"

"They are simply movers."

"Mules you mean."

He shrugged. "Perhaps. They lost seven boxes, three contained GreenTarts. Lollipops and straws."

"Shit!" Their worst nightmare was about to hit the streets. Dicer steeled herself. "And the aliens?"

"The driver says an alien appeared in the cab and ran him into the pole. Half an hour ago, they started shooting at the sky, saying we were pod people waiting to take them to the aliens." He shook his head.

"They're trying a mental?" Dicer asked trying to see into the van from behind the barricade.

"They're making a reasonable attempt at it. Abrams phoned that new shrink too. She should be here soon."

"Great, just what we need, someone to humor our little abductees." Dicer reached for someone's fieldglasses to look inside the van. The driver turned his head and her stomach flipflopped. "Fucking asshole!" She threw down the glasses and swiped the megaphone, stepping from behind the barricade. "Kenny! You stupid sonofabitch, throw down that weapon and get out." A volley of shots was their response.

"Hold you fire!" Lt. Watson shouted. "Are you crazy?!" he yelled at Dicer who had ducked back behind the barricade.

"The jury's still out," Aviles said, suddenly at his side. "I take it you know them?"

"I'm in a bad TV movie. That's my cousin Kenny."

"And the other fellow?" Aviles asked picking up the fieldglasses.

"I didn't get a good look at him." Dicer massaged her forehead.

"Lt. Watson, shouldn't you be negotiating their surrender?" Aviles asked evenly.

Watson glanced at Dicer. "I'm doing the best I can with my limited experience with extraterrestrials ma'am."

"I beg your pardon?" Aviles lowered the glasses to look at him.

"They say aliens caused their crash and we are agents for the E.T.s, ma'am."

Aviles groaned. "The press is going to eat this up."

The words were not out of her mouth as a piercing *SHREEEEK* filled the air and the yellow van exploded. The forceful blast shattered windows in nearby buildings and rocked police cars, knocking several officers to the ground.

"What the fuck was that?" Aviles shouted as she huddled behind a car.

"Fucking missile!" Lt. Watson shouted as he ventured from behind the barricade towards the burning van.

A second *SHREEEEK* ended with the explosion of the EMT van on the opposite side of the street.

"Move! Move! Move!" Watson waved his people back not knowing if they would be targeted next. The EMT team stood helplessly watching the remains of their van. "Get them out of there!"

Watson shouted. Two members of his team sprinted towards them as an awful caustic smell filled the night air.

Numb Dicer stared. "You need a chemical spill team," she said softly.

"What?" Aviles asked.

Dicer shook herself out of her stupor at watching her cousin die. "Chemicals; they were carrying ether and acetone and who knows what else," she said pointing to the burning ring around devastated van.

"Shit!" Aviles raised the megaphone to her lips as she held her phone in the other. "Stay back! Do not approach the suspects' vehicle! Do not approach!"

Sirens sounded in the distance while a dozen officers stood helplessly watching.

Watson, face glistening, yelled into his radio. "It had to come from somewhere!" He looked up in the sky as if expecting another attack or aircraft. "Anything large enough to carry anything bigger than a shotgun. . . . I know goddamn it. Close the whole goddamn city if necessary . . . I don't give a fuck . . . No! No!" He thrust the radio into Aviles hand. "You tell them!"

"Someone should wake the mayor," Dicer mumbled and turned away.

"Where are you going?" Aviles called after her.

"Tell my aunt her son is dead." With a little help from her mother.

Carolyn Goddard-Dicer knew someone was dead when she saw her oldest daughter's strickened face as she opened the door.

"Who?" she asked, pulling her robe closer against the icy fingers of death.

"Kenny." Dicer walked into the front room of the northtown condo. She never appreciated how successful her mother was until she entered the condo her mother had bought to avoid upkeep around the house. The condo was her sanctuary from the outside world. Like Dicer, she preferred not to bring her work home, thus spending long hours in her office, including weekends.

"What happened?"

"He was transporting drugs, the van hit a pole, then someone blew it up?"

"The police?"

Dicer shook her head. "A missile. We don't have those," she sneered.

"A missile?" Carolyn asked frowning. Things like that did not happen in Metrox. Did they?

"Where's your television?"

"Den." Carolyn turned away to get dressed.

The media was all over the story on a slow news Monday in July. The mayor and the chief made statements to repudiate early reports that the police had blown up the vans and to declare that such unlawfulness would not be tolerated in their town while assuring the public that their best investigators were on the scene. "No, your best investigator has been yanked. Again!" Lou Ayers yelled at the screen in the break room. It was his first day back and he had to tell Dicer that she was off the case if he could find her; downtown thought she was no longer objective given the identity of one of the victims. Somewhere the fact that drugs were involved had been completely overlooked in their statements. Even the media was downplaying it against the missile attack as being an attack on the city, which it was. However, Mickey had filled him in on their latest theory and the Mexican mafia.

The screen flashed the names of the two victims who had been tentatively identified, as Ramon Wallace and Kenneth Goddard. "Fucking buzzards!" Ayers exclaimed again as they connected Kenneth to Dicer showing her photo. "How the fuck they expect her to do her job with them flashing her picture on the television like that?"

"I think that's the point," Cafferty said from the doorway. The motherly commander of the Gamin Station crossed the room to pour herself a cup of coffee. "And for once I think she should back off."

"Why?"

"You think it was a coincidence it was her cousin who died by a missile?"

Ayers' blood ran cold. "You don't think . . . ?"

"I keep out of your cases, but I can't help but pick up tidbits here and there. She knows something, but can't prove it. That makes for a very precarious position in this town." She looked at him. "Or have you forgotten your own house?" She walked out.

The rain fell softly, mirroring Dicer's mood as she entered the Laredo street building on her way to V-Sec Security on the fifth floor. Until two years ago, the historical granite building had been an eyesore, but like much of the area it had received an extensive makeover.

The elevator let her off on the fifth floor, but her progress was stopped by a layer of security doors.

"Identification please?" a disembodied voice said.

Dicer took out her wallet and waved it around until the first set of doors slid open, then the others allowing her into a typical gray and burgundy corporate office. She nearly grinned at the big-haired receptionist waving a nail file as she gossiped into a headset smacking gum; then she remembered where she was.

"Quite a performance," said a quiet voice behind her.

Dicer turned to see the auburn-haired woman who had pushed her in the van. "Nice to see you again."

"This way, lieutenant," she said motioning down the hall to her right.

"Why do I feel I was expected?" Dicer asked as she entered a small cozy office with an early lunch laid out.

"You were." Sparrow motioned to a chair at the small table. "Please, have a seat."

Her empty stomach led her to accept the invitation to lunch. "Thank you."

"We must keep our strength up." Sparrow filled their glasses from the chilled pitcher.

"How's Fuentes?" Dicer asked.

"I have no idea." Sparrow raised one of the stuffed pastries to her lips. "Don't be shy."

Dicer tentatively tried a pastry and found herself ravenous for the seafood. "Have you seen the news?"

"You're off the case," Sparrow informed her.

Dicer didn't doubt the validity of the statement. "Figured as much."

"Why did you come here? Are you looking for a job?"

"No, I'm looking for answers. Answers that I believe you have." Dicer helped herself to the juice.

"Depends on the question."

"How do I get to Pablo Menendez?"

"Not by banging on the front door."

"What do you mean?" Dicer asked.

"Remove surveillance from NFC."

"Can't do."

"Yes, you can. The brass is already complaining about the manhours on this. Humor them."

"How do I know you're not working for Menendez?"

Sparrow shrugged. "You came looking for me. How'd you piece it together anyway?"

"One of my officers saw you in Ydyllic."

Sparrow smiled. "Wasn't me, but that's irrelevant at the moment."

"You were telling me how to get to Menendez," Dicer said after a long pause.

"Can't do that."

"Can't or won't?"

"Can't." Sparrow met her eyes. "He's not in the city and the feds have been after him for years. What makes you think you can get to him? Or build a case against him?"

"Unlike others, I want him."

Sparrow chuckled. "Well that is a sufficient reason. Lt. Dicer, I am not unfamiliar with the innerworkings of your department nor your chief's uncharacteristic support of your unorthodox style.

Yet he's allowed Stein and Aviles to yank your chain for the last
two weeks. Why do you think that is so?"

Dicer shrugged. "What does this have to do with Menendez?"

"Could it be you have exhausted your usefulness to him? Or is
he distancing himself from you? Have you been too successful in
your mission? Has Aviles been too close to you recently? What will
be her reaction when she discovers your relationship with Fuentes?
What of the allegations that you are living way beyond your means
in the canyon? Do you think that inventory was just a diversionary
tactic? When was the last time your team was evaluated? Your
books audited? How long do you think captains will come to you
for miscellaneous, though valuable, equipment before they decide
to deal themselves into the game? You took them by surprise before, but they have sharpen their own skills and are ready to do
battle. The only problem is that you don't know which war you
should be fighting. When they splashed your mug on the tele this
morning, it became one and the same." Sparrow rose, retrieved an
envelope and handed it to Dicer.

"Sun Tzu reminds us that a good strategist must create a situation to which his enemy must react. Pablo Menendez has been
successful because that is his strategy. You must not allow him to
dictate the time and place. I say to you now, lieutenant, gather
your troops around you and defend yourself.

Dicer shrugged. "I always believe the best defense is a good
offense."

"Not when your strength is inadequate and your enemies know
your strategy."

"I can't sit back and do nothing; that was my own flesh and
blood killed out there this morning."

Sparrow shook her head. "Perhaps you misunderstood me;
defending yourself you must be active in doing so. Some may be
willing to sacrifice their troops, but you're not. This I know; therefore, you shall defend them against your enemies' attacks. Believe
me, the situation will arise where your preparation can be used to
your advantage."

Dicer studied her. "What are you saying?"

Sparrow pursed her lips. "Remember the three little pigs?"

"The three little pigs?" Dicer stared at her. "You've gone from ancient military strategy to fairy tales?"

"They do have their points. Consider Menendez the big bad wolf and your survival depends on how you built your house."

The door opened, a bearded man looked in. "They're waiting on your go ahead."

"I'll be there shortly," Sparrow told him and turned her attention back to Dicer. "Never let your enemies know your true strengths or weaknesses; he can always adjust.

Pull the surveillance off of NFC. Warfare is riddled with deceptions. I'll see you out."

Dicer returned to the Gamin Station and indeed withdrew all of the surveillance on the NFC and its leadership. Then she ordered everyone on regular patrol until further notice, everyone except Mickey and Merlo. She had a special assignment for them.

CHAPTER 15

When Toni Jensen arrived at work that morning, three times the normal number of claims were in her bin. Her complaint fell on deaf ears. When there were even more after her return from lunch, she again went to the supervisor's office.

"We all most share the load," he told her, then dismissed her.

Throughout the afternoon, he checked in on her every half hour, even reprimanding her for a restroom break. Knowing he was baiting her, she held her tongue until most of the workers had clocked out at five.

"Mr. Coombs," Toni called walking towards him as he headed for the front door.

"What is it now?" he asked. "I have an appointment."

"What are you trying to accomplish by loading me down with work?"

"You have a normal workload, if you can't handle it, say so and I'll find a position more suitable to your intellectual abilities."

Toni was taken aback. "You're jealous, pure and simple."

"Ms. Jensen, I suggest you use this time to catch up on your files. Excuse me." He walked off.

"Little dick motherfucker," she muttered and turned around to put in another hour or so.

"Toni!" Jill called coming through the glass door.

Toni turned with a smile. "Hey. What are you doing here?"

"Passing by, saw your car and remembered that you still owed me dinner. I'm here to collect. What do you say?"

"Let me get my things. Come on back."

For two days Dicer cooled her heels, tightening up her defenses and plugging holes, real and imaginary. She was operating under the assumption that her enemies were closing in fast and they would go after her team to weaken her position first. After distributing thirty-one memos, she received a summons from the chief to meet him at the Regency Club.

Chief Harmon waited in a private room with a tray of cheeses and crackers. He waved her towards the leather chair across from him as he popped a cracker into his mouth.

"How are you?" Dicer asked.

"Better if you would stop the paper sorties."

"Just following procedures." To the letter.

"Going page by page." He refilled his wine glass. "Six of your officers are working patrol?"

"Yes, sir. Cafferty is short-handed with vacationing officers and they are very good at what they do."

"No doubt, they have the largest vocabulary on the streets, which they use in their beautifully written reports. Johnson should try his hand at fiction, the flowery sonofabitch." He sipped his wine. "When I came up, none of your officers would have made it through the probationary period. If they did, they would have been one tough bastard. No, instead of weeding them out, we ship them to you to tap into their police officer souls and bring it forth to serve and protect. You know what I don't like about you, Dicer?"

"No, sir."

"Your goddamn lack of ambition. If I were given half the leeway you were given—"

"You wouldn't be half the man you are," Dicer told him.

He nodded. "Some cocksucker would have put my head in the toilet. But no, these bastards write fucking memos when they should kick your fucking ass."

"Try to, you mean," Dicer corrected.

He chuckled. "Yes, try to kick your ass." He picked up another cracker. "Stein was not thrilled at the two file boxes and basket of peaches you sent him. Nice touch. I didn't think you had such subtlety in you."

The peaches had been Mickey's idea. "Chief—"

He raised a hand. "Ahh. I called this meeting. You listen."

Dicer settled back into her chair. "Freeing NFC and writing those seemingly innocuous memos, not to mention your reports have left them wondering about your emotional stability." He pulled an envelope from under the table. "That's why I'm sending you to therapy five days a week, starting tomorrow. Your refusal will result in automatic suspension."

"For what?"

"You did watch your cousin die with a truckload of drugs. There's enough conflict to work out for anyone and given the events of the past month, it is imperative that we can be assured of your fitness for duty."

"I have a right to face my accusers."

"I say go to the shrink. The new one is a woman so that should suit you just fine. No excuses."

"Can I speak now?"

"No, you've been talking too much this week, albeit in written form. Go, write more memos, just don't send them my way; I may consider it insubordination."

"Yes sir." Dicer rose. "Can I ask you one question?"

"If you promise not to write a memo reminding me of this conversation."

"Wouldn't think of it. Which one of us is expendable, me or Aviles?"

"To answer that would weaken your respect for me and I couldn't live with that. Good-bye, Dicer."

"Bye, sir." Dicer quickly left the club and into her car to open the envelope. "Sonofabitch!" She hit the steering wheel.

As she drove toward the Gamin Station with every intent of kicking serious ass, she heard the Sparrow's voice warning her that all warfare was based on deception. A block from the stationhouse, she turned north.

Carolyn Goddard-Dicer met her daughter at her office door. "I just got off the phone with your father; he'll be here tomorrow evening for the wake. Nikki is picking up Kylar about now."

"Any word from Keven?"

"If he can make it, it will be Saturday morning."

Dicer flopped onto the settee and perused the office. "I don't know why I'm here, mother."

"I'm glad you stopped by anyway." Carolyn sat next to her daughter, then took her hands in hers.

"Up until now, it's all been so easy for me. Now I don't know who I can trust or what is true anymore. Hell, I don't know if I'm awake or dreaming." She ran a hand through her hair. "The chief is sending me to therapy to see if I'm fit for duty. The funny thing is, I don't quite know myself."

"You and Kenny were close once."

Dicer rose. "Every time I look out my window and see that little crooked capstone, I tell myself that I could have done something more to steer him off the path he was headed down."

"You can't beat yourself up over this, Ki. You did more than anyone; you couldn't have done more without becoming the enabler his mother was. Even Irene." Carolyn shook her head. "She's really taking this hard."

"That's what Kris told me." The phone buzzed, but her mother didn't bother to answer it. "How's Mae?"

"About what you'd expect."

The door opened and a young man entered. "Excuse me, but Pritchard is in a state."

"I'll be right there."

"Yes, ma'am." He let himself out quietly.

Dicer sighed. "I need to get back to Gamin."

"You want me to come by after I leave Mae's this evening?" Carolyn asked.

"If you like, but you should call to see if I've made it home; my days are unpredictable."

"I will." Carolyn walked her daughter out.

At nine o'clock the next morning Dicer waited alone in the waiting room of a Boxtown office. She noted the room's sports art and three magazines, Women's Sports & Fitness, The Advocate, and Mountain Biking.

The inner door opened and a uniform officer exited, glanced at Dicer, nodded and let herself out. Dicer turned around to find a thirtyish woman in excellent physical condition accentuated by the tight-fitting pants and snug sleeveless polo watching her.

"Lt. Dicer?" she asked.

"Dr. Ochoa?" Dicer rose. If she had known her therapist looked like that, she would have feigned mental anguish earlier.

"Yes. Please come in." Dicer entered and she closed the door behind her. "Have a seat."

Dicer chose a folding chair. Ochoa pulled another to face her.

"I don't understand why I have to come five days aweek," Dicer said.

"You're being punished," Ochoa responded with a wink.

"Thanks for clearing that up. I thought I was crazy or something." Dicer sighed.

"Would you like some juice or milk?"

"Milk?"

Ochoa smiled. "Juice then." She rose and poured a glassful.

"Thank you," Dicer said taking the glass.

"Welcome. Now what's up with you, lieutenant?"

Dicer started to laugh. "You're not very shrinky, doc."

"I'm not very anything. May I call you Ki?"

"Sure. Your juice." Dicer took a sip of the yellowish juice. "Good."

"Now what do you want to talk about?"

"You."

"I'll tell you about me, if you tell me about you first."

"Why does this sound like kindergarten?" Dicer relaxed slowly. "What you want to know?"

"Whatever you want to tell me. Why don't we start with your memo blitz."

"Oooh you are up to date. How do I know you're not one of them?"

Ochoa leaned forward slightly. "One of whom?"

"The aliens. Isn't that why they called you out the other night. You counsel abductees?"

"I have. But we're reversing the order here."

"Does that make you uncomfortable?" Dicer asked.

"No, but I'd like to know why you'd think it would."

"Now you're sounding shrinky."

"Is that good or bad?"

Dicer opened her mouth to open, then smiled. "Don't you have some ink blots or something? Word association, I like that."

"You don't like giving up control do you?"

"Are you supposed to be that direct? At what point do you blame my mother?"

"Do you blame your mother?" Ochoa absently adjusted the wide silver bracelet on her right arm.

Dicer's eyes fell on it, slid off, then back. The insignia on the bracelet was familiar. "I think I should see the other shrink."

Ochoa raised her eyebrow. "Why?"

"I don't trust you."

"That paranoia is expected, but I'm sure—"

Dicer rose suddenly knocking over her chair.

Ochoa rose as well. "Lt. Dicer, please."

Dicer grabbed her wrist. "Who else does Sparrow have in the department?"

Ochoa reached over with her left hand and pressed the nerve on Dicer's arm causing her to release her right wrist. "Next time you put your hands on me, prepare to lose it. Now sit the fuck down."

Dicer stared at Ochoa, saw that she backed her threat with a dangerous confidence. "My apologies, doc." She sat, needing to know what was going on here more than she needed to win the point.

"No harm."

"Now, I'm who and what I say I am. What my patients tell me

is confidential. Like you, I do not share my confidential files with friends and relatives."

"So you are admitting you know Sparrow?" Dicer accused.

"Yes."

"Then you know why you can't be my therapist."

Ochoa nodded. "I can understand why you feel that way; however you may find your visits even more beneficial."

"I doubt it." Dicer took a minute to cool down and process this new information. Was there a way to get a list of which officers saw her? There was one sure fire way, but it was time-consuming. Going through official channels would send off alarms, which she couldn't afford at the moment. "You ever read Sun Tzu?" Dicer asked abruptly.

"Yes."

"If all warfare is deception, how can you trust anyone? Is all deception a form of warfare? Are all who deceive us our enemies or tools of our enemies?"

"I could think of two situations where your answer would be of utmost important."

"What?" Dicer asked.

"In war of course, and in love. As the adage goes, all's fair in love and war. Is that possible because they are the opposite sides of the same coin?"

At that particular moment, Dicer was thinking about another adage, keep your friend's close and your enemies even closer.

Friday morning Toni Jensen arose with Jill, hating to go to work for the first time in her life. Two people had quit and she had worked on her day off until nearly nine just to catch up and she would go in early this morning. Now she knew how Jill had felt in the 5th. That petty bastard Coombs was intent on making her life unbearable there. If they had not bought that damn house she would quit, but they were taking full possession of it this weekend.

"I don't want to hear it," Jill said as Toni let loose her first volley.

"I can't believe you said that."

"I did. Do something about it. Confront him, go over his head, or something."

"Each time I do that, he gets worst."

"Then complain to someone who will make a difference." Jill laughed nastily. "Why don't you ask Xorron to find you a job in one of her many holdings here?"

Toni threw a pillow at her back. "So you can have a fit."

"Like you're not giving me one now with this Coombs dude. Shit, shoot the sonofabitch."

"Don't say that." She hated when Jill carelessly said things like that.

At work later than morning Toni opened the door of her cubicle to a commotion outside. "What's going on?"

"Coombs called the cops on Dante."

"For what?" Dante was a slender part-time college student who barely said good morning.

"He threatened to jack him up. Coombs fired him. He left and came back to carry out his promise."

Toni pushed her way to the front as two officers led the young man out of the building. Toni followed them out. "Excuse me, officers," she called.

The darkhaired officer turned to her. "Yes?" They had felt the hostility directed towards them in the building.

"What are you going to do with him?"

"Take him in." The other officer pushed Dante into the backseat of the cruiser.

"He was provoked. Coombs has been on a rampage. Someone was bound to do something. It could as easily have been me."

"Lucky, it wasn't."

"Who do I call to see what happens? What if he needs a lawyer?" Toni asked.

The officer took out a card. "Here, but the lieutenant will probably kick him loose. He didn't actually hit him."

"Thank you." She looked into the car. "It'll be okay," she assured the young man. He only dropped his head.

Toni returned to the building, where Coombs waited on her with a disapproving and malicious grin.

"What were you saying to them?"

"You're a nasty sonofabitch and you're lucky someone hasn't capped your redneck ass, you toothpick dick, motherfucker."

"You're fired, you cunt-eating dyke."

Toni hit him, knocking him against the wall.

Coombs raised a hand to his lip, smiled and reached for the phone, pushing 911 and reported the assault.

Jill drove across to the 5th to pick Toni up. "I can't believe you hit him."

"You said do something."

"Not hit the man." Jill yanked the car door open and got in.

"It was a primordial response; I didn't think."

"Now there's a change."

"Look on the brightside, I can work on the house the rest of the day."

"Yeah, you ought to find the nearest soup kitchen, because we'll need it." Jill laughed. "You actually hit him. I don't fucking believe this. You hit somebody."

They swung by and picked up her car before heading home to their nearly bare apartment. "What are you doing?" Toni asked as Jill unbuttoned her uniform.

"Dicer gave me the rest of the afternoon off, told me she needed me at ten tonight. Let's move the bed after lunch." And that would complete their incremental move. The Sunray house had a king-size bed in the master bedroom and they could have been staying there, but they wanted to close this chapter of their life, which Toni had done with a bang. All afternoon, Jill would burst into a fit of laughter for no apparent reason, but Toni knew it was more than the thought of her hitting Coombs; it was the entire situation, the dire financial circumstances in which they suddenly found themselves.

They were debating the position of the microwave when the phone rang. "We have phone!" Jill exclaimed reaching for the phone. "Busted are us," she answered jovially.

"I'd be concerned only if it were your spirit. Good evening, Ms. Merlo."

"Good evening, Xorron. You have impeccable timing."

"Do I?"

"Yes, I was just telling Toni that perhaps you could help her find a comparable job after she slugged her supervisor and got herself fired."

"What?" Xorron asked after a long pause.

"Yep." Jill danced away from Toni. "Busted his lip and got herself hauled downtown. Workplace violence is something else."

"Yes, it is. May I speak with Ms. Jensen please."

"I don't know. You may be a bad influence. She never hit anyone until she met you," Jill told her chuckling.

"Perhaps she never had to, for I'm sure Ms. Jensen would not engage in wanton violence."

"You're right about that. So prove your power and find her a job."

"Last week if I had made that suggestion, you would have been greatly offended."

"Don't get me wrong, I'm not asking for a handout; she's no slacker. She—"

"Yes, I understand. Vengar-Metrox is looking to fill a number of key positions. There should be something suitable to her needs available. In fact, I believe they do interviews on Saturdays this summer."

"Is there anyone in particular she should see?"

"No, Just show your foundation card. That's the best I can do for her. Now may I speak with her?"

"Yes, and thanks."

"Glad I can be of service."

Jill handed the phone to Toni. "See, that wasn't so hard. Just ask."

Toni rolled her eyes. "Hello?"

"I really do like you partner."

"That makes two of us. What's up?"

"End of the week review and I came across that guy's name from Houston. Do you still want it?"

"Yes. Yes." Toni scrambled for a pen.

"Horace Uribe."

"Great, thanks. I'll look him up."

"And Toni?"

"Yes?"

"Don't go around hitting people."

"Oh, all right, if you insist."

"Goodnight," Xorron said chuckling.

"Night." Toni hung up and turned to Jill. "What was that all about before?"

"Getting you a job. You're not being unemployed around me. Shit, we need to rent out a room or two."

"If push comes to shove."

"Well, it's a helluva push now."

Toni would have felt better if Jill accompanied her to Vengar-Metrox for moral support, but she had not returned home until six, dirty and exhausted. Instead she arrived alone at the East Laredo building where more than two dozen cars populated the parking lot. A sign near the counter directed applicants to the second floor for applications, examinations, and interviews.

Upstairs, she sidestepped a man exiting a room shaking his head. "Rough?" she said.

"Like you wouldn't believe." He carried a test booklet and a handful of pens.

Toni watched him as he crossed the hall and entered a room with a pasted sign on the door, STEP 5. How many steps were there? At the end of the hall, a fiftyish woman sat behind a table filled with color-coded forms, booklets, and pens. Her nametag said Gertrude.

"Good morning," Gertrude greeted her with a smile.

"Good morning. Is . . . is this for employment with Vengar-Metrox?"

"Yes." The woman passed her a clipboard with forms and a several pens, then pushed a sign-in sheet to her.

"How long will this take?" Toni asked.

"Depends on the type of position you're applying for, anywhere from two hours to six for executives."

"And you make decisions today?"

"It has happened, but usually we notify the applicants Tuesday."

"And what is the percentage that you hire?" Toni pushed the sign-in sheet back to her.

"Ten to twenty percent of those who complete the process." Gertrude pointed to the door to her right. "Go in there and fill out those five forms, then take them to that room, Step 2." She pointed to the door to her left.

"Okay." Toni took the forms to the room which only contained one man who was double checking his forms while eating a donut. After the usual demographics, she thought the questions became rather strange, asking of eating and reading habits, music and personal preferences. The final statement instructed the applicant to have a quick snack if s/he had not eaten.

Step 2 was eye, hearing, and hand-eye coordination tests. Step 3 involved several aptitude, attitudinal and interest assessment tests. Step 4 was an essay on justice and a topic of your choice. Step 5 was a food break while they assessed the prior four steps. Step 6 was the first or last interview. Toni waited an hour as the applicants came and went from three interview rooms. She noted few people went into Number 3, but they stayed longer. Listening to the other applicants discuss their process, she realized that they really were trying to match the applicant with the right job. Additionally she learned, she was not asked for a urine and blood sample, nor did she sign a background check waiver and a few more items as the others had done.

The interview room was a stark closet size room with two chairs facing each other. Toni took the vacant seat across from the red-haired woman.

"You're going to need flexible hours when school starts?" the woman asked without prelude.

"Yes."

"And when is that?"

"August 26, but registration the week before that."

"So we're looking at a month of full-time work." She scribbled on a large index card. "And how many hours can you give us a week during school?"

"Forty if the schedule is flexible."

"Reasonable hours."

"Thirty. I'm accustomed to working long hours when necessary."

"But graduate school is a different beast." She scribbled again on the card, then turned to a computer to her left. "We'll put you down for thirty." The small printer spat out a sheet.

"Flexible?"

"Of course." Red-hair handed her the sheet of paper. "Go there Monday at 10:00. Goodluck."

Toni blinked. "Is that it? I'm done?"

"Yes. Enjoy your weekend."

"You as well." Toni quickly exited the building and went to her car. She pulled out her map; 3847 Edison Drive was in the neighborhood. She decided to drive past to get an inkling of what it was.

Edison Drive circled around and through the small industrial park. Sansori Communications owned a local Latin American radio station and cable channel.

Sunday morning Toni Jensen walked out on the patio and took in the large backyard with the green lawn that needed mowing in the next day or two. They did not have a mower, nor had they settled on whether to hire a lawn service. Neither had much of a lawn growing up, but for some reason she wanted to take care of it herself to make it feel like her own; however, after a summer that feeling may go away rather swiftly. All of her life, she wished for an old-fashioned home to call her own; hoaky or not that's what she wanted. By some strange twist of fate, she had gotten what she wanted; now they had to make the most of it.

"Too late to have second thoughts." Jill brought out a pair of folding chairs, then retrieved matching spillproof mugs with their names below the Vengar logo.

"Fourth and fifth." Toni settled into the chair.

"That really is a bigass yard, Toni. You sure you want to mow it?"

"No." Toni laughed, shaking her head. "But I'm going to. As soon as you buy a lawnmower."

"Me? You're the on wanting to mow."

"Division of labor. I labor, you get to watch." Toni shifted her chair to lean against Jill. "How long before the heat becomes unbearable out here?"

"All we need is a pool."

Toni glanced up at her. "Uh huh. Who's going to pay for it?"

"Okay, a hot tub."

"Put a chair under a sprinkler."

"Oh you have great ideas."

"Why thank you, very much." Toni relaxed against her, thinking of their relationship and the time spent on picnics in the park or under any tree they could find. They were so close now, given their rather disastrous first encounter and their protracted feud forestalling any courtship. "Know who we should call?"

"Who?"

"Teri Knotts."

Jill chuckled. "Yeah. I bet if we told her we had a new place and a spare bed, she'd hop in that old Caddy and head our way."

"Yeah, she would." Teri spent a year trying to get them together.

Jill jumped up, nearly sending Toni sprawling. "Let's call her."

"She's not up this time of morning."
"If we wait, she won't be home."
"Maybe not."

A quarter before ten Monday morning, Toni drove to 3847 Edison Drive home of Sansori Communications. Once inside the complex, she was directed to the fifth floor, to the second floor, then to the sub-basement in search of her contact T.Z. Aragon. As she entered the dim, cavernous sub-basement, the idea of a wild goose chase crossed her mind.

"You're late," called a disembodied voice.

Toni looked around and didn't see anyone. "Where are you?"

The lights flicked on, illuminating a work area of tables and electronic equipment in the far left corner; green, blue, red and black numbered lines were painted on the white floor.

"Are you, Jensen?" a woman in a white coat with many stuffed pockets strode across the open floor.

"Yes. Are you Aragon?"

"Yep." The woman removed a rubber glove, but not her red tinted goggles.

Toni shook the offered hand. "No one seems to know where you are."

Aragon shrugged. "Naw, they just don't care." She gave Toni the once over. "You look real professional, but I need you in something more . . . um . . . less restrictive. Rubber, nonblack, sole shoes, an old-fashion pair of sneakers will do just fine." She turned and walked back towards her work station.

Toni followed her. "What will I be doing?"

"Making films. Congratulations you're an assistant producer." Aragon glanced at her. "Don't let it go to your head. We just run simulations down here. You're going to be wired to a computer and experimented on."

"Is it dangerous?"

"Hell no. Unless you walk into a lake with the shit on."

She chuckled. "We have a different setup for wet work. You have done some scuba diving right?"

"Just a tad." Toni was sure she had been given the wrong assignment.

"That's all you need."

"So I won't be processing claims or anything?"

"Nope, but you will be processing data." Aragon walked to the wall and pressed a lever; a panel slid back, revealing a bank of monitors and more computer equipment. "You're also an editor. I hope you like watching movies, for that's the other part of your job."

"What will I watch for?"

"Depends on the assignment." Aragon slipped into a comfortable-looking high chair. "Sit. It looks intimidating at first, but it's easy like working your VCR, cable, computer and stereo at one terminal." Toni sat and allowed herself to be propelled through a crash course on editing and videography.

When they broke for lunch four hours later, Toni inquired about the paperwork and was informed that all had been taken care of except a few signatures which would be done later if Aragon was satisfied with her performance. Her favorite discovery of the afternoon was the international videolibrary in another annex of the sub-basement. When her day ended at seven that evening, Toni had mixed emotions on her new and creative job. It was the creative nature of the job itself that provoked those mixed feelings, on the one hand it was stimulating and imaginative, on the otherhand going frame by frame, as they had done all afternoon, could be as monotonous as filling out health-care forms.

"Ms. Jensen!" the new on-duty guard called as she left the elevator.

Toni turned to the older man in his fitted black blazer. "Yes, sir?" How did he know her name? She had been in the basement all day, even eating lunch there.

"You're wanted in 732A."

"732A?" The building only had five floors.

"Next door. There's a connecting corridor in the basement."
He pointed to the west wing. "There's an elevator as soon as you
push through the double doors. It should be a couple doors down."

"Thanks, uh.."

"Earl."

"Thanks, Earl." Toni followed the directions with only one
wrong turn. Room 732A was a vice-president's office or so said the
brass plate outside the door.

A dark-haired male behind a desk turned towards her as the
door clicked behind her. "Yes?"

"I'm Toni Jensen; the security guard Earl told me I was wanted
here."

He reached for the phone. "You wanted to see Miss Jensen?"
he asked lazily, listened then shrugged, hanging up the phone.

The inner door opened and the red-haired interviewer in a
spiffy, creme suit walked out. "Toni, please come in. I won't keep
you long, knowing T.Z. has filled your head all day."

Toni was a little confused, but vowed to roll with the punches.
"You're a VP?"

The veep nodded. "Val Trujillo. I'm a firm believer that if you
want good people around you, you must choose good people. How
did you find T.Z.'s work?"

"Different."

"T.Z. is different and hard to please. Apparently she was in a
good mood today, no one complained of her storming through the
complex." Val Trujillo pulled a sheaf of papers from her desk. "In
addition to assisting T.Z., your responsibility is to keep the project's
budget straight. T.Z. will not stoop to such an odious task. She
has two people out, so by the time school starts, your in-studio
burden will have lessened allowing for school and this task. T.Z.
has a habit of ordering equipment without proper authorization,
which only means I approve it; but I do like to know where two
hundred thousand dollars goes down there when I'm asked to explain it. That's your responsibility now. Any questions?"

"Several. For instance, pay and benefits?"

Trujillo rolled her eyes. "See what I mean." She reached for the phone. "Daniel, where's Toni Jensen's paperwork?. . . . Would you print a summary of her salary and benefits please? She'll be by first thing tomorrow to sign everything." Trujillo hung up. "Daniel will have that for you on your way out. Anything else?"

"How will I keep track of T.Z.'s spending or whatever?"

Trujillo handed her the folder. "Here's all the forms and contact people you'll need. As to getting your hands on invoices and price lists, just tell her you'll handle that from now on. You have any problems with T.Z., throw your weight around; but I'm pretty sure you won't though."

"Okay." She had no idea what weight, but she could see how T.Z. would be so focused on her cameras and computers that mundane budgeting tasks would be delayed, indefinitely.

"Good and keep up the good work. With Dawn out, no one is running interference for T.Z., thus T.Z. has been running rough shod over everyone except for today."

Toni nodded, remembering T.Z.'s first words this morning telling her she was late and the lunch deliveryman who was whispering when he entered the basement and visibly relaxed when he saw her. Yet, they had had no notable disagreement except over Jodie Foster.

Trujillo patted her on the back. "Relax, I'm sure you can handle what she throws at you. You have a whole month to get a groove going." They were headed for the door. "Oh, one more thing."

As Trujillo went back to her desk, she wondered about that pat on the back. Every time she encountered one of Xorron's "women" they acted a bit familiar. Now there was no doubt, that Trujillo was one of the hands-on managers, Xorron reportedly favored.

Trujillo returned with a blue velvet jeweler's bag. "A little token." She poured out a silver and crystal amulet on a silver chain. "It's also an emergency beacon. Just snap it open and press the bud. It sends a signal to our satellite, alerting security who pinpoints your position using a global tracking system and helps on the way."

"A cell phone would have done the trick," Toni said, taking the amulet.

"Yes, but this is so much more attractive." Trujillo walked her to the door.

"Thank you. I really must be going."

"Yes. Enjoy your evening."

Toni took the lavender envelope Daniel held out to her and headed back the way she had come. In the car, she opened the envelope, looked at her salary and gasped. For a full 40-hour week, her pay had doubled and she discovered she was a junior executive with a multimillion dollar budget, T.Z.'s of course, but still. What the hell were they trying to do to her? She had trouble managing their money at home. . . . Hell, that would be a helluva lot easier with her pay. She wondered if they would give her an advance. Realizing they would if she asked, she dismissed the idea. She would not take anymore advantage of her exceptionally advantageous position at the moment. She would enjoy it, but like all good things, it would come to an end soon. Like T.Z. said, she still had to prove herself in the sub-basement.

CHAPTER 16

At midnight Dicer paced her office, waiting for the phone to ring, anxious to do something beyond covering her ass. When the phone rang, she snatched it up before the first ring ended. "Yes?"

"Two-fifteen at 94833 Belfry Lane. No guarantees."

"Thanks."

"Be careful." The phone clicked off.

For the last three hours, Dicer hand been debating over who she would use if that call came. Now she had to make a decision. Circumstances left her no choice but to use Mickey and Merlo, although she would have preferred Gomez. Yet those two knew the most about what they were up against. As Mickey's phone rang, she had second thoughts, but proceeded to give him instructions when he answered, the same with Merlo. At the last minute she dialed Gravelli who had made herself scarce of late.

At two o'clock hidden in a courtyard across from 94833 Belfry Lane, Dicer reminded herself that this was a reconnaissance mission only to verify her suspicions. She had cautioned her people to do nothing, no matter what transpired with their suspect. There were exceptions to that rule and the longer she waited the more her spine tingled, forewarning danger. She had talked herself into calling the whole thing off when the black Ford pulled into the darkened drive of 94833 Belfry. No one got out until a second vehicle arrived; this one a dark minivan. Raising the nightvision glasses, Dicer got her first glimpse of Pablo Menendez as he got out of the van. Slowly he turned in her direction as if seeing her there. Dicer held her breath. Then a squeal of tires came from both directions, followed by sirens.

"Fuck!" Dicer exclaimed under her breath. "Remain where you are!" she commanded her small team.

"Oh shit!" Mickey exclaimed a split second before the police cars converging on 94833 exploded.

"Holy mother," Gravelli breathed into the mike; she was in a yard two doors down and one of the cars was directly in front of her.

"Merlo, call for backup and prepare for our retreat," Dicer told her.

"Gotcha." Merlo started the engine of the surveillance van a street over.

During those few seconds, Dicer had lost sight of Menendez and the van was pealing out of the drive. "Where's Menendez?" she asked.

"In the van," Mickey told her.

"Gravelli?" Dicer asked. No answer. "Gravelli?"

"Near the van. Which way?" Gravelli called, her breath coming in spurts as she raced for Merlo and the van.

"Don't follow! They'll hit you!" Dicer exclaimed as sirens sounded in the distance.

"Got to!"

"Merlo, don't move!" Dicer commanded.

"Get out or drive!" Gravelli's voice came forcefully over the mike as she gave Merlo her option.

"She's got a gun on me," Merlo said.

"Get out!" Dicer commanded.

Merlo opened the door just as a volley of small arms fire strafed the passenger side of the van. Merlo dove to the ground as a rush of feet came her way. "I've got company," she said and looked up at the ugly assault rifle.

"Who are you?" asked the ski-masked man in a heavy Spanish accent.

"Police," Merlo said softly wondering where Gravelli had gone.

"The same police with sirens?"

"No," Merlo said vehemently; something telling her it was a bad idea to associate with them. "We were here to observe."

"Tell Di-cer, next time." He stepped back and shot the van tires. "Stay." He faded into the darkness which was now dotted with lights.

Merlo gushed out a breath, noting she was soaking wet and not from sweat. She knew she was dead. She don't know how long she laid there listening to the night's emergency noises before Mickey squatted down before her and she raised her head.

"You okay?" he asked.

"No," she admitted to him, knowing she would not have admitted it to another soul.

"What happened?"

"You didn't hear?" She tried to set up and groaned with sudden pain in her thigh.

"What is it?" Mickey flicked on his flashlight.

"My leg."

He ran the light over her leg and pulled out a tiny dart. "What the fuck?"

"I hope it isn't poisoned," Merlo said and fainted.

Around the corner, Dicer was learning the identity of the officers in the two cars and it made her furious, one had been Phil Grant. "Who the fuck ordered this? Three good officers are dead over this foolishness!" She searched the gathering crowd for Aviles. So intent on looking for Aviles, her mind at first didn't register the military-bearing of deputy chief Scott Stein. "I'll be fucked!" she shouted and headed for him, but was intercepted by a solid female body.

"He's waiting to blame this on you," Alexis Guzman told her. "Don't give him the satisfaction of taking your badge in public."

"He got those men killed!" Dicer shouted through gritted teeth. She moved her hand to shove Guzman out of the way when Mickey's urgent hails caught her attention. She side-stepped Guzman to get to Mickey. "Where's Merlo and Gravelli?"

"Gravelli's nowhere to be found and they're taking Merlo to St. Mary's." He held up the dart in a baggie. "This was in her leg."

"Fuck, let's go."

"The van's on a flat."

"I got a car," Guzman said, tugging at Dicer's sleeve.

"Mickey, call—"

"Toni; I'm on it." He followed several paces behind as he dialed Toni.

Toni raced across town to St. Mary's. Mickey was the first person she saw as she entered the emergency room. "What happened?"

"Shot with a poisoned dart."

"Is she okay?"

"I don't know." He saw the naked fear on her face. "I mean, she's not in danger of dying, but she's experiencing a little numbness in her left leg. But I don't know how she is, you know."

"Where is she?"

"Taking tests. Besides saying it's a poisoned dart, which I figured out, they don't know what's happening."

An hour passed before Toni could see Jill Merlo who had been moved into a room near the nurses station. Jill's eyes were sunken, cheeks hollow and lips dark. Toni only stood staring at her in the dim light.

"The only thing they know is it isn't contagious," Jill said reaching for her.

Toni walked over holding her close. "I was so afraid coming over. Does it hurt?"

"No, I can't feel anything."

Toni extracted herself from Jill and pulled a chair close. "You should get some sleep, you look like hell."

"I feel like hell, but they want me to stay awake."

"Then glad I'm here," Toni said, attempting a smile.

"So am I, but you have to go to work."

"Fuck work."

Jill chuckled. "No, one of us needs to work. I'll feel better knowing everything is going on as usual. One guy said it could wear off in a couple of hours, twelve at the most."

"Thought you said they don't know what it is?"

"They don't, but speculated it was a concoction from a blowfish or frog or something like a zombie drug causing area paralysis."

"Paralysis!" Toni groaned.

"Not total, just enough to cause numbing of my left leg." Jill fought off sleep. "Tell me about your day again."

Toni smiled feebly. "I thought you wanted to stay away."

"You know you enjoyed it."

"Maybe a little," Toni recounted her day, but at daybreak Jill fell unconscious and couldn't be awakened.

Meanwhile Dicer battled her superiors as internally no one took responsibility for the police action that ended with three officers dead and a state bureau agent missing and no sign of Pablo Menendez. Nevertheless, Scott Stein had taken the foreground in cleaning up the mess and placing the mop bucket at her feet. She met the chief at his side door to his restroom.

"It seems awfully suspicious that the mole in my unit was one of the three who was blown up," she told him.

"Which is why Stein is looking to nail this to your forehead." Harmon pushed open the door, not bothering to stop Dicer from entering.

"I'm being set up."

"Told you that." He entered the stall.

"What?" Did her ears deceive her?

"I told you to sit your ass down and shut up."

"You have any idea what I had to do to get that info on Pablo Menendez?"

"Which you were not going to do anything with, which is why Stein moved on it." He let out a long sigh as his bladder drained.

"And you knew of this?"

"No, he called me this morning and his report should be on my desk."

"Stein's a pencil pusher. What does he know about operations? That ineptitude is what got those officers killed."

"Or your primary dereliction of duty," Harmon said stepping from the stall.

"My dereliction of duty? They've thrown roadblocks up every step of the way. How many people have died since the first day Buchova tossed me out of the cathedral? How many more will die before you act like the chief and call off the dogs?"

"At least you now know who your enemies are, within and without." He vigorously washed his hands.

"Where's Aviles in all of this?" Dicer asked.

Harmon turned to her, looking her directly in the eye. "You tell me, Dicer, which one of them are you willing to trust?"

"Neither."

Harmon shook his head. "But you have to choose, my dear."

Dicer clenched her jaw. "And you, chief, where do you stand?"

"You still have your badge." He walked out and into his office, closing the office door behind him.

"Sonofabitch," Dicer spat and turned on her heels.

Reporter Eduardo Trujillo waited at her car when she came down. "They wouldn't let me inside," he complained.

"That makes two of us." Dicer unlocked the doors and got in. Trujillo joined her. "What do you want?"

"Same as you do, lieutenant. Why is deputy chief Stein suddenly in the spotlight? Where is Aviles? Why is he telling the media you are no longer available for comment? Are you under a gag order? Was this your operation? Who were you after? Stein says an international drug lord. Was it Menendez?"

Dicer started the engine. "Have you had breakfast?"

"No." He lied, but it had been hours ago.

"Then you don't mind fixing it while I shower."

"I'm honored." He knew he would not have had this opportunity if Lin Gao was not on vacation.

Toni called T.Z. to explain her situation and was surprised at the number of questions the woman asked. She was even more surprised when a woman with a striking resemblance to T.Z. arrived several hours later with a medical bag and a stack of release forms. "I'm Ren Aragon."

"You're a doctor?" Toni asked.

"Yes, at the Children's AIDS Hospice and Roxboro Clinic." She handed Toni the clipboard. "I need you to indicate that I am Ms. Merlo's primary physician and authorized to use nontraditional, even experimental treatments."

Toni hesitated. "Experimental like what?"

"Not drugs." Aragon extracted several colored bottles of oils from her bag, then a large black velvet jeweler's bag. "I know what this is and am 95% sure I can cure it."

"Without drugs?"

Dr. Aragon nodded solemnly. "The sooner the better."

Toni signed the forms and took them to the nurses station. When she returned Dr. Aragon was rubbing the oils over Jill's body, then covered her with a gauze sheet. She placed crystals on her forehead, chest and right leg. Around the puncture she placed a generous amount of yellowish-green putrid gel. Taking two silver rods, she held one in the gel and the other against the crystal on Jill's chest.

"Turn off the light," Aragon told Toni.

Toni did what she was told and stood against the door to watch. Aragon, hands on both rods, closed her eyes, taking several deep breaths. Expecting chanting, Toni was taken by surprise as the crystals began to emit a faint red light and the rods vibrated with tinkling zings. An acidic smell filled the room as the crystals changed from red to orange to green to blue to a near black before going clear.

"Ow!" Jill exclaimed knocking the crystals from her forehead.

Toni walked to her, pushing her back down as she tried to sit up. "Stay still."

Aragon scooped up the spilled crystals, then wiped the now-black gelatin from her wound, then covered it with a red substance.

"What's that?" Toni asked.

"Iodine." Aragon chuckled. "Nature's a majestic bitch."

Toni laughed wiping tears. "How'd you do that?"

"Just a little energy to stimulate her body to expel the poison." Aragon quickly packed her nontraditional equipment, then picked up a more traditional stethoscope and thermometer. "Of course, they'll say the poison just wore off in due course. Your heartrate and temperature should return to normal in a few minutes."

"Who're you?" Jill asked thickly.

"Dr. Aragon. Would you get her some ice chips?" Aragon asked Toni.

"Sure thing." Toni left the room relieved and intrigued at what had just happened. If she had not seen it for herself she would not have believed it.

After giving Trujillo an earful and writing up her own report of the early morning fiasco and complaints against Stein for IAD, the chief, and the commissioners, she hand delivered them, then headed to see Sparrow.

Sparrow met her at the front desk as usual. "Tough break, lieutenant."

"Not necessarily, except for those deaths. Stein made a tactical error."

"He revealed himself too early." Sparrow led her back.

Dicer nodded. "And left records of his bugging of my phones. The sonofabitch records everything."

"You have copies?"

"I'm getting them now. I also filed several complaints on him."

Sparrow glanced at her as she opened the office door. "Feels good to be back on the offensive?"

"Yes." Dicer noted this was a different office, more of a real one with work stacked in small piles. A large screen with a grid of the city covered a large portion of the left wall.

"Sounds like you have everything in order. What can I do for you this time?"

"Did you have people on Menendez?"

"No need to, we had his itinerary until your people rode in like the cavalry." There was an edge to her voice Dicer had not heard since Fuentes.

"You lost him?"

Sparrow sighed. "For the moment."

"But you do have someone on the inside?"

"Not for long. We're pulling them out as we speak. Menendez has a habit of wiping out everyone in a cell to make sure he gets the leak. Don't be surprised when several corpses missing tongues appear in the morgue." Sparrow pinched the bridge of her nose.

"That's not good."

"You're telling me." The two women felt each other out in the silence.

"One of them left me a message."

"What was it?" Sparrow asked anxiously.

"'Next time.'"

Sparrow shook her head, reaching for the phone. "That's not good." She spoke rapid Portuguese, then restrained herself from slamming down the phone. "We've lost contact with our man. If he doesn't make his rendezvous point in two hours, then he's dead."

"Damn."

"And you're next on his list." Sparrow opened a drawer and took out a pack of chewing gum. "He'll want to talk before shooting you. You'll have one shot to get him. The end pieces are explosives. Chew and stick."

"What?!"

"Saliva acts as—"

"No. No. I'm not putting explosives in my mouth."

Sparrow pulled the pack back to her, then pulled out a pen. "Laser, one burst can blow up a car, but one burst is all there is."

"You're a regular James Bond." She reached for the pen.

Sparrow covered her hand. "If he gets it, you're dead."

"You make it sound as if I'm dead if I encounter him anyway."

"Not necessarily. As I told you before, he will want to talk to

you, boast of his ability to remain free, and demonstrate his brutality." Sparrow finally removed her hand from Dicer's. "You may
be more fun for him alive than dead."

"What do you mean?"

"He likes to slowly turn good cops bad. I'm sure he's done a
psychological profile of you, your strengths and weaknesses. I would
imagine you'd be a prime target."

"And how do you know so much about Menendez? Besides
the obvious infiltration."

"Extensive background research. Consulted a few experts and
interviewed his living victims." Sparrow reached for the ringing
phone. "Yes?" She listened then hung up. "Jill Merlo is awake."

Dicer took a deep breath. "Thank goodness."

"It wasn't goodness." Sparrow rose. "Do you have time? I want
to show you something."

"Yes." Dicer rose, just as her beeper went off.

"Use the green one," Sparrow said pointing to a phone on a
stand by the door.

Dicer slipped into a seat at the back of the small darkened auditorium as the speaker commentated on the violent video images projected on a large screen behind her. The screen went blue as the
lights near the podium came on; the speaker's voice switched tim-
bre.

"Narcopolitics has never been confined to Colombia, Mexico
or the U.S.-Mexico border. Like other types of corruption and
graft, it thrives here in Metrox. Law enforcement is enmeshed in a
battle not only with the criminals but with ferreting out internal
and government moles and malefactors who are at the least impeding investigations. On the other end of the spectrum, we have
deputy mayors conspiring with an international criminal organization, getting caught, then placing the blame at the feet of investigators, who are then pulled from the case after linking that incident to others in the past two months." A web of intersecting

events appeared on the screen, a web that was essentially a more stylized version of the board in Dicer's office. "Shit!" Dicer exclaimed and rose, moving forward. "What you see is what the mayor and the chief refuses to acknowledge. It is difficult to attribute this interaction of people and events to mere coincidence, especially when evidence exists, which of course is being suppressed." The projection changed to a stock photo of Pablo Menendez. "Pablo Menendez, 54, is the proverbial mastermind behind this scheme. Menendez rose rapidly through the underground economy of Mexico and set up shop in Tijuana, later San Diego and El Paso, establishing a network of illegals that outlasted dozens of Colombian takeover attempts, governmental interdiction, and assassination plots. However, the explanations for his ability to survive in this violent and treacherous world has risen to mythical proportion. Cults have risen around him with majestic monuments from Mexico City, Cozumel to Tijuana, San Diego, El Paso, St. Louis and . . . " Color photos of estates and palatial properties appeared on the screen as clicked off each city. "And Metrox," she finished as a series of New Faith Cathedral photographs appeared with angles making sure the audience recognized the streets and neighborhood.

The speaker allowed the murmur to continue and spoke over it as if to a silent hall. "Last month, three ministers were killed in the New Faith Cathedral. Evidence exists linking the deaths to a cult that not only worships Menendez, but receives the majority of it's revenue from him as well. Much to my dismay, I can present no more without offending the police lieutenant standing there wishing to ring my neck for divulging more than I already have. However, I would like you to focus on the screen again for a final video clip. Judge for yourself. Lights off."

Dicer stood mesmerized as two shadowed men discussed containing her and her team and distracting them with idiot assignments. That piece was followed by several clips of them at scenes, then a discussion speculating on her sudden withdrawal from NFC and Aviles' public disappearing act.

When the clips ended and the lights came on, the podium was empty.

"Shit!" Dicer exclaimed looking for the speaker. A young man thanked the audience which was buzzing with information overload. Dicer realized they were all carrying videos and folders. Taking out her badge, she approached the tawny young man in gray slacks and blue dress shirt as he boxed up material from a table next to the podium. "I'm Lt. Dicer, Metrox PD."

"I know who you are," he said handing her a videotape and folder.

"Where's that woman?" she asked him.

"What woman?"

"The speaker. You are aware she may be guilty of slander and libel and other offenses in violation of . . . " she trailed to a stop at his patient grin. "Who are you?"

"Danilo." He snapped the top of the plastic packing box.

"How can I get in touch with the speaker? What's her name at least?"

He shrugged, retrieved a stray flyer of the lecture and wrote down an address. "Nine o'clock, give this to the doorman. Otherwise . . . "

"Shit out of luck," said a woman towering over the young man.

Amazon was the only description Dicer had for the six-six woman in a form-fitting pleated jumpsuit. "Who are you?"

"Not of your concern." She effortlessly picked up the box. "Time to go, Brother Danilo."

"Brother Danilo?" Dicer asked reaching for his arm. "Are you a priest?"

"In a fashion." He followed the woman out.

Dicer turned to the remnants of the responsive audience and began to question them about the lecture and speaker, discovering it was a summer lecture series on international affairs and commerce. Tonight's lecturer had been called out of town abruptly and the speaker introduced as an expert on Metrox-foreign relations. No one remembered or could pronounce her name as Danilo Morales, the director of Latin American Xport Institute, LAXI, sped through it.

At the Gamin stationhouse, Dicer searched the databases for information on LAXI, discovering it was a thinktank on Central and South American economies. Danilo was older than he looked and had dual doctorates in economics and Latin American Studies. However, what intrigued her most was the institute's Broadway address across the street from Metrox Towers in the city's premier financial district.

Pushing that fact to the back of her mind to ferment, she slipped the video into the VCR expecting to see video clips of Menendez as in the lecture, but instead the video contained a documentary on the historical and current economic impact of Latin America on Metrox business. The earlier waves had included Cuban investors in the fifties to Mexican exports in the seventies to Colombian financiers in the eighties to new Mexican entrepreneurs in the nineties and to the recent wave of Brazilian small businesses. Although interesting and well-done, the video disappointed Dicer. She packed it in her bag to give to Nikki who would enjoy the history lesson.

Dicer was on her way out for the nine o'clock meeting with the "lecturer" when a van pulled alongside her car and the side door slid open. She stopped in her tracks, glancing back at the stationhouse then at the van with its door open. Against her better judgment, she walked toward the open door of the van.

"Who did you expect?" Sparrow asked from the interior.

Breathing a sigh of relief, Dicer stepped closer to see into the van. "What are you doing here?"

"Hop in."

"I have an appointment."

"Won't take long."

Dicer got into the cargo van with the bolted row of seats. The door automatically closed. "What's up?"

"Our man made it out, not in good shape, but well enough to warn of an impending strike by Menendez."

"What or who?"

"No idea, except a structure is most likely. A structure relevant to who he believes is antagonizing him."

"Me?"

"I don't think so, but you should be careful just in case he's had a change of heart." Sparrow held out the pack of chewing gum.

Dicer shook her head. "No."

"Let me post a guard on you," Sparrow offered.

Dicer took a look around the sanitized gray interior. "I've been wracking my brains to figure out why you're helping me specifically. Not just the fact that we're both after Menendez. Why me? Fuentes?"

Sparrow shrugged. "You have a chance to take him down legally. I've been in one war or another most of my life, so killing a man is not unfamiliar to me; however I would prefer not to if I have a choice."

"Me?"

Sparrow nodded imperceptibly.

Dicer knew but she had to ask. "And if I fail?" She did not doubt Sparrow's ability to fulfill her deadly promises.

"I won't." The van's door slid open. "Step lightly, lieutenant."

As Dicer drove in the waning sunlight to the Oldtown address to meet Danilo Morales' lecturer, threads of the last several weeks dangled in her head as she tried to weave each and every one into a rational pattern. She could see the much of the larger picture, but it was the hidden motives of the peripheral players that had her strung out and jumpy. And Sparrow? What was her angle? It was more than Fuentes; worst she felt an irrational bond to her, a comfort at a level that went beyond the short time they had spent together. Intimate but not sexual.

The address on a Boxtown backstreet turned out to be an old Catholic school undergoing serious renovations on three of the four structures, new fencing was being supplemented with fast growing hedges on both sides. Dicer drove around until she saw signs of life, a half dozen cars stood in a dimly lit side parking lot at the fourth completed structure. Getting out of the car, she was hit by the spicy aroma filling the night air reminding her that her last meal was seven hours ago. Somewhere around the back a door slammed and playful children's voices yelled out.

At the only door visible, Dicer knocked on the heavy door with the brass knocker after failing to find a doorbell. The door opened and she took a step backward as an imposing big man in a monk's cassock opened the door.

"Yes?" he asked.

Dicer handed him the flyer with Danilo's scribbling on it. She had not been able to decipher it and had contented herself in making a copy, later to be faxed to a linguist.

"No weapons allowed inside, detective. You'll have to leave them in your trunk or check them with me."

"My trunk." Dicer quickly disarmed and headed back for the door where the monk waited patiently. Her stomach growled as the aromas engulfed her as he led her through a room of tables with chairs stacked on top into a brightly lit kitchen with gleaming pots and pans hanging everywhere. Three women chatted as one stood at a counter next to the restaurant size oven, one set a long-table for a dozen or so and the third mixed blue kool-aid in a gallon pitcher; three full pitchers were already on the counter.

"Hello," the table-setter greeted Dicer.

"Hello."

"You're just in time for dinner," said the older cook holding out a slice of freshly baked bread she was cutting.

"Bless you," Dicer said mouth watering. She stifled a moan as she bit into the heavenly bread. As she savored the bread, her eyes wandered around the large room and out the window into the well-lit courtyard a squeaky rocker provided a constant rhythm for the three or four children darting about.

"What are you doing here?" the kool-aid woman asked. She was in her late twenties or early thirties and wore a perpetual amused expression. Her bright eyes shone with humor.

"Danilo Morales told me to come." Dicer realized the big man was gone.

"Oh." Kool-aid woman filled a tumbler and sat it on the counter. "Here, sit, drink, dinner's in ten minutes."

An athletic teenage girl came in carrying a book. "Is it ready?"

"No."

"What do you want me to do?" the teenager asked.

"Round them up and get their hands clean," the cook said.

"No prob," the teenager said walking across the long room to the sliding door. She didn't say a word but the children suddenly filed in making funny faces at her as they passed. The Amazon from earlier came in behind them, closing the door, locking it, and drawing the blinds which created a peaceful mountain view on it.

Dicer silently counted the people coming through the kitchen/dining room. She was at ten including herself when Danilo came in carrying a baby. "Lieutenant, how are you?"

"Fine. How old is the baby?"

"Nine weeks." He held the baby for her to see.

"A new one." Dicer wondered if they were Mormons. The teenager sitting in a chair near the door laughed aloud, then returned to her book.

"Come help, Sig," the cook said as she began to fill bowls from the large pot. The teenager filled a tray with the bowls and quickly distributed them around the table. Platters of fruit, vegetables and breads were strategically placed on the table.

Sig showed Dicer to a large spotless, gleaming restroom to wash up for dinner. Dicer appreciated the granite counters. She was admiring the masonry when the Amazon opened the outer door and looked in.

"Are you okay?"

"Yes." Dicer followed her out. "I would love a tour when it's all done."

"Tell Danilo."

They entered the dining room where the children were spaced evenly between the adults. The baby was in a bassinet at a corner of the table near Danilo. Dicer took a seat between Danilo and Sig and directly across from a woman she had not seen in the kitchen before, but earlier at the small auditorium. The big man took his seat and a long silence followed.

"May the goddess be as free with her blessings tomorrow as today," Sig said.

"May the goddess be kind," came the mumbled responses.

"Now let's eat, I'm starving," Sig said reaching for the nearest platter.

"What is Sig short for?" Dicer asked.

"My father thought I was a real pistol," she said chuckling.

"Still are," Danilo told her handing Dicer a bowl of rice.

Dicer listened quietly to the family bantering and recount of the day's adventures. The children had taken a tour of the downtown library's summer exhibit with the Monk. The cook had worked until four. Kool-aid played softball. The table-setter was a pediatrician and had just gotten home at eight. The lecturer said little, only answering direct questions from the two children flanking her.

"What you do today?" the young girl with the braids asked Dicer.

"I worked all day."

"Doing what?"

"Paperwork, visiting people asking questions. What's your name?" No one had addressed anyone by name all the time she had been there except Sig.

"My apologies," Danilo said wiping his mouth. He went around the room identifying each. Her lecturer was Kwan.

After dinner Sig led her to a comfortable turn of the century furnished study with all the modern technologies along one wall. "What do you want with Kwan?" Sig asked pointedly.

Several indicators during dinner had led Dicer to surmise that Sig for whatever purposes was the leader of the little group. After the last few weeks, nothing would surprise her at this point. "I just want to ask her about where she obtained the information in her lecture this evening."

"Why?"

"I have a few questions she may be able to help me with. She seemed to have had unusual access to Pablo Menendez's world."

"Yes, she has, which is why she's lecturing on it. It's for her spiritual cleansing as well as social duty." Sig glanced at the clock. "They should be in the baths. You're lacking sleep and emotional balance. You should join them and spend the night. We have a free bedroom. It locks from within," Sig added with a half-smile.

"I'll just talk to Kwan and go home."

"If you want to talk to her, it'll have to be done downstairs in the baths." Sig left no room for compromise.

"Fine. Show me the way."

"You know the routine? Shower before entering." Sig rose. "I expected you to be more difficult."

"I'm tired," Dicer admitted.

"Which is why you should stay. Would you like me to call a friend of yours to reassure you that we're safe?"

Dicer chuckled. "And who would that be?"

Sig snagged a phone on her way out, pushed several numbers. "Hi, I have a friend of yours contemplating a long session. Do assure her we're nonviolent." Sig stopped at the basement door and handed her the phone.

"Hello?" Dicer said eyes rolling, wondering what nut was on the other end.

"Kiwi?" Kylar said.

"Kylar?!" Dicer exclaimed drawing to her full height. "Where are you?"

"At your house about to go for a swim. What are you doing with Sig? Are you suddenly in need of spiritual guidance?"

"Guidance yes. What do you know about these people? Are you in another cult?"

Kylar laughed. "Go take a long hot bath and relax. I'll see you on the weekend."

"You're going back with dad?"

"Yes, I'm letting him persuade me to move back." He took a deep breath. "Kiwi, be careful what you think around Sig."

"You're telling me she's telepathic?"

"Just be on your good behavior, they're good people. Night."

"Night." Dicer punched the phone and looked around for Sig. Everyone was doing a disappearing act on her. She took the stairs down and followed the soothing music around a corner to several bubbling, steaming baths. Only one was occupied by the cook, Zora.

"Showers are around that corner," Zora said pointing.

Dicer showered quickly, dressed in one of the light robes and returned to the baths where two others had joined Zora. Kwan walked in wearing only a thin shift which she doffed without effort revealing a superbly fit body despite the long scars crisscrossing her body. She turned to give Dicer a view of her checkered back before stepping into the yellow bath at the end. Dicer removed her robe no longer self-conscious about the nakedness and joined Kwan in the bath.

"Want to talk about it?" Dicer asked as her body adjusted to the heat and water jets pummeling her body as the tangy medicinal aroma filled and cleared her head.

"I attempted to rescue a woman who had fallen into Menendez's clutches. We were caught going back for another person. My back is from his electrical and chemical torture; the scars across my stomach and thighs are from my escape through a plate glass window and over a roof covered with shards of glass designed to keep out a combat team," Kwan said in a cool tone.

"When was this?"

"Last year outside of Tijuana. I was lucky to be rescued before I bled to death." Kwan closed her eyes and slipped lower into the bath.

"What happened to the others?"

"Shot on their knees before me." Kwan expelled a long breath. "I'm sorry."

"Not as sorry as I am."

They were silent for a long spell and Dicer dozed as the jets massaged her body. She came awake at a sudden eruption of laughter. She looked over as the others left the baths, all with athletic bodies. When she turned her head back, Kwan was staring at her.

"You wanted information?"

Dicer nodded. "If you don't mind."

"There's brandy in my quarters," Kwan said rising.

Dicer awoke refreshed in the cool chamber, feeling better than she had in weeks. Before going to bed she had quizzed Kwan for two hours on Pablo Menendez and his operations. Kwan filled in gaps and corrected mistakes from the San Diego report. Her respect for the woman grew; Kwan had gone into the heart of Menendez's lair knowing the man's cruelty and penchant for acid torture to save a young woman who had been led astray by Menendez's power and position in the narco-underworld. Afterwards there was no doubt that she was the expert Sparrow had been consulting; just as there was no doubt Sparrow had been the one who rescued Kwan after her escape from Menendez. More importantly, Sparrow wanted something more from Menendez than his death which was why he was still alive. However, his time may be running out given the treatment of Sparrow's infiltrator which she was not too happy about.

CHAPTER 17

Dr. Aragon examined Jill Merlo before signing her release papers warning her that she had been lucky and additional exposure to the toxin may be fatal. She recommended several natural herbs to build up her natural immune system.

"And I want to see you every week at the clinic to get a blood sample and make sure there aren't any nasty, unexpected side effects. Starting Friday." Aragon scribbled on an appointment card.

"What time?" Jill asked taking the card.

"Call early to see what's available. It's not necessary to see me to give a blood sample and that shouldn't take over ten or fifteen minutes. If you feel anything strange, double-vision, queasiness, headache, come in."

"Okay."

Aragon put a finger under her chin and looked into her eyes. "Don't play with this, Jill. Anything out of the ordinary, come in."

"I hear you."

"Good, finish dressing and I'll be at the nurses station."

"Thanks for everything."

"You're welcome. Just be careful of shooting darts." Aragon patted her on the shoulder and walked out.

Toni walked in. "Well?"

"She wants me to see her Friday at her clinic." Jill waved the appointment card at her. "It's near you."

"Good, I can make sure you go. Mickey said he'd come by at lunch."

"Any word on Gravelli?" Jill asked.

"He didn't say."

"I can't believe she just disappeared in thin air." One moment

Gravelli was there with a gun, the next she was gone as gunfire riddled the van she was trying to commandeer to chase Menendez. Had she grabbed another vehicle? Had someone grabbed her? Those were her questions, as well as Dicer's.

Returning to her office after briefing her officers for their daily patrol, Dicer had not gotten comfortable when the blue flasher went off in her office. "Oh shit!" She reached for her headset, keying in the dispatcher downstairs. "Peggy, what you got?"

"Bomb threat on police headquarters. Call just went out to evacuate the whole block." The whole block was dedicated to the administration of justice, including police headquarters which housed the overpopulated city jail, the courthouse next door and several state and federal enforcement offices.

"What about the prisoners?"

"Gotta transport them to D.C. most likely. They should be putting out the call for all available officer."

Dicer's phone rang. "This should be it. Put the team on standby. Get Gomez and Mumford up."

"Gotcha."

Dicer clicked over. "Hello?" she answered in a tight voice.

"Is this your buddy?" Aviles's voice came over the line, noise in the background.

"I do believe so. You got my e-mail?"

"Yeah. You get anything else to help us out with this?"

"No, except it should symbolize who he believes is of immediate threat to him."

"Why not you?"

"Long story. Where are you?"

"Getting the hell out of the building." Aviles waited for Dicer to say something smart. When she didn't and the line remained opened, she asked, "What's going through your head?"

"I don't think he'd warn the targets like this." Dicer emptied her bag on the table looking for the tape she had gotten from

Kwan which she used during the lecture. "Let me get back to you. Keep an open line."

"Will do."

Dicer rushed across the room and slammed the video in, fast-forwarding it trying to find the section describing Menendez's strike pattern. As she stared at the bombed building, cars, and boats and Kwan's voice pierced her. "Narcopolitics!" she exclaimed and scrambled to call Aviles.

"Yes?" Aviles answered on the first ring.

"Aberdeen compromised his operation pushing Stein to upgrade his attacks on me. Experts describe him as a premier player in narcopolitics and narcoterrorism."

"What the hell are you rambling on about?" Aviles shouted over the background uproar.

"Evacuate city hall too!" Dicer shouted back. If police headquarters were shut down, the logical alternative command center was city hall.

"What?" Aviles yelled, a second before their connection was severed.

"Shit!" Dicer exclaimed, grabbing her keys and racing for the door nearly bowling over Commander Cafferty.

"I'll ride with you," Cafferty said, falling in behind the long-legged lieutenant.

"You hear anything else?" Dicer asked over her shoulder.

"No, just a bomb threat at H.Q."

They drove the Cat-mobile downtown as officers turned motorists around and directed traffic out of the center of the city. Several irate motorists were out of their cars yelling at the officers and anyone who happened by as emergency vehicles were allowed. Dicer and Aviles were still blocks from their destination when an explosion rocked the car.

"Oh, my god!" Cafferty breathed.

Dicer slammed on her brakes as a pickup truck swerved into her path. "Fuck." At a standstill, Dicer jerked the suburban into a loading zone. Cafferty was already out and moving.

Their trek was a half block shorter for they could see the damaged city hall; the three minidomes with the flagpoles atop were obliterated. Century old columns at the front of the building were cracked and crumbling as dust settled around the blast site. Hundreds of people cried, stood, collapsed, yelled and stared in disbelief as rescue workers and evacuees were assisting survivors out and around the building as acrid smells assaulted the nostrils.

Dicer spotted Guzman and angled her direction. "Where's Aviles? What happened? Had they started evacuating the building?"

"She called it in when you were disconnected, then ran over here to make sure they obeyed. That's the last I saw of her."

The downtown horse patrol rode in and began to urge everyone farther back from the building; they were afraid a gas line had been ruptured. Threat of an additional explosion further panicked the crowd. Rumor began to circulate that the mayor and his staff did not get out. Still disbelief reigned as the citizens wondered how such a thing could take place in their city. Remembering Oklahoma City and New York and the embassies, they speculated on who could have delivered such a horrific blow to the heart of the city. An Islamic terrorist? A militia group? An anti-abortion group? A mental degenerate feeling wronged by the city? Who? Who? Why? Why? Lay citizens and proclaimed experts anguished over the questions as the National Guard moved in and the ATF and FBI took over the case.

Aviles, covered head to toe in fine gray powder with splashes of blackening blood, found Dicer and Guzman busy in the trenches. She encouraged them on and went on to direct her troops. The day was still early and it would only get longer as the casualty list grew.

Four hours later the mayor was declared missing and Aberdeen, despite the cloud over her head, took the reins of the city. She reminded everyone of the explosion (which could have been a bomb) at her house. Slowly the enormity of what had happened swept across the city as shock and disbelief gave way to grief and despair. National news networks were showing local feeds of the tragedy.

On the sofa, a disgruntled Jill Merlo watched it all unfold on the television. Toni had not left when the bomb went off and stayed to ensure Jill remained home. A call to T.Z. Aragon received a quick brush off; she needed techies to repair or bypass a communications grid that apparently suffered collateral damage from the downtown explosion.

"We're in deep shit," Jill muttered as Aberdeen called a press conference announcing the state of emergency for Metrox and implore the citizens to remain calm.

Tired and aching Dicer trudged back towards the Cat-mobile leaving Cafferty to supervise support efforts for the survivors and rescuers. According to the FBI special agent in charge (SAC), hundreds of lives had been saved by a tip and the pulled fire alarm. As she approached the vehicle, she saw a plain white envelope with her name printed in block letters. Before she opened it, she knew who it was from. Getting out an evidence bag and gloves, she carefully opened the envelope. The sheet of standard bond paper had one typed line on it: *Victory is mine. Surrender.*

The FBI SAC, Jonathan Griffith, looked from Dicer to the bagged note. "And you say this is from the guy, Pablo Menendez who you have sent out almost daily flags on?"

Her patience wearing thin, Dicer nodded. "That's what I'm saying." She knew by his manner he had been warned about her, so she didn't add that Aberdeen was a Menendez flunkie, a flunkie who was now acting mayor.

"And what do you believe is the purpose of the bomb?"

"Terrorism, pure and simple. He's flexing his muscle, demonstrating his power to subdue this town, bring it to its knees. For whatever reason, he wants this town," Dicer told him echoing Sparrow's words.

"Thank you, we're not dismissing any theory at the moment. Write up your report and submit it post-haste to Agent Doughery."

His glance slid over her shoulder. Stein came their way with a head of steam, looking every bit like the man in charge.

"Lieutenant, they have a traffic problem on Wyoming, see if you with all of your gadgets can unsnarl it." He dismissed her, turning to Griffith. "Jon Jon, let's see what we can do about this jurisdictional issue . . . "

Dicer's pulse quickened as she thought about slugging not one but both of them as they walked away. "What the fuck's going on here? Does anyone care that Pablo Menendez has masterminded the takeover of the city?"

"I do," said a voice behind her.

Dicer turned to see Eduardo Trujillo and Yvette Yemen in a sky-blue pantsuit. "Ms. Yemen, Mr. Trujillo." What was Trujillo doing with the owner of the giant competitor? Nothing was making any sense at the moment.

"Lieutenant, can we go somewhere to talk?" Yemen asked.

Dicer's mind raced, but her curiosity got the best of her. "Okay, but I need a shower in the worst way."

"This is urgent. We have executive quarters at the Globe," Yemen informed her, ran her eyes over the young lieutenant. "We can also find you something clean. Those need to be trashed."

"I'll meet you there," Dicer told them. "I may not be alone."

"I'll leave instructions at the front desk," Yemen called.

By the time Dicer was satisfied she was clean, she realized her hunger. In the bedroom, she dressed in soft cotton pants and a colorful hospital scrub top. When she emerged from the bedroom, she was taken off-guard by the number of people in the front room, mostly women, most she knew by sight, a sitting judge, two councilwomen, a representative, business and community leaders, all powerful women. "What's going on?" she asked Yemen.

"Aberdeen is unacceptable. We don't intend on allowing her to sell our city for a few dollars to this glorified drug dealer," one of the councilwomen said vehemently.

"She wouldn't sell it, she'd give it to him." Dicer remained standing. "Does this place have anything to eat?"

"I ordered you a platter from Gusto's," Trujillo told her. "It should be here shortly."

"And you, Eduardo? What are you doing here?"

"Our headlines will not be the bomb, but a call for the removal of Aberdeen from office. She if your accusations are correct is a conspirator in that bombing. She's responsible for blowing up city hall and the mayor. Was it a coincidence she was not there? We'll put the facts to the people and let them decide," he said forcefully.

"So will ours, if you give us something concrete," Yemen said.

"Although we're prepared to come out as a block against her," said councilwoman Ferguson.

"We'd prefer hard evidence," Judge Minski added.

Dicer walked to the bar and helped herself to the scotch. She knew exactly what they were asking her to do, cross the line from police officer to concerned citizen violating several ordinances in the process.

"You'll just be an unnamed police official," Trujillo offered.

Dicer turned to him. "We both know, everyone will know where you got your information." She took the bottle to an open spot next to Stanley Lichmann, owner of Lichmann Industries. "Who's going to pay my legal fees?"

Judge Minski cleared her throat. "You have nothing to worry about, Dicer."

"Tell me that after you've heard the story." Dicer wondered if Menendez had a contingency plan for this. She then chided herself for giving him more power; then reminded herself of his evil cunningness and what he had done to Kwan. Thinking of such a monster running a city with Nikki and Katie made up her mind. Some things just couldn't be tolerated. And to her own surprise she said, "I want my mother."

Several suppressed their smiles, some openly sighed with relief. They were convinced that Dicer possessed information crucial to bringing down Aberdeen and her political machine that she was building in the shadow of the mayor's laissez-faire leadership.

While calling her mother from the kitchen, she heard the deliveryman arrive and her hunger pangs reasserted themselves with a vengeance. Her mother would be there in fifteen minutes. When she returned to the living room a new woman had arrived and was introduced as the CEO of Vengar-Metrox. Dicer froze and stared, not getting her name. Whatever was taking place in this room, and she surmised with Menendez's strategy, Vengar-Metrox was taking an active role in it. There was a connection she wanted to know before she continued; for if she suspected were true, then the CEO had her own sources of hard evidence. But could she produce it without suspicion? Of course, Trujillo indirectly worked for them.

"So tell me, if your intention is to oust Aberdeen, then obviously you have someone in mind, who is it? A coup cannot be complete without a replacement."

"A coup is a little harsh," Ferguson admonished. "This woman by your own reports consorts with drug dealers and killers."

"However we do have a candidate to put forth for the emergency election."

Dicer wished she had paid closer attention to civics. "And who might that be?" she asked sweetly taking one of the platters to a table. Two others had done the same.

"Arnetta Bilbray."

Dicer looked at each one slowly. "Are you serious?"

"She has impeccable credentials," Minski replied.

"No doubt about that." Bilbray headed the city's economic development programs and was credited with the city's economic recovery and continued growth in the last seven years. She was known for her unflappable honesty and even-handedness in distributing the dollars across the city and between the recipients. Yet she wouldn't hesitate to yank the financial rug out from under a firm she found lacking. She ran her division so efficiently, few at city hall or the general public paid any attention to those who questioned her relationship with her "roommate" NSU's women's basketball coach. If she ran for mayor, that would change. "Damn," she said and focused on her meal as the others made strategic plans.

CHAPTER 18

As if Mother Nature tried to cleanse the city's poisoned soul, heavy rains battered the city starting before day. If the bombing of city hall and the apparent death of the mayor (his body not recovered) had not done enough to the spirit of the city, two morning papers declared that Aberdeen must go and outlined her circuitous involvement in the bombing as well as a list of questionable practices that caught Dicer by surprise. Again she wondered why she had been put on the spot if they had all of this other abuse of power evidence.

In a bold and dangerous move, the Virada printed a list of businesses with alleged ties to Menendez. Talk radio and commentators fueled the debate as citizens were spoon fed the legalities of the case. Meanwhile, Dicer waited for the call downtown that by three o'clock had not come; even Aviles had not called.

"Started the war without me?" Lin Gao asked catching up with Dicer as she left an afternoon briefing.

"Not me." Dicer headed upstairs with Gao following.

"Can I get a few quotes? I'm writing the follow-up piece for tomorrow."

"I've never known you to collaborate on a story." One of the Globe articles was a joint effort between Gao and the religion editor.

"Not on you."

In the darkness, Dicer reached for the ringing phone. "Yeah?" she answered drowsily.

"Dicer, I need to see you," an urgent voice said.

Dicer sat bolt upright, coming fully awake. "Gravelli?"

"Yes. Meet me at 33400 West Lafitte."

"Where have you been? What have you been doing? What are you doing out there?"

"Tell you when you get here."

"What was that number again?"

"33400." The line clicked off.

Dicer sped through the night to the outskirts of the city through warehouses stopping just short of the airport at Al's Body Shop. A slither of light escaped through a crack of the ill-fitting office door. Even in the darkness the wear of the old corrugated steel building was evident to the observer.

Checking her weapons, Dicer got out, looked around and listened intensely to the night sounds. Nothing seemed out of the ordinary, yet the hairs stood up at the back of her neck. Moving cautiously to the door, she reached out and turned the knob on the door; it gave way and she gently pushed open the door. Hesitating, she stepped in with her gun drawn.

"Please close the door behind you," a deep male voice said as another man held a gun to Gravelli's head as she sat tied up in a chair.

Cursing herself, Dicer closed the door behind her. The speaker stepped from the shadows and relieved her of her weapon, then frisked her taking two more off her.

"Someone knows where I am."

"Please, don't insult me," said a third man with a heavy accent as he stepped from the shadow of the soda machine.

Dicer recognized Pablo Menendez. "I thought you'd be in Tijuana by now gloating over the razing of the city. Why destroy what you want?" Her eyes followed him as he circled her. "Or is it that you must destroy what you can't have?"

"It's not the city I want; and you're going to get it for me."

"And what might that be?" Menendez circled closer and Dicer noticed the lesions, a purple one on his temple near the hairline. He had AIDS.

"I want the healer."

"Excuse me?" Dicer thought he said healer.

"The healer, the one who cures with her hands."

Dicer's jaw dropped. "A faith healer?" Had that been the reason for the deaths at New Faith Cathedral? Had those ministers failed to heal him and paid the ultimate price for their deceptions? "There's no such thing."

"She's real," Menendez said softly. "I've seen her work."

"You've been sniffing too much of your shit. Ain't no fucking faith healer in—" She didn't see the fist coming until it landed on her jaw, rattling her teeth. He may have been ill, but he had not lost any quickness.

"She's here! I want you to find her and bring her to me."

"How am I suppose to find her?"

Menendez nodded to one of his men who produced a blurred photo. Despite the blur and the dim lighting, Dicer recognized her at once.

"The sooner you find her, the fewer of your relatives will die."

Dicer's blood ran cold. The heat inside was stifling, she wiped her forehead. Her hand drifted down to the amulet. "What do you want with this healer? I can barely make out the person here. She looks like a kid."

"Don't let that fool you." Menendez turned towards Gravelli. "Let her go."

"What?" exclaimed the guard who had held the gun to her head.

"Do it," he spat. "The search will go quicker with the two of them."

Dicer saw that he was sweating profusely; then flicked the amulet open and pressed the nubby button inside. "Where should we start? This is a large city. She may not even be here." Knowing what the man was capable of she wanted to get as far away from him as she could; yet she had to stall for time in case Sparrow was near and would respond to the beacon. But why would she, no one knew where she was.

"She's here, I can feel it." Menendez mopped his face with a white silk handkerchief.

"Feel it?" She should be content to get out alive with Gravelli and worry about protecting her family later.

"Yes." He waved the handkerchief in the air as if that motion explained it all.

Gravelli rose wobbly from the chair rubbing her hands where the handcuffs had cut into them. A canister crashed through the blackened window with a hectic hiss. Gravelli dove behind the desk. Dicer went for the sofa cover as her eyes watered and throat constricted. Gunfire peppered the night.

The last thing Dicer heard before going unconscious was a muffled voice saying, "drag the coppers out before they die too."

Dicer awoke flat on her back on a stretcher with an oxygen mask over her face which she pushed aside to vomit barely missing the EMT's feet as he jumped back.

"Wash her mouth out," a gruff voice instructed.

Dicer looked up, saw Stein, and bent double in pain.

"Put the oxygen back on her," a commanding female voice ordered.

"Who are you?" Stein blustered.

"Her personal physician." Dr. Aragon filled a syringe with a blue substance and injected it into Dicer's arm. "Now breathe," she said gently.

"Gravelli?" Dicer asked coughing.

"On her way to the hospital; she caught a bullet in the shoulder." Dicer nodded and fell back on the stretcher. Then she sat bolt upright. Aragon pushed her back down. "Let's get her to Roxboro. No need to take her to the others, they'd just transfer her to us."

"I need to ask her questions," Stein said as the other officers worked the scene.

"Later. We need to oxidate her." Aragon pushed him back so the EMT's could load her.

"Where's Roxboro?" Stein asked Aragon.

"Boxtown." Aragon headed for her car.

Dicer awoke on a cot in a small yellow room dying of thirst. She wore cheerful smiley-face scrubs with velcro fasteners. A pitcher of water and a cup with a straw were on the small lucite table next to the bed. Sitting up, she drank three glasses of water before her thirst saw any relief. Standing she stretched and took several deep breaths, almost no pain, only a scratchy throat. Going to the door she opened it and was met with the screech and laughter of a room full of children at play.

"What the heck is this?" she muttered as a small boy threw a block at her.

One of the young attendants looked up from the floor. "The kiddie waiting room slash nursery."

"Where are my clothes and that lady doctor?" Dicer asked, counting eight children.

"I think your clothes went to the cleaners and we have four female doctors." She pointed through the glass double doors. "Ask Dana at the lab desk."

Dicer walked out into the much quieter lab area. Only four people waited to give blood or urine or something. Dicer asked after her clothing and the doctor.

Dana looked at a chart. "Aragon admitted you and your clothing isn't back yet."

"Where's Aragon?"

"She's seeing patients down that way." Dana pointed to another hallway; the lab was the hub of four hallways. "Let me get your x-rays to take to her."

Dicer, brown envelope clutched to her chest, went in search of Aragon and was told to take a seat. A brochure informed her that the Roxboro clinic had six full-time practicing doctors, two dentists, two psychologists, an AIDS counselor, two social workers, an herbalist and a host of support staff including the research lab. She was reading a brochure on immunizations when she heard a familiar voice in an unfamiliar tone.

Jill Merlo was whining about seeing the doctor. She stopped short at the sight of Dicer. "Lieutenant!"

"Merlo. Ms. Jensen."

"No one knows where you are."

"Stein does."

"Well, he didn't tell." Jill and Toni flanked Dicer. "How are you doing?"

"Not puking my guts out anymore. What are you doing here?"

"My new doctor is here." Jill nor Toni had told anyone about the unorthodox "cure" performed by Dr. Aragon.

"What happened to Menendez and his men?" Dicer asked Jill.

Jill's eyes bucked. "Menendez? No one saw him. Two men were dead in the bodyshop, but that's all."

Dicer contemplated the meaning of that. "What time is it?"

"Ten-fifty," Toni informed her.

"You've been in?" Dicer asked.

"Six to ten-twenty. My appointment's at eleven. My lunch break."

"Not chastising you. What is the official line on this?"

"You and Gravelli were meeting a snitch and the two ambushed you. You took them out," Jill said as if asking a question.

"No. I'll need a ride back to Gamin."

"No problem, Toni walked over."

Dicer frowned. "What?"

Jill grinned. "Didn't I tell you, she has a new job."

"Congratulations," Dicer said as her frown grew deeper. Coincidences were beginning to mount up.

A woman came out clutching a plastic baggie of samples, then Aragon came out, saw them sitting together and walked over. "Good morning. Jill, I'll need you to give blood, urine, and saliva samples at the lab. They're expecting you. It's right through there at the intersection. There shouldn't be much of a wait."

"Only four people when I came through," Dicer said offhandedly.

"Lieutenant, if you'll come with me, we'll check out your lungs and trachea and send you on your way."

"My clothes aren't back," Dicer complained as she rose. She didn't add that she would have preferred they not take them. There could have been trace evidence on them, like the gas used.

"They should be back soon." Aragon led her in and gave her a complete once over.

"Why did you happened to be on the spot?" Dicer asked.

"I got a call that someone had been exposed to cyanogen chloride."

"Which is?"

"A blood gas. Actually it was just a sternutator. I think."

"You think?"

"You're alive."

"Why'd they call you?"

"Exotic toxins are my specialty."

"Which is how Jill Merlo ended up as a patient?"

"Yes and no."

"What's that supposed to mean?"

"I can't discuss another patient with you."

"We're not discussing patient confidentiality; we're discussing a police matter on how you keep turning up in our case."

Aragon closed her chart. "You're doing just fine. If the nausea or vomiting returns call me. For now drink plenty of liquids and try to rest."

"Rest my ass," Dicer muttered. She didn't know what game they were playing with her but she'd find out.

After finally getting her clothing and Aragon gave Merlo a full bill of health, Dicer directed Merlo to V-Sec's office. The receptionist informed her that her party was out of town.

"When did she leave? Where did she go? When will she be back?" Dicer demanded.

"I don't know."

"Who would know?"

"No one. She doesn't work here."

"What?" Dicer nearly shouted.

"She only rented space on a temporary basis."

"So you have no idea where she is?"

"That's correct."

Dicer threw up her hands in abject frustration. "That's just peachy. No one knows a goddamn thing."

A young man carrying a large stuffed envelope entered through a side door as they turned to leave. "Lt. Dicer, I have a package for you."

Dicer grudgingly took the heavily taped package. "Thank you."

"Yes, ma'am." He sauntered out.

"Let's get the fuck out of here," she said to Merlo.

In her heart of hearts, Dicer knew Sparrow disappeared Menendez; for what purposes she didn't know. Had he been killed in the attack? Was Sparrow a bounty hunter? If he were alive, what did she intend to do with him? Regardless, two more men were dead; whether they deserved it or not was irrelevant. The bottom line was that whenever Sparrow went into the field people died. Sparrow had told her in no uncertain turns that she would take care of him if she didn't, which she had not.

Dicer waited until she returned to her office before carefully unwrapping the package from Sparrow. It contained two video-tapes, six audio cassettes, the laser pen and a folded sheet of V-Sec letterhead with a handwritten note.

"*There are many battlegrounds on which Evil can be fought with normal force; however there are times when only the extraordinary can prevail. Yet we all can use a little help now and then. Thank you and may the goddess treat you kindly.*"

"What the fuck does that mean?" Dicer asked aloud in her empty office. "I've been played like a fucking fiddle; that's what that means." Yet she could not determine why she had been targeted, used and double-crossed at ever turn. Frustrated she slipped the first video in and took out a soda as gray snow was clicked off by each passing seconds. Just when she was reaching to fastforward, the screen blanked, then jumped into focus. Aberdeen and Stein were sitting in a well-appointed darkwood study discussing the changes to be made when she was mayor and he was chief. Framing Dicer was near the top of the list, as was getting rid of that communist dyke, Bilbray, and getting portions of the population hooked on GreenTarts. With references to Menendez as Saddam, their entire strategy was laid out as was their plan to doublecross him by not delivering what he desperately wanted, the Healer.

Had the bombing of city hall been a message to Aberdeen and Stein? Or were they responsible for the bomb themselves? And who killed those ministers? Now she wasn't so sure it had been Menendez, yet it still fit the scenario, sorta. Who had her shot? Who blew up Lou's house? Who killed Kenny? No matter which ordered it, they were all responsible.

Dicer quickly made copies of the first tape. She had ignored her buzzing phone by turning it off; therefore when a key turned in her lock, she drew her weapon and trained it at the door.

"Jesus H. Christ!" Lou Ayers exclaimed closing the door behind him. "Put that thing away," he said when she kept the gun on him.

"May your goddess treat you kindly."

"Yeah, whatever. Everyone is looking for a piece of your ass. Stein is going ape-shit at the D.A.s office calling for a full-fledged investigation of the connection between you, Menendez and Fuentes."

"Then he's scared." Dicer tossed a copy of the tape to him. "Put that somewhere safe. And arrange for me an escort downtown, our team only and in riot gear."

"What for?" A mixture of excitement and dread ran down his spine

"To arrest the mayor for conspiracy to distribute a controlled substance, murder, bribery, treason and anything else I can think of for that matter." She picked up her phone and punched in the numbers. She waited five minutes before the chief came on line. "Want me to tell you what I'm doing?"

There was a long pause. "Just do your goddamn job! I don't
have time to do everyone's job for them. I don't want to hear from
you until it's done!" He hung up.

Shaking her head, Dicer dropped the phone into the cradle.
After putting on a vest, she took the remainder of her tapes to Dr.
Otu who put them in a timed vault.

The acting mayor had set up temporary offices at the historical
Wiltshire Hotel. All morning she had been drawing power to her
in the guise of keeping the city on its feet as protestors picketed on
the sidewalk. The city council was scheduled to meet that evening
to address the situation.

When Dicer arrived late that afternoon, Hernandez was there
with his team in combat gear stationed outside the Wiltshire's
entrance. She walked up to the chopper pilot. "Well?" She did not
want to fight her own people to get to Aberdeen. The picketers
had stopped marching and were watching the encounter closely
wondering if this were the coup that everyone was talking about.
News cameras inside and out were trained their way.

Hernandez pulled to his full height. "Lou said you wanted
only your team. We started this together; we'll finish it together."
He stepped aside.

Dicer walked into the extravagant lobby. "Seal the exits.
Hernandez, Gomez, you're with me. Lou, clear our exit."

"You'll be safe as a baby coming out."

Dicer, Hernandez, and Gomez entered the suite serving as the
mayor's temporary offices. The middle-age woman behind the desk
reached for the phone, but Gomez in two quick steps placed her
hand on the receiver.

"Metrox PD. Where's Aberdeen?" she asked with unbridled
menace. Her patience wasn't as great as Dicer's and she was long
tired of being jerked around.

She motioned over her shoulder. "In with several . . . "

Hernandez flung open the double doors. Eleven pairs of eyes

stared at him, as he moved to one side and Gomez to the other.
Then Dicer stepped in, her weapon drawn.

"Susan Aberdeen, you're under arrest for conspiracy to commit murder, sixteen counts of murder, destruction of public property, vandalism, public disturbance and others I haven't come up
with yet."

An ex-linebacker stood up. "This is ludicrous. We're in the
process of—"

"Sit the fuck down," a second white-haired man said. "Let the
officers do their jobs."

Aberdeen snapped her head around to the man. "David?"

"It'll save me from wringing your neck," he said softly.

The three officers glanced at each other and tried not to smile
for David Aberdeen was her ex-husband and still her most ardent
supporter. Well, was until that moment.

Dicer and Gomez strode to the opposite end of the room.
"Please let's make this as easy as possible," Dicer said gently taking
her arm, helping her to her feet.

"You have the right to remain silent," Gomez began, as Aberdeen stood dumbfounded, more at David's betrayal than the fact
that she was being arrested by Ki Dicer.

When they led Aberdeen out of the conference room, reporters were jockeying for position in the hallway. So Lou had leaked
their purpose and let them through. He was still smarting over the
loss of his house. Dicer reminded herself to buy him a bottle of
bubbly.

Reporters shouted over each other as Gomez pushed their way
through spinning a baton. Outside, bulbs flashed and more reporters shouted questions. No one had bothered to cover or try to
conceal Aberdeen.

Downtown, Stein got the call and switched on his television to Channel 6. Going to his safe, he gathered the duffel he had stored there.
He buzzed his secretary telling her to hold his calls and slipped out
the side door, then took the stairs down to the parking garage. As he

approached his car, he pressed the key-lock. Nothing happened. Repeating it, nothing happen.

"Technology is a bitch when it doesn't work," Aviles said stepping from behind a pillar, as did six others, including Dicer.

"You're not the only one who can jam communication grids and send false signals," Dicer said stepping forward. "You're under arrest, you despicable sonofabitch."

Stein thought about his chances.

"Go ahead, Guzman would love to put one right between those baby blues," Aviles sneered. She removed his service weapon and badge with surprising adeptness as Mickey yanked his arms behind his back.

As they led him away, Dicer felt curiously disappointed and Aviles saw it in her face.

"I, too, wished he wouldn't have surrendered so easily; but that's the coward's way. Killing him wouldn't have made you feel better, only emptier as you fell into the abyss with him."

"Maybe for a while it would have." Dicer walked off. She had paperwork to do on those two.

Dicer should have been happy by the way things turned out; instead a heavy sadness rested in her chest like an anvil. There were too many dead bodies and too many unanswered questions for her to be anything other than morosely relieved. She looked up as the clock chimed midnight. Somewhere in this big city someone was having fun with friends and family while she sat writing up reports that could wait, but which she preferred not to delay, wanting to put this behind her. That would not be so easy as the pundits were already criticizing the handling of the case, stating it could have been done in a less public manner, with less force. Given the nature of the previous attacks, less force would have been suicidal if that pattern continued and they walked into an ambush.

When she had not typed a word in ten minutes, Dicer saved her narrative and packed her bags for home. Perhaps she could

start on that wall tomorrow. Opening the door, she stepped back
as Chief Harmon stood with a hand raised to knock on her door.

"Chief," she said in a lethargic tone.

"Lieutenant, burning the midnight oil as usual." He stepped
into her office, then leisurely surveyed the contents. "If I remembered
how large your space is, I would bust you down a grade or two."

"Yes, sir."

He glanced at her quickly; that was not her usual retort. "You
must be tired."

"Not physically."

Harmon nodded. "Why don't you take a couple weeks off.
Aviles and the DA can handle it from here."

"I would prefer to oversee this myself."

"You've done your job; let others do theirs." Harmon stopped
in front of her board still full of diagrams, outlining the connections between NFC, Menendez, Aberdeen and all of the people
and offenses in the case.

"Did you want something, sir?" Dicer asked after an extended
silence.

"No, just to send you home." He turned to look at her. "The
city owes you a great deal of gratitude, Dicer."

Dicer shook her head. "Just doing my job."

Harmon flashed her a quick smile, that quickly disappeared.
"Despite your superiors."

"Some of them."

He shrugged, then headed for the door. "I, of course, look
brilliant."

"As usual," Dicer said, closing the door behind them.

"We're a good team." He put a hand on her shoulder. "Now if
only we could stir that latent ambition."

"No, sir. I like myself."

He glanced at her. "Yes, I believe you do." They went down
and out to the parking lot in silence. "Some mysteries are meant to
remain unsolved," Harmon said as he turned away from her.

Dicer turned to watch his retreat. What the hell did that mean?

Dicer resisted the urge to go to the compound, as she referred to the renovated school where she had met Kwan and Sig; but by early evening she could not resist any longer. When she arrived at the Boxtown compound, a work crew was just finishing a day's work on one of the buildings. Since her previous visit they had completed the exterior of the nearest building which had been surrounded by scaffolding. A small brass plate had been added to the brick posted sign proclaiming the structure the Temple of the Seven Sisters. On the backside, the small parking lot was full, forcing several cars to park along the side of the newly paved drive which circled the compound. Following suit, Dicer got out and only then noticed the adjacent park where a volleyball game was in full swing. One of the members of the four-women team looked like Sig, so Dicer veered in their direction cutting across the freshly mown lawn. The sand court, the two rows of bleachers and the electronic scoreboard indicated that they were serious about their volleyball. An adjacent basketball court was occupied by what looked like neighborhood kids who occasionally glanced over at the volleyball players.

"Dammit!" one exclaimed as she landed on the sand missing a save.

Dicer sat on the end of the bleachers with four other spectators as the women finished the highly contested match. From her perspective, their foul language and intense competiveness was not very nun-like if that's what they were.

"You had an explosive week," Sig said coming over with a water bottle and towel.

"I did and you don't sound like a nun cursing at your opponents like that."

Sig laughed. "Believe me, I'm no nun." She hung the towel around her shoulders.

"What are you?"

"A volleyball player." Sig sat down as the others drifted back to the compound. Lights flickered on around the courts as the teenagers continued their own game.

"What happens when it gets cold?" Dicer asked watching one young woman steal the ball from the young man she was guarding.

"Hopefully the gym will be finished by then. It's last on the list. Someone thought we needed a kitchen and living space." She giggled like the teenager she was.

"What do you do here?" Dicer asked.

Sig waved a hand. "This, read, study."

"That's not what I mean. Who are you in the scheme of things here? What makes you so special?"

"If I were so special, we would have won." Sig jumped up. "I need to shower. You can wait in my chambers if you don't want to listen to the others bullshit."

"I might learn something. What is this Temple of the Seven Sisters going to be?" Dicer asked as they walked back towards the compound, the size of the structures coming into perspective.

"A small alternative high school for one. They've just gotten approval from the school board for fifty students to start, but enrollment is only expected to reach twenty-five or thirty, mostly teenage girls. There are five state certified teachers to handle them." Sig skirted the front of the building and opened a gate to the courtyard. "The classrooms are in the east building, the wing that looks like a pregnant bug is the gym."

Dicer followed Sig through a garden path to a set of stairs which they took up to the fourth and top floor, then along an enclosed terrace to a heavy oak door. Dicer was not surprised when Sig placed her hand on a scanner to disengage the locks. Inside were a manual deadbolt and security chain.

"Someone's serious about security," Dicer said turning around to appraise Sig's spacious quarters. Everything had a distinctive Latin American flavor, from the vivid paintings to the Mayan sculptures to the tiled flooring. "How many rooms do you have?"

"Including the bathroom? Four. That's plenty. We take all our meals downstairs, but I do have a refrigerator and microwave. So help yourself to something to drink. I won't be long."

"How old are you?" Dicer asked as she retreated toward an open door across the room.

"Twenty-three."

"You're kidding." She was so accustomed to young people trying to look older and looking older from hard living, that a fresh scrubbed twenty-three year old looked Nikki's age.

"Nope." Sig closed the door.

Dicer sat down at the table of books which she quickly discovered was not casual reading, but reproductions of ancient tomes in a language she didn't know and several technical manuals on electrical system. At least those were in English. Another stack was on city planning and administration. She was reading a well-highlighted section on power brokering when Sig came out in t-shirt and shorts, carrying a pair of fisherman sandals.

"You have quite divergent interests," Dicer said to her motioning to the books.

"Don't we all." Sig slipped on her shoes. "What are you looking for, Dicer?"

"Answers," Dicer told her. "That's why I ask questions and why you keep avoiding them."

"I'm not avoiding your questions; you don't like the answers."

"How about this one: Are you aware that Pablo Menendez was actively looking for you, believing you could possible cure his AIDS?"

"Yes."

Dicer blinked. "You were?"

"Yes."

Dicer rose to pace. "Then why in heaven's name did Danilo bring me here to see you, knowing I was after him and knowing if I . . . " She stared. "You were baiting him using yourself and me?" she asked in disbelief.

Sig shrugged.

Dicer sat on the creme sofa. "You're behind all of this? Does Sparrow work for you? Who are you?" Anger began to creep into her voice. "What gives you the right to play god with people's lives like that? Because of you Kenny's dead."

Sig shook her head. "No, we were latecomers to the game. If we had not run interference, your city would have lost more than its mayor and bricks and mortar. You would have lost your soul and the will to fight back. If you analyze the samples from that truck, you'll discover that it has traces of cyanide. He wasn't trying to addict those people, he was planning to kill them. We stopped the truck. Your foolish cousin started shooting at you which gave Menendez time to blow the truck up. We did what we could to save lives, not lose them. We are a people of peace who have not known much in the last twenty years. We must protect each other for history has shown that no one is willing to do it for us. They destroy our villages, steal our children, torture us to prove our powers and pursue us across the hemisphere. I refuse to run anymore, lieutenant; we will make our stand here and I'll be damned if Fuentes, Menendez, Aberdeen, or anybody stops me."

"And you'll do it if you have to take over the city."

"If that's what it takes, yes!" Sig waved an arm outward. "Look around you, you see it, you know it, these people have fucked up a good thing. No one cares about anything besides what they have for themselves and at any cost to everyone else. Somebody needs to step forward and show people that there's a better way. We have been in the shadows far too long. We have been too easy of a target for far too long. Not anymore. We don't want your city, but given what has been happening neither does anyone else. We didn't come here wanting to get into your politics or your social problems. All we wanted was something of our own, for our people. Yet when we arrived, it was impossible to sit back behind iron gates and do nothing while the rest of the city marched into hell with their heads held high. Unlike others, we refuse to do nothing and allow the poor to suffer for the evils of the corrupt. Evil is real, as you know, and it was here in Metrox."

"No doubt, but I want to know where Evil is now?"

"Evil is always here, it just takes different forms."

"I want the form of Pablo Menendez to answer for his evils."

"I don't know where Pablo Menendez is," Sig told her quietly.

"You mean you don't know or that you don't know what they did with him?"

"I have no idea where Pablo Menendez is."

"I don't believe—" A soft klaxon went off.

"Supper," Sig said and headed for the door to the interior of the building.

"A little late for eating isn't it."

Sig opened the door. "Not around here. And you weren't shy about the other night."

Dicer glanced at her, looking for the cue to the sudden change. One minute she's talking about taking over the city, the next she's teasing her about her appetite.

Downstairs instead of going to the kitchen where they had eaten before, they entered the cafeteria style room that had been dark and deserted that night; now the room was brightly lit and the tables were full of people settling down. Dicer did not fail to notice they were mostly women, superbly fit, bright-eyed, intelligent women. A few children were interspersed.

"Is this some type of conference?" Dicer couldn't help but ask.

"No, just one of their confabs to make sure everyone is doing okay." Sig led them through to a table with Rex Xorron and two other women.

Dicer took a second to realize that the caramel woman with the unruly hair and dancing eyes was the woman she had come to believe was somehow involved with Fuentes and was doing a fairly good job on Toni Jensen.

"Good evening," Dicer heard herself say as she sat, her eyes riveted on Xorron.

"Everyone this is Lt. Dicer; she doesn't like strangers calling her by her first name," Sig said, then introduced the others. "This is Elizabeth Arana, Val Trujillo and Rex Xorron you know, but never met."

Dicer turned to Trujillo. "You by chance know a young reporter by the name of Eduardo Trujillo do you?"

Val nodded. "My younger brother."

Dicer sighed, shaking her head. So she had been played four ways to Sunday. And how close were they to taking over the city? At that moment she wouldn't have been surprised to see Bilbray or Yemen walk in.

"We're working on them," Sig said.

Xorron poured them glasses of the iced tea. "What are you two so worked up about?"

"Evil," Sig said.

"It'll always be with us, but there's no reason to let it ruin such a pleasant end to a productive day." Xorron raised her iced tea glass. "May your goddess keep you from the abyss."

"May your goddess treat you kindly," the others intoned.

"May your goddess keep you on the right side of the law," Dicer added derisively.

"We hope that as well," Xorron said, meeting Dicer's eyes.

Dicer went home with a full belly and overflowing mind. Some of her outstanding questions had been answered, little good that they would do her professionally. Yet others remained as to what they were planning in the future. Sig had made it clear that she would not sit idly by and let evil take over without a fight. Dicer would bet that a month working Carrollton would change her mind for in this city as in most, evil was diversely perverse and did not wear a single face that could be picked out of a line up.

Yet she could not help but appreciate the breadth of the programs they were supporting, not only for their people, but the others in the community. But they had only told her of the good deeds they were doing. What of the bad? There was always the downside, wasn't there? Time would tell and she'd be watching.